M000284014

# LOVE, CLANCY:
# DIARY OF A GOOD DOG

### By W. Bruce Cameron

*A Dog's Purpose*            *The Dogs of Christmas*
*A Dog's Journey*          *A Dog's Perfect Christmas*
*A Dog's Promise*              *The Dog Master*
*Emory's Gift*                *A Dog's Way Home*
*A Dog's Courage*

#### THE RUDDY McCANN SERIES

*The Midnight Plan of the Repo Man*
*Repo Madness*

#### HUMOR

*A Dad's Purpose*
*8 Simple Rules for Dating My Teenage Daughter*
*How to Remodel a Man*
*8 Simple Rules for Marrying My Daughter*

#### FOR YOUNGER READERS

*Bailey's Story*                *Lily's Story*
*Bella's Story*                *Max's Story*
*Cooper's Story*              *Molly's Story*
*Ellie's Story*              *Shelby's Story*
*Lacey's Story*              *Toby's Story*
*Lily to the Rescue*
*Lily to the Rescue: Two Little Piggies*
*Lily to the Rescue: The Not-So-Stinky Skunk*
*Lily to the Rescue: Dog Dog Goose*
*Lily to the Rescue: Lost Little Leopard*
*Lily to the Rescue: The Misfit Donkey*
*Lily to the Rescue: Foxes in a Fix*
*Lily to the Rescue: The Three Bears*

# Love, Clancy

# DIARY OF A GOOD DOG

### W. Bruce Cameron

Tor Publishing Group

New York

LOVE, CLANCY: DIARY OF A GOOD DOG

Copyright © 2022 by W. Bruce Cameron

A Forge Book
Published by Tom Doherty Associates / Tor Publishing Group
120 Broadway
New York, NY 10271

www.tor-forge.com

Forge® is a registered trademark of Macmillan Publishing Group, LLC.

Library of Congress Cataloging-in-Publication Data

Names: Cameron, W. Bruce, author.
Title: Love, Clancy : diary of a good dog / W. Bruce Cameron.
Description: First edition. | New York : Forge, 2023. |
"A Tom Doherty Associates book." |
Identifiers: LCCN 2022034352 (print) | LCCN 2022034353 (ebook) |
ISBN 9781250163547 (hardcover) | ISBN 9781250163554 (ebook)
Subjects: LCGFT: Novels.
Classification: LCC PS3603.A4535 L68 2023  (print) |
LCC PS3603.A4535 (ebook) | DDC 813/.6—dc23/eng/20220725
LC record available at https://lccn.loc.gov/2022034352
LC ebook record available at https://lccn.loc.gov/2022034353

Our books may be purchased in bulk for promotional, educational,
or business use. Please contact your local bookseller or the
Macmillan Corporate and Premium Sales Department
at 1-800-221-7945, extension 5442, or by email at
MacmillanSpecialMarkets@macmillan.com.

First Edition: 2023

Printed in the United States of America

0  9  8  7  6  5  4  3  2  1

*For Scott Miller: a rare, decent man
who came into my life as my literary agent
and has remained as a friend.*

# LOVE, CLANCY:
# DIARY OF A GOOD DOG

Dear Diary:

The cat is despicable.

Even her name is dreadful: Kelsey. My name, Clancy, carries with it all the fun and love that a wonderful dog can bring to the world. The name Kelsey has none of those qualities. The name Kelsey sounds like, well, a cat.

I don't understand it, but before my person, JayB, brought me home, he was living here by himself with this deplorable creature.

Meanwhile, I had been looking for JayB in the world. As a puppy, I lived with a nice woman with many dogs, then a tired woman with a baby, then a man with wonderfully dirty fingers, but never with anyone who felt quite right, because they didn't seem to have the time for me. A dog needs more than shoes to chew and bowls of food to eat—without a person, our person, we are lost—and we know who our person is: it is the human who commits to loving us unconditionally. All the people liked me, of course, because I am a wonderful dog, but none of them completely opened their hearts to me.

Then I met JayB, who I loved from the moment I sniffed his outstretched hand.

When I bounded in the door for the first time, Kelsey was standing in the hallway. Let it be known to all dogs and humans that I was willing to be friendly, even loving, toward this tiny, strange animal. I could only assume she would feel the same way about me. Who doesn't love a happy dog?

Kelsey, that's who doesn't love a happy dog.

Her eyes became slits and her sneering lips drew back from her evil teeth and her back arched impossibly high and *her claws extended and she emitted the most awful spitting sound, like a snake, or something getting ready to attack a snake. Then she turned and fled—something she came to do less and less as she became accustomed to my presence. Now she is not at all intimidated, which is humiliating.*

*She pads around the house, silently looking for victims. Oh, she has JayB fooled: his pants are often befouled with her rank odor from the way she presses up against him, rubbing her head and making that hideous, weird purring sound she emits while pretending to be an animal capable of affection.*

*She's putting her scent on him so I'll know she was there. Everything she does in the house is deliberately provocative.*

*This is not an animal to be trusted.*

*And so, today, I am making the decision. Actually, I have known it for quite some time, but I finally am allowing myself to admit it.*

*I must get rid of the cat.*

 Love,
Clancy

# One

JayB bent over in the hallway to put on my leash and I could barely restrain my excitement. My nose told me that the winter cold had finally been pushed away by an increasingly insistent sun. Walks would last longer, and we would encounter more people and dogs.

I shoved impatiently against the outer screen door as my person opened it, but then he and I both stopped in surprise. A strange car was parked in our driveway, and standing beside it was a woman I'd never seen before.

JayB slowly descended the cement steps. A complicated churn of dark feelings wafted off the woman in our driveway, strong as any scent. I eyed her anxiously. She was scowling. Her light hair was longer than JayB's, falling to a blunt end in line with her chin. She was shorter than he was, though built more solidly. Her smell was powerfully attractive, meat odors and other food aromas embedded in her clothing.

But JayB seemed anxious. Was this woman a threat? If so, shouldn't we go back inside the house?

"Hello, Maddy." JayB greeted her cautiously as we approached.

The woman put her hands on her hips. "Don't 'hello' me," she replied. "I made a list."

"A list?" my person repeated.

The woman nodded vigorously. "I'm calling it the eight simple rules you have to obey for us to get back together again."

There was a long pause. JayB cleared his throat. "I'm not sure what you're saying to me, Maddy. To get *back* together, don't we have to have *been* together in the first place?"

The woman (Maddy?) shook her head, her expression stern. "Okay, I'm going to have to add another rule. That's exactly what I'm talking about, which is why I made a list!" She raised her phone and looked at it.

I sat attentively. No one has ever thrown a phone for me to chase, but that doesn't mean it can't happen.

Maddy moved her lips for a moment, then nodded decisively. "Okay. Numeral one: you didn't call me after we broke up. Who does that? Talk about cruel and unusual."

"You told me not to call you ever again in this lifetime or the next."

"Not for *after we broke up!* You always call someone after you break up. If you don't, it means you're a bad person."

"You didn't call *me.*"

I yawned, relaxing, because JayB no longer seemed agitated.

Maddy rolled her eyes. "It's the man's job. God. What magazines do *you* read? This is why women do everything in our country. Okay. Number—two—and this is the one deal-breaker for me, so I want you to take it as seriously as all the others—JayB, *you act like nothing ever makes you angry.* You're so full of hidden fury you're afraid to show it, or you might, I don't know, take hostages. At some point, you're going to explode and I don't wanna be collateral when that happens. Everybody agrees with me on this."

"Collateral? Why do I always feel like I need an interpreter when I speak with you?"

"Because you don't listen!"

"Wait, who's this 'everybody' who agrees with you? We don't have any friends in common."

"Everybody I tell about it. Duh."

Obviously, we weren't going to go for a walk any farther than we already had. Well, I had enjoyed it while it lasted.

JayB looked thoughtful. "I don't think I'm actually as angry as you say, though. I don't *feel* mad. If I were so full of fury, wouldn't I know it?"

"That's my point: if you don't get angry, you're going to be furious. Do you know what it's like to be in a relationship with someone who's steaming under the pot, waiting to spew all over everyone?"

"No, I don't."

"Well, it's no picnic in the Bay of Pigs, I promise you. Okay, and this one is big, number three: you've got to stop trying to plan everything. Sometimes life is meant to be lived like it's a train wreck, and not all in order according to some sort of *strategy*. You need to learn to be spontaneous, to do spontaneity. Come up with stuff that's completely surprising, even to your own brain. Stuff that makes you *cry*."

"What kind of stuff?"

"Like, surprise me by suddenly saying we're going to London and we don't have time to pack or even put on underwear. We're just like, all of a sudden on a private jet to London. Or, we go to Target and have a huge shopping spree in the electronics department. My printer crapped out, so that would be a good one for today. Or something simple, like—you make me close my eyes, and when I open them, we're at the top of a Ferris wheel somewhere."

"I don't think I can come up with those on my own."

"Why not?"

"Because you just said them. So they won't be my ideas."

Maddy made a disgusted noise. "Okay, I'm going to have to add another rule, which is that you stop being so logical all the time. Would it hurt you to give a fun and completely stupid reply to something? Stop *thinking*. Like, when I ask a question, your answer should be completely random for once. Just *talk*."

"Icicle pancakes."

"What's *that* supposed to mean? You sound crazy."

"Are these rules written down somewhere? Because maybe it would be easier if I just read them and got back to you."

"You've made me lose count. Now I have to start over."

JayB held up a hand. "No, *please*. Please don't. I think I get what you're going for here. In order for us to get back together, I would have to become a completely different person in every single way."

"Exactly. Also: I don't like your name."

"What's wrong with my name?"

"It makes no sense. J-A-Y-B. It's like you're a rapper or something. If you were under oath, you'd have to take a fifth, a name like that."

"My given name is Jago Burr Danville. Would you prefer I go by Jago? That's what my parents call me, but I've always hated it, and when I started using 'JayB' in middle school, the teachers said it was fine as long as I was expressing who I was. So, JayB is who I am. Expressed."

Maddy frowned. "And what I am saying is, the point of the rules is I don't *like* who you are. You need to change. *All* men need to change. You can ask any of my friends."

"I think this might be a good time for me to remind you that you broke up with me, not the other way around."

"That's another rule, maybe the most important one. Now that we're back together, it's bygones be gone. You'll have to let go of this thirsty need for revenge. I'm sorry I broke your heart, but boo-hoo. You're thirty-three years old, for God's sake."

"And doesn't it seem that to break up you have to be seriously dating in the first place? We only went out—what, twice—and you told me you wanted to break up both times."

"First, it was two *and a half* times, and second, you just applied confirmation. You never took me seriously. I was the best thing that ever happened to you, but luckily you have a last chance now. You blow this one, and you'll spend the rest of your life the way you were before we met."

"Happy?"

"Oh. Okay, sure. Happy," Maddy snorted scornfully. "Well, because we're getting back together again and you'll probably want to take me out to dinner someplace nice, I'm going to ignore you. We both know you were a broken man when I put that burger in front of you. Then you left me a huge tip. I don't get many tips. So I thought, okay, he's what I've always wanted, a fool rushing in. Oh, wait, I almost forgot, and this is the one deal-breaker for me: you've got to get a job. I can't be expected to support you for the rest of my life. I mean, what if we have children?"

"Of course I'm going to get a job. I just need to figure out what I'm going to do next. I can afford to take some time."

Maddy vigorously shook her head. "Not if we're getting back together, you can't. I spoke to my manager and he said he'd be happy to give you a shot at waiting tables during the graverobber shift."

"Thank you for doing that, Maddy, but I don't want to be a waiter. I have an advanced degree and I'll find something soon. But I do agree, this one sounds like a deal-breaker. Thank you so much for giving me all these ideas on how I can improve myself. I'll just have to accept that you've moved on. Years from now, I hope, when you're married to a wonderful man that you've completely remodeled to your satisfaction, you'll look back on this time and remember me fondly."

I glanced up in surprise as Maddy, sobbing, ran to JayB and threw her arms around him. He looked unsure and glanced down at me, but all I could do was wag. She put loud, wet kisses all over his face. "Okay. Okay. I *knew* you were worth it. I take back everything I told my girlfriends about you. So, I know you want to buy me a shower of gifts, but I'm even later for work than usual, so I'd better go. But call me, okay? We'll make plans to do something spontaneous."

I wagged because she held a delightfully aromatic splay of fingers toward me. "Who is this?" she wanted to know.

JayB cleared this throat. "That's Clancy."

"Hi, Clancy! I'm going to be your new mommy!" Waving, Maddy jumped back into her car and drove away.

I looked up at my person. Walk?

Walk! As we left the driveway, I didn't need to turn around to know that Kelsey had bounded silently up to her habitual perch in the window and was watching us with those unloving, unwinking eyes. I didn't care about her now; I was devoted to making sure JayB had all the fun a person could experience with a dog at the end of the leash.

We turned up the sidewalk and I was happy to find places to mark which, while not new to my nose, had been painted over by male dogs I had not met. I saluted them with a leg lift of my own, communicating my acceptance of their trespass without surrendering what was, after all, my territory.

Before long, I spotted Odin pulling his person on his own leash. I knew Odin well. He was a much older dog, thin, with light-colored, smooth, short fur, an inquisitive face, droopy ears, and a placid disposition. His person was a woman much older than JayB, and much smaller, too. In fact, as I watched, Odin was dragging her toward us and she was slapping her feet on the pavement in an attempt to stop him.

"Hello, Helen!" JayB called cheerfully. "How're you this morning?"

Though Odin was a male and very often tried to pee where I had already marked, I actually enjoyed the old fellow. I could hear him at night sometimes, out in his own backyard, barking. His voice communicated the clear, uncluttered thoughts of a dog who had started barking, couldn't remember why, and was unsure whether to stop.

When I reached Odin, he was more interested in greeting JayB than sniffing politely behind my tail. That was another thing about Odin—he was much more into humans than dogs. His method of greeting included lifting his heavy paws and plowing his nose dead center between my person's legs. JayB bent over with an *oomph* sound.

Helen shook her head. "I'm sorry," she apologized. "I've never been able to teach him not to do that."

"I imagine," JayB opined, "that when he does it to you, he comes pretty close to knocking you over. He probably weighs more than you do."

Helen laughed while Odin and I examined each other for new smells. "You're right," she acknowledged ruefully. "They told me a coonhound would be easy to train, but I don't know how."

"I've never met a dog who was easy to train. Clancy sure isn't."

I was happy to hear my name.

"Remind me again what kind of dog Clancy is."

"Well, when I rescued him, they said he was yellow Lab, but it's sort of clear that he's got a little something else in him."

"Are you taking him to the dog park?" Helen asked.

I glanced up at my person as he nodded because I knew what "dog park" meant. Did that mean we were going to the dog park?

I could not imagine anything more wonderful.

Dear Diary:

A dog park is a place where people go to sit on benches and watch in amazement how much fun it is to be a dog. Off-leash and free, canines express their full personality. Odin is of the sniff-and-leg-lift persuasion, as it turns out, while I'm more inclined to pursue the female dogs, my nose aimed under their tails.

Some dogs are completely fixated on a toy and seem unaware of anything else—I ignore them because, though I do love a toy (especially a ball!) as much as the next dog, I only give chase if my person throws it. To do otherwise is to miss the whole point.

I could spend all day, every day, at the dog park. There is just so much to do there.

Plus, no cats.

 Love,
Clancy

# Two

I'm envious," Helen told JayB a bit wistfully. "I used to take Odin to the dog park, but lately I've been having so much trouble getting around. I'm afraid I'm not giving him all the exercise he needs."

I glanced up at JayB, who was fidgeting for some reason. "Well," he observed, "I could take Odin with us. I pretty much walk this time every day, and it would be no trouble at all."

Helen brightened. "Really? That would be wonderful."

Odin seemed to register that people had just uttered his name. I watched as he looked around to find a lamppost or tree trunk to mark in celebration. He started to move, his leash growing taut as he stepped toward a nearby fire hydrant. JayB reached out and took the leash from Helen's hands. "Hold on, Odin. Stay."

"Stay" is a word I hear a lot.

"I would, of course, pay you," Helen told JayB.

"Oh, no, that's not necessary, not at all."

"I insist. If you're going to be walking Odin, I should give you . . ." She paused. "Twenty-five dollars a day?"

"No, really," JayB protested.

"Well," Helen said patiently, "I've noticed that you don't have a job yet, JayB. Times must be tough for you, and I have more money than I need. Please accept this arrangement."

JayB laughed, but under it I heard mild irritation. "I haven't found a good fit, yet, but that doesn't mean I'm broke," he assured her. "My house is free and clear and I still have savings from when I moved from Walnut Creek."

"Well, I'll tell you what," Helen decided. "You take Odin with you now, and we'll discuss it when you bring him back."

I wasn't sure what to think when, moments later, my person clutched Odin's leash in the same hand as mine and walked us up the sidewalk. This had never happened before, and Odin and I were both a little uneasy with each other, not sure what this new arrangement meant.

Odin didn't realize we were most likely headed to the dog park, so his steps weren't as lively as mine. There was no quickening in anticipation of the off-leash fun we were about to have. In fact, Odin kept stopping and looking back over his shoulder for Helen, who'd gone back into her house.

Odin, I knew, adored his person. This is as it should be—dogs are meant to take care of the people we're with. For Odin, though, the love was somehow deeper, his dedication more complete, than with many other dogs I knew. I sensed it in the way he kept his eyes on her, and I felt it now in his increasing distrust of JayB, who was leading us away from Helen. Odin did not like that we were leaving her behind. He seemed to be waiting for the leash to loosen so he could run back.

The street was quiet and a light breeze moved the tree limbs. We passed house after house, grass still brown and matted from the snow that had so recently pressed it down.

Resigned to our journey, Odin began to match my pace.

Then something completely unexpected happened. JayB pulled us up short, our leashes yanking without warning. "Oh no!" he blurted, staring down the street.

Odin and I both glanced in that direction. We saw and smelled nothing remarkable, only a man with light-colored hair walking a strange-looking dog toward us. The wind was at our tails, so I wasn't sure about this new dog, but I could tell from its gait it was about my age and, when it paused to lift its leg at a fire hydrant, that it was male.

JayB turned and began moving briskly in the direction from which we had come. Perplexed, Odin and I increased our speed, trying to keep up. Odin glanced at me for an explanation, but all I could do was give him a vacant gaze.

"Hurry! Come on!" JayB urged. We reached a corner and darted around it, still trotting ridiculously fast. Fences and signs and yard decorations called out to us for examination, pleading with us to over-paint the enticing smell of other male dogs with our own urine. But we couldn't stop because JayB was pulling us so forcefully. We were nearly at a gallop and my person was starting to pant. I could tell from Odin's reluctant jog that he thought whatever we were doing was absolutely foolish.

"Come on, dogs!" JayB gasped at us. "Don't let him see me!"

I still had no idea what was going on.

Eventually, JayB slowed and we turned more corners, finally arriving at the dog park, albeit from an odd direction.

Whatever was pursuing us had apparently lost our scent. I wondered briefly if it had anything to do with the man and his weird-looking dog.

In the dog park, our leashes were released from our collars with a *snick* and Odin and I were free to run.

Odin made a big, nose-down circle around the fence, raising alternate rear legs. Meanwhile, I homed in on two smaller dogs—both females, one white and one brown and mottled, who had been playing with each other. They froze as I approached—I hoped it was because they recognized how smart I was. All dogs are intelligent, but I thought it was pretty apparent that I was a standout. I know how to do Sit, Stay (sometimes), Bark (not an actual command, but something that I can do without being told), and Shake. With the exception of Bark, I often received rewards for performing these astounding tricks. In fact, I knew that JayB had a pocketful of treats on his person at that very moment. The tantalizing odor of chicken filtered through his pocket and out into the world.

The two female dogs were playful and we chased each other, kicking up wood chips.

"Odin!" I heard JayB call.

Odin snapped his head around and trotted affably to my person. I raced ahead so that I arrived first, because of those chicken treats.

"Odin," JayB said more quietly. "Can you do Down? Down?"

Neither Odin nor I knew what he was saying, but he was using the same intonations as when he said "Sit." I figured something was up.

"Odin, Down." JayB crouched and patted the ground in front of him. We both looked. There was nothing there. He was just patting the grass. "Down," he repeated.

I was beginning to think there was something about the word "Down" that we were supposed to know.

"Tell you what," JayB decided. "Odin, can you Sit? Sit?"

Oh, I knew that one. I immediately put my butt on the ground, drooling at the thought of the chicken to come. Odin sat too, but his expression remained puzzled. Perhaps he didn't realize that JayB had a reputation of being generous with his treats.

"Good dogs," JayB praised both of us.

I loved hearing that, though it made me suspect that JayB wasn't planning to produce chicken.

We spent a lot of time with this whole Down thing. When JayB put a treat between his fingers and patted the ground with that same hand, I shoved Odin out of the way and plunged my nose forward.

JayB shook his head. "No, Clancy."

There are many words I do not like. I would put "no" in the same category as "cat." I felt bewildered and a little hurt. He had a treat in his hand, I'd been doing Sit. How could "no" possibly apply to this situation?

JayB was still patting the ground with those delicious smells coming from his fingers. I saw the treat, right there, but JayB's other hand kept pushing my chest, keeping me away. "Down, Odin," he reiterated patiently.

Odin had had enough and pounced. Both of his front paws hit the ground and he dropped his nose to JayB's hand and, to my shock, began crunching.

JayB had given Odin my treat!

I stared at JayB, wounded. Something very wrong had just happened.

"Okay, pay attention now," JayB lectured. "This is your new and most important command, Odin. Down."

Odin was still lying with his belly on the ground but willingly took the treat anyway. *For doing nothing!*

JayB clapped his hands and we both jumped to our feet, shaking ourselves off, glad that foolishness was over.

"Odin, Down."

This was how we spent a good portion of what should have been our free, fun time in the dog park. That strange command, "Down," repeated over and over. I became distressed when I noticed that whenever Odin put his belly to the dirt, he received a treat. How was *that* in any way related to what we were doing? For that matter, why was Odin even here? This was *my* person, *my* dog park, and now Odin was eating my treats.

My opinion of Odin, which until now had been high, was beginning to change. Did he think he was part of my pack now? Did he think he was going to come and live with us and eat my food and sleep in my place on the bed?

I watched in befuddlement as Odin responded to the word "Down" by getting a treat for doing nothing, just sprawling in the grass like he was going to take a nap. Odin was well-known as a lazy dog, so I hardly thought this was behavior to be rewarded. The high energy I brought to every situation was, in my opinion, vastly preferable.

"Don't you know what we're doing, Clancy?" JayB asked me.

Something in the way he said my name caused me to pause. "Down." Odin went to his belly and got a treat. I was beginning to associate the word "Down" with Odin flopping in the grass and getting chicken. I puzzled it through. Did "Down" mean "lie in the grass"? That seemed awfully complicated. But there was no denying the fact that Odin was happily scarfing down treats and I was getting nothing, even though I was JayB's favorite dog!

I couldn't stand it any longer. The next time JayB uttered "Down," I tried lying down in the grass.

JayB fed me a treat!

I was excited and triumphant, but still confused. When my person clapped his hands, I ran a little bit in the dog park, shaking off my bewilderment. When he called me back, I did Sit next to Odin without being asked. Surely, more chicken was due for that.

Alas, not.

"Down," my person commanded.

Odin went to his stomach and I did too, and we got treats, and then I understood. I was getting a treat for doing what Odin was doing, even though Odin was doing nothing. This is how people are, and there's little we dogs can do about it because humans have the treats in their pockets.

Dogs don't even have pockets.

My person seemed happy, though, so I felt happy, too. Happy went with dog park the way Down went with chicken.

We all turned and looked when we heard the familiar sound of the dog-park gate rattling.

I wagged at a new dog coming in. She was a female, large and light-colored with white markings.

"Oh," JayB whispered.

Odin was still sprawled on his stomach, expecting more treats, but I heard something in JayB's voice that focused my attention on him. He seemed distressed.

"Okay, dogs," he murmured. "That woman's walking straight toward us. Do me proud; don't jump up on her, Odin. Don't get on the bench with her, Clancy. Okay? Be *down* dogs. Good *down* dogs."

I heard some words I recognized but had no idea what was being asked of me. I saw a tall woman with long, black hair smiling and striding toward us, but my attention was mostly on her female dog, who was sniffing where I had previously left my mark. Obviously, she found me attractive.

"Stay," JayB told me.

Stay meant we weren't going to have whatever fun I thought we were going to have. It meant "remain right where you are until you forget why."

The woman approached and JayB stood up from the bench, something that smelled like fear releasing into the air with his movement.

"Hi." She greeted shyly. "My name's Dominique."

"Hi. I'm JayB."

The woman extended a calm hand and my person seized it briefly. "Very nice to meet you," she said. "Are these your dogs?"

"Oh, no, Clancy here, the yellow Lab, he's mine. But Odin belongs to my neighbor. I'm just walking him."

The woman smiled. "Great. This is Phoebe."

JayB turned to us. "Okay, dogs!" he said with a clap. This was the signal that whatever had been going on was no longer going on and that we were allowed to go back to being dog-park dogs. I stepped up to the new female while Odin remained at the bench. He probably figured JayB was good for a few more chicken treats.

Up close, I inhaled the fragrance of this new, magnificent animal. She stood still for my examination of the area beneath her legs. Then I turned so that she could admire the same parts on me. When I play-bowed, she wagged and did a little turn.

This new dog, whose name I would come to learn was Phoebe, was possibly the most captivating beauty I had ever sniffed. I breathed in her fragrance and, in that moment, knew I had found my true mate.

Dear Diary:

A dog can always tell what a person is feeling. The strong emotions—anger, fear, love—pop off the skin with an unmistakable scent that is unique to each individual but full of subtle characteristics common to all people. Happiness and sadness appear on the face and in the tone of voice, while surprise ripples through the whole body.

What a person is thinking, though, is almost never evident. I know if I were a human, I'd be thinking about all the bacon in the refrigerator. I'd be planning the next car ride, or plotting how best to throw a floating toy into a big pond.

If dogs and humans traded places for even one day, people would realize how much more wonderful life can be, because the best emotion of all is happiness.

 Love,
Clancy

# Three

Whenever the wonderful new dog and I dashed past the bench where JayB sat with the woman with long hair, she called out "Phoebe! Hi, Phoebe!" and that was how I learned her name: Phoebe. Such a magical, lovely sound.

I escorted Phoebe to where a large pan was constantly replenished with fresh water by a trickle from a metal faucet. I felt that by guiding her to the water, I was communicating that I was willing to show her all the wonders of my world.

Eventually Phoebe and I sprawled in front of the bench with Odin. I was delighted to see that, though a male, Odin wasn't particularly interested in her. Perhaps he had gotten to an age where he was no longer captivated by such a rapturous scent.

"I moved out from California," JayB was saying, "but this is where I grew up. Prairie Village, I mean. It's nice: quiet, low crime, good schools. Besides, my dad lives here."

"Is he infirm?" the woman asked delicately.

JayB shook his head. "No, he's in good health. He looks younger than he is, and he's only sixty. No, it's more that my dad's just kind of a dreamer, you know? He'll have a job, but then he'll get bored and move on to something else. How about you, Dominique? How long have you lived here?"

The woman's name was Dominique.

"Kansas City? Less than a year. I moved from Boston. I accepted a position as an art director at Hallmark."

JayB raised his eyebrows. "That's supposed to be a great company."

"Oh, it is. I love it. But life's been so busy, it's been hard to meet people. I've felt so guilty about not taking Phoebe for walks. I'm glad I decided to bring her here today."

"Me, too."

I could tell that JayB and Dominique were growing comfortable with each other. As I sniffed at Phoebe to see if she sensed the same thing, she suddenly lunged to her feet to greet a long, low dog coming into the park. I chased after her, and we wrestled until Dominique called, "Phoebe!"

I watched Phoebe being led out of the gate of the dog park, trying not to be overcome with disappointment that she hadn't glanced back at me once. Wasn't our time together as special for her as it was for me? Didn't she realize we were meant to be together?"

"Come on, dogs," JayB said to us. With a *snick,* my leash was back on my collar. He grinned down at me. "Okay, Clancy. This is like maybe the best day of my life."

I was a little disappointed when we didn't follow Phoebe's scent, though I had learned long ago that people don't smell things as well as dogs do. Instead, he led us in the unmistakable direction of home. "Even her name is beautiful. *Dominique.* I haven't asked a woman for her phone number in maybe ten years, Clancy, but I just did it without thinking. I don't know . . . there was just this connection."

He was saying my name, but he showed no signs of reaching in his pocket for chicken.

"I haven't been on a real date in forever. You know, if this thing goes anywhere, we'll probably spend time together in the dog park. That means you get to play with Phoebe some more, Clancy. Bet you'd like that—you're covered in her spit."

There it was, something I *did* recognize: my name and my Phoebe's name spoken at the same time. JayB understood that I'd met my dog. That's how I thought of her, anyway: Phoebe was my dog, and I was hers.

"I need to come up with a way to explain why I'm not working now, that I've got enough money that I can take my time deciding on a new direction. Luckily she didn't ask me what I do for a living. What do you think, should I call her as soon as I get home? Would that be lame? I don't know, I don't want to play games, be the kind of guy who deliberately holds off calling a woman so she'll think he's aloof and cool. That's not me. No one has ever seen me as cool.

I'm enthusiastic. Some people might say it's charming. Well, I *hope* somebody would say that. I'd say that. If I were Dominique's best friend, I'd say, 'You've got to meet charming JayB Danville. He's got a charming house on a nice street. He's got a dog and a cat. He's got a kind heart. He's working through some things professionally, but he's financially secure. No, no, this dog-walking thing is just a favor for an elderly neighbor.' See? Charming."

I had heard the word "cat" and assumed it was a mistake. We were on a walk. Two dogs, two leashes, a wonderful day filled with exotic odors wafting up from the grass. Even thinking about a cat at such a moment could spoil the mood.

JayB was nodding to himself. "Okay, that's it, Clancy. I'm going to call her the second I walk in the door."

I had a thought, then. I pictured Phoebe coming to live with us at our house, spending the days wrestling with me and helping me terrorize Kelsey. Right now, though, Phoebe obviously lived with Dominique. But what if I could get Dominique to move in with us?

Could a dog possibly make that happen?

At Odin's house, we turned up the driveway, as I expected. Odin, who never seemed to get excited about much of anything, strained to get back to his person. He was quivering with joy.

Being separated for any time at all from JayB made me anxious, and I was always ecstatic to be back with him. That's just how dogs are. But Odin seemed particularly frantic. I realized, watching his desperation, that he didn't only crave being with his person. He was acting like he'd been *worried* about her the whole time we'd been gone.

We mounted the steps to the front door. "Now, Odin," JayB warned, "You're going to have to do a better job. No jumping up. You understand?"

Odin heard his name, but didn't react, except to keep wagging energetically. His nose pressed against the crack between the door and the house, huffing in the scent of his person. After JayB pushed a button, we heard some sounds, then the door opened, though we were still separated by a screen.

"Hey, Helen," JayB greeted.

"Hi!"

Odin jumped up, putting his paws on the screen.

"Do me a favor," JayB requested. "Back up a few steps. I want you to see something."

With a curious smile on her face, Helen backed down the hall-way.

"Okay, I'm going to open the door and I want you to say the word D-O-W-N real firmly, okay? Keep repeating it."

She nodded. When JayB popped the door open, Odin surged forward.

"Odin," Helen commanded sharply, "Down."

Odin looked as if he hadn't heard her properly. He froze.

"Down," Helen repeated.

That was a word I thought I recognized. Hadn't I recently heard it?

Odin dropped to his belly. Helen clapped her hands together. "Oh my," she exclaimed.

With that, Odin, feeling her excitement, crawled toward her on his stomach.

JayB laughed. "Well, that's technically down," he observed. "Don't let him jump up, though."

Odin dragged his now-dropped leash across the floor, pulling himself with his front paws, gliding along the smooth hardwood. When he reached his person, Helen said "Down," again, though it seemed to me Odin was already doing Down.

Having reached her feet, Odin flopped onto his side, wagging furiously.

I could sense what he was feeling. He was being good and he knew it. He was so happy to be a good dog for his person, he thought a belly rub would help things.

Helen's knees issued cracking noises as she knelt down and stroked his stomach. Odin closed his eyes and groaned. "Good dog, Odin," Helen murmured, "Good dog." She smiled up at JayB. "That's amaz-ing. How did you do that?"

"He's a really smart dog. All I did was give him a few treats and he figured it out. The crawling thing is his own invention, though. I only taught him to lie down on the ground."

"Could I give them both a treat?"

"Sure."

Odin and I both went alert when Helen reached into a crinkly package and threw two small bits of turkey at us.

For a dog, almost nothing beats being fed a morsel from a human hand. Usually, we have no idea why treats are being given, but in this case, I thought I knew—this Down thing, crawling on one's stomach, really seemed to please people.

Walking home, JayB reached into his pocket and pulled out a small slip of paper that I recognized. Dominique had handed it to him in the park. He put it back in his pocket and smiled down at me. He was happy.

We strolled past the few houses between Odin's and ours. As we came to our driveway, I sensed an immediate change in JayB's mood. His shoulders slumped, and his steps faltered.

That same car was back in our driveway. The driver's door opened and the same woman, Maddy, climbed out of it. She looked angry, either again or still.

"Oh, boy," JayB muttered.

"When were you going to call me?" she demanded. "And don't tell me you dropped your phone in the toilet. Men always think that one works."

"But you were just here a couple of hours ago," JayB protested.

"Yes, and didn't I say this is a very delicate time?"

"No, you never said that."

"Well, I shouldn't have to! I can't believe I drove all the way over here and you're still deaf to my tones."

"But, I mean, you could have called me, if you wanted to talk."

"No, that's one of the eight simple rules. You're supposed to call *me*, JayB."

"But, I mean, how often?"

"As often as it takes!"

I nosed the pocket with the chicken treats. Things seemed tense and I knew what would cheer us all up.

There was a long moment of silence. "JayB," Maddy said softly, "did you ever think maybe you should see a psychiatrist?"

I turned as another car pulled in our driveway. This one was black and shiny. I immediately picked up the smell of a dog coming from within. Both front doors opened.

"Look who I found walking around your neighborhood!" announced a man I recognized. I had met him many times before. His name was Walter, though sometimes JayB called him Dad. He was a very nice man, though he'd never once thought to carry dog treats in his pocket.

I knew the scent of the man standing up out of the other side of the car. He was the person I had smelled from afar when JayB had suddenly pulled our leashes, and Odin and I had run to keep up, bewildered by our change in direction. The strong odor of dog wafting out of the car was familiar too—it was the dog accompanying the man when we all ran down the sidewalk.

I felt JayB's posture change. Were we going to run away again? I tensed. JayB seemed even more unhappy than when he'd spotted Maddy in our driveway. "Hey, Rodney," he responded with no joy.

The new man—Rodney?—was grinning as broadly as Walter. "Don't 'hey Rodney' me," he chided. He came walking around the front of the car, his arms stretched wide, and enveloped my person in a broad, backslapping hug. JayB reached a hand up and tentatively tapped some fingers between Rodney's shoulder blades.

"You moved back to KC and never thought to call me?" Rodney demanded. "Should I be pissed?"

JayB shrugged.

Maddy approached from beside her car and stood with the group of people, glaring like a cat. "Who's this?" she challenged suspiciously, nodding at the men.

Rodney held out a hand. "My name's Rodney Spitz," he replied.

"I'm JayB's oldest friend. We met in grade school and have been like brothers ever since."

Maddy shook his hand. "Maddy Pine," she stated sternly. She turned an accusing look at JayB. "You never told me about Rodney."

"Maybe I was waiting for the right time."

Though we could all smell the male dog in the car, no one was making any moves to let him out. I decided he must be a bad dog. I glanced at the house and saw Kelsey in her customary place in the window.

No one was letting her out, either.

Maddy turned a fierce expression on Walter. "And who are you?"

A round of laughter ensued. Maddy scowled.

"Isn't it obvious? I'm Jago's father. Walter," he boasted, showing all of his teeth. "How do you know my son?"

Maddy squinted. "I'm JayB's girlfriend."

Walter shot JayB an incredulous look. "You never told me you had a girlfriend. Especially not such a beautiful one."

"This is great," Rodney enthused. "I'm only two blocks over, myself. I'm living in a house rent-free while I remodel the kitchen."

"Is that what you do now?" JayB asked. "Like a carpenter?"

Rodney shook his head. "More like a freelance entrepreneur. This is just my current project."

"So, how's the remodel going?"

Rodney smiled, "Well, I'm living there rent-free, so you know, no hurry." He winked. "Hey, I need to introduce you to somebody." He went to the back door of Walter's car, and when it opened, out sprang a stocky and strangely wrinkly, light-brown dog about my size.

"Is he a beagle?" Maddy asked.

"Shar-pei," Rodney replied.

I stared. I had never seen a dog like this before. His face was pushed in and jowly, with folds of skin collapsing over his eyes. His ears looked too small to be functional, his tail too short for his body, almost a stub. "This is Spartan," Rodney announced proudly.

"This is Clancy," said JayB.

Hearing my name and "Spartan" made me think that Spartan was this dog's name. He was ignoring me, carefully sniffing where I had marked a post that morning and then lifting his leg with contempt. I wasn't going to allow this insult to stand, so when JayB dropped my leash, I moved swiftly over to inspect Spartan's mark and pee all over it. Then the two of us circled each other, his poor excuse for a tail held stiff. We uneasily examined each other between the legs. A ruff of fur rose along the ridge of Spartan's back. He seemed extremely unfriendly.

"This is going to be a lot of fun," Walter proclaimed.

"I don't know what would lead you to say something like that," JayB replied.

"What do you do, Walter?" Maddy inquired.

"I'm an investor."

JayB looked away, shaking his head slightly, but Rodney brightened.

"Investor?" Rodney repeated. "Does that mean you invest in things?"

Walter nodded cheerfully. "I'm diversifying as we speak."

"I don't like financial language," Maddy interjected. "Better to just tell the truth."

Rodney nodded. "Exactly. Walter, we need to talk about this sweet deal I just came across. Put in a million, maybe a million and a half, and get back ten or twenty, easy."

"That's exactly the sort of thing I'm looking for." Walter beamed.

"It does sound easy," JayB agreed cheerfully. "What is it?"

"Okay, on the surface, it's a restaurant," Rodney replied.

JayB folded his arms. "No."

*Dear Diary:*

*One of the most loathsome sights conceivable is a cat sitting on a window ledge, staring out through the glass. Their cold, unwinking eyes and unloving faces are so different than a dog's. A dog would be happy, panting, perhaps pawing the glass, yearning to join the fun. Kelsey, however, sits and glares malevolently. She is so bitter not to be a dog that her entire face squints.*

*I have no doubt she would be terrified to be outside. All cats I've encountered in the out-of-doors have rightfully run away from me, except for one that didn't. A cat knows a dog is a superior predator. They flee in terror because, for a cat, to leave the house is to be in mortal danger.*

*And that's when it occurs to me: all I have to do is figure out a way to force Kelsey out of the house. Once in the yard, she would have to run away.*

*I picture her scampering down the street, a pack of dogs in pursuit, and it makes me wag.*

Love,
Clancy

# *Four*

The word "no" always makes me anxious, especially when delivered with a stern coldness. I did not know what I might have done to have that word spoken by my person. I lowered my head guiltily.

"Hear me out," Rodney pleaded.

"No."

JayB said it *again*. He turned to Walter. "A million and a half? In a restaurant? No way."

"Hey, I work in a restaurant," Maddy objected. "Are you saying I'm a waste of money?"

"I think," Walter observed dryly, "you're forgetting who's the father and who's the son, here, Jago. I can make up my own mind, don't you think?"

Rodney nodded eagerly. "Walter, it's like God gifted me to you. We need to talk. Seriously."

"Excellent idea. Why don't we all go out to dinner? I'll buy," Walter suggested grandly. He smirked at JayB. "In a *restaurant,* I mean."

"Oh, I can't," JayB objected quickly. "I've got some things I've got to work on."

"What are you talking about? You're *unemployed,*" Walter chided.

"Just because I don't have a job, doesn't mean I don't have a life," JayB responded reasonably. "This is all very nice, but I have plans."

Maddy whirled on him. "See, that's for sure on my list of eight simples. You plan *everything*. Can't you for once just go with the flowing?"

Rodney and Walter were grinning, but JayB was not.

Maddy turned to Walter. "I'd love to," she advised, "but I have to work tonight. I only stopped by to reassemble our relationship again."

"Aw, I'm sorry to hear that," Walter replied. "I was so looking forward to getting to know you. I thought we could all go to Pierponts."

Maddy brightened. "Pierponts! Okay, for that, I guess I could take the night off. I was going to skip work anyway, but JayB apparently forgot we had a date."

I noticed JayB's hand going into the pocket with the piece of paper Dominique had given him. "Have fun!" he told them.

Walter shook his head. "That's my son," he observed sadly. "Never up for a good time."

"Tell me about it," Maddy affirmed. "Every date we've ever had has been a huge disappointment."

"Nobody ever said that about me," Rodney boasted. "I'm the proverbial life of the party."

Moments later everyone else, including Spartan the saggy-faced dog, departed—Maddy in her car, Walter and Rodney and his dog in Walter's shiny black one. JayB and I went in the house and Kelsey dropped off the window ledge, rightly concluding that I had come up with a masterful plot to rid her from our lives. JayB opened a fragrant can of fish and put the contents into a bowl on the counter. He had never learned that when it was up there, Kelsey could reach it, but I couldn't.

Eventually, he would place food in my bowl on the floor as well. I could reach that, of course, but the strong fish smells coming from the counter were maddeningly provocative.

After a time, JayB pulled out his phone and the piece of paper from Dominique. I instantly picked up a gust of nervousness. He glanced down at me. "Okay," he told me. "Here goes."

I wagged, concerned that he seemed afraid. All I ever wanted was for JayB to be happy and maybe cook up some bacon.

"Oh, hi," he told his phone. "Dominique." He listened for a moment. I did not know why he was saying her name. "JayB, you know, from the dog park. Yes, hi. I was thinking . . . oh. Okay, yes! When? Oh, wow. Yeah, of course. Tomorrow would be great. Sure, it's a date, noon. Okay. Hang on." I watched as JayB fumbled for a pencil and paper. He glowed with relief. "Okay, ready." He listened, and then smiled sunnily. "You live really close by!"

Then he said, "Oh, sure. Right. I'm sorry, I didn't mean to interrupt anything. Okay. Okay. Well, then, tomorrow noon. See you then. Okay. Bye, Dominique." He lowered the phone and beamed at me. "Clancy, I've never had anything in my life go as well as this."

I wagged with happiness.

The next day I sensed added energy in my person's movement as he took a shower and got dressed. He stood and looked at himself in the mirror, then put on a different shirt. He brushed his teeth and hair and turned to me suddenly. "Oh, you know what, we should go to Helen's and see if she needs me to take Odin for a quick walk."

I heard the name Odin and guessed what was coming—we headed out the door and up the street, JayB holding my leash. I smelled Rodney and Spartan and turned, looking over my shoulder. The two of them slowed as they ran by.

"Hey, buddy!" Rodney panted. "You should have come out with us last night."

"Hi, Rodney. You talk my dad out of a million?"

Rodney laughed. "I'll let him tell you." He passed us, and then started running backward so he could keep talking. "Your Maddy's a hoot. We did some shots. Walter's hilarious, just like I remembered him. Want to get together later? I'm not doing anything." Rodney stopped running, jogging in place now, still facing us.

Spartan greeted me stiffly. This was a strange dog. We knew each other now, so he should have been much more effusive, but instead, he stared coldly at me through dark eyes concealed between creases of flesh.

"Actually, I have a date."

"Oh!" exclaimed Rodney. "Tell Maddy I said hi, then."

"Uh, sure," JayB said agreeably. Rodney turned and ran, and Spartan followed him without a backward glance at me.

"Actually, her name's Dominique," JayB observed quietly—so quietly that Rodney didn't turn around. He glanced down at me. "Dominique," he repeated.

He seemed so happy.

Up ahead, Rodney passed Helen, who was in her driveway. Odin was not with her. She was stooped over, trying to pick up some rolling cans that had fallen through a hole in the paper bag she was carrying. Rodney glanced her way and kept running.

"Rodney . . ." JayB muttered, shaking his head. We picked up our pace. "Hey, Helen, let me help you there." Moving swiftly, he snagged loose cans and gathered them in his arms.

Helen smiled at him. "Right on time! Thank you, JayB. Come on in, I know Odin will be happy to see you. Odin!" she hailed as she opened her front door.

We went inside and I heard Odin's nails clicking as he ran toward us, but at the last moment, he fell to his belly and crawled the final little bit to his person. He flopped over for a tummy rub, his tail whapping the floor.

"Good dog!" JayB praised. I liked hearing those words. He put the cans down while Odin greeted me properly.

"I have some good news for you," Helen said, beaming.

"Oh?"

The doorbell rang. Odin and I both barked in case the people didn't know intruders were threatening to come in.

"Hey," JayB scolded. "That's enough."

We didn't know what he was saying, but it was clear he was as angry with the doorbell as we were.

"In fact," Helen declared, "that's probably them now!"

Odin and I reached the threshold at the same time. The smell of canines came to us through the crack under the door. We both lowered our noses to it. Helen made her way between us. When the door opened, Odin and I were surprised to see two women around Helen's age standing and carrying their dogs.

They were little dogs, white with curly hair. The dogs stared at us and we stared at them. I had been picked up off the ground before, of course, but there seemed to be something different about this arrangement. Usually, I'm carried to the bathtub, my body collapsing into dead weight in protest, but that did not seem to be where these two women were headed. They stepped in and laughed excitedly, hugging Helen. "Hello, hello!" Helen greeted.

They put their dogs on the floor, and the two of them skittered over to sniff Odin and me. They were scarcely larger than Kelsey, but much friendlier, their tiny tails wagging furiously.

"Oh, this is going to be so much fun," the shorter woman enthused.

"JayB, these are my friends, Cindy and Lindy," Helen introduced.

JayB smiled.

"The dog walker!" the taller one exclaimed.

"Oh, well, not exactly," JayB replied, which made everyone else laugh.

"That one's Tillie and mine's Millie," the shorter woman announced. "They're sisters, just like we are."

"We are so thankful for you," the taller woman said.

JayB frowned. "Thankful?"

"We always feel guilty when we leave the dogs alone. Knowing they're with a reliable dog walker takes a huge weight off our minds."

I glanced up at JayB, sensing discomfort.

"We're going out to lunch!" Helen told him. "Haven't done that in ages!"

All of the women laughed. JayB did not.

"It's twenty-five dollars, right?" the shorter woman asked.

JayB was silent for a long moment. "Yes," he finally replied. "That's right."

Soon we were back outside and, as far as I could tell, headed to the dog park, but now we had these two silly little dogs with us. They were both females and did not seem to understand why Odin paused at strategically located signposts and fireplugs. They sniffed curiously at our markings at first, then ceased doing that and simply trotted along to stay even with JayB. Some dogs just don't understand what's important.

JayB was unhappy—I could smell it on him. Yet we were out for a walk with dogs—how could he be anything but elated?

We made a turn and headed down a street we'd never walked

before. JayB pulled a piece of paper from his pocket and stared at it, and then glanced down at me. "You know what? We'll look back on this someday and laugh about it, I promise. I mean, talk about awkward first dates. . . . We'll eat takeout or something at the dog park and it'll be fine. Right, Clancy?"

I had heard a word or two that I recognized and looked to his hand, but it did not go into his pocket to retrieve anything for me.

We walked up some steps, and that's when it struck me that I could smell Phoebe. *She was inside the house in front of us.* I wagged and panted with excitement. My person was capable of many wonderful things and this was just one example: he'd found Phoebe for me!

When he pushed a button, I heard her bark from within, and Odin and I glanced at each other, sharing the knowledge that there was a dog in the house. I wondered if Odin knew it was Phoebe.

The door opened and a man stood there, tall and shirtless. "Hey," he greeted. "You JayB?"

JayB didn't speak for a moment, then nodded. The man held out a hand. "I'm Bedford. Nice to meet you." He turned and looked over his shoulder. "Hey, Dominique! The dog walker's here!"

We dogs all went on alert because the man had yelled something and now had an air of expectancy. He turned back to JayB. "She said you guys didn't talk about price. That's Dominique . . . she doesn't think about things like that."

"Oh," JayB said. "Right. It was mostly . . . social."

"I'm thinking what, maybe twenty dollars an hour?"

JayB was still standing motionless and I gazed up at him curiously. Then, I whipped my head around at the thundering steps of Phoebe. She squeezed past this new man (Bedford, I decided). I was heartened she came to me first, then sniffed Odin, and then lowered her nose to the little dogs. I was so happy my whole body was wagging, from my tail forward.

"So, how long've you been a dog walker?" Bedford asked.

JayB cleared his throat. "It's twenty-five dollars for a couple of hours. That's what I've been charging."

The man grinned. "Well, hey, I guess I just can't get used to how cheap things are here. I moved out from the east coast. I like it, though."

I looked up as Dominique joined us. She put a hand on the man's arm and held out a leash to JayB. "It's good to see you again," she greeted with a happy smile.

"Yes. It's good to see you, too."

For a moment, everyone stood there, and then JayB bent down and put the leash into Phoebe's collar. "Okay then, I'll see you in a couple of hours."

"Nice to meet you. I'll have your fee, in cash," the man advised with a wink.

"Okay," JayB agreed, a little woodenly.

He turned and descended the steps, and, of course, we all followed on our leashes. I wanted to feel concern for my person, who was radiating disappointment as he trudged along, but Phoebe's irrepressible joy filled me with so much love that it was all I could think about.

We made our way to the dog park and I played and played with Phoebe. The two little white dogs tried to keep up with us for a while, but eventually were content to sprawl next to Odin, who had decided he wasn't going to run around today.

*Phoebe. Phoebe.* That's all I cared about.

The next several days went the same. There were no little white dogs, but we would stop by Helen's and pick up Odin, then proceed to Phoebe's house. Usually, it was Dominique who answered the door, and Phoebe and I would immediately start wrestling. JayB would talk to Dominique, and they would both laugh. When that happened, JayB was happy.

Then we'd head to the dog park, and then we'd take long walks around the neighborhood. Eventually, we reversed the process, stopping to drop off Phoebe, then going to Odin's house, where Odin would crawl on his belly to Helen and then flop down for a tummy rub. The same trick, every time, but it never ceased to delight his person.

As long as I was included in the turkey treats, who was I to question the arrangement?

We spent our days outside, away from Kelsey. I saw Phoebe all the time. I'd never been so happy. This was how I wanted my life to be forever.

Then, one dark, late night, I heard Odin.

Dear Diary:

A dog's voice is easy to understand. I can hear a bark, or a howl, or a whine, and know exactly what that dog is feeling. Most of the time, the dog is happy. Dogs are happy because they get to be dogs.

But sometimes a dog conveys something else. The rich tones of a dog's vocalizations can communicate mourning, and grieving, a sadness so deep it hurts all the way to my bones. A dog's wail lifting up into the night sky can speak clearly of these things.

There is no sound more lonely.

 Love,
Clancy

# Five

It had been dark for a while. JayB was sleeping. I did not know where Kelsey was and did not care. But the sound that came to me, drifting on the night wind, was forlorn and unmistakable.

Odin was howling. Howling a sad, grieving wail. It sounded like he had pressed himself through his dog door and was in the backyard, his nose to the sky.

The howl went on, and on, and on.

I was impatient with my person the next morning. He had not heard Odin during the night, and was therefore unaware of any urgency. I sat and watched anxiously while he stirred his coffee and stared blankly out into the backyard. When I nosed him, his hand dropped down and stroked my forehead, but otherwise he didn't react. When I was finally on leash and we were heading down the street, I lifted my leg only to attend to my internal pressures—this was not the time to mark territory. I strained as we made our way up the sidewalk toward Odin's house. At the door, the echoing bell that followed my person's thumb on the button elicited a strained barking from my dog friend on the other side. Odin's voice was hoarse and weak from having spent the night addressing the moon.

I waited with increasing impatience as JayB fidgeted and finally rapped on the door. Then, with a glance at me, he pushed the door open. "Helen?" he called. With a scramble of nails across a wooden floor, Odin raced toward us and thrust his face frantically at JayB. "Hey, Odin," my person greeted. "How are you doing, buddy? You okay? What's wrong?"

JayB pushed Odin back, frowning. Odin panted. He was quivering, his eyes wild. Saliva flecked his jaws. When he looked at me, he didn't see me, and when I sniffed him, he acted as if my nose hadn't touched him at all.

"Helen!" JayB called more loudly. He cocked his head and listened. I watched Odin. JayB advanced cautiously into the house. He called several times and each time the three of us paused, listening for something.

Then JayB looked down at Odin, his eyes widening in understanding. His shoulders slumped. "Oh no," he murmured.

We entered a room at the end of the hall. Helen was there, and she was not there. Her smells had changed. The tiny sounds a person makes while moving through the world had silenced. This was why Odin had cried all night. He panted now, watching JayB, hoping my person could do what humans always do, which is to fix something gone terribly wrong.

There was, apparently, no fixing this. JayB spoke with his phone to his face, and then a bewildering succession of people came and went. Odin was mistrustful but obedient when JayB pulled us gently into an empty room. "Oh, Odin. Oh," he crooned softly. Odin wasn't wagging and his ears were down. He was still panting but he would lift his head and go silent at some noise within the house, straining to hear some sign of Helen out there with the other people. I kept by his side, sniffing him to let him know that he had a good friend.

Later, JayB gently urged Odin to his feet and led us down the street, not to the dog park, but just along some bushes for me to do my business more properly. Odin was distracted and actually squatted instead of lifting his leg. As soon as he was finished, he wanted to go home. I knew, though, that he'd never really be able to go home again.

That night, Odin stayed with us. The only break in his grief was when he saw Kelsey—with a deep-throated growl, he went after her hard and fast. She bolted and JayB shouted "No!" and I cringed from that word.

After that, Odin lived with us, but he and Kelsey always had a closed door between them unless he was restrained by an indoor leash. "You're a hunting dog," JayB told him. "But I can't let you hunt my cat, Odin."

Odin did not want to sleep on the bed, so JayB put a blanket by the front door, and that was where Odin remained whenever he was in the house.

I understood what was happening for Odin. How can a dog trust a world when his person is no longer in it?

Most days we started our mornings by walking up the street. Every single time, Odin tried to pull us up the driveway toward Helen's house. And every single time, JayB would gently say, "No, Odin, she's not there anymore. Come on, buddy, come on."

Sometimes those women who carried their dogs like squeaky toys—whose names were Cindy and Lindy, I learned—brought Millie and Tillie to our home. The first time this happened, the women cried and hugged JayB. They were very sad. I thought it probably was because of Helen.

Most mornings we would go get Phoebe. I was sad for Odin but my mood evaporated the moment Dominique or Bedford brought the dog I loved to the door. Odin ignored her, so she was all mine. We had bonded, Phoebe and I, the way two dogs bond because they belong together.

One day, I found a dirty ball along the sidewalk. I instantly had a brilliant idea for what to do with it: when Dominique sat on the steps with JayB to talk and laugh, I would put it in her lap. The ball would delight her so much that she'd want to come home with us so she could keep it.

By the time we arrived at Phoebe's house, I'd chewed that ball so much that it was soggy with my saliva. When Dominique came out and sat down, I pushed right past Phoebe and spat the ball into her dress, between her legs.

She sprang up. "Yuck!"

"Clancy!" JayB cried. "Dominique, I'm so sorry."

Phoebe jumped on the ball. I patiently waited for Dominique to draw the obvious connection between the ball, Phoebe, and living at our house.

"It's okay," Dominique assured JayB. "I need to go change, though. I have an appointment."

For some reason, Dominique didn't come with us that day, and when we returned, it was Bedford who greeted us. Dominique wasn't waiting for us at our house, either, despite the ball I had shown her.

People are so unpredictable.

One morning we were all walking briskly toward the dog park—Millie and Tillie with us—when I heard a voice calling from behind. "Hey, JayB, wait up! JayB!" The full pack reacted to the voice, but JayB seemed unaware. If anything, he picked up his pace.

"Wait up, buddy!" the voice called.

I recognized it as belonging to the man who was Spartan's person. Rodney. I did not want to smell Spartan, so I was happy to trot with my person.

"Slow up!"

Finally, my person stopped. "Hi, Rodney."

Rodney was a bit breathless. He was wearing shorts and no shirt, and he and Spartan were both panting. "Hey." He put his hands on his knees. "You need to fix your phone or something, I've been texting you and you haven't responded once." He laughed. "It's like you're avoiding me or something. Anyway, I need to make use of your services."

"Excuse me?"

"Yeah, I've got a real problem with Spartan. We'll be running and then he smells something and stops, wants to lift his leg. Practically yanks my arm out of the socket."

JayB nodded. "Right, that's what dogs do. They like to smell things. It's in the dog owner's manual."

Rodney laughed again. "Yeah, ha. So, when I run, I'd like you to watch Spartan. Like, starting now. Okay, bro? Thanks."

JayB was quiet for a moment. "Rodney," my person finally stated evenly, "I'm not actually a dog walker."

"Oh," Rodney jeered. "So—let me count—one, two, three, four, five reasons why everybody knows you're a dog walker. That means Spartan's number six, okay? Keep track of what I owe and I'll write you a check at the end, or maybe I could, like, build you a screened-in porch in trade."

"I already have a screened-in porch."

Rodney waved his hand. "Okay, whatever. Thanks."

JayB accepted Spartan's leash, Rodney ran away, and now we had Spartan with us.

It changed everything.

Phoebe and Spartan sniffed each other with rigid backs, their tails stiff in the air. I assumed that she would find Spartan as loathsome as did I. He didn't play, he didn't bow, he didn't even run, he just stood around. In fact, he didn't behave like a dog at all—he was more like a cat.

That was it! Spartan was a cat in a dog's body.

Things really started going wrong a little later, at the dog park. Off-leash, Spartan seemed to think his place was by Phoebe, who didn't act at all disturbed by this strange canine with his collapsing face. Spartan was so unfriendly that when I approached him, he would give me the coldest of stares and even *growl*. Growling at *me*, Clancy, everyone's favorite dog!

I forgot this insult when JayB produced a plastic disc and let it fly with a graceful snap of his arm. It soared through the air and the three of us, Spartan, Phoebe, and I, joyously pursued it. I had previously learned that Phoebe was much faster than just about any dog on four legs. Her pursuit of a sailing disc inevitably meant that she would get to it first. She didn't, however, know what to do with it when she reached it. I had learned long ago that the proper thing to do with a disc was, after mouthing it a little bit, return it to the person who threw it. Phoebe, however, thought the point of a disc was to capture it and then trot around with it held high in her jaws. I indulged her in this behavior because she was so precious to me. Eventually, she'd drop the disc and I'd spring on it and then race back to JayB, who would throw it again, repeating the cycle for all of us. I assumed that Phoebe was enjoying this as much as I was.

Spartan was slower than either of us and so I had no worries that he would ever catch the disc. But then the worst possible thing happened, which was that Phoebe's joyful, chewing run resulted in her dropping the toy in front of Spartan. He scooped it up triumphantly, but he didn't prance like Phoebe did. He didn't return it to the person who threw it, like any sensible dog would. He didn't wag or act at all happy with his prize. He just stood there.

Phoebe and I danced around impatiently. And then Spartan did something extraordinary. As Phoebe darted up close to him, he opened his mouth and let the disc fall. She snapped it up and dashed off gaily.

Spartan had given Phoebe the toy.

I frantically pursued Phoebe and finally she released the disc and I was able to snatch it. I returned it to JayB. Once again, the disc soared, but this time Phoebe, when she caught it, only batted it around playfully and Spartan got his jaws on it again.

I was heartsick. Phoebe and Spartan were playing disc with each other. It was as if I wasn't even there.

Seeking reassurance, I ran back to my person, who extended a friendly but distracted hand. I put a paw on his leg, beseeching him to notice that there was no fun in the dog park anymore. I looked to Odin, whose sadness still weighed on him like wet fur after a bath. He didn't seem to understand, either.

We escorted Spartan to a house that smelled like him and also Rodney; I would come to learn that this was their home. Then we stood at Phoebe's house so JayB and Dominique could talk.

JayB spoke to me on the way home. "She's perfect, Clancy. Except that she's with Bedford. I don't know what she sees in him . . . he doesn't even own a *shirt*."

When Odin and I set off on our leashes the next day, JayB in the rear, I was unsure if it would be a Millie and Tillie day, or a Phoebe day, because we were leaving the house so much later in the day, for some reason. Humans decide dog schedules, but as far as I was concerned, life was better if every day was exactly the same. As usual, Odin dragged us toward Helen's driveway.

JayB sighed. "Okay, Odin, okay. I guess you have to see for yourself." My person led us to the front door. JayB twisted the knob and pushed it open, straightening in surprise. "Oh! Well, that's not good. It shouldn't be unlocked."

Odin was trembling. JayB knelt and undid his leash. In a flash Odin was down the hall to the room where he had last seen his person.

Odin would need some time on Helen's bed with her scent in his nose. I elected to stay with JayB, who wandered aimlessly into the kitchen.

I became conscious of someone behind us and turned to look. A woman had stepped through the doorway. She held something in her hand, pointing at my person. "Stop," she ordered in a very loud and angry voice.

JayB froze.

"Don't move," she commanded, "I have a gun."

JayB held very still.

"If you try to turn around," the woman threatened sternly, "I will shoot you in the back."

Dear Diary:

I guess Odin lives with us now. He is not happy. He was always a dog who preferred a nap over a run, or to watch a ball rolling past his nose instead of launching himself in frantic pursuit. But now his mood has turned somber. He isn't eating much, and it is up to me to finish his dinners.

He understands what we found at Helen's house. He knows what it means that Helen no longer fills the air with her breath. When dogs are separated from their people, they feel it, and their distress is clear and evident to any canine they encounter.

To be severed in this final, absolute way means Helen is not coming back, not ever. Odin knows this, but I am not sure he accepts it. Will he, in time, learn to adapt to living with JayB?

It doesn't seem so. His grief is too profound. Plus, there is an unwillingness within JayB that Odin and I can sense, a reluctance to fully embrace Odin as part of the pack. For some reason, JayB doesn't seem to want Odin to live with us, to become Odin's person.

I know this: when it comes to Kelsey, Odin is my brother. There's nothing fun about his determined lunging at the cat—he wants to hunt her, rid her from our lives.

At every attempt, JayB speaks sharply to Odin, who lives on the leash, even inside the house.

Kelsey's reaction is to flee in terror. She finally understands how to behave around fierce canines like Odin and me.

"This isn't good, Odin," JayB says.

*Thus far, he's been successful in keeping Odin and Kelsey separate.*

*I'm wondering if I can change that.*

Love,
Clancy

# Six

Both JayB and the woman standing behind him seemed tense. I noticed that JayB had raised his hands into the air. There was a long, anxious silence. I wagged, but only half-heartedly, because I wasn't sure what was going on.

I hoped we could soon get back to doing something fun, meaning go to Phoebe's house and take her to the dog park without Spartan.

I regarded this new woman. She carried a flowery smell—much less attractive than Maddy's. She was also shorter and thinner than Maddy, though her hair was similar, just off her shoulders. And she seemed equally angry. Of all the women we had met recently, I preferred Dominique.

"Could I ask a question?" JayB asked.

The woman did not reply.

"See, if I turn around, how are you going to shoot me in the back? Wouldn't you wind up shooting me in the front?"

The woman seemed to think about this. "Are you trying to get smart with me? I'll remind you, I'm holding a weapon pointed at you right now."

"Thank you for that reminder."

"I am going to call the police and if you try anything, I will shoot you."

"You've made that point, and I'm not going to argue. And I think it's a great idea to call the police."

She frowned. "You do?"

"Of course. I'm not here with any criminal intent."

"Then what are you doing in my mom's house?"

JayB looked surprised. "Helen was your mother?"

"You knew Helen?"

"Yes, I'm her neighbor. I live just a few houses down. Can I turn around? I mean, I really don't have time to get shot today. Maybe if you could wait until the weekend, we could do it then. I have most of Saturday free."

"Okay, but very slowly and keep your hands in the air, and don't try anything."

"Just for clarification, it seems like you're asking me to *try* to keep my hands in the air. So I have to at least try *that*, right?"

"What is it with you?" she demanded. "Can you not treat anything seriously?"

"I think maybe I'm just a little nervous. This is my first attempted assassination."

"It's not assassination. It's the Make My Day law. You're in the house, so I can legally shoot you."

"Not in the back, though. That's not allowed," JayB pointed out. "That's the Go To Jail law."

The woman considered. "You're right. Turn around."

"You know, I think now that we've decided you can only legally shoot me in the front, I'm more comfortable with our current arrangement. Didn't you say something about inviting the police to the party?"

The woman bit her lip. "Okay, if you turn around and keep your hands up, I won't shoot you."

"You'd be surprised at how often people say that to me."

"*What?*"

"I'm kidding. Okay, I'm turning around, and you're not shooting me. Let's focus on how friendly that makes this." Carefully, awkwardly, my person pivoted until he was facing the woman, hands still raised. Then his shoulders relaxed and he dropped his hands. I wagged, glad he was no longer upset.

"Hey!" she barked at him. "What do you think you're doing?"

"Well," he replied reasonably, "you're not really going to shoot me, no matter what I do."

"Oh, yes, I am," she insisted.

"No, you're not."

"Am, too."

"See, that's not a real gun."

The woman stared at him. "What do you mean? How would you know?"

JayB pointed his finger and the woman took a step back from him. "That orange thing in the front, that's on there so that if you ever were to point the gun at law enforcement, they would know it was just a toy."

The woman looked offended. "Nobody told me that," she complained. "I've been carrying it in my pocket when I go for walks at night."

"You could always throw it," JayB suggested. He focused his gaze. "I can see the family resemblance. You have Helen's blue eyes and blond hair. Are you the doctor or the teacher?"

The woman frowned. "I'm the bookkeeper. And you still haven't answered my question. What are you doing in my mom's house?"

"I'm her dog walker. Well, I mean, I'm not actually a dog walker. That's not what I *do*. It's just that I would walk Odin as a favor that she insisted on paying me for, and then when your mom passed away . . . and, oh, by the way, I'm so sorry for your loss. . . . It must have been a real shock."

The woman lowered her eyes. "Yes," she agreed quietly.

"I took Odin to my house because no one knew what else to do. I think your mom's friends, Cindy and Lindy, already called . . . is it your brother and your sister?"

The woman nodded bitterly. "Right. No, they were called, but my siblings are both too busy to do anything about this, so it's up to me. One's a teacher and the other's a doctor, so my job isn't important. Did you say 'Odin'?"

"Yeah. Hey, Odin!" JayB called.

I raised my head expectantly and heard the jangle as Odin came out of his person's bedroom, wagging a little.

"Oh my God, *Odin*," the woman exclaimed, kneeling with her hands open. Odin ran to her, wagging. Now the woman was crying. She had her arms around Odin, who seemed a little confused. "You're a good, good dog," she murmured.

Odin seemed to know who she was, but wasn't reacting to her the way dogs treat old, trusted friends. He was hesitating, and I knew it was because he still really couldn't accept that Helen was gone and was worried that this woman being here meant even more things were changing.

"You can tell he's met you before. I'm JayB Danville, by the way."

The woman wiped tears from her cheeks. "I'm Alana Knox. Hi."

"Hi, Alana." There was a pause. "Well, I'm so sorry," JayB apologized. "I didn't mean to frighten you, though I guess you weren't too frightened. After all, you had the gun."

Alana laughed a little. She stood up from petting Odin and looked around her surroundings. "I just got here a little while ago and was walking through the house. My God, my mom has all these boxes in the basement. I guess I'm supposed to go through each one and figure out what to do with everything. This could take months, if I let it."

"I'm sorry," JayB repeated. "It must be hard."

Alana nodded, biting her lip. "Would you like to sit for a moment?"

"Sure."

Odin curled up in the corner of the room on the carpet, and I lay down with him.

"Is there anything you need, anything I can do for you?" JayB asked.

The woman shook her head, "I don't think so. I took an Uber from the airport and I've got my mom's car keys, so I can go buy boxes and shipping stuff. . . ." Her voice trailed off. "It's pretty overwhelming."

Odin was lying on his side and it occurred to me that this was how he positioned himself for a tummy rub. My thoughts flashed to Dominique and I realized I had the answer for how to get her to move in with us: I would sprawl out like Odin. No human can resist a dog's offered belly. Dominique would rub my tummy and want to come to our house with Phoebe so she could do it again!

"Um . . . Alana? Would you like me to take Odin with me to the dog park today?"

We all looked at Odin at the sound of his name.

Alana thought about it and nodded. "That would be nice."

"Okay, then." JayB stood. "I need to go pick up a couple more dogs and head out. Want to go to the dog park with us? Odin?"

I wagged excitedly. Odin peered at my person without enthusiasm.

Alana stood as well. "What makes this really hard," she said mournfully, "is that my mom and I weren't speaking. I hadn't spoken to her for two years or more. We got in this huge fight. She didn't like my boyfriend and, well, we had words."

"I'm really sorry."

"No, I'm the one who should be sorry. I shouldn't dump that on you, we barely know each other."

"I think pointing a gun at me sort of broke the ice."

Alana laughed.

At Phoebe's house, I executed my brilliant plan and sprawled out for a tummy rub, but Phoebe, not understanding the strategy, went completely berserk and jumped on me, so Dominique was not lured into stroking my belly. I would have to try again.

Bringing Dominique and JayB together was proving to be much more difficult than I expected. And then there was my other plan: to get rid of Kelsey.

Being a dog takes a lot of concentration.

After playing with Phoebe at the dog park, Odin and I dropped her off and returned to Helen's. Odin picked up his step as we turned up the driveway, wagging in anticipation. His person might be gone forever, but he still drew comfort from his home.

Alana opened the door. Her eyes were puffy, and she smelled different somehow.

"Thank you," she greeted quietly. "Would you like to come in?"

JayB shook his head, "Oh, no, I don't . . ."

"Please," Alana interrupted. "I could really use some company right now."

"Sure."

Odin and I found the same corner of the room. The people sat in the same chairs as before.

"This is going to be so hard," Alana lamented. "Like, look at this." She held out what I recognized as a book, though it was larger than the ones JayB propped on his chest in bed at night. "It's Mom and Dad's wedding album. They were so young!"

"Is your father still with us?" JayB asked delicately.

Alana shook her head. "No, he died a long time ago. And you know I have a brother and a sister."

JayB nodded.

"They're older than I am. Mom was forty-three when I was born. It's like my siblings are a different family. I was the baby and kind of an only child, if you think about it." Alana opened the book in her lap and shook her head. "They look so happy," she murmured. She smelled very sad. Her eyes were wet and she gave JayB a trembling smile. "I guess I won't ever have a wedding album. My boyfriend—his name's Guy, Guy Trulock." She paused and waited for JayB to say something and then continued. "He doesn't believe in marriage so much."

"I have a lot of friends like that."

"Have you ever been married?"

JayB shook his head. "No. I lived with a woman for several years and right about the time we started thinking about getting married, we realized we weren't really suited for domestic life with each other. That was back in San Francisco."

"And now you live here in Kansas City," Alana observed, a question lingering over the statement.

"Right. I bought a house out here almost on impulse. I have a half brother, Tim, who lives in Vancouver, whose job, as far as anyone can tell, is to ski and get government assistance. He never calls. My dad lives in this area—he recently came into some money and bought a place in Mission Hills. I thought about maybe moving somewhere else, but I don't know where that would be." He shrugged. "My dad and my mom got divorced when I was young.

Her name is Celeste and she lives in Florida with her third husband. My dad's name is Walter, but I was really raised by my stepfather, Howard. Just a few blocks from here, actually."

Alana gave him a small smile. "Howard and Walter: Celeste likes traditional names."

JayB laughed. "Well, now she's married to a guy named Twain Wolfe, if you can believe it, so no."

Gradually, Alana's smile faded. "I opened maybe three boxes the whole time you were gone. It's going to take forever. My mom seems to have kept everything."

JayB inhaled. "Well, I hate to add to your burdens, but I'm hoping you'll keep Odin here with you."

She sighed. "I didn't realize that all this would include taking care of a dog." Her eyes widened. "Oh! What happens to Odin?"

I was hearing Odin's name a lot, but not mine, and wasn't sure what to make of that.

"What do you mean?" JayB asked.

"I can't take Odin back to Marina del Rey with me," the woman explained. "So . . ."

JayB shook his head. "Odin's a wonderful dog, but he's mostly a breed called Treeing Walker Coonhound. He's a hunter. His instincts tell him to attack my cat, so I'm having to spend all my time keeping them separated. Meaning, I have been *watching* him, but I can't possibly adopt him."

"I have a cat, too," Alana informed him in a small voice.

"Oh, but that doesn't necessarily mean Odin will be hostile toward it," JayB advised. "Kelsey, my cat, runs away—she's a literal scaredy cat. She runs, so his instinct is to pursue. A cat that stands its ground is always a different story."

"Yes, that's her," Alana acknowledged with a rueful laugh. "She's backed down whole *packs* of dogs."

"Problem solved, then," JayB offered with a smile.

Alana regarded him, a troubled expression on her face. "My boyfriend—we live together?—he doesn't like dogs. He would never agree to take in Odin."

"Oh." JayB and Alana both turned and gazed at Odin. "So I guess we're back to your question," JayB concurred. "What happens to Odin?"

Both Alana and JayB seemed restless and sad. "Well, I don't need to do anything right now," she decided after a long moment. "I have a million boxes to go through first. Like, I found a reel-to-reel tape recorder. I don't know if I should donate it or try to sell it."

"I think something like that you could sell. Maybe on eBay?"

"I don't really know how to do that."

He shrugged. "Well, I could help you."

Alana gazed at him steadily. "What do you mean?"

"I mean I could, you know, help you go through the boxes. Personal stuff, obviously, you'd need to make a decision on. But like, old electronics, things like that, I could sort them out, decide with you what needs to be sent to a charity and what you might want to try to sell, like in a garage sale or something. Garage sales are very big around here. Your task would go faster with two people, I think."

Alana smiled at him. "That's so nice. I would like that, thank you."

"Okay, my schedule. Most days I get a much earlier start. I walk a dog named Phoebe." I glanced up sharply at her name. "And sometimes a dog named Spartan. And your mom's friends have two little dogs named Millie and Tillie. But I usually take care of them for just a few hours, and then I'm free the rest of the day. So I could come by and help in the mornings, and some afternoons."

"That would be great. I'll go for a run," Alana speculated, "and be ready when you get here."

They smiled at each other. "It's a deal," JayB declared. "Do you want to start now?"

"Honestly, I'm completely drained, and right before you got here, I realized somebody cleaned out the refrigerator. All there is is ketchup and mustard, stuff like that."

JayB brightened. "Oh! Why don't you come to my place for dinner, then?"

Alana shook her head. "Oh, no, I couldn't do that."

JayB raised his hands, palms up. "Why not? You're going to have to eat eventually. Please, it's the least I can do."

"All right. Thank you. So, is everybody in Kansas City as nice as you are?"

"No," he told her. "It's pretty much known that I'm the nicest person here. I've won awards."

JayB and Alana each held a leash as Odin and I escorted them to our house. When we arrived, a grinning man was standing next to an automobile.

It was Walter.

*Dear Diary:*

*Most days, Spartan's person shows up, panting, on the front steps. Rodney shoves Spartan through the front door. "Thanks, bro!" he shouts.*

*I can feel JayB's disgust when this happens, and can only assume it has to do with Spartan's appearance. A dog's eyes are not meant to be hidden under the collapsed skin of its forehead. Dog's mouths are meant to convey a variety of expressions, but Spartan remains solemnly blank no matter what we are doing.*

*Other days, instead of Rodney bursting through the front door, we walk to Spartan's house to retrieve him.*

*I am agonized over the fact that Phoebe doesn't see Spartan as an intrusion into our relationship. She wags and play-bows in Spartan's presence. Is she doing that to torment me?*

*Surely my feelings are as obvious to her as hers are opaque to me. Phoebe is a happy, guileless, fun-loving canine, so full of life I have trouble getting her to pay attention to anything important.*

*Spartan's presence only adds to the distraction.*

*To a dog, every day is worth living and no day can really be ruined, but for me, a day at the dog park with Spartan is practically pointless.*

Love,
Clancy

# Seven

JayB's reaction to seeing Walter was to suck in a breath, and I glanced at him curiously. "You bought a *Ferrari*?" JayB demanded.

Walter flashed his big smile. "Yeah. I've always wanted one. I had to pay cash for it, can you believe it? I guess my credit isn't what it should be." He shrugged and laughed. "Who's this pretty lady?"

I sensed some discomfort as JayB turned and gestured to Alana. "This is Alana. Remember Helen? I told you about her. This is Helen's daughter. She's here from Marina del Rey."

"Oh, I'm sorry about your mother. I never met her, sad to say."

"Thank you."

"I'm Jago's father, Walter. I'm an investor."

JayB made a snorting sound and Walter glared at him. "What?"

"An investor?" JayB chided. "Really?"

Walter waved his hand. "How else do you explain that I have a Ferrari and own a house in Mission Hills while your house is here in Prairie Village?" Then he shot a look at Alana. "Not that there's anything wrong with Prairie Village."

JayB turned to Alana. "What my dad's not telling you is that his 'investment' was in a Powerball ticket, along with all the other employees in shipping and receiving."

"And it paid off, didn't it?" Walter bragged. "All you did to get *your* money was be beaten up by a woman."

"Thanks for that, Dad."

Alana frowned. "I feel like I'm missing some backstory."

Odin and I turned as a car pulled up. I wagged because I recognized the scent of the woman who got out of the car. It was Maddy. She slammed her door and, as the car drove off, came striding up to us.

"Who's this?" she asked suspiciously, jabbing a finger at Alana.

"This is Alana Knox. Her mother, Helen, is the woman who died," JayB replied emphatically. "Alana, this is Maddy."

"Hi, Maddy."

Maddy looked Alana up and down and said, "Oh."

"We are very sorry for her loss," JayB stated pointedly.

Maddy blinked. "Oh. Of course. I'm sorry your mother died. I never said I wasn't. I just didn't expect to make a surprise romance visit to my boyfriend and find him talking to a woman in shorts."

JayB frowned. "Maddy . . ."

"Thank you, Maddy. Well, I should be going," Alana observed.

"Oh no, you can't leave yet," Walter boomed. "Jago's about to tell you how he makes a living being punched in the nose by women."

JayB shook his head and sighed.

"Oh," Maddy joined in, "I *wish* I could get paid for that. I'd be rich."

"Besides, Alana," Walter continued, "I want you to meet Jago's best friend, Rodney. He's on his way over—I just called him from the Ferrari."

JayB stared stonily at his father. "And why," he asked Walter, "would you do that?"

"To see the new car, of course."

"You have a surprisingly busy social life going on in your driveway," Alana remarked.

"As well he should," Maddy interjected.

"Tell the story," Walter urged. "She'll love it."

Alana eyed JayB. "I can see that whatever we're talking about is painful for you. Please don't feel like you need to say anything for my benefit."

"No," Maddy objected. "Men should always do what they don't want."

"It's okay," JayB assured her. "Anything to amuse Walter. But there's not that much to tell. So, back in Walnut Creek I was an HR director for a tech firm that needed to lay off some people."

"This was before I made all my money," Walter interrupted. "Otherwise, I might have bought the company, saved my kid's job."

"Thanks, Dad. Anyway, so it was in the procedures manual that the company was required to have a security guard on site whenever mass firings were taking place, in case, you know, of violence. Or people with toy guns."

Alana smiled.

"Toy guns are *worthless*," Maddy sneered.

"Well, the CFO, my boss, decided we couldn't afford a security guard," JayB continued. "So I started having meetings with people to tell them they were being laid off, and this one woman got furious and threw her laptop at me."

Alana winced. "That sounds painful."

JayB grinned. "Well, she missed, but the laptop got hurt pretty bad."

"Come on. *Then* what happened?" Walter prodded impatiently.

JayB gave him a long look. "And then," he responded slowly, "the woman came back with her husband. He also was unhappy, I guess, and he punched me."

"Oh! no," Alana said.

"I would have beaten him to a pulp of blood," Maddy declared.

"Then he held me while she punched me."

"Wait," Alana objected. "The *woman* hit you?"

"My grandma stabbed a guy once," Maddy remarked.

JayB nodded. "Yeah, and what made it worse was that she actually hit harder than her husband. So I settled with my company and bought a house here in Kansas City. I figured my dad needed moral support because he had just been fired himself."

Walter arched an eyebrow. "Well, I have a different take on what happened."

"Oh, do tell, Dad."

Walter turned to Alana. "See, I had some innovative ideas for what we should be doing in shipping and receiving. I wanted to expand the business."

"As I understand it," JayB interrupted, "you were taking boxes and selling them to moving companies."

"Exactly," Walter agreed triumphantly.

"That's brilliant," said Maddy.

Walter grinned at her. "It represented a, what you call it? A separate income stream. We bought the boxes so cheaply, and then I figured you mark them up a little bit, you sell them, and bingo, Walter gets a bonus."

"Except in this case, you paid yourself the bonus instead of giving the money to the company," JayB pointed out.

Walter shrugged. "Every business has startup costs. Anyway, what Jago here is *not* saying is that, even though I was temporarily seeking new and better opportunities in my profession, I was continuing to contribute to the pool every week for Powerball. I mean, I know a good investment when I see one. And then, of course, it paid off."

"I don't think I've ever heard a story like that," Alana said.

Walter nodded again. "I know. Call me a dreamer, and maybe I am, but I've always said, if you do what you love, the money will follow."

"You should write a book," Maddy told Walter. "I'd for sure watch the movie version."

"I really should go," Alana decided. "You've got company."

"No, I invited you to dinner."

"Hey, that's great," Walter proclaimed brightly. "Let's all get dinner. I'll buy."

"Excellent!" Maddy enthused.

"We'll order when Rodney gets here," Walter declared. He turned to Alana. "You'll like Rodney. Man has a real head on his shoulders. We're doing some business together." He winked. "Rodney is Jago's best friend since they were little boys."

Alana glanced at JayB. "Jago," she repeated.

"First name Jago, middle name Burr. JayB," my person explained. "So, Dad, you mean to tell me you're actually going into business with *Rodney?* Wait, this isn't the restaurant, is it?"

"Oh, it's way more complicated than that," Walter boasted.

I looked up then because I could hear and smell a dog approaching. I knew instantly who it was: Spartan.

Spartan, of course, barely acknowledged there were two other dogs, though both Odin and I would have been willing to exchange butt-sniffs.

"Whoa, look at that Ferrari! You gotta let me drive it, Walter," Rodney hailed. His eyes widened when he saw Alana. "Hell-lo."

JayB gave Alana an apologetic look. "This is Helen's daughter Alana," he told Rodney.

"I am so glad to meet you!" Rodney told Alana. "This is going to be great!"

Alana seemed puzzled by this.

We all entered the house together. Spartan busied himself sniffing the corners. Kelsey made a haughty appearance, but when she spotted Spartan and Odin, she vanished down the hallway.

Everyone sat in soft chairs. Odin folded his legs to lie down, watching me for a clue as to what to do. When I eased down on the floor next to my person, Odin relaxed a little.

"Have you ever been to Kansas City before, Alana?" Walter wanted to know.

Alana shrugged. "I visited Mom a couple of years ago, but otherwise, no."

Rodney grinned. "I've lived here my whole life, if you can believe it. Went to Shawnee Mission East, even though there's no such place as 'Shawnee Mission.' That's just part of the allure. I'll have to show you around. It's really a great town. I have a lot of friends here, of course."

Alana nodded. "Okay."

"Well, if you've never been to Kansas City, then the choice for dinner is obvious," Walter declared heartily. "We'll get barbecue. Kansas City's known for its barbecue."

"Let's get Jack Stack, that's my favorite," Rodney said decisively.

"Just don't tell them it's for me," Maddy cautioned. "I got thrown out of there when I went back after the incident."

Later, a man brought fragrant bags of meat to the front door. Odin and I reacted to this promising development by leaping to our feet and making our presence known to all the people assembling at the table. Spartan, however, reacted not at all. What kind of dog ignores food? I mean, it was *meat in a bag*, something that was absolutely dog business. Fine, let him do what he wanted. As far as I was concerned, all the people were happy, so it was only logical that some food items soon would be tossed onto the floor. Odin and I decided to do Sit. Sit is one of those dog things that humans find irresistible.

"How long before you leave?" Maddy coldly asked Alana.

"I don't know," Alana replied with a quick look to JayB. "It depends."

"On what?" Maddy challenged. "On *JayB?*"

"Oh, no. I mean, I have to take care of all my mother's things. I don't know how long that's going to take. JayB's offered to help."

"Oh, JayB's offered to, quote, *help*, unquote, has he?" Maddy asked, with two fingers bending in the air. She stared accusingly at JayB. "Like I haven't heard that one before."

"Please don't misinterpret anything," Alana objected mildly. "I live with my boyfriend back in Los Angeles."

"He have a name, this anonymous LA boyfriend?"

Alana laughed a little, nonplussed. "Of course."

Everyone was looking at Alana expectantly. "Guy Trulock," she finally admitted with something approaching reluctance.

Rodney guffawed. "What kind of name is that? Is he a Muppet?"

"Good one, Rodney." Maddy admired. "I totally agree."

"I do understand it's an unusual name," Alana acknowledged.

"Oh yeah. Try this one on for size," Walter interjected. "Twain Wolfe. I mean, that's got to be straight out of witness protection or something. Nobody has a name like that."

"Well, except at least one person does," JayB commented.

Maddy waved her hand dismissively. "Those fools in witness protection are worthless. At least the people in prison are honest."

"Right? Tell that to my son."

Thus far, no food had fallen to the floor. Odin and I glanced at each other in concern. Sometimes people get so busy talking, they forget that their dogs are right there doing a good Sit.

"I didn't know when I took this remodeling gig that my best buddy lived right around the corner," Rodney announced. "This changes everything."

Maddy nodded. "Sometimes things happen for a reason, even in the presence of deficiency."

Walter was smiling. "I love having everyone here like this. It's like a family. The only person missing is Celeste."

JayB gave him a bleak look.

"So, Alana," Rodney speculated slowly, "you've never been to Kansas City. You need someone to show you around. That's me. What're you doing tomorrow?"

Alana looked surprised at the question. "Oh, well, mainly just taking care of my mom's house, I guess. Packing things up and going through boxes. Going to the store. Things like that."

"I'll tell you where the best grocery stores are," Rodney promised. "Everybody knows me by name at those places, I've been going there for so long. They'll give you a special deal if you tell them Rodney sent you."

Maddy gave Rodney an admiring look. "So, you're like, famous or something?"

Rodney nodded. "Famous? More like well-known, really. Locally, anyway. Hey, JayB?" Rodney stood. "I need to talk to you about something really important. In private."

JayB looked around. "Can it wait?"

Rodney shook his head. "Actually, no. I need to talk to you *now*."

*Dear Diary:*

*Kelsey eats in the most unappreciative manner. Dogs consume dinner with gusto, letting everyone know from the sounds we make that we love the food that has been given us by our people. Cats, on the other hand, eat silently, without gratitude or acknowledgment. It's disgusting.*

*If JayB didn't so reliably set out the fragrant cans of food on the counter, I'm not sure that Kelsey would even live with us.*

*I'm thinking about that counter, about her can of food. Could I climb up there? If I could get on top of that counter, I could eat her food.*

*That would change everything.*

Love,
Clancy

# Eight

Everyone went quiet at Rodney's dramatic pronouncement. When my person, looking resigned, stood, I naturally followed him into the kitchen, though Odin remained behind with the food. Sometimes being a loyal dog means walking away from potentially lucrative opportunities.

In the kitchen, JayB gave Rodney a puzzled look. "So, what's up, Rodney?"

Rodney winced. "Can you keep your voice down?" he whispered.

"They saw us come into the kitchen. I think they pretty much know we're in here. Is this about the restaurant?"

Rodney drew back a little. "What did Walter tell you about it?"

"Actually, my father has told me nothing. What I'm telling you is you can*not* rope him into investing in a restaurant. Understand? I'm serious."

"It's not *just* a restaurant. You need to talk to Walter about this."

"I'm talking to you, Rodney, because it's your idea. My father . . . my father isn't very good at managing his money. Or anything else, really. He likes to take leaps of faith. But I read a book about restaurants one time—the title of it was *Never, Ever, Ever, Ever Invest in a Restaurant*. Can you guess what the conclusion was?"

"A *book?*" Rodney mocked. "This is far better than anything in a book. But no, that's not what I need to talk about." He stared intently into my person's eyes. "I have to tell you something really serious, and I mean it. This is me being really serious. Can you tell the difference?"

JayB shrugged noncommittally. "Actually, you look constipated."

"It's about Alana."

"Yeah?"

"I call her."

JayB frowned. "What does that mean?"

"What do you think it means?" Rodney snapped. "This is man-to-man talk. It means I *call* her. I know you saw her first, but you have Maddy."

JayB shook his head. "I don't have Maddy. I don't think anybody has Maddy. I'm not even sure *Maddy* has Maddy."

"Okay, but still, I'm calling Alana, here. You have to honor that."

JayB folded his arms. "That's ridiculous."

"What are you saying? You're gunning for Alana, too?"

"No, I'm not *gunning*. Gunning? I'm not sure what you're saying."

"I'm saying she's new in town. She's kind of vulnerable right now. She doesn't need a lot of guys sniffing around her. She needs to settle on somebody like me, to protect her."

"You don't even get how offensive that statement is, do you? How is it you're walking around in an adult body when your brain is still back in middle school?"

"That's exactly what I'm saying. It *is* like middle school. I was always there for you in middle school."

JayB snorted. "You were *never* there for me in middle school. Remember Susie? I told you I loved her, so you asked her to the winter dance."

Rodney thought about it, then laughed. "Well, yeah, I guess I did that. But you were still trying to work up your nerve. I had to pounce."

"Right," JayB agreed sarcastically.

"Okay, so, this one will make us even, then."

"What kind of math do you do?"

"I'm just saying I think we have an understanding here."

"Actually, an understanding is where at least two people understand. In this instance, I think we're one person shy."

Rodney clapped him on the shoulder with a cupped hand. "I appreciate this."

I followed them back out to the table.

Maddy was glaring at them suspiciously. "Everything okay?"

"Oh, yeah," JayB assured her. "Rodney was just lifting his leg on something."

Rodney laughed.

Maddy turned back to Alana. "Well, anyway, I can't run. I have non-standard knees."

Rodney was immediately energized. "Run? Who's a runner?"

Alana shrugged. "I run."

"Have you ever done organized races?" he asked eagerly.

Alana shook her head. "Oh, no, nothing like that."

"Well, I have," Rodney informed her breezily. "My time in a 5K is under thirty minutes now. That puts me in pretty serious competition. A lot of the younger guys can't believe it when I blow past 'em. They say, 'There goes the Rodster.'"

JayB nodded. "I'm sure that's exactly what happens."

"I'll take you running, Alana," Rodney offered slyly. "I'll show you the routes. It'll be great. And don't worry about Odin. I have the best dog walker."

JayB sort of smiled at this.

"This is wonderful," Walter rejoiced, opening his arms as if to hug everybody. "Let's call Celeste."

My person groaned aloud. *"Dad."*

"What?" Walter protested innocently. "We're having a party. Everybody's here. I think we should call her."

"Who's Celeste?" Maddy asked suspiciously. "Your anthropologist?"

"She's JayB's mom," Rodney supplied helpfully. "She used to make me pancakes with bananas in them. I forget what they're called."

"Banana pancakes," Maddy advised primly. She shrugged. "You learn a lot, being a waitress."

"Why would you call Mom?" JayB asked Walter.

Walter laughed. "Because I want to talk to her, of course. That's why you call people. I've tried a bunch of times, but every time I do, the phone's answered by some guy."

"That's her *husband,* Dad. It's his phone, which is why he answers it."

"Well, you can see why it's awkward for me."

"I hate it when that happens to me," Rodney interjected. "So like I'll be dating some girl and her ex-boyfriend will call and I'll answer and he'll be all stuttering and weird about it."

"I don't *stutter*," Walter corrected irritably. "I just hang up on him."

"Oh, yeah," Rodney agreed with a laugh. "They do *that* a lot, too. *Click*." He glanced at Alana. "But I'm not dating anybody right now. I'm completely available." He winked and then grinned at JayB.

They ate some more, and finally a few pieces of succulent meat fell from my person's fingers. Moments later, Alana surreptitiously lowered a cupped palm and Odin gratefully licked something from it. Good people know they should share food with their dogs.

Rodney didn't give anything to Spartan. Maybe that's why Spartan didn't care when the food arrived.

People stood and began carrying things into the kitchen.

"Well," Rodney announced, "I'll walk Alana home, so you guys"— he nodded to Maddy and JayB—"can clean up and, you know, do whatever else you feel like doing."

Maddy flinched. "Oh, excuse me? So that's what this is? Some sort of tag team on me?" She turned to JayB. "I'm going to have to make that one of my eight simple rules."

"Sounds good," JayB agreed affably.

"Oh, I better go too, then," Walter observed. "Hope I don't wake up the neighborhood." He gave a soft chuckle. "The Ferrari's engine is like angels making thunder under the hood."

Rodney laughed. "Thunder under the hood," he repeated. "That's probably what my ex-girlfriends say about me."

Maddy rolled her eyes. "Oh, please. You don't even *have* a hood."

Rodney looked puzzled, and JayB grinned.

"I really don't need you to walk me home, Rodney," Alana said mildly. "It's only a few houses up the street."

Rodney waved a hand. "Don't worry about it. You can repay the favor someday."

Odin went out the door with Alana and then it was just me, the cat (hiding somewhere in hostility), Maddy, and JayB.

Maddy folded her arms. "So," she sneered, "I guess you got what you wanted."

"What I wanted? I wanted more ribs, but Rodney ate them all."

"No." Maddy pointed to herself. "Alone at last."

"Right, sure, there is that."

"I took a Lyft to get here. So if you want to have some champagne or something, okay."

JayB seemed uncomfortable, and I raised my head to regard him alertly. "Maddy, I think maybe Rodney gave you the wrong idea about something."

"You can say that, but I know how men are. They always want two birds in their hands, unless they're driving. So you don't have to worry, I figured I'd give in eventually. This is technically more than our third date."

"That's what I'm trying to talk to you about."

Maddy raised an eyebrow. "Oh, you want to talk first?"

JayB sighed.

Suddenly the front door opened. "Hey, you two," Walter greeted sheepishly. "I'm sorry to interrupt."

"You didn't," Maddy assured him. "We were about two minutes away from that."

Walter laughed awkwardly, then turned to JayB. "Okay. Hey, would you do me a favor? I got the Ferrari started, but I can't figure out how to get it into reverse."

"Sure."

We all went outside. I took the opportunity to lift my leg. The night had cooled and the bugs were singing to each other.

JayB sat in Walter's car. "Okay, you do it like this. See?"

Walter nodded. "Oh, okay. Got it."

JayB climbed out of the vehicle. "Hey," he said brightly, "you know what? Maddy doesn't have a ride home. Could you maybe give her a lift?"

Walter beamed. "Oh, I'd be happy to. Want to see what this baby can do?" he asked Maddy.

Maddy frowned at JayB, then turned and looked at Walter. "Okay, fine." She walked past JayB, giving him a cold look.

"Goodnight, Maddy," JayB said to her.

"Good*bye,* JayB."

"Take care, Jago," Walter added. "I'll see you tomorrow, son."

With a lot of noise, he backed the car into the street and then drove off, his tires screeching.

"Come on, Clancy, let's get you a proper dinner," JayB told me.

There are many words a person can say, but "dinner" has to be the most wonderful of all.

Later, JayB was staring at a book in bed when I heard an odd sound coming from the back bedroom. I trotted down the hall and looked in to see Kelsey at the open, screened-in window. Cooler air flowed in past her, carrying her cat stench straight to my nose. A moth was popping against the screen and Kelsey was batting at it spastically. She was so frustrated in her attempts to spear the innocent moth that she kept leaping onto the screen with all four claws extended, clinging to it. Then she would drop back down to the ledge, which was a short distance from the top of the mattress. It would be an easy leap for a cat—and for a dog, for that matter—to reach the bed where she was conducting her fruitless attack.

I watched her, growing more and more incensed. JayB was lying in bed and deserved to have the attentions of his animals. But this one, this cat, did not care. She only wanted to hunt an innocent moth. Without even thinking, the next time she went all-four-claws onto the window covering, I leapt from the floor to the bed and threw myself against the screen.

I dropped back to my feet as the screen fell out into the night, the cat still attached.

Kelsey was outside.

For a moment, I reviewed events, trying to figure out what had just happened. Did *I* do that? No, I decided, it was Kelsey who had jumped up on the screen, just like it was Kelsey who was now crouched in darkness.

We would never have to see her again. Wagging joyously, I turned and went to check on my person.

JayB held a book on his chest, but I could tell by his breathing that he would soon have the best night of sleep he'd ever had. No cat to leap on him in the middle of the night, making her ridiculous, deep-chested purring, rubbing herself all over his face so that his skin carried her insufferable odor the next morning.

And then I heard an odd yowl, a low moaning. I lifted my head and began panting, as much to mask the racket as to work off the tension I felt.

"What is it, Clancy?" JayB asked. He set the book down. "I heard it too." He cocked his head, listening.

I wanted to think of something dramatic that I could do to convince him to keep his attention on me, but I couldn't imagine what that would be. Growl, lift my leg on the dresser, throw up? The best I could come up with was to leap nimbly to the floor, go to my water bowl, and lap up water as loudly as I could manage, deliberately rattling my steel collar tags against the ceramic rim.

It wasn't enough. Clearly rising above the distraction was the louder repeat of the same unwelcome noise.

JayB threw the blankets off his feet. "Kelsey?" he called. "Kelsey, is that you?"

I watched in dismay as he found the screenless window. He thrust his head out into the night. "Kelsey, what are you doing out there?"

I could only hope he was telling her to go away and that all her food would be given to the dog. He turned from the window.

He did not go back to bed.

I watched sullenly as Kelsey scampered in the door the minute JayB slid it open. She gave me a single, haughty look, but otherwise devoted her efforts to smearing her scent around and around JayB's ankles until he picked her up and stared into her face. "What did you do, Kelsey? How did you get through that screen, you silly cat?"

I was hoping to hear words like "No!" and "Bad!" but I did not.

I was no longer as happy as I had been.

*Dear Diary:*

*Odin is unable to understand where he belongs. His house, still redolent of Helen, feels like home—but dogs know that home is wherever our people are. I can see he finds comfort in lying in his dog bed in its familiar corner, but he remains uneasy, thrust into uncertainty because Helen is gone.*

*Will he accept Alana as his person, now? I don't know if he can manage that.*

*Odin looks to me to lead him toward understanding because I am a dog with a person, and he knew us before Helen was wheeled away by the softly speaking people. But I don't know anything except that humans will decide everything, as has always been true.*

*Alana and JayB speak of Odin sometimes. We both look up when we hear his name.*

*"What happens to dogs like Odin?" Alana presses JayB. "An old guy, his owner dead. Where will he live?"*

*"He's a wonderful dog. If he were a different breed, or if Kelsey were a different cat . . ." JayB shakes his head. "I just can't take him. I don't know what happens."*

*"Poor Odin," Alana says sadly.*

Love,
Clancy

# Nine

The morning light was barely beginning to filter in through the windows when I reacted loudly to a knock on the door, earning a stern, "No barking. Stop that barking!" from JayB. I didn't know what he was talking about, but he went to the door clutching his fragrant coffee and opened it, peering out through the screen.

It was Rodney and, unfortunately, Spartan.

"Hey, buddy," Rodney greeted cheerfully.

I stepped out with my person and went to sniff Spartan. Despite the fact that we were arguably part of a pack, Spartan remained wooden and unfriendly. He allowed me to examine him a little and then spun and looked me directly in the eye, a clear act of hostility. I went over to mark the shrubs in front of our house, putting him on notice that the entire yard smelled of my urine for a reason.

"So, hey, how do I look?" Rodney wanted to know. He was wearing pants that left his legs bare and a shirt that did the same for his arms. He hoisted his hands up and curled them, grinning. "I pumped a little iron."

"You look like someone who's brought his dog over to my house too early," JayB replied. "You're not due for another half an hour."

"I know. I couldn't wait any longer. I texted Alana to tell her, so it's okay." Rodney turned. "So, check out my butt. That's all Alana's going to see on this run . . . get it?"

"Thanks, I'd rather not look at it."

Rodney turned back. "Hey, I want you to know, I'll never forget how you set the two of us up. I mean, we'll probably talk about this for a long time. You're a good wingman, JayB."

"I don't feel like that's at all what happened."

"Oh, come on, you saw the sparks. You got to admit"—he leaned forward and lowered his voice—"she's really hot. Don't you think?"

"Yes, that's what I think," JayB admitted reluctantly.

"And smart. Do you get that she's smart? I mean, nobody wants a woman who's too smart, of course. That's the worst. But I think she could keep up with me easily, long as it's the right topic."

"There's no doubt in my mind about that."

"So. Now you get it. You meet a chick like that, you do your inventory on her. Looks: check. Brains: check. Not crazy: check."

"I like your list better than Maddy's."

"Point being, I'm not going to let this opportunity pass me by." Rodney glanced at his watch. "Time for me to meet up with her."

"Come right back," JayB admonished.

Rodney looked nonplussed. "What do you mean?"

"I mean, come back and get your dog. This is a Saturday. I'm not walking any other dogs today. I'm just watching Spartan as a one-time, what-was-I-thinking favor to you."

"A favor to me and *Alana*," Rodney corrected. "Well, 'come right back,' you say, but I mean, what if things start to get, you know, friendly?"

"I promise you that's not going to happen."

Spartan watched his person run off without him and did not change expression. Maybe the animal *couldn't* change expression. There was something so wrong with his face, he seemed capable of nothing but staring.

I had no use for a dog like Spartan, but apparently we had traded Odin for him, since JayB put us both in the backyard. While JayB was out there with us, he lifted the screen up and pounded it back into its place over the window. I pictured Kelsey hurtling out of it, clinging to the screen, and couldn't help but be a little happy with the image.

There were, I knew, more moths to come. Kelsey might once again ride out into the night.

Some time later, a loud panting sound drew our attention. Spartan didn't move but I went to the gate and wagged as Rodney staggered up the driveway. He was breathing heavily, his scent strong with salt and sweat.

"Hey, Spartan," he called over the top of the fence. Spartan stood up but did not wag.

The slider opened and JayB stepped out to join us. "How'd it go?" he asked Rodney. "Should I expect a save-the-date card?"

Rodney nodded but seemed to have trouble breathing enough air to make words.

"Wow, you look completely wiped out. How far did you run?"

Rodney held up some fingers.

"Four miles?"

Rodney nodded.

"She have trouble keeping up?"

Rodney found his voice. "You could say that. Come on, Spartan."

I was glad to see Spartan ease through the gate.

"You're welcome," JayB called.

Rodney waved dismissively and walked his dog away.

Later, we wandered up the street to visit Odin. Alana opened the door, smiling. "You really *are* the nicest man in town. I'm so grateful for your help."

"No problem. So how was the big road run? I guess you went four miles?"

Alana laughed. "If that. Rodney had a lot of trouble keeping up. I kept waiting for him so I could see where to turn. But it was nice out. There were so few cars, and the park was mostly empty, so it wasn't like running along the bike path in the Marina, where you have to dodge people every ten yards. A lot of folks had dogs with them. I don't know why he didn't take Spartan. I figured Odin wouldn't be up to it."

"That's true. If you want to drop Odin off next time," JayB offered, "I'll be happy to watch him for you. No charge, of course. You're a premium customer."

They smiled at each other.

Soon, we were down in Helen's basement. There were several musty boxes opened on the floor. Alana gestured. "I guess . . . I don't know. Just start. I'm taking the top boxes and opening them up and dividing everything into piles. There's a pile to keep that's mostly nostalgic stuff. There's a pile of items I think might be worth selling. That's the smallest pile. And there's the stuff I hope that charity will take, because if they won't, we'll send it straight to the dump."

JayB nodded. "I've heard that there are companies that will come and buy everything in the house, all the furniture, the clothing. They want it all. So if they don't sell it in an estate sale, it all goes to a charity that they find for you. They'll even clean up the house after they've taken everything."

"Oh, I never knew that. I guess I could have looked online."

"I'd be happy to kind of investigate that for you, if you'd like."

"That would be really nice, JayB. Thanks." She gave him a searching look.

"What?"

She shook her head. "Nothing."

A little while later, JayB pulled coffee mugs from a box. "None of these match. Do you want them?"

Alana laughed ruefully. "I can't imagine having any sentimental attachment to a Royals coffee mug. Oh, look what I found." She waved some papers and then sat on the basement floor. "It's a letter from my dad to my mom."

"You okay?" JayB asked, concerned.

I glanced at Alana. I could feel strong gusts of emotion coming from her now. I looked over at Odin, and I could tell he felt it too. Alana took a deep breath, and when she spoke, her voice was soft. "Just give me a moment."

Odin and I glanced at each other, and Odin eased to his feet. He felt compelled to go to Alana as she sat cross-legged on the floor. He thrust his head forward and gave her a concerned kiss.

Odin was a good dog.

Alana wiped her face, gesturing with the papers in her hand. "I never knew anything about this. My dad wanted to take a transfer to Texas, a big career move. And he wrote down all the reasons why they should go." She looked up at JayB with a half smile. "My mom wrote back, 'Can you imagine someone like me *living in Texas?*'"

Alana laughed bitterly. "That's so my mom. She would make up her mind about something and that was it. There was no changing it." Her smile faltered a little bit. "Obviously, we didn't go to Texas. As much as it meant to my dad."

"Career stuff is really hard," JayB observed cautiously.

Alana nodded. "Yeah, I know. Tell me about it." She looked at JayB. "So, what, those people hit you and you sued or something?"

"Settled," JayB corrected. "No lawsuit." He sighed. "I have a master's in human resources, and worked in the industry for quite a while before I realized I didn't really like it very much. You spend most of your time listening to employees tell you things they hate about the company, and then it's your job to report what you've heard. And then we had to lay people off, people considered 'non-essential,' like there's any such thing. My job was to get them to sign the paper. It was soul-killing. So, when I got punched, I hired a lawyer and the company's insurance wrote a check. I decided it was a reset, an opportunity to start over and see what I really want to do in life. I'm still trying to figure that out, though apparently I'm a natural as a dog walker." He smiled ruefully.

Odin put his head in Alana's lap.

"I always saw myself as an entrepreneur," she said, stroking Odin distractedly. "Not like what Rodney means when he says it—actually, I don't know *what* Rodney means. But it just wasn't wired into me to go to work for some big company somewhere. Maybe it comes from being the baby in the family, the caboose. I had to make up ways to entertain myself. Anyway, so I scraped together my savings and opened a retail shop. It was so cool, JayB. I had anything and everything it occurred to me to carry. Clothing and costumes and cowboy boots and decorative items. It was called Alana's Closet. I was so happy, but I struggled just to break even. Then I hit on an idea to put crystals on a motorcycle helmet. Every night, I sat there for hours, gluing on these Swarovski crystals, one by one. When I was done, the thing was amazing, so beautiful. And I sold it for three thousand, five hundred dollars. I bought a bottle of champagne that night. I thought, 'Thirty-five hundred on a single sale!' That's a lot more than I usually made in a month. Then my boyfriend pointed out that I'd probably put eighty hours into that project. By the time you costed out the materials—and then, you know, rent and electricity, California taxes—I was making less than minimum wage. . . ." Alana trailed off wistfully.

"Starting a successful business is supposed to be almost impossible," JayB speculated. "I've never done it."

Alana nodded. "That's when it occurred to me: people always say to do the thing you love, but that doesn't mean you're going to get rich or even make enough to survive."

"What did you like most about it?"

"Well, I guess it was the *creative* nature of running a business, you know? I mean, every day it was something different. One day, the toilet backed up, and when I found out how much it would cost to hire a plumber—this is after the landlord told me it would be a month before he'd have time to fix it—I knew I'd have to figure out how to handle it myself. And there was something so not-romantic about running a snake down through a toilet into the bowels of the planet. But in the end, I was exhilarated. I ran into a problem, and I took care of it. And then I sold a vintage leather jacket for a two-hundred-dollar profit that same day. Most nights I went home with a smile on my face. Not at all like what I'm doing now—answering emails all day long. Tracking invoices. Filing. Every day the same. I mean, I had to have a job, and owning my own business meant I learned how to handle bookkeeping, bills, all of that. So I took that skill out into the job market, and that's how I wound up where I am."

Alana looked sadly at the papers in her hand. "My dad loved my mom so much. They were childhood sweethearts. In fact, they were always kind of fuzzy about how long they'd known each other. They'd never had another person in their lives. His death was a shock. He just had a stroke one day and that was that. He treasured me, though. Treasured me, treasured my mom. I remember, growing up, it seemed like such a happy home. I don't remember my dad ever once talking about who was paying for what. They were married. It wasn't like now—Guy and I track every penny on a spreadsheet, I'm good at that sort of thing—and settle up at the end of the month. We're completely independent of each other, even though we live together. If he buys an expensive meal, it's up to me to catch up with something else so that he isn't, as he puts it, 'out of pocket.'"

She gave JayB a look as if challenging him to comment.

He said nothing for a moment. "I get what it's like to feel a little trapped by circumstances. I was stuck in my old job, wondering how I was going to get out of it, and then the solution walked up and punched me in the nose."

Alana laughed. "I can't imagine what it's like to be free to do whatever you want."

"Try," JayB invited.

"Sorry?"

"Put yourself in my position. Imagine you can do what you want, live where you want. What would you do?"

*Dear Diary:*

*If I eat the cat's food, she will be forced to leave here and go find a home where there are no dogs.*

*I cannot leap onto the counter the way Kelsey does. She launches herself with no effort. I guess I could, too, if I were that small and had such a surly attitude.*

*But dogs are much smarter than cats. While Kelsey makes her leap in a single bound, I'm intelligent enough to realize that if I could put something between me and the counter, such as a chair, I would be able to use a two-stage assault to achieve my goal. Kelsey could never come up with a plan like this. She's too busy licking herself in her obsessive-repulsive way.*

*There's a chair in the kitchen that's often close to that counter. JayB sits in it to talk on the phone, or to click something, or to rustle through some papers. The chair doesn't appear to be close enough for me to make the jump from it to the counter, but I won't know for sure until I try.*

*As I put my front paws on it, something unexpected happens. The chair moves, rolling away from me so that I have to walk with my back legs to keep up. Finally, it bumps into a wall and stops.*

*Now that the chair is no longer scooting away from me, I can climb up on it, but I'm all the way across the room. I drop my front paws and look around in confusion.*

*I've managed to move the chair.*

*It seems there might be something I could do with this newfound discovery, but I can't figure out what that might be.*

Love,
Clancy

# Ten

JayB and Alana went silent for long enough that Odin drowsily opened his eyes, sensing something.

"Maybe, if you had the freedom, you'd open another store?" JayB suggested.

Alana frowned. "The point is, I don't *have* freedom. I'm on leave of absence, but my job's waiting for me when I get back."

"All right."

"I hate conversations like this. Let's talk about something else."

"Sure. So . . . what was your mom doing living in Kansas City?"

"Oh, yeah—Mom's sister, Aunt Ellen, got really sick. So my mom came out to take care of her. And then, when Ellen died, Mom inherited this place"—Alana looked around—"and then, I don't know, she decided she liked it out here."

"Everyone says it's a great place to live, but not exactly the most exciting place to visit."

Alana smiled. "We came out one time, Guy and I. He made fun of the whole trip. It started at the airport. He said the airport was stupid, too far away. Though, in LA, a lot of people live hours from LAX. We're lucky, we're just up the road, takes us less than thirty minutes. Anyway, he said Kansas City was a hick town. Made fun of the food, the clothing, the culture, and especially the people. To Guy, the Midwest has absolutely nothing going for it, so if you live here, you must be a moron. My mom took about all she could stand and then they had a huge blowout. And of course, there I am in the middle, trying to make peace." Alana shook her head. "My mother could make an argument into a take-no-prisoners kind of thing. She called Guy self-centered and pig-headed. Guy doesn't like it when people argue with him—who does?—so he pretty much made me choose between my mom and him. They *both* made me choose. I mean, Guy's the love of my life. What was I supposed to do?"

Alana's voice had gone soft and low. Odin stirred, looking up at her.

"So what happened then was, we stopped talking to each other," Alana finished. "I can't believe how long I let that fight come between me and my mom."

Suddenly, she was sobbing, crying those racking, tearful, gasping sobs people do now and again. She stood and so did JayB. Odin, his tail wagging uncertainly, went into a Sit. JayB stepped over to Alana and folded her into his arms.

I wasn't sure what to do. I could feel the distress and other strong, sad emotions around this embrace, but there didn't seem to be a role for a dog.

Suddenly, Alana straightened and went a little rigid. "Oh," she exclaimed. She literally put her palms on JayB's chest and pushed him back. "Oh, wait. Sorry."

"No, there's nothing to be sorry about."

She shook her head wildly. "This was—oh God. I don't know what I was thinking. Hey, I think I need some time. Could you just go? I need to be alone right now."

"Alana . . ." JayB protested mildly.

"Please," Alana urged.

I followed JayB up the stairs and to the front door. Odin went with us, confused. My last sight of him was his lost expression as JayB escorted me outside.

JayB put my leash on my collar and shrugged. "Something just happened, Clancy," he told me. "But I'm not sure what."

Early the next day, JayB walked me outside on the leash, and we were doing a good job of marking the area along the driveway when a car pulled in. I recognized it as the one that had belonged to Odin's person, Helen. The woman who stepped out of it, however, was Alana. Odin followed her and trotted over to me for a morning sniff.

"Hey," she greeted. "I brought a peace offering—coffee cake from Dolce's. Do you like coffee cake?"

JayB considered this. "I don't think I'd want to be associated with anyone who *doesn't* like coffee cake."

Alana laughed.

"You drove here from your house?" JayB asked. "I thought you were this big runner."

Alana laughed again. "Went shopping. I can't believe how cheap everything is here. I mean, eggs, coffee, even gasoline. I felt like I was rich."

"Why do you say the coffee cake is a peace offering? Are we at war?"

Alana shrugged, looking sheepish. "Well, I sort of overreacted. I mean, it wasn't your fault. You were just being nice, and then I don't know, I started feeling guilty or something. Like . . . I mean, I know you weren't trying to do anything, JayB. I know that you were just being compassionate, but in that moment, I was not in a good place. I took it the wrong way."

"No, of course. I know that you have a guy. I mean, Guy . . ."

Alana nodded wearily. "I do wish he had a different first name."

"Anyway, I respect that. I can't speak for Rodney, however."

Alana rolled her eyes.

JayB grinned. "So maybe we should try it again."

Alana frowned. "Try what again? Hugging?"

"Yeah, why not?"

"Okay," Alana agreed slowly. She reached into the car, pulled out a square, sweetly fragrant box, and set it on the roof. Then she shut the door and walked up to JayB, suddenly seeming shy. Each held out their arms and they embraced. I glanced at Odin, wondering if this was something we should get involved in. Dogs always help when there's an affectionate situation, as opposed to cats, who simply make people feel bad about themselves.

I contemplated the way JayB's scent changed as he held Alana.

As soon as they began hugging, I heard the full-throated roar of a big machine. I glanced up and saw what I had come to recognize as one of Walter's cars. It sped toward us, making a lot of racket, and the tires squealed slightly as it swung into the driveway and came to a rocking halt.

JayB and Alana stopped hugging.

Walter struggled out of the front seat, grinning. "Good morning."

"You know, Dad," JayB observed, "a lot of people would call before they just show up at a house."

Walter laughed, "Are you kidding? In this car, it's like a five-minute drive from my place to yours. It takes longer to dial the phone. Good morning, beautiful," Walter hailed Alana. "You're particularly lovely this morning."

"Thank you, Walter," Alana replied, looking amused.

Walter slapped his hands together. "We need to drink some champagne tonight. I've got something big to celebrate."

JayB looked wary. "Oh?"

"Yeah. Our man Rodney was absolutely right about the restaurant. It's the proverbial diamond in the rough. Close to the river. It's in operation right now, but the owner is tired of running it and looking to get out from underneath."

"The restaurant," JayB repeated woodenly. "What do you and Rodney know about restaurants?"

"It's like minting money."

JayB and Alana exchanged glances. "It's more like minting money and then throwing it out the window," he corrected. "Do you know how complicated it is to run a restaurant?"

Walter grinned. "What I know is you can pay like six cents for some pasta and sell it for eight bucks. That's the kind of margin an investor like me is looking for."

"Yeah, sure," JayB allowed. "That may be true, but you've got health codes and you have all sorts of personnel issues. It's a really bad idea, Dad."

Walter looked annoyed. "Yeah, right, I get it. Human resources." He grinned at Alana. "We had HR. I think their one contribution

84 W. Bruce Cameron

was to make a sign that said to remove food from the refrigerator on Fridays." He turned back to JayB. "Son, this is a business. Something, I'll remind you, I know a thing or two about."

"A thing, maybe. I'm not sure about two."

Alana laughed, but Walter didn't.

"Seriously, Dad, there must be some reason the owner is willing to walk away, and it can't be because he's making too much money."

"There's a top-secret plan to it, yes," Walter acknowledged, "something I can't talk about yet, but even still, it's a good deal." He pulled out his phone. "I will use my *phone*, thank you very much, to call Rodney to come over and explain the deal to you so you'll understand."

JayB shook his head. "Oh, please, don't."

"Maybe I should go," Alana offered. "I don't think I should hear the secret."

JayB glanced at her. "No, we're going to have coffee cake. You promised."

"Coffee cake!" Walter agreed with a grin. He turned away to talk into his phone.

JayB looked challengingly at Alana. "The peace offering is no good if you leave."

Before long, we were all in the house, and I was just settling down underneath the table when the door opened and Rodney came in, followed by his ridiculous dog. Odin had his head between his paws and didn't look up, but I felt obligated to go and greet the newcomers.

JayB looked exasperated. "Sure, just walk right in."

Rodney grinned. "Oh, come on, we're neighbors." He sat down and reached for a piece of coffee cake. "This is so great," he enthused, his voice muffled by food. He smiled at Alana. "Let me guess—Dolce's, right? Man, I need to give you that city tour, or you're going to find every place on your own."

"That would be okay by me," Alana replied lightly.

Rodney guffawed. He reached out and put his hand on Alana's

arm and she snatched it off the table. "Well," he observed magnan-
imously, "it's a good thing I live close by."

"Yeah, it's great," JayB stated flatly.

"So, this restaurant, you're not going to believe the opportunity,"
Rodney told JayB.

"That sounds accurate," JayB observed.

"Okay. Sarcasm. Ha," Rodney replied. He turned to Alana, "JayB's
never had what you might call the vision thing, you know? He was
more like the follower. Which was okay by me, because I was the
leader. Every general has an army. Every rancher has a cow."

"Every bank has a robber," JayB suggested.

Alana laughed.

Rodney rolled his eyes. "You see? He'll probably find a hundred
things wrong with this deal, but it doesn't matter, because there's
one right thing."

"And what's that?" Alana asked.

Rodney was holding a finger up in the air and now he stared at it
as if there was beef on the fingernail. "The one thing is: it's brilliant."

"Oh," JayB admired, "as long as the reason's *that* good. . . ."

Rodney and Walter exchanged a glance. "No, I mean there's
something about this deal that even the current owner doesn't
know. Something genius. Like you know how people are always going to garage sales and buying an old dresser and in the bottom
drawer there's a Picasso? This is like that. So, while everyone's distracted, thinking, 'Oh, Rodney and Walter are running this wonderful restaurant, let's go eat there,' they won't even realize what's
about to happen."

"Tell you what," Walter enthused, springing to his feet, "I hate
wasting time. Rather than sit here and talk hypotheticals, let's just
go. To the restaurant. We'll show you what we're talking about."

*Dear Diary:*

*People and dogs form packs in a similar fashion, creating ever-changing groups out of whoever happens to be there. For a dog, this can mean other dogs and even humans but not Kelsey.*

*Over time, though, some packs become more or less permanent. Odin and I see each other nearly every day now, so he and I and Phoebe are a pack, and I guess I would add Millie and Tillie, though probably not Spartan—to be in a pack, a dog has to want to belong.*

*I think Alana and JayB and Rodney and Walter and Maddy are in the process of forming a pack, but as is often true with dogs, they're having trouble deciding how each of them relates to the other. I think part of the problem is that none of them pees outdoors. It can be very difficult getting to know someone under those circumstances.*

Love,
Clancy

# Eleven

Before long, we were taking a car ride—a car ride made less enjoyable by the fact that Spartan was in the vehicle with us, in the back with Odin. I was in the middle seat, and JayB and Alana were sitting up front. Rodney had gone with Walter. At a corner, we heard a loud squeal of tires and Walter's car sped away from us.

JayB watched it go. "Well, I guess we won't be following them, since I'm not willing to go ninety miles an hour in a thirty-five."

"I'll navigate on my phone," Alana assured him.

"Okay, thanks."

"It's a good thing you have an SUV, now that you're a full-time dog walker," she teased.

"It's a regular dogmobile."

"So, if you don't mind me asking, how long have you and Maddy been together?"

JayB shook his head. "Never."

Alana smiled. "That's not what Maddy thinks."

"Right, I do get that. But we only went out a couple of times, and she broke up with me each time."

"So if you're not dating, why's she always around?"

"Meaning, why don't I tell her to go away?" JayB looked thoughtful. "I can't really think of a gentle way to do that. And . . . I don't know. I guess I spent most of my childhood trying to help my father get over losing Celeste. It seems better to let her decide to leave on her own than to force the issue. Besides, when I'm with Maddy, I feel as if I'm learning English as a second language."

Alana's grin broadened.

JayB nodded. "How about you and Guy? How long've you two been together?"

Alana's smile winked out. She turned and looked out the window for a moment, then turned back. "A few years. You'd like him. He's nice."

JayB nodded noncommittally.

"He does things I can't stand to do myself, like negotiating our new lease, or getting the moving company to pay for some holiday decorations they broke."

"That's great."

The car drove on, stopping occasionally. The dogs got to their feet every single time, then flopped back down when it became obvious we'd fallen for a false alarm.

"You know," Alana remarked after a time, "I always thought it would be fun to open a restaurant."

"You can't be serious."

"I'm not kidding. I worked in one for a while; started as hostess, then waitress, then in back as a cook. Your dad's right, in a way—the operation's not that complicated. It's the same everywhere—take the order, cook the food, serve the food, clean the dishes. It's the decisions you have to make about what kind of place you're running, the menu, all of that—that's what can trip you up."

"And it's in those types of decisions," JayB observed shrewdly, "where you thrive."

Alana regarded him carefully. "You really pay attention to the things I tell you. Not too many men do that."

They exchanged small smiles, then Alana's expression turned cautionary. "Just don't tell your father I have experience. I'm afraid I'll get dragooned into working for him."

"Oh, my dad is *not* going into the restaurant business. I've had to talk him out of crazy schemes before, like when he wanted to start a professional basketball league where no one could be taller than five-nine."

Alana laughed.

Soon, Odin and I were lifting our noses with interest, because we could sense a change outside the car. A grassy smell was coming to us, with the promise of open terrain. We were both wagging with our noses pressed to the glass when we stopped. Walter and

Rodney were already in a parking lot, standing next to Walter's car and laughing. JayB opened the doors and we all scrambled out.

We dogs assessed where we were, sniffing along tree stumps and lifting our legs. The ground was flat, the grass fresh and cut. I saw a fenced-in area with an open gate that led to another fenced-in area with an open gate that led to another, like a series of dog parks all linked together. Some of them were cement pads instead of grass.

It was so alluring that Odin couldn't resist; suddenly shaking off the cloud of sadness that he'd been carrying, he began to play like a regular dog, jumping up and twisting and rolling on his back in the grass.

Watching him cavort, I realized how much I'd come to treasure Odin. He was my best dog friend.

I hoped this would be one of those destinations that my person elected to revisit, because Phoebe would love this place. I imagined her galloping, her sleek fur ruffled by the breeze, the two of us leaving stolid Spartan far behind.

The image made me wag.

I readied myself to run, but then the leash clicked into my collar and I realized this was not a day for running.

"Rodney and I made an executive decision on the way down," Walter told JayB. "We figured that, of all of us, the only one with experience in this industry is Maddy."

JayB briefly closed his eyes.

"So we're going to invite your girlfriend to be part of the team," Rodney interrupted.

"The team?" JayB repeated cautiously.

Walter grinned. "This is bigger than us. We called her from the car. She should be here any minute."

I followed JayB as he and Walter and Alana and Rodney filed into a big building. Spartan was uninterested in going, and Odin seemed tired after his brief burst of energy and elected to sprawl in the shade under a tree in their pen. Dog parks are for off-leash running, but apparently not for these two.

Rodney stopped just inside the door. Delicious food smells wafted to my nose. I wagged. "So, see this room here, it's a closet or something right now," he said. "We're going to take all this junk out of here and make this into an office for me, and then that area across the hall will be where my assistants will sit."

"Sounds like a good plan," Walter admired.

"Yeah, thanks."

JayB frowned. "So that's, what, you and two assistants on top of the restaurant staff?"

Rodney nodded. "I know. It's a lot of people, but that's okay. We're going to need an HR director, JayB. Know anybody good?" He grinned.

"What was the fenced-off area we just saw?" Alana wanted to know.

Rodney shrugged. "I don't know. It looks to me like they had animals here. Minks, maybe. I don't think they were raising them for food." His eyes brightened. "But, you know, we could do that. We could put buffalo or something in there. Ostriches. Start a ranch, make a little extra money on the side."

JayB considered this. "Or, instead of on the side, you could make money upfront, even—like, by running a restaurant. This place seems ideally suited for that."

Everyone laughed, so I wagged.

"So right now, this room is being used for food storage," Alana noted. "Where are you going to put the food storage if you take it over as an office?"

Rodney pondered this. "I don't know. I hadn't thought that far ahead. I guess maybe I could add on a room."

"Or build an office building," Walter suggested sunnily.

"Now that makes sense," said JayB.

Alana smiled at him.

We followed Rodney down the hallway into a big empty room with many tables and chairs. Two men were sitting on high stools, watching a television and sipping liquids.

"Hey, come over here, I want you to meet somebody," Rodney

called across the room. A large-boned woman with short gray hair and glasses approached us without smiling.

"Oh goodie," she greeted, "more executives?"

"You're not going to believe her name," Rodney told us. He turned and grinned at her. "Tell them."

The gaze she gave him was wearily patient. "My name is Des-Moines, like the city. That's where I was born, so that's what my mom named me."

"What's your last name?" Rodney wanted to know. "Idaho?"

Alana stepped forward and held out her hand. "I'm not an executive. I'm just a friend," she informed the woman. "Nice to meet you, DesMoines."

All the people, except Rodney, reached out and held the woman's hand briefly.

The woman seemed tired. "You know," she said, "though we aren't serving food to anybody right now, this is technically a restaurant, which means our furry friend here shouldn't be inside." Her knees popping, she stooped and held out both hands. They smelled wonderfully of different meats. I sniffed them, wagging, and closed my eyes when she stroked underneath my chin with one finger.

"That's Clancy," JayB informed her.

I glanced up at my name.

"Okay, we'll take the dog outside," Rodney agreed affably. "You can go back to, you know, whatever, DesMoines."

DesMoines nodded. "Thanks, boss," she said wryly.

JayB held up a hand. "Hey, DesMoines, do you mind if I ask you a question?"

She shook her head.

"How would you describe what you do here?"

"Oh," Rodney interrupted. "Mostly she just enters stuff in the computer and then, I don't know, I see her in the kitchen a lot."

JayB looked blandly at Rodney. "Thank you, Rodney." He turned back to DesMoines. "Does that helpful description cover everything, or is there something you'd like to add?"

DesMoines nodded. "I'm not a bookkeeper, but I do keep track of everything in the system like I was trained. I schedule the staff, take care of paying the bills, order the food, make sure the place opens and closes on time, schedule vacations. I hire people and sometimes have to fire people." She shrugged. "The usual."

"Okay," JayB said. "Thanks. Oh, one more question."

DesMoines waited tolerantly.

"So, I think I heard the restaurant isn't making any money."

DesMoines shook her head. "We're *losing* money," she corrected firmly.

"All right then, you're losing money. Why is that?"

DesMoines spread her hands. "No customers," she explained simply.

"Ah," JayB said. He and Alana exchanged glances.

"When the county decided to turn the south edge of the property back into wetlands," DesMoines continued, "it made the road a dead end. People used to come down it all the time as a shortcut. With no traffic, we've sort of fallen off the map."

We went back outside. I joyously ran over to say hello to Odin and to ignore Spartan. Then I returned to JayB's side. "So, Dad," he was saying. "This is a business without customers. Is that the big secret you've been dying to tell us? That if you just had *customers,* you'd be making *money*? Because I have to believe the current owner already knows that."

Walter and Rodney chortled.

"Not even close," Rodney declared.

Alana eyed Rodney. "A money-losing operation with no people coming to eat. What is it I'm missing?"

"Look around you," Rodney suggested, waving his arms expansively. "Do you see what I see?"

"Way over there I can see the Walmart Garden Center," JayB responded. "It's very pretty."

"Hint, hint," Rodney said slyly. "Look *down*."

The people all looked at the grass, so I did, too.

"The land," Walter advised impatiently. "The business *owns the land*. Two acres of it."

"I wanted them to guess, Walter," Rodney grumbled.

"It was taking too long."

"But what fun is a secret if you don't make people guess for a few minutes?"

"Wait," Alana interrupted. "The business doesn't lease the property. So what?"

"That *is* the so what!" Rodney declared.

Walter swept his hands through the air. "We're going to put up housing, maybe some retail. From the upper floors, you'll have a view of the river."

"So you're going to turn this into a huge residential development," JayB translated.

"Well," Walter disagreed, "not me so much. You know me, I don't know a jackhammer from a . . . a . . ."

"Plumb bob?" JayB suggested.

"What? What the heck's a plumb bob? My point is, Rodney's got this handled."

JayB turned to Rodney. "Can you really do something like this?"

Rodney grinned. "Of course. What do you think I've been doing all this time?"

"Honestly," JayB replied, "I think you've been doing *nothing*."

"I don't know much about construction," Alana interjected cautiously, "but I know it takes time to get permits and all that. Have you factored that into your calculations?"

Walter waved a hand. "Yeah, in San Francisco it takes forever, I'm sure. But this is Kansas City. All you have to do to get a permit is stand in line for about ten minutes and get a form stamped. It's nothing." Walter snapped his fingers, and I looked at him curiously.

Sometimes JayB snaps his fingers because he wants my attention, but this did not seem to be that kind of finger snap.

A car pulled up and I recognized its sound and smells, especially when Maddy got out.

I wagged.

Maddy looked upset as she stalked over to us. Her eyes were on JayB. "How come I had to get a call from your father on this?" she demanded. "Are you going to forget our anniversaries too?"

"Oh," JayB replied mildly, "I would have called, but I thought you had to work today."

"I did! But something like this is more important than work. I came as soon as I heard. I left two tables waiting for me to take their order. That's how serious I am." She turned to Alana. "But he called *you*, I see."

"Oh, no, it wasn't like that," Alana objected.

"Do you ever wear anything but shorts?" Maddy challenged. "You've got legs, we get it. Some of us don't."

"I was just telling my son about our vision to build condos and shopping on this site," Walter advised. "Jago isn't particularly enthusiastic."

Maddy smiled. "I love it when you call him that."

"It's a wonderful thing," JayB agreed.

Alana laughed.

Walter made another wide gesture. "My wife's going to be blown away. We'll probably name a street after her. Celeste Boulevard."

"Your *wife*?" JayB repeated incredulously. "Dad, when was your last psych evaluation?"

Walter laughed heartily.

"I think it's terrific," Maddy enthused.

"Okay, but, Dad," JayB stated patiently, "you heard DesMoines. There are no customers. If you invest in this place, it's a black hole."

Maddy shook her head angrily. "That's what you do, JayB. You just keep stomping on the throat of dreams. That's one of my eight simple rules. You've been doing it to me since we met. I never wanted to be a waitress. I want to be an actress, but you've never supported me in that."

JayB looked helpless. "I never knew you wanted to be an actress."

Maddy put her hands on her hips. "Can you see why that makes you a bad boyfriend?"

Walter looked disappointed. "Well, I'm sorry to hear you're departing the industry, Maddy. I was really hoping you'd come work for me."

Maddy brightened. "Manage the restaurant? I'd love that."

Rodney frowned. "Well, sure, but I'm still the boss, okay?"

Maddy shrugged. "A lot of women let men think they're the boss. We can do that here, if you want."

"You're hired," Walter told Maddy.

She squealed and gave him a hug.

"Well, Walt," Rodney objected, "I hate to be the wet blanket, but shouldn't a decision like that go through me?"

Walter shrugged. "You're right, I'm new at this CEO stuff. Okay, what do you think, Rodney?"

"I think she'd be great."

Maddy squealed and hugged him, too. "Okay," she said eagerly. "The first thing I want to teach the waitstaff is never to write anything down. That way, you get the order wrong, no one can prove it."

JayB gave Walter a suspicious look. "You're talking as if you've already done this, Dad."

Walter gave JayB a tolerant smile but didn't say anything.

*Dear Diary:*

JayB seems different around Alana now. It reminds me of the way he reacts to Dominique. There's a slight straightening of his posture and a tension coming off his skin. He also seems to laugh and smile more. Does this mean my hopes of having Dominique and Phoebe live with us won't be realized?

I have another problem, as well: I can't communicate much of anything to Phoebe. My plan to entice Dominique to rub my tummy will never work, as long as Phoebe goes berserk and leaps on me. When JayB and Dominique sit on the steps and talk, I behave as happily and attractively as I can, thinking that, surely, the two humans will get up and walk together back to our house, dropping off Spartan along the way.

So far, that hasn't happened.

Love,
Clancy

# Twelve

"Dad?" JayB said insistently. "Please tell me you did not put your money into this place."

Walter shrugged. "Well, I mean, I wrote a check and signed some documents. I don't know . . . I'll leave that to the paper-pushers."

"Then you have to get out of the deal!" JayB urged. "This is insane!"

"Like you would know insane if it threw up your breakfast," Maddy mocked.

Rodney beamed at Maddy and Alana. "You know what? The four of us should go out sometime. That would be a blast." He reached out as if to put his arm around Alana, who stepped back smartly. "Hey, Alana, let me show you where the condos are going up."

Walter grinned and nodded. "Good. I need to speak to JayB privately."

Maddy crossed her arms. "Yeah, but I need to speak to JayB privately, too, and my stuff is life and sudden death, so bring him right back."

Walter nodded. "Sure, okay."

With a helpless look at JayB, Alana let Rodney steer her away. Walter led us over to the shade where Odin was stretched out. The way Odin lay on his side reminded me of how he crawled across the floor when he saw Helen and then flopped down on his side for a belly rub.

JayB gazed intently at his father. "Dad. I mean it. Get a lawyer and get *out*."

Walter grinned. "You worry too much. I can afford it."

JayB sighed. "Why won't you listen to me on this?"

"Because I've got something more important going on. I sent your mom two dozen roses."

JayB stared at him. "You sent Celeste two dozen roses," he repeated. "Why would you do that?"

"They're her favorite flower."

"No, Dad, I mean why would you send Mom flowers at all? How's her husband supposed to react to something like that?"

Walter looked disgusted. "You mean Twain Wolfe? Like I care. Whose side are you on? I'm your father. This guy's just . . . I don't know, number three."

"He's the man my mother's married to. He's who she picked."

Walter straightened himself and looked JayB in the eye. "Your mother and I belong together. I've known it from the moment I met her. Surely, you can't be on Mark Twain's side. "

"I'm on your side *and* I'm on Mom's side," JayB explained patiently. "Now, how much money does this place lose?"

Walter waved a hand. "DesMoines gives me all these printouts, but when I ask her what they mean, she says she's not a business person. And I guess she's got it all needlessly complicated. There's a payroll system. There's a vacation-scheduling system. All this stuff on one computer printout, all these different reports. It's an utter mess."

JayB gave his father an exasperated look. "That's how business works. It's great that your payroll feeds into your accounting system, and scheduling vacations is important because vacations accrue value. If someone quits with outstanding vacation days, the law says you have to pay them for those days. Same with outstanding sick days. So all that needs to be tracked and it becomes a liability in your profit and loss statement."

"Yeah, I get it. HR."

I saw that Maddy, who had been standing with her arms folded watching from some distance away, was now striding across toward us. She seemed very unhappy.

"Okay," she announced when she reached us. "Time's up." She turned to JayB. "We need to talk, stat. That means now."

JayB nodded. "I know what stat means, but wouldn't it make more sense for you to sort of add up your issues and then we could clear them all at once? Sort of like your eight simple rules. This would be eight simple issues to talk about at the same time. You could email the list, even."

Maddy shook her head. "This is much more disastrous than that." She reached out and seized JayB's shirt in her fist. She pulled him away and I followed, glancing back at Walter, who nodded approvingly.

JayB allowed Maddy to drag him over to a space under an awning off the building. Alana and Rodney were still walking at the far end of the field, and I could see Rodney pointing into the air.

"Okay, Maddy, why don't we stop here before you rip my shirt."

"Oh, you *wish* I'd rip your shirt." Maddy released her hold. "So, what's with you and Alana?"

"Alana? I don't know what you're talking about."

"Yes, you do. Pot calling the kettle black, here. I see the way the two of you look at each other."

JayB was silent for a moment. "You mean she looks at me differently?"

"Oh, come on. I'll tell you this right now. If she thinks she's going to steal my man, she's the one who goes home without the glass slipper."

"But I'm not. Your man, I mean. We broke up."

"No, now we're back together on probation, but not with you drooling over Alana's shorts."

"I guess I don't see things the way you do, Maddy."

"Oh yeah? Like I'm not supposed to notice how you're always smiling that fake smile of yours at her? At your *neighbor*? So-called?"

"I didn't realize I have a fake smile. How's it different from the real one?"

"I'm going to take off the gloves and throw them at her feet," Maddy fumed. "If a person's not willing to fight for what she believes in, we might as well all get back on the Mayflower. First, I'll file a restraining order. She comes within fifty yards of you, she goes to jail. Where they don't allow *shorts*."

"I'm not sure that'll work."

"No, it will. I've had them filed against me, so I know how it goes."

"I think you're missing something, which is that Alana has a boyfriend waiting for her back in LA."

"Oh yeah. She has a *boyfriend*. She calls him 'Guy.' She can't even make up a real name for him. Women like her don't have boyfriends. That's why she wants mine—I've turned you into eligibility. And what do you do with it? You put your head in a noose of your own making. Didn't you promise your best friend you wouldn't make any moves on her?"

"No, I never said anything like that."

"So you admit it!"

"Admit it? Admit what?"

"Be a man. Don't try to steal Rodney's girl, because if you do, two people can waltz that tango."

"All right."

I wagged because Alana and Rodney were walking back toward us. Rodney was smiling.

"Well," JayB hailed Alana, "what did you think of the grand tour? Is it a good plan?"

"It's certainly ambitious," Alana responded cautiously.

"That's me," Rodney agreed with a grin.

"So, listen," JayB announced. "I need to get back to dog walking. I have Millie and Tillie this afternoon." He glanced at Alana. "Would you rather ride back with me or be strapped to the hood of the Ferrari?"

Alana grinned. "I think I'll go back with you."

"Okay," Maddy warned Alana, "just this once. And don't think I won't be watching the whole time."

We got back in the car. I was disappointed to see that Spartan was coming with us. I thought he should stay with Rodney, but apparently JayB found something in Spartan to like, the same way he found something in Kelsey to like. I was glad my person had such a loving personality, but I wished he wouldn't waste it on animals like them.

Alana regarded him. "Rodney tells me your dad already bought the restaurant."

"That does seem to be the case." JayB glanced at her. "Any ideas on how we could keep this from becoming a disaster?"

Alana pursed her lips. "Maybe. But is that even your responsibility?"

"Oh, you mean help my father out of a jam he's gotten himself into?" JayB shrugged. "I suppose not. Except that was sort of my job as a kid. I worked really hard so that everyone else would think we were a normal family. Like when I negotiated with the repo man to turn in Dad's car so they wouldn't have to send the sheriff."

"Sorry." Alana looked out the window. "The leaves are so green. The side streets here, the tree branches overhead make them like tunnels. And the birds in the morning! The first few times, I thought my TV had popped on with a nature show."

"They do take getting used to."

"You want to hear something funny? When I first came out to visit my mom, I thought there would be no trees at all. I mean, Prairie Village? I pictured a tiny little sod town. Completely flat. But Kansas City is so hilly."

"You should see it in the fall, when the leaves change."

Alana frowned. "No. I mean, I have to get back."

"You mean to Marina del Rey?"

"Yes. That's where I live, JayB." She regarded him stonily. "I am not going to help with the restaurant, okay?"

I picked up something in her tone and glanced at her.

JayB nodded.

"I've got the estate sale people coming tomorrow. Everything's going out the door except what I need to stay there. I'm shipping a lot of items back to California. They're taking care of that, too. I just point and they wrap it up."

"And then what?"

"And then I list the house. Could you keep Odin all day tomorrow? I think he'd just be underfoot at the estate sale."

"Sure. I'll come over right after your run."

"Good."

They were silent for a while.

"So, how do you feel about selling all your mom's furniture?"
JayB ventured carefully.

Alana gazed at him coolly. "It's just furniture. That's all."

"Okay."

"God," she muttered under her breath.

"What is it?"

Alana shook her head. "Sorry. No. No, you're just being nice. I
don't know why I'm so irritated. Can we talk about something else?"

The next morning, when JayB walked me up to see Odin, there
were trucks in front of the house and a lot of people milling around,
some carrying boxes.

"Hello?" JayB called.

"Oh," Alana replied, coming into the hallway, "thank God you're
here, JayB. It's Odin."

"What's wrong?"

"He's been crying all morning. He seems really upset. I had to
lock him in my bedroom. Do you think he's somehow . . . I mean,
do dogs get attached to objects, like furniture?"

"I don't know. Maybe Helen's scent is on them."

"Oh, that never occurred to me. Poor Odin."

When Odin joined us, his eyes were wild and the distress rolled
off him as JayB put him on his leash. I was touched that my person seemed to know what was going on, even if I didn't. "It's okay,
Odin," he murmured gently. "Come with us."

Later we had Spartan and Millie and Tillie. I was worried JayB
would consider this to be enough dogs, but we went straight to
Phoebe's house. I was ready to charm Dominique, but it was Bedford who came out with Phoebe.

With the full pack on leashes, we headed to the dog park.

"You know what, Clancy?" JayB remarked, "I've got to get myself
a real job." I glanced behind me at him because of my name, but

kept even with the other dogs in front. "I can't have Alana seeing me as nothing but a dog walker."

In the dog park, Phoebe took off and I pursued, unable to keep up with those long legs of hers. Odin predictably collapsed at the base of a tree and Spartan sniffed around in the grass, but otherwise ignored us. It was the most wonderful time.

I noticed a woman walking over to JayB, and trotted up to be friendly. "This is my dog, Clancy," JayB informed her. "He's a yellow Labrador."

"Oh, that's nice. So the other dogs aren't yours?"

"No."

"I see you here with them most days. Are you a dog walker?"

"*No,*" JayB responded forcefully.

The woman blinked. "Oh, sorry," she apologized. She did not sit next to him on the bench.

A little while later, I was over by the fence, lying on my back, letting Phoebe chew on my face. It was glorious.

"Clancy!" JayB called.

I jumped to my feet and saw him crank his arm back. With a snapping motion, a ball arced through the air and bounced near us. I beat Phoebe to it, snatching it, and after chewing it just a moment, trotted back to JayB for him to throw it again. He gave it a heave and Phoebe left me behind as she raced after it. When she grabbed it, she shook her head and it flew from her jaws. As it rolled across the bark chips, a large black and brown dog came storming up to us.

I paused, unsure of the bigger dog's intentions. Phoebe was standing with the ball on the ground between her front paws, her tail wagging uncertainly. The big dog stalked up to Phoebe, a low rumble in his chest. Phoebe's ears went back. She glanced at me and I felt helpless. What should I do? Then I caught sight of motion out of the corner of my eye. Spartan was streaking across the dog park straight toward us, his face as expressionless as always.

*Dear Diary:*

*I am a good dog. When I have gotten into brief altercations with other dogs, my person has always been very cross with me. If I'm on a leash when I engage angrily with another canine, he pulls me back with a yank. I have learned that dog-on-dog violence, even if justified, displeases him, and therefore I will back away from a fight.*

*A good dog is friendly to dogs and people, though not necessarily cats.*

*I suspect Spartan doesn't know these things.*

Love,
Clancy

# Thirteen

Spartan dashed up to us and stopped so abruptly, the folds of skin over his brows appeared to roll forward, and I half expected that his entire face would fall into the dirt. The brown and black dog with the broad chest and big head who had challenged Phoebe for the ball turned to Spartan and they stared at each other. I cringed because this was not good dog behavior. Gazing directly into the eyes of another dog could mean only one thing.

I was right.

Spartan lunged and, with a snarl, was on the other dog, who rose up on his back legs. The air was split with their horrible shrieking growls as they snapped at each other. Instantly, I heard a woman screaming at me, or at least I interpreted it as being at me, communicating fear and anger and the word "No!" From behind me, I heard JayB yelling and I knew he was running in our direction.

"No, Spartan!" he was shouting. "No!"

Even though he was calling out to Spartan, I felt like a bad dog.

When Spartan and the other big male dropped back to all fours, Phoebe gleefully dashed in, grabbed the ball in her mouth, and fled the altercation. JayB reached down and seized Spartan by the collar. But as he pulled Spartan away, the other dog snarled and lunged.

The woman ran up and grabbed the collar of the big dog. "Bernie, no," she scolded. She whirled on JayB. "Your dog is too aggressive to be in the dog park!"

JayB shook his head. "I saw what happened. Your dog attacked first."

The woman put up a hand, palm out, facing JayB. "You're wrong and you should be ashamed. You're supposed to be a dog-trainer."

"I am not!"

"Come on, Bernie," the woman huffed. She turned, pulling her dog, who wouldn't go willingly. His fur was still up.

"Come, Spartan."

We all sheepishly followed JayB back to the bench where he had left our leashes.

Phoebe did not seem traumatized. In fact, she actually bumped up against Spartan in a playful manner. When he turned to her, she bowed, chewing the ball with a wide-open mouth so it fell into the dirt and rolled to Spartan's feet. Spartan sniffed at it. I stared at it as if fascinated, but really, I felt sick inside.

Phoebe wanted to play with Spartan, not me.

It seemed to me that I might have lost my only love to a dog with no personality and a face made up of piles of folded skin.

Later, when we walked back, Phoebe smelled like Spartan. When she mounted the steps, wagging, so that Bedford could let her into the house, her glance back was for Spartan, not me.

Odin could sense that I was unhappy and sniffed me in support, but I was too miserable to appreciate the gesture. I was happy to see Rodney arrive to take Spartan away. I hoped I would never see Spartan again, but I knew that was unlikely. People get stuck in a pattern and there's little a dog can do to help them out of it.

Odin spent most of the rest of the day with us at home, and I felt his spirits lift a little when he surged to the end of his leash and Kelsey fled. My mood improved as well.

The next morning had a different feel to it, which I took as a hopeful sign that Spartan wasn't coming over. JayB seemed less inclined to hurry, and I got the sure sense that we probably were not going to go visit any of the other dogs. As disappointed as I was over not seeing Phoebe, I actually felt some relief. I didn't know if I could face her scent after her betrayal of the day before.

I was tracking JayB with my eyes, mindful of the smell of his breakfast, and thinking it would be appropriate for him to share some of it with his good dog doing Sit, when the phone rang.

"Hey, Alana," JayB greeted the caller, then listened for a moment.

"Take the dogs for a walk," he repeated. "Sure, we could do that. I never get to do that." He laughed. "No, it's fine. We'll be up in a little bit. Okay. Thanks." He pulled the phone away from his ear and set it on the counter and looked at me. "She wants to talk to me, Clancy." I heard my name and thought there might be some bacon coming my way, but I was wrong.

JayB trotted down the hallway, his quick motion alarming Kelsey, who dashed away. I pointedly followed JayB, wagging, then waited as he showered and toweled himself dry. Next, he played with his face, covering it with soap and then scraping it off. And then he messed with his hair and gazed into his mirror. Finally, he dressed and put the leash in my collar.

Kelsey was cowering somewhere, still afraid.

I wasn't surprised when we turned up Odin's driveway. I noted that all the people who had been wandering around the day before were gone. The heavy door was open, but the screen door was shut. JayB rapped his knuckles on it, and I heard Alana stepping out of the kitchen.

"Come in!" she called.

JayB and I entered the house. I looked around. Everything was different. All the furniture seemed to have been taken away. Helen's smell was still there in the carpet, but it was mostly gone from the house now.

Alana had her phone to her ear. "I know, honey, I get that we don't have much room, but what was I supposed to do? I'll get a storage unit or something. We'll figure it out." She listened a little longer while JayB waited, looking awkward. "Okay, sure," she agreed. "How's the cat?"

I reacted to that word, but there was no sign of a cat in the house. Odin was sprawled in his dog bed, and I went to see him. He flapped his tail once but did not greet me with any sort of joy. His sense of loss was particularly strong today, covering him like a heavy blanket.

"I know," Alana continued soothingly. "I'm going to put the house on the market soon. I've been talking to the realtors. It's complicated.

Okay." Then she said, "I love—" and blinked, pulling her phone away from her face with a frown.

"Hey, Alana," JayB greeted.

Alana smiled at him. "Hi. Thanks for coming over. Odin, you want to go for a walk?"

Odin did not want to go for a walk. I could tell in the reluctant way that he left his dog bed, climbing out of it the way a dog slogs out of a river, the water dragging him back.

He stood without wagging while Alana put his leash on his collar. "Okay." She beamed at JayB. "Let's go."

Back outside, I lifted my leg and noted that Odin did the same, though he didn't sniff the result.

When a male dog doesn't sniff another dog's mark, there's something seriously wrong.

"So, something on your mind?" JayB asked.

Alana gave a rueful laugh. "It's about your friend, Rodney."

"Okay, you promoted him to friend, not me."

She laughed again. "I'm just hoping you'll have some ideas on how I can get rid of him."

This made JayB grin. "I have to tell you, I've been trying to do that my whole life."

"Seriously? I get the sense you're not kidding."

"I'm really not. Except that, if not for me, I'm not sure Rodney would have any friends in the world. He's always been that way. He's not evil, he's just . . . Rodney. And with him dragging my father into his delusions, I *really* can't get rid of him now. I sort of need to keep an eye on him to make sure he doesn't get Walter involved in something illegal. Why, what'd he do to you?"

"It's just that when we go running, he *won't stop talking*. I mean, the entire time. I try speeding up so that he'll be panting too hard and he starts calling for me to wait. He wants me to set a pace so that he can keep jabbering. It's driving me crazy. And anyway, I never said I wanted to run every single day, but now he thinks we've got a standing appointment. He'll be over soon, I promise. And if I'm not outside waiting for him and I don't come to the door, he'll sit there on the stoop. Oh, except for the one time he came into my house. I mean, literally just walked in and poured himself a cup of coffee, because I'd gotten delayed. Is that like a thing here, going into other people's homes? I see Walter doing it to you, too."

"It's a thing here, but usually only at my house. So, how often do you want to run?"

"Oh, I don't know. Just maybe a couple of days a week. I like it, and it helps keep my weight down."

"You know, since I started walking dogs every day, I've lost eight pounds."

"Oh? Well, you don't need to lose any weight, JayB."

They gazed at each other for a moment. "You don't, either," he finally told her.

She glanced away.

JayB frowned thoughtfully. "All right. I don't want to make light of this if he's really bothering you. Can you just tell him you don't want to run with him anymore?" JayB asked.

Alana stopped and gave my person a long, dark look. "Just tell him. *Just,*" she repeated, sounding surly.

"What's wrong?"

Alana turned and stalked away.

JayB hurried after Alana, and I hurried after JayB. A dog who just lets a person run off is no kind of dog at all. Odin, on leash, followed Alana. "Hey, I'm sorry, Alana. I didn't mean to make you angry."

"I'm not angry," she snapped.

"Upset, then."

"Could you stop with telling me how I feel, please?"

JayB nodded silently, falling into step with her. For a long time, nothing was said. I tracked their unusually unhappy body language, feeling anxious for both of them.

"I get that I'm not good at that," Alana sighed. "I mean, I'm *terrible* at it. Telling people what I want, what I don't want. I try to please everybody, and I *hate* that about myself."

"It's not the worst of qualities, though, is it? Couldn't it be that you're just *nice*?"

"Too nice."

There was a warmth on the breeze, promising a hot summer, and the air felt heavy with scents from flowers and thriving grasses. Odin clearly felt that the smells would be vastly improved with a few strategic leg lifts, but our humans had adopted a brisk pace that suggested stopping would not be tolerated.

"I'll talk to him. Rodney," JayB said. "Make him understand."

Alana shook her head. "I'm not asking you to do that."

"Still . . ."

"No. Please, JayB. You do that and he'll come right to me, wanting to talk about it. You wouldn't be solving anything."

We walked along at a slower, less-tense pace for a while.

"Okay. Here's a different plan," JayB suggested. "When we see Rodney next, you tell him that I've offered you a position in my burgeoning dog-walking business. We're expanding, and I've made you vice president of global operations."

Alana laughed. "That could actually work. If I tell him I'm dog-walking, he won't know what to do. He's not going to want to walk *with* us, right?"

"If he does, I'll assign him to Spartan."

I couldn't tell if the dog park or Phoebe's house was the intended destination—it didn't seem like Alana and JayB were taking us in either direction.

"It was strange walking into your place and seeing all the living room furniture gone," JayB remarked.

"I know, I actually cried a little as they took the stuff away. I didn't really associate this house with my mom so much, but when they hauled out that soft chair, I pictured her sitting on it and reading under the lamp. And now it's all gone."

They were quiet for a moment. Alana wiped her eyes.

"I'm sorry that I overheard you on the phone. Was that Guy the guy?"

Alana nodded. "That was Guy. He's upset because some boxes arrived. And he has no idea how many more will be coming, now that the estate sale people are finished. I mean, there's just stuff that I wanted to keep, you know? My siblings aren't interested in anything, they say. My brother is the executor, but he's been too busy to even send me the will. I guess I get the proceeds of the house sale, which pisses him off, of course. But his wife's family has money, my sister does really well as a physician—I guess Mom was hoping to give me a boost." She wiped her eyes again. "My realtor said it's going to take a while to sell the place because the wallpaper and appliances are really old; so are the kitchen cabinets." Alana shrugged. "She's going to decide if I should paint over the wallpaper or what. Rodney says we should do a complete remodel."

"Oh, that'd be nice . . . for him. Give him a house to squat in when he gets kicked out of his current place."

Alana grinned.

"So. Now you list it and then just leave?" JayB asked nonchalantly. I picked up some tension in his voice.

"Not immediately. I want to meet the folks who buy it and be comfortable with them, you know? I mean, Mom really loved this house. I just wouldn't like it if people started a meth lab or something."

JayB laughed.

Odin had had enough and planted three of his paws on the sidewalk and aimed a stream at a stop sign pole. Our people halted and I followed Odin's mark with a high-quality effort of my own.

Alana searched JayB's face with her eyes for a moment. "I do need to get back. I think Guy's getting lonely without me. Our last couple of conversations . . . it seems like he's really suffering. And I miss my cat. Rhiannon."

"Your cat's name is Rhiannon?"

"Yeah. Not from the song, from a book I read when I was a little girl."

I was hearing "cat" a lot. It's not my favorite word.

We were all back at my house, in the kitchen, when the front door popped open. Odin and I reacted immediately, barking so ferociously that we knew whoever it was had to be terrified.

Disappointingly, it was only Rodney and Spartan.

"JayB!" Rodney called. "Where are you? I need you to watch Spartan for a few days. I have a critical situation."

# Dear Diary:

A dog knows that humans decide our fates. They decide where we live, when we will eat, and what dinner will be. They determine if we are good dogs or bad dogs, and if we're going to go to the dog park or lie on the rug. All dogs know this and all dogs accept this.

But that doesn't mean we always comprehend a situation—human decision-making can make us anxious.

I'm upset because Spartan is apparently living with us now. This started after a brief conversation during which Rodney said JayB had "better not try anything with Alana." Then Rodney was gone, and his dog stayed here.

Spartan remained as expressionless as ever while he watched Rodney go.

Normally, when a dog sees their person leave, the dog feels distressed and apprehensive and will pace and yawn and nervously drink water. Not Spartan. Spartan just sits there with his cold eyes underneath his overlapping brow. Does he care that his life has completely changed? I can't tell. He's on a leash a lot, restrained from lunging at Kelsey, who spends her days cowering. He doesn't seem bothered that I am off-leash while he is on.

To a dog, a person's decisions always seem like forever. As far as I know, Rodney is never coming back and JayB has decided Spartan permanently belongs in our pack.

Why couldn't it be Phoebe instead?

Love,
Clancy

# Fourteen

Rodney started in surprise when he rounded the corner into the kitchen. "Oh wow, Alana! I was just going to call you."

"Oh?" Alana replied blandly.

"Since you're here, come on in, Rodney," JayB invited.

"So I can't go running with you today. I mean, obviously." He pointed to his pants. "I'm sorry, babe."

"Oh," Alana lamented neutrally. "Too bad."

"I've got some really important stuff going on," Rodney continued, laughing at himself. "You're not going to believe this. I've got to go to Canada. The country, I mean."

"Canada," Alana repeated.

"The country," JayB added.

"Right?" Rodney agreed. "I'm as amazed as you are. That's the kind of stuff that happens when you're in my business. It's a huge deal."

"Sounds great!" JayB gushed. "See you later."

"I'm sorry I can't take you with me," Rodney asided to Alana. "I mean, it's all very last-minute and honestly it's a little hush-hush."

"Okay."

"I'm really not supposed to tell you anything about it. That's what I mean by hush-hush."

"Okay."

"All right, look, it's a gold mine," Rodney blurted. "I mean a real gold mine, like, a tunnel with gold in it. I know how cool it sounds. I'll see if I can bring you back a chunk."

"Have fun," JayB urged.

Rodney frowned at him. "You can't have fun, it's *Canada*. Anyway, that's why I need you to watch Spartan for a few days. Or however long it takes."

"Oh, a few days? Like overnight? That kind of a few days?"

"Yeah," Rodney replied scornfully. "Overnight, *obviously*. You don't go all the way to Canada on a day trip. It's north of Alaska."

"Where in Canada?" Alana wanted to know.

Rodney turned to her and frowned. "What do you mean? It's Canada."

"I know, but what city?"

"How would I know?"

"Okay, good enough," JayB agreed cheerfully. "But I thought you were going to stay around and learn the restaurant business."

Rodney snorted. "What's there to learn? It's kind of the simplest business there is."

Alana sighed.

"Plus, your dad's got so much going on, and he and I are partners on the thing in Canada." Rodney focused on Alana. "I'll call you, of course."

"Oh, but you're going to be so busy."

Rodney grinned. "Yeah, but never too busy for you, babe. JayB'll watch the dogs when you go for your run."

"So, yeah, about that," Alana responded, taking in a deep breath. "I'm actually going to help out with the dog-walking thing now. *Instead* of running, I mean."

Rodney stared at her. "I have no idea what you just said."

"I said," Alana repeated slowly, "JayB needs help with his dog-walking. He's going to expand the business, so I'm going to help him walk dogs."

"Help JayB?" Rodney shook his head. "I still don't get it."

"Rodney!" Alana snapped, exasperated. "I'm going to walk the dogs with JayB to help him with his business, so I won't be going running with you when and if you return from mining gold in Canada."

Rodney looked at JayB, then at Alana, then back at JayB, and then at Alana again. "If you knew how rich this gold mine is going to make me, you wouldn't worry about money," he grumbled.

"Well, sure," Alana concurred, "but that's in the future. And right now, I'm going to pick up a little extra money working for JayB."

"Okay," Rodney turned to JayB. "You and me."

"You and me what, exactly?"

"Let's go into the other room for a second. *Bro.*"

"Okay, bro," JayB responded genially.

I followed the two men as they walked down the hall and ducked into the living room, because I wanted to be there if JayB needed me. Rodney leaned forward. "What the hell's going on?" he hissed. "Alana's going to work for you now?"

JayB shrugged. "Don't worry about it."

"Don't worry about it? You took an *oath*. You pledged to keep your hands off Alana."

"I never said anything like that." JayB was speaking calmly, but seemed annoyed.

Rodney stared. "So this is it, then. This is how you betray me. Behind my back."

"I'm not betraying anybody. And I'm standing right in front of you."

Rodney fell quiet for a moment, then narrowed his eyes. "Well, you just wait," he seethed. "Wait until I tell Maddy about *this*."

Rodney departed soon after that. Odin and I were unsure what to make of the fact that Spartan remained behind.

"So, how about I walk with you tomorrow?" Alana suggested. "I have an appointment with the dog groomer today."

"Tomorrow's perfect."

"Yes, boss."

Then Alana left, taking Odin. Very baffling, but after we collected Phoebe, I concentrated on trying to play with her and only her, though Spartan kept shoving his stiff chest in the way.

Later, I waited for Rodney to show up, growing tense when Spartan was given his own bowl of my food. When JayB went to bed and Spartan was still in the house, I realized my life had changed forever.

The next morning, I wagged when I smelled Odin approaching our front door and was there to greet him when he and Alana mounted the cement steps. Her knuckles rapped briefly on the doorframe.

"Come on in," JayB sang out. He walked out from the kitchen to greet her. "How was the dog groomer?"

Odin smelled *terrible*. His eyes were hooded with shame at the strong, offensive odor he carried with him.

"Great. Though Odin acted like he was being tortured."

JayB grinned. "Clancy's like that, too."

"So: I'm reporting for dog duty."

"Okay, it's just Spartan, Odin, and Clancy today."

"I have to ask you something," Alana said. "It's about Odin."

JayB lifted an eyebrow.

"He's just so restless. He wanders around and sometimes he cries a little bit. I'm really concerned."

"Well," JayB speculated, "maybe he's still having trouble getting over Helen."

Alana thought about this. "Do you think dogs understand death? I mean, what it even is?"

JayB nodded. "I do, actually. I think we can tell when a person or an animal is dead because we can see it. I think for a dog it's the smell. They smell the change. Odin knows Helen is gone. What I'm not sure about is whether he believes Helen is ever coming back."

"Poor Odin."

"He was really devoted to your mom. A few weeks before she passed, he learned to do this crawling-approach thing because he was always jumping up on her, and we wanted to change that. Here, watch this. Odin, Down."

Odin looked at JayB, as if unsure of what he'd said.

"Down," JayB repeated, holding out a flat hand.

Odin sank down to his stomach. I contemplated the fact that I didn't see anybody's hands digging into pockets for a treat. Otherwise, I would have done Down myself.

"Now, call him," JayB suggested.

"Hey, Odin, Come," Alana commanded.

Odin rose to his feet and went willingly to Alana, who gave JayB a questioning look.

JayB shrugged. "I guess he did it for Helen and nobody else. He would crawl across the floor, like a Marine making his way up the beach, and then when he got to your mom, he'd flop on his side and wag his tail hard while she gave him a belly rub. It was pretty cute."

"Oh, Odin, you're such a good dog." She gazed helplessly at JayB. "Any more thoughts about what I'm going to do about him?"

"You mean, where he's going to live?" JayB shook his head. "I love him, but I have to keep Spartan and Odin on leashes whenever Kelsey comes out from under the bed. I'm okay with it temporarily, but eventually I'd forget, and then Odin would be on her in a second."

Alana looked really unhappy. "I asked him again. Guy, I mean. He said absolutely no dogs."

"Is Guy's issue the same—his cat?"

"No. And she's *my* cat. Rhiannon was living on the streets when I found her. She learned how to take care of herself there. I've never met a dog willing to mess with her." Alana gazed mournfully at Odin. "It's just that Odin's so confused right now. I hate the idea of sending him off with strangers. He'll think everyone he cares about has abandoned him."

For a long moment, they gazed at Odin, who felt their stare and looked back uncertainly. They were probably as bothered by his smell as I was.

"Then don't," JayB said finally. "If Guy won't accept Odin, get a new guy." He gave her an ironic grin.

"Oh, really? So am I not supposed to get the completely unsubtle point you're making here?"

"What?" JayB replied innocently.

"You don't understand. Guy is good for me, JayB. He stands up for me. When he's around, no one can step all over me."

"What about standing up for *me*? You're my new partner in my dog-walking empire. You leave and it'll all collapse."

"I somehow think you'll get over it."

"Yeah? I think maybe you're underestimating your powers."

"My powers."

"Your impact on people."

"People? Meaning you?"

"Exactly." There was a silence. "Let me take you to dinner tonight," JayB suggested suddenly. "Give me an opportunity to talk you out of leaving Odin and me."

Alana nodded mockingly. "Sounds good. You, me, Maddy, your dad. We could go to Walter's restaurant—I'll bet we can get a table. We'll Zoom with Rodney doing his journey to the center of the earth."

"Or," JayB countered, "what about just you and me?"

They were both smiling.

JayB's phone made a chirp. Frowning, he reached for it.

"It's my dad," he informed Alana and put the phone to his ear. "I'm kind of busy, Dad. What's up?" He frowned. "When? Oh. Bye." JayB put his thumb on the phone. He looked to Alana. "That was Walter. He's on his way here. Actually, he's here. He just pulled in."

With that, the front door opened and I wagged over to greet Walter, the friendly, treat-less man. Spartan and Odin elected to eye him from the floor.

"Hey, Dad, pretty short notice."

Walter was smiling. "And there's beautiful Alana," he observed delightedly, then switched his gaze to JayB. "I called you in advance, just like you asked."

"Yeah, from my driveway." JayB looked over Walter's shoulder out the front window. "Where's the Ferrari?"

"Oh, the Ferrari," Walter answered, waving his hand.

"Or the Cadillac?"

Walter made the same gesture.

"So, what's going on?"

"Well, I kind of lost my license."

"You mean you left it somewhere?" Alana asked.

Walter shook his head. "No, it was sort of revoked. I was on I-35 and I lost track of my speed."

"How fast were you going?" JayB asked.

"Well, they said a hundred and fifteen, but I don't trust those radar things."

"You were going a hundred and fifteen on I-35," JayB repeated.

Walter nodded. "Yeah. Twice."

"You mean you got two tickets for going over a hundred miles an hour?" Alana asked.

"It's okay," Walter told her and held up his phone. "See? Rodney programmed my phone so that whenever I want to go somewhere, one of his friends will come pick me up."

"That's just Uber, Dad. *I* have Uber."

Walter frowned. "Jago, look, I realize there's a little bit of competition between you and Rodney, but he's your oldest friend."

JayB groaned softly.

"You and Rodney seem to have gotten close, Walter," Alana observed carefully.

Walter beamed. "Rodney's like the son I never had."

JayB blinked. "What does that make *me*?"

"You," Walter responded evenly, "are the son I *had*." Walter turned to Alana. "Jago was always so serious. He had everything planned out. He made spreadsheets of his homework assignments when he was in high school."

"How would you know that?" JayB interrupted. "You weren't even here when I was in high school."

"Because I know people. That's what makes me so successful. Plus, Rodney told me."

"I am so comforted to think you and Rodney have been discussing me."

Alana laughed.

"Rodney understands life is meant to be lived," Walter continued. "Go for the moment, at the moment. He's a risk-taker, just like me. Anyway, I came over because I need your help."

"My help with what?"

"Yeah, well . . ." Walter hesitated. "Maddy fired a waitress for being fat."

*Dear Diary:*

*Every time we return home from wherever we've been, whether a car ride or a walk, I hope Kelsey will be gone. I can't really explain to myself how she could leave or where she might go, but I comfort myself with the idea that JayB will push open the door and her odor will have vanished from every room.*

*Thus far, I've been disappointed.*

*I'm not being selfish—I'm looking out for JayB. A dog is loyal, but a cat is not. A dog can't wait for a person to return from being somewhere else, but a cat doesn't care in the slightest.*

*A dog's biggest fear is being abandoned by his person, but a cat seems to live in a state of self-imposed abandonment.*

Love,
Clancy

# Fifteen

I sensed that Walter had just said something alarming. JayB and Alana exchanged a glance.

"She did what?" JayB asked.

"Fired someone for being fat. So, would you mind coming down to the restaurant and sprinkling your HR dust around, get everybody settled down? Nobody wants to do any work right now. They're all pissed off, just standing around complaining."

"Where's Maddy?" Alana wanted to know.

"She locked herself in the room where we store the wine."

"That does not sound good," JayB observed. "So, what about Rodney? He's the boss, right? Why don't you ask him to sprinkle the HR dust?"

Walter shook his head. "Rodney's in Canada working on our gold-mining project. We're partners."

"Partners. How much money is Rodney putting in?"

"Rodney's share is sweat equity."

"So, Rodney has a shovel and is walking around Canada, digging up dirt, looking for gold nuggets?"

Alana laughed.

"No," Walter said testily, "not like that."

"So basically, you came over here to tell me Rodney is the son you've never had and you need me to help you with your new restaurant business."

Walter beamed. "Exactly."

JayB turned to Alana. "I'm sorry I won't be able to give you your dog walker training today. I was really looking forward to it."

Alana smiled. "Me, too. There's so much I don't understand. Like, do I put the leash on the dog or on me?"

"I've found it works better on the dog."

"Right, right, on the dog," Alana acknowledged with a nod. "Man, this is complicated. No wonder you need an advanced degree."

"Do you want me to call one of Rodney's friends or do you want to drive?" Walter asked.

Jay B sighed. "I'll drive."

We took a car ride without Alana and Odin. I was in the back middle seat and Spartan was all the way in the back. My person drove and Walter sat next to him.

"I may only be the son you've always had, but I can read you, and I can tell something's going on," JayB observed.

"What do you mean?" Walter responded innocently.

"You seem . . . tense. I can tell the difference between your fake happy and your real happy."

"Fake happy." Walter snorted.

"No, I mean it. Like when I was a kid and you lost your job, but still went to 'work' every day? You'd come home all jolly. I knew something was up."

"I was *looking* for work. That's the same as work."

"Sure. You want to tell me what's bothering you?"

Walter sighed. "It's just that business is not good. We don't seem to serve food."

"I'd agree that serving food is one of the things that restaurants are supposed to do."

"It's like the place is off the beaten path a little bit and no one thinks to go there."

"So, are you losing too much money, Dad?"

"Heck, I don't know. That's not my thing. I asked DesMoines to give me some of the printouts. I thought I'd let you look them over. I'm more of the big-picture guy."

"Big picture," JayB repeated.

I lifted my nose because I smelled a familiar place. I realized we were returning to the building with the food smells and what I had come to think of as our personal dog park. I glanced to see if Spartan registered the odors and, of course, got nothing but a stony face full of wrinkles in return.

"But it doesn't really matter, does it?" JayB asked. We stopped in front of the building, and I got to my feet, wagging. Spartan stood too, but he didn't wag. "I mean, the restaurant's just a placeholder. The big money comes from the development, right? Multimillion-dollar project, hundreds of condos, rollercoasters, indoor water skiing, catapults. You'll make, what? Half a billion dollars, each, you and the Rodster, right?"

There was an edge to JayB's voice that I did not recognize, and I wagged again, this time uneasily. Walter was staring out the window, silent.

JayB reached over and tapped Walter on the shoulder. "Hey, what is it you're not telling me?"

A tense silence followed.

"Well," Walter finally muttered, "it got all fouled up."

"What do you mean?"

"I mean, as it turns out, even though this is America, I'm not free to put up my condominium buildings on my own property. There's a zoning rule against it. Something to do with the swamp."

"The wetlands?"

Walter didn't answer.

JayB sat for a moment. "So," he mused, "you can't build. Didn't you make that part of the purchase agreement? Your plan to develop the land had to be approved, as one of the contingencies?"

"No," Walter huffed. "Of course not. We didn't want them to find out our secret. If they'd known our plans, they wouldn't have sold us the property."

"Okay, so how much are you out? I mean, what'd you pay?"

"I know this is going to be hard for you to understand, but in business there's this thing called 'blue sky.'"

"I know what blue sky is. It's a higher price paid for an asset, based on profit potential and not the actual value."

Walter shook his head. "No, it's the price of *optimism*. If you know things are going to go well, you pay more because you don't want to lose the deal. No clouds, no silver linings, just blue sky."

"Okay, sure. So, you paid a lot in blue sky, then?"

"Well, I mean, if it weren't for these crazy regulations confining my ability to develop *my own land in America,* I would be making millions and millions of dollars right now."

"Now? I don't think you know the speed at which Rodney works."

"Well, okay, not *now*," Walter corrected himself irritably.

"Bottom line: you paid more for the operation than you can sell it for," JayB translated.

"Yeah, and it turns out you can't really sell a business that's losing money."

"You can if the buyer's my father."

"The thing is, I don't *want* to run a restaurant. It's too much routine. It would drive me crazy. Every day you do the same thing over and over again."

"Like a job," JayB suggested.

Finally, we got out of the car. JayB held both our leashes while Spartan and I marked different areas of the parking lot.

Walter came around the car to be with us dogs. "I need your help, son. I need you to make the business profitable so I can get out from underneath it."

"That may not be possible. I can't conjure up customers. Are you saying you're worried about money?"

"Not worried. Nobody's worried. I may have maybe bitten off more than I can chew, is all."

"You said you were fine; you had millions and millions of dollars from your wise investments in lottery tickets."

"I *do* have millions, but I don't want to blow it all on this dump."

"Then you might have to shut it down."

"No. *No*," Walter flared. I shrank back from his anger. "And fire everybody? I would never do that. I will never be that guy, lay everybody off just because of money. You know what that's like? To lose your job because of management decisions? No, Jago. It's not the employees' fault nobody eats here. I'd rather jump from a cliff than lay people off." He sighed. "Please? This thing is just bleeding money and your girlfriend keeps calling me with all these questions."

JayB frowned. "Alana's calling you about the restaurant?"

"Alana? No. *Maddy*." Walter stared at JayB. "What are you saying here, son? I say girlfriend and you say Alana? You do know Rodney's sweet on Alana, don't you?"

"Everyone seems to know that."

Walter held up a finger. "Don't steal another man's woman, Jago. Don't do to him what Howie did to me."

I'd never heard JayB laugh the way he did now. It was a bit of an ugly sound. "What are you talking about? Celeste met Howard two years after your divorce."

"That's what she says now, of course," Walter said icily, nodding to himself. "But how else can you explain why she left me? Had to be because of Howie."

"Dad, you were in *prison*."

"No." Walter shook his head. "No, I was in lockup. Briefly."

"For kiting checks."

"Yes, but I got off on a technicality, remember?"

JayB groaned.

"I would think you'd *want* your parents to get back together," Walter observed coolly. "I would think you'd *want* to help your father's business."

"I thought your other son Rodney was going to run the restaurant."

"Rodney has bigger fish to fry right now. This is why you went to grad school, isn't it? I tried to talk to the employees, and I think I got Maddy calmed down, but everyone else is really angry."

"You do realize that since you made Maddy part of management, anything she does is in your name. This woman she wrongfully terminated could sue *you*."

"I don't know what the world has come to," Walter lamented.

"All right. All right. Since Rodney is off frying fish, I'll see if I can fix anything. But that's it. I'm not going to run this restaurant for you."

A few minutes later, we were sitting at an outside table. It was a beautiful, warm spring day, marred only by the scent of Spartan sitting under a tree. JayB was talking to Maddy, whose legs were bouncing under the table. I've learned that when there's no food smell on the table and people's legs are bobbing up and down, there will be no treats given, no matter how good a Sit a dog might execute. I sprawled in the dirt.

"Why don't you tell me what happened," he said to Maddy.

"What happened," Maddy declared forcefully, "is I was giving direct orders and the waitress, Savannah, refused to obey so I had no choice."

"All right, what were the orders you issued?"

"I mean," Maddy complained, "what is it with this place? Savannah, DesMoines, am I going to have to change my name to Green Bay? Rapid City?"

"Just walk me through it, if you don't mind."

"Okay, but don't listen to anybody else. Everybody's got a big fat opinion right now that's polluting the crime scene."

"Well, we'll see. So what happened? What were the orders?"

Maddy folded her arms, scowling.

"Maddy?" JayB prodded. "What did you tell her to do?"

"I don't see the point in answering that until there's a full investigation. I have more experience than anyone you know—I'm *still* having experiences, in fact. I know my rights."

"Why don't we regard this as a full investigation, then."

Maddy stared at him. "An *investigation*? Are you saying I need an attorney? Because I'm not paying for that."

"No, that's not what I'm saying at all. Please. I need to understand what's going on. Tell me your side of things."

"I'm running this whole operation here and not getting any support from headquarters. Like, isn't there supposed to be a 1–800 number for me to call for mental health? My last job had one. I called it all the time."

"I'll look into that. Just, please, tell me what happened."

Maddy sighed, and I closed my eyes, thinking of what a waste of a table this was, to sit and talk without dropping any food for a dog.

"Okay," Maddy finally agreed, "I'll spill the beans and rat out everybody else, but if I waive my fifth amendment, you have to promise not to be mad."

"Okay. I won't get mad."

"That's because you *never* get mad, not because you love me," Maddy pouted.

"What was it you asked Savannah to do?"

"I told her my car needed an oil change," Maddy mumbled, her eyes sliding away.

JayB stared at her.

"Look, if you don't change the oil, the engine blows up or something. I don't know. I just know that there's a sticker in my windshield that was never there before."

JayB held up a hand, "Okay, I get it, you needed an oil change. But why would you ask Savannah?"

*"Because she reports to me,"* Maddy exploded. "She has to do whatever I tell her."

"Actually," JayB corrected her patiently, "that's not really true. She has to do things related to her job description, but vehicle repairs aren't on that list."

"Of course you would say that," Maddy snapped. "Of course there's a *list*. You never wash my back. You should be taking care of me as your number one responsibility always, first thing, before you even open your eyes in the morning."

"I know . . . the eight simple rules for remodeling JayB Danville. I'm just saying you fired her for no good reason. You can't do that."

"That's not true. I get fired for no good reason all the time."

"From what I understand, Savannah's a good employee. She's been here for two years."

"Good employee." Maddy snorted. "Right. Have you seen her socks?"

"Sorry?"

Maddy's eyes narrowed. "Isn't the real issue here that you're trying to steal Rodney's girlfriend to get back at me?"

"No, I can honestly say that's not the real issue."

"Oh, I just caught you in the biggest lie since sliced bread. Did you really think Rodney could keep your secret in his pants? I thought I was throwing up when he told me your ploys. I couldn't see it more clearly if I had my eyes open. So, no."

"No?"

"No to Alana."

"I see."

Maddy stared off for a minute and then turned back. "Well, that's it then. You don't need 1–800 to see how hard this is for me mentally. I'm taking my sabbatical, starting now. Paid, obviously—I don't work for free."

JayB shook his head. "We don't offer paid sabbaticals."

"Walter told me we do, and he owns the place. You're just the dog walker. You've never once commented about my hair, and I changed it twice in the past week."

"That seems . . . true."

"At last, you admit something! You're like prying teeth." Maddy stood and I lazily regarded her. "I'm dismissing this conversation, now, but don't think it won't return when you show up to apologize. FYI, I like tulips. Or jewelry."

Maddy left the table, and I put my head back down.

*Dear Diary:*

*Every time my person speaks, his voice stirs a love within me. It's a different sort of feeling than what I experience when I think of Phoebe—this is the pure devotion a dog has for a person.*

*I suppose I could find fault with some of his choices. Having a cat live with us, putting her food out of reach, inviting Spartan into our pack to live with us. These cause me aggravation. Or I could dwell on the wonders he has brought into my life: Phoebe, chicken treats, our new place of so many dog parks, car rides. . . . But truthfully, none of that really matters. JayB is my person, and that's more important than anything else.*

*I think of Odin, of the deep, aching wound within him. I cannot imagine what it might be like to have a person and then lose her.*

*I wish there was something I could do to help my dear friend Odin, but a dog lost is a dog lost until he finds a way to open his heart to another person.*

Love,
Clancy

# Sixteen

Later, JayB talked to a woman who cried and several other men and women, and finally sat with DesMoines.

"So, hey, DesMoines," JayB said wearily, "kind of a weird day."

She shuffled her feet. "You could say that. I've seen weirder, though."

"I'm going to speak to Walter. Obviously, if Savannah will take her job back, the position is still open for her. I think I'm also going to ask her to agree not to pursue any other remedies against the organization or Maddy or anybody in management, and, in return, give her a settlement of some kind."

"Seems fair," DesMoines agreed slowly. A long silence followed.

"I would like to offer you a bonus as well. You've had to put up with a lot of tumult over the past several days while the restaurant transitions away from how it has always worked, toward one that's more . . ."

"Insane?" DesMoines suggested.

JayB laughed.

"I was wondering if you were going to talk to me."

JayB looked wary. "Oh?"

DesMoines nodded. "You're the only one of your crew with any sense, far as I can see. You and maybe that Alana. So, tell me the truth, please: should I be looking for another job? I don't want to stay where I'm not wanted, and I for sure don't want to find myself suddenly unemployed."

JayB gave her a level look. "My honest answer is, I don't know. Maddy's going to be on . . . on leave, but I don't actually know how long my dad will want to fund the business. He's got lots of money, you know, but he gets impatient. If you'd give me a printout of all of our financial statements, vacation schedules, anything you've got, it

would help. I can promise that if we're shutting down, I'll make sure
you get a generous severance. I'll get on it as quickly as I can, try to
figure out what's going on."

"What's going on is, your father bought into a money-losing business and made it worse."

After that, we took a car ride! But we parked at home and I resigned myself to seeing and smelling Kelsey. Then JayB surprised
me by walking from the driveway up to Odin's house. Alana answered the door when he knocked.

"Hi. So what was the big problem at the restaurant?" Alana
asked, letting JayB, Spartan, and me inside.

Odin flapped his tail briefly when he saw me, but elected to stay
in his dog bed. I've had naps like that. You get so involved in being
comfortable, it just isn't worth it to get up for anything short of a
meal. Spartan ignored Odin completely.

"The biggest problem was Maddy, but luckily she's gone on sabbatical."

Alana gave him an odd look.

JayB nodded. "Yeah. So, I know that you're not really interested
in doing this kind of thing, but I wonder if you'd do me a big favor
and look through all these reports and see if you can make sense of
the numbers. I haven't looked at financial statements since a class
in college."

Alana tilted her head. "I thought the restaurant was just something on the side until Rodney could fire up the bulldozers."

"Yeah, that was Plan A, but it turns out the property isn't zoned
for anything except a dilapidated restaurant with a huge piece of
land that's divvied up into small, fenced-in ostrich pens."

"Huh." Alana reached for the sheaf of papers. "Is it possible that
this'll all unwind over the business license? I've heard of businesses
that can't get to that final stage. It happens in California a lot, and
if you can't transfer the business license, you can't keep running the
operation, and all bets are off."

"That makes a lot of sense, but if I know my father, he waived any right to cancel the deal under any circumstances, including having a huge meteor wipe out the building."

Alana smiled. "Well, it's going to take me a while to figure all this stuff out. It's a big favor, so"—she gave him a speculative look—"maybe if you buy me that dinner you promised . . . ?"

Odin and I lifted our heads at that wonderful word. Even Spartan seemed to be paying attention.

JayB grinned. "Deal."

A short time later, a woman came to the door and handed over some wonderful-smelling sacks. Odin and I gave this development a lot of consideration. JayB and Alana sat at the table and talked and laughed. Spartan watched the gaiety from the corner.

"You know," Alana observed at one point, "your restaurant—"

"My *dad's* restaurant," JayB interrupted.

"Okay. Your *dad's* restaurant could use a menu reboot. Nothing wrong with burgers and fried chicken, and I actually like the veggie stir fry, but why not branch out? Did you know DesMoines managed a Cajun restaurant for ten years?"

"I had no idea."

"Yeah. In New Orleans, so she must know what she's doing. Why not add a little gumbo?"

"That's a great idea. And maybe barbecue?"

"Oh, I would not try barbecue in Kansas City. That'd be like taking hockey to Canada."

"I think that's what Rodney's doing right now."

Alana laughed. "But seriously, maybe add some spice to, I don't know, the lasagna."

"Cajun lasagna?"

"I don't see why not. Get a reputation for something besides empty tables." Alana tossed down chicken pieces, even throwing one across the room to Spartan.

I was starting to adore Alana.

"So," she remarked, "your girlfriend called me."

JayB sighed. "Could we call her something else?"

"All right," Alana agreed, smiling. "Maddy called me. She said she needed to warn me that you're not spontaneous."

"That's not true. I plan to do something spontaneous Tuesday."

Alana laughed.

Later, the paper bags were stowed away, and JayB and Alana moved about in the kitchen, mostly silent while water ran, occasionally bumping into each other and smiling.

"Well, hey," she offered, "I'll walk you home."

"Thank you. This is a pretty high-crime area."

Alana laughed. We headed outside. Odin and Spartan and I dutifully lifted our legs. Night had fallen, and with it had come some warm, moist air, hinting at impending summer. It was the kind of night that gave a dog energy, and Odin and I both responded, stepping briskly, smelling eagerly, hoping to encounter a creature to hunt, or a dog to inspect.

Suddenly, Alana stopped. "What's that?" She pointed to a space between houses filled with shrubbery. In among the bushes, I saw some bugs.

"Oh! Those are lightning bugs," JayB replied. "Have you never seen them?"

"They're *real*," Alana exulted with a squeal. "They're really real!" She dashed across the street and JayB and our pack of dogs quickly followed. She stopped and gazed into the bushes with wonder. "I thought," she explained in a tremulous voice, "that fireflies were only in Disney movies. I didn't realize they truly existed."

"Really?" JayB responded.

"They're magic. Look at them!" Alana turned to JayB with shining eyes, and I felt something strong rise inside JayB and come off his skin . . . something like joy.

"This is the most wonderful night," Alana whispered.

They spent several moments cupping their hands and looking into them. "It's like a miracle," Alana breathed. She looked up at JayB and he gazed at her, and they both smiled.

I wagged when she stepped into his arms and they kissed, the bugs flashing all around them. When they parted, though, I felt

Alana's mood change. She stepped away, and when JayB reached for her, she backed up even farther.

"I'd better say goodnight," she whispered.

"Alana . . ."

She shook her head, reaching for Odin's leash. I watched her leave and felt JayB's mood change.

Human beings are utterly baffling.

The next several days were so similar to each other that I accepted them as how life would be from now on. Spartan still lived with us, watching me from hooded eyes, barely reacting to anything except for his bowl of food, set out by my person at mealtime. Spartan did sniff and mark whenever I did, but he took no joy in it. It was merely the mechanical reaction of a male dog to a provocative scent.

We did not see much of Odin, for some reason. JayB took us to Odin's house one time, and I was curious to see how awkward he and Alana were with each other. The breezy, happy exchanges had been replaced with silences and averted glances.

As we were leaving Odin's house, Alana spoke: "JayB."

He turned with a questioning look.

"We'll . . . talk."

We had apparently forgotten the way to the old dog park—instead, we now took car rides to our new, personal dog park. Phoebe and Spartan and sometimes Millie and Tillie romped in the big, fenced-in spaces, though Phoebe had far more energy than any of us.

DesMoines paid more attention to me than to the other dogs. Her hands were strong but gentle as they stroked my fur. She had figured out that (probably unique to me, as a dog) I really liked bacon. She often gave me a crumble or two.

Maddy often came to see me as well. While JayB was speaking to people, she would go up to him and hug him from behind and he would stop talking for a minute. At one point, they were sitting in the shade under a tree at a wooden table, and JayB said, "Maddy, why are you here every day? I thought you're on sabbatical."

Maddy shrugged, "I see myself more as a paid consultant now.

I'm the only one with any experience in the underworkings of the restaurant. Certainly, *you* don't know anything about it."

"Well," JayB acknowledged, "I suppose that's true, although I do have DesMoines."

Maddy rolled her eyes. "Oh, please. She's always working. You can't trust that type."

One morning, we stopped to pick up Odin, and Alana invited us inside and gave me a turkey treat. She gave one to Spartan as well, but I couldn't really complain about that. I've noticed that most people treat dogs equally. She was probably hoping Spartan would change expression, but he never did.

"Well, I have news," JayB announced.

Alana raised her eyebrows.

"The business is all his now. The restaurant, I mean. It got transferred over to Walter's name. He's now Kansas City's newest and most inept restaurateur."

Alana smiled. "I finally finished going over the books. They're a little . . . well, let's just say they haven't been kept very up-to-date, but it was easy to piece things together once I understood the system. There are some pretty big issues."

"You seem really stressed," JayB observed.

She shook her head. "It's not about that. I'm in the offer/counter-offer period of selling the house. It's weird because, where I'm from, you put a house on the market and all of your offers come in higher than the asking price. That's not what's going on here, and I don't know anything about selling houses. I just want the whole thing to be over, you know?"

JayB nodded.

Alana was silent for a moment. "So, back to the restaurant. I don't know if you knew this, but Walter and Rodney and Maddy have salaries. Really *big* salaries. Money that can't be justified by cash flow. Taken together, it's by far the single largest expense."

"That sounds about right."

"Yeah. So, the place is running solidly in the red, but it wasn't always. When you go back and look at the books from a long time ago, it was actually making money. A *lot* of money. It had customers. There's huge capacity in that dining room, plus the deck and patio seating when the weather's nice. All you need now is to reduce your, let's call it *executive overhead,* and get some people in the door. Maybe advertise. There needs to be a hook. The way it is now, there's no particular reason for people to go there. You might as well put up a big sign that says 'Food.' Put some pizzazz into marketing, so people get curious and want to check it out."

"Pizzazz," JayB repeated dubiously. "Man, that is not me. I can hire staff, I can maintain systems, but I don't know how to generate pizzazz, attract patrons. And Walter sure doesn't."

Alana laughed.

"Rodney's still mining gold, which is a good thing. DesMoines is like me—she can keep the operation running, but attracting customers isn't her thing, either. To succeed, this business needs a really flexible thinker, a person who's innovative, who can improvise, good on her feet, creative, someone with that spark."

Alana shook her head, a small smile on her face. "You know, JayB, I love how you listened to me about what I really want in a career, but I'm not staying in Kansas to help run a restaurant. I *can't.* I'm selling the house and going back to California."

JayB nodded but didn't say anything.

Alana sighed. "Okay. About the elephant in the living room."

"That's not an elephant, that's a shar-pei."

Alana smiled, but her smile quickly faded.

*Dear Diary:*

*I have been unable to conquer the moving chair.*

*The two times I've tried to climb up on it, the chair has run from me as if alive, forcing me to trot along on my hind legs to keep up. Eventually, when it hits the wall, it stops, but by then I'm so far from the counter where Kelsey's food sits that getting on the chair would make no sense. (I know because I tried it. Both times.)*

*I am doing that now. I am pushing the chair and it is moving at random, scooting across the floor. Kelsey watches inscrutably with slitted eyes. I imagine that seeing a dog exert such power must be terribly intimidating and she is frozen in shock (otherwise, she would flee the room and go live with someone else).*

*Spartan is in the other room, walled off by a new gate in the doorway.*

*I'm on a different trajectory today, scooting across the floor, the chair swiveling slightly so that I am disoriented when the thing finally stops, but then I smell it: Kelsey's fishy meal on the counter.*

*I'm right where I want to be.*

*How did this happen?*

*Scarcely daring to believe it, I nimbly leap up on top of the chair. It swivels, then stops, and now the counter is an easy step. I claw at the slick surface, and then I'm up!*

*I lower my face to the small bowl of delicious, fragrant morsels. I've done it! Kelsey will never again enjoy a meal in this house.*

*If only Phoebe could see this, she would be amazed.*
*This is going to work!*

Love,
Clancy

# Seventeen

Alana sighed. "I am so sorry about how I kissed you the other night."

"I'm not."

"I didn't mean to lead you on. I was just caught up in the moment."

"I don't feel led on. Is that why you've been avoiding me?"

Alana glanced away unhappily. "I'm just not good at things like this," she finally explained in a small voice.

"Things like what?"

"You know. Confrontation. Disappointing people."

JayB watched her until she met his gaze. "It would be more disappointing to me if you stopped seeing me just because of a kiss."

"Okay," she whispered.

"Okay," he agreed.

I yawned, thinking that if we were going to stand around like this, I might as well take a nap.

"So," Alana announced in a more business-like tone, "once the restaurant is current with your suppliers, you won't be on a cash basis. Do you understand what I'm saying here? Right now, you're cut off. Nobody's extending any credit because you fell so far behind on your payments. Not Walter's fault—it was under previous management that all this happened, but the upshot is that you're having to buy your supplies from the grocery store, which is a recipe for disaster. You need wholesale prices. Does that make sense?"

"It does, but it won't matter if we don't get butts in the seats."

"That's true. Well, the land must be worth something, even with the zoning. If Walter decides to shutter the place, cut his losses, he won't be out *everything*."

JayB was shaking his head. "My father might be a lot of things, but heartless isn't one of them. I think he'd spend every dime he's got to keep from laying off the staff. I admire that. Last place I worked, the CFO acted like the people were no more important than, I don't know, bugs."

"Except the one who punched you in the nose," Alana reminded him with a smile.

"Oh, her? She was irreplaceable. Had a left jab like Tyson Fury."

"Well, I don't know how rich Walter is, but even Powerball isn't an endless pile of money. And didn't you say he split it with everyone from his work? So yeah, he might actually spend every dime he's got."

"Can you explain all this to Walter?"

"I thought I was explaining it to you so *you* could explain it to him."

JayB chuckled. "Oh, no. He'll listen to it coming from you, but if I start telling him, he'll just roll his eyes and say I've joined the hordes of paper-pushers who are ruining the country."

"Could it maybe be the two of you need to have an honest conversation with each other?" Alana asked tactfully.

"Right, sure, like I've been trying to do since . . . oh, I don't know, age nine?"

Alana laughed.

"I think Walter looks at me and sees Howard—my stepfather—because I'm less . . ." JayB trailed off, thinking.

"Unstable?" Alana suggested.

Now JayB laughed.

"What happened to him? Howard, I mean."

"Oh. He passed like eight years ago. Heart attack."

"I'm so sorry."

"He and my mom were getting divorced at the time. It sort of put some distance between us. My mom and me, I mean. It's like *she* thinks that *I* think that Howard died because she left him. I've never said anything like that, of course." JayB sighed. "So, can I buy you lunch at my father's restaurant? The place might lack pizzazz, but DesMoines added a fish special."

Alana nodded. "Sure. But . . ."

"But?"

"We're good? About the kiss and everything, I mean."

"Sure. Long as you don't try something like that again."

Alana laughed, and later, we all took a car ride!

Odin and Spartan and Phoebe came with us. We also picked up Millie and Tillie, and when we did, we met a new dog, named Woo-Hoo, who was at Millie and Tillie's with another woman. Woo-Hoo was even smaller than Millie and Tillie, but a lot more yappy. Nothing happened that Woo-Hoo didn't snap at or bark at. I thought of Woo-Hoo as Woo-Hoo the Bark Dog. Finally, Spartan had met a dog who was as unfriendly as he.

In the car, Millie, Tillie, and Woo-Hoo the Bark Dog occupied the back while Odin, Phoebe, Spartan, and I crowded together in the middle seat. There was not a lot of room, but I made sure I was firmly pressed up against Phoebe, inserting myself between her and Spartan.

Alana stared out the window. "Such a pretty day," she observed wistfully. "I love the clouds here. In LA, it's usually completely sunny."

"Well, but we get that slate-gray Midwest sky a lot, especially in winter."

"I'm really going to miss this."

"Miss Kansas City?"

Alana nodded. "Yeah, I am."

"Well, you haven't been here in August."

"What happens then?"

"August is when the humidity and the temperature both go above eighty. You take a walk around the block at night and your T-shirt's soaked."

Every time the car eased to a stop, all the dogs would alert, but then it would start moving again. This happened now as Alana said, "JayB." She reached out her hand and touched his briefly. They regarded each other. "I'm not going to miss only the city. I'm going to miss you. You've become a really close friend, a very special friend to me. I can't tell you how much I appreciate everything you've done, the way you helped me with my mom's things. I don't know too many people who would do something like that."

"Well, after all, I am officially known as the friendliest person in Kansas City," JayB reminded her with a grin. They looked at each other and his grin faded. "I feel the same way about you, Alana," he murmured. He drew in a breath, preparing to say more, but honking began behind us.

Alana's glance flicked up and out the window. "Oh, green light."

Our car moved on. "So, has Rodney called you at all?" JayB asked. "Or is there no cell service at the bottom of the mine shaft?"

"He left one message, but mostly he texts, like a lot, every day."

"What does he text, if you don't mind me asking?"

"A lot of emojis, like biceps, martini glasses, flowers, and kisses. It's like getting messages from an eight-year-old."

JayB laughed. "That's all he does, is send hieroglyphics?"

"No. Here, I'll read you a couple of the more amusing ones. Okay, here he says, *'Hey, I know I promised to call, but Canada is so LOL. More meetings now. Glad I brought my sweater.'* Then there's a selfie."

Alana showed JayB her phone. He glanced at it. "Nice."

"There's a couple more in his sweater if you want to see them."

JayB shook his head.

"Okay, then here's one: *'I know you wish you were here, Alena.'*" She looked up. "He spelled my name wrong. *'But believe me, I'm working hard.'* Then there's a selfie of him eating dinner in a restaurant. There's a half-drained beer and an empty shot glass. So, you know, working hard. *'Everyone knows me by my first name, of course.'*"

"Of course."

"Okay, this one's my favorite: *'Alena,'*—still doesn't know how to spell it—*'don't tell Walt, meeting an attorney because Canadian law. Here's a pic of me at the pool a couple years ago. Six pack under my arm and in my stomach. LOL.'*"

"Wait, he has six-pack abs?"

"Um, well, not visibly. And then here's what he sent a day later. *'Hey, no fair. I sent you a pool picture, you didn't send one back. What's with that? LOL. I ♥ bikinis LOL.'*"

"LOL," JayB concurred. "Let me guess, there's a selfie."

"Oh, yeah. And then here's the one from yesterday: *'Hey, Alena, I hope to come home soon. Looking forward to your BIG WEL-COME. LOL.'*"

"You're probably spending a lot of time planning that welcome."

"You bet."

When we stopped, we'd arrived at our personal dog park.

"Want to stand with me and watch the dogs for a while?" JayB offered. "It's one of the best perks of my job."

Millie, Tillie and Woo-Hoo the Bark Dog wound up in one fenced-in area while Spartan, Odin, and I frolicked with Phoebe in the other. Well, not frolicked. Odin circled around himself for a nap and Spartan just ran after us, growling and thrusting out his chest. Phoebe seemed fine with this, but I was appalled.

DesMoines walked up to JayB, and when I trotted over to the fence, he let me out and she offered me little bits of bacon.

It's good to be a dog.

"Hi, Alana. So, JayB," DesMoines ventured, "could I ask you a question? It's maybe a little personal."

JayB sort of straightened and looked wary. I alerted to the quick change in his mood. "Sure," he responded tentatively.

"It's about this woman."

"What woman is that?"

"Celeste. Who is Celeste?"

Alana smiled.

"Oh. Celeste is my mom."

"Your mom?" DesMoines arched her eyebrows. "I thought your parents were divorced."

"Oh, they are."

"How long now?"

"It's been more than twenty, twenty-two years, I guess," JayB cal-culated after a moment.

"Twenty-two years," DesMoines repeated. She gave JayB a shy smile. "He's a handsome man, your father. He makes me laugh. He comes in and we sit and talk. When it's not busy. Which is always."

"Well, sure," JayB acknowledged, "but there's probably a lot you don't know about him."

"What I know is that a ship without a rudder will stop drifting if you anchor it."

"Ah. Well, I'm not much of a sailor, but Alana's from Marina del Rey." They all grinned at one another, then JayB and Alana watched DesMoines walk away.

"Well, Skipper," he said, "I have to say that with all the anarchy my dad's brought to her restaurant, I'm surprised DesMoines hasn't thrown Walter overboard."

"I'd be willing to give up the nautical references now."

JayB laughed.

"I know what you mean, but DesMoines is right; he is handsome, and he's kind and generous and courteous. And don't you think she's a good catch for your father? You have to love her dark hair, blue eyes combination. Great smile."

"I think my father lives in the delusion that winning Powerball means my mom will come running back to him. Until he rejoins reality in progress, he won't even notice other women."

I turned as I smelled three dogs—a young male and two older females—and two women coming toward us. The dogs were smaller than me, but certainly larger than Millie and Tillie.

"How does this work?" one of the women asked as she arrived.

We were all sniffing each other politely while our people spoke.

"I'm not sure what you mean," JayB said tentatively.

The other woman pointed to where Odin was sleeping and Phoebe was fruitlessly trying to entice Spartan to play.

"What I mean," she explained, "is do we pay for the dogs individually or as a group?"

JayB was clearly perplexed by the question. Alana reached out and put a hand on his arm. "No fee," she informed them. "As long as you eat here, you can let the dogs run free in the park."

Both people grinned. "That's fantastic," the second woman enthused. "The place where we've been going, there's a twenty-five-dollar fee for the dogs, and then the food is terrible. Just microwaved hot dogs and stuff. We're supposed to be letting these two old girls run around more, but in the house, it's impossible. Digby here is only nine months old and he crashes into everything."

"Well, there's nothing to crash into out here," Alana observed.

"Exactly."

"Are they friendly, or do they need to be by themselves?" JayB inquired.

"I think Digby is as friendly as they come, but he doesn't really know the rules to being a dog yet, you know? He'll jump all over, and sometimes the older dogs need to correct him."

"Well," JayB responded, "Phoebe over there is pretty young. I'll pull her out and put them together in one of the fenced-in areas."

The woman smiled at me. "Who's this?"

"This is Clancy." JayB reached down and patted me on the side, and I closed my eyes halfway in sheer pleasure. "He's around six years old now, a rescue, yellow Lab, sometimes a good dog, sometimes not."

I loved being called a good dog by my person.

Soon, the dogs were all behind fencing except me. I was torn. I hated that I wasn't in the fenced-in area with Phoebe, because she and the young male were playing together frantically, but he was so young that I did not see him as competition.

For a moment, we all just watched the dogs play, then Alana turned and gave JayB an amazed look. "Do you realize what just happened?"

## Dear Diary:

Well, somehow other dogs found out about our personal dog park, because now the place is crowded. I appreciate that there are separate pens—our first dog park sometimes made me anxious, with all the dogs crowded together inside a single fence.

I know the old dog park made Millie and Tillie nervous, too. Some dogs react to the presence of a large, strange pack by challenging every canine with hackles up and tails stiff. The little white dogs were cowed by this and would cringe, lowering themselves to the ground like Odin crawling to Helen.

I personally don't understand aggressive behavior in the dog park. Isn't it better to be friends with everyone? I think unfriendly dogs want to be seen as in charge. Which is ridiculous—dogs are not in charge, people are in charge.

At our new, personal dog park, people decide which pen to put their pets in, and I accept JayB's decision without protest. But I am distressed when I'm in one pen and Phoebe's in another, especially if Spartan's in there with her.

I don't know how to get JayB to understand that I belong with Phoebe and Spartan doesn't. People, it seems, are not good at understanding relationships.

Love,
Clancy

# Eighteen

A few days later, JayB was sitting at an outdoor table with one of the people I thought of as DesMoines's friends. This woman often worked with DesMoines inside the building at our personal dog park. She had long yellow hair and was always nice to me, though she never gave me anything to eat. (Dogs find it even easier to like the people who hand out treats.)

"This is a liability waiver," JayB explained to her. "It's pretty simple. We have to ask customers to sign one before we can let them put their dogs into any of the pens."

As JayB was saying this, I saw Spartan, alone in one of the smaller pens, lift his head, go alert, and then jump to his feet. He was actually wagging his stubby tail and he raced over to the gate. Obviously, something was happening.

I looked in the direction he was staring and spotted Rodney climbing out of a car. He was carrying a big box with a handle on top. The car drove off, a cloud of dust chasing after it.

I realized at that moment that Spartan did care about somebody. He cared about Rodney. Rodney set down his box and let Spartan out of the pen. Spartan jumped and twirled at his feet. I had never seen this dog bring so much energy to anything. It made me reassess Spartan. Perhaps he was not a cat in a dog's body, because no cat would ever exhibit such joy.

Rodney brought Spartan over to our table and peered at the papers on it. "Shouldn't you run that past me?" he challenged JayB.

The nice woman with the long hair stood and went back inside the building while JayB gestured. "Things have changed since you went on your international spy mission, Rodney. I don't know if you noticed, but we have people here eating lunch—actual customers."

Rodney peered around, unimpressed.

I wagged because Maddy came outside. Spartan did not react to her approach.

"Well, hey, Rodney," Maddy greeted. "How was Canada?"

Rodney shook his head. "What happened in Canada was so bad, I can't talk about it this century."

"Why, hello, Maddy," welcomed JayB. "I didn't expect to see you here. Again."

Maddy sighed. "I'm thinking about ending the monotony of sabbatical, because things're really falling apart."

"Don't worry, I'm back," Rodney assured her.

Walter came out to join us, a big grin on his face. "Hey. Look who it is. The conquering hero."

"Walter, I won't charge you for this, but we need to attract a better-looking clientele," Maddy declared flatly. "I think it's time to make a task force to listen to me."

Rodney spread his hands, palms up. "Hey, Walter. I'm really sorry about what happened. I couldn't believe it when there wasn't any gold."

Walter clapped Rodney on the back. "Well, there's a life lesson there for you, Rodney. Better to take a risk and lose everything, than have the burden of crushing obligations."

JayB nodded. "That makes all kinds of sense." I leaned up against his leg so he'd know how much I loved him.

"Besides, we still have the Korean deal," Walter reasoned. "Right?"

Rodney brightened. "Yeah. As far as I know, the boat is just sitting there, a fortune of scrap iron piled up on it, ready to go to China as soon as we put up the money."

"And," Walter added expansively, gesturing, "look around you. We turned this place around. We're making money."

"No," JayB corrected. "We're losing *less* money, which I'm glad you brought up. I need to talk seriously with the three of you."

Walter shook his head. "Oh, come on. Don't dampen the mood, Jago." He turned to Rodney. "Call your girl, Alana. Let's get her down here for a big celebration. Send one of your Uber buddies to get her."

"Tell her I said it would be a good time to go over a few things with all of the salaried executives here," JayB agreed. "Business things."

"On it," Rodney replied.

I was happy to see Odin arrive a little while later, jumping out of a car from the back seat ahead of Alana. I had been chasing a fast dog who held a tennis ball in his mouth and could outrun me as he made tight circles inside our big dog park. When I gave up, feeling I was fruitlessly wasting effort, he would dance toward me, chewing the ball in his loose mouth, even dropping it in front of me. But when I lunged, he would snatch it, and then we'd be off again. We did this over and over and over again.

Some dogs never learn.

Rodney ignored Odin but spread his arms wide and enveloped Alana in an expansive hug, which she stood inside until he released her.

We sat at a big outdoor table—Maddy and Walter, Alana and Rodney, and my person. Delicious meal smells floated down. Odin and I stationed ourselves between Alana and JayB while Spartan curled up at Rodney's feet.

Several moments went by with people talking and not feeding dogs.

After a pause, Alana spoke: "Could we talk about the restaurant's cash flow for just a minute?"

"Absolutely not," Walter replied.

"Dad," JayB sighed.

"Now that I'm back, things'll improve, I promise," Rodney vowed.

"Like, people have *got* to stop bringing their dogs here," Maddy stated vehemently. "There has to be a code of health."

"That reminds me," Walter interjected. "Alana, I need your help managing my money. I get all these statements from the bank, and with Rodney's special projects starting to bear fruit, I need to understand the big picture."

"Oh, no, I'm not a money manager," Alana protested.

"That's more my specialty," Rodney claimed.

"Then I should get paid, too," added Maddy.

"You're too busy for this kind of thing," Walter told Rodney. "Besides, with Alana on the job, business here's finally picking up."

"Actually," said Alana, "it's JayB running ads about our dog pens that's been bringing in people."

"Right," Maddy snorted.

"It was your idea to market this as a place to bring dogs," JayB reminded Alana.

"Which I'm still against," Maddy informed them. "I think I need to veto on this one."

"So whatcha been up to with me gone, Alana?" Rodney asked.

"Well, I just found out the buyer's financing fell through. I have to put the house back on the market," Alana replied mournfully.

"Oh, I'm sorry," JayB responded.

"You don't sound sorry," Maddy challenged.

"To tell the truth," Alana said, "I'm just exhausted. I need a break. I'm going to go meet my boyfriend and cat in Vegas."

I raised my head suspiciously at the word "cat." Why would any person seated at a big table with lots of food use such a word in the presence of three wonderful dogs?

"Afterward, I'll bring Rhiannon back so she can stay with me while we show the house." Alana turned to JayB. "Would you be willing to watch Odin for a few days?"

"Of course."

"Why Vegas?" Rodney wanted to know.

"Oh, it's because of Rhiannon. My cat is crazy. When she's on an airplane, she just screams. No idea why, because she's fine in a car. I had to take her off the plane the one time I tried it."

"Well, wait," JayB objected. "You're going to *drive* to Las Vegas?"

"Yep. Taking my mom's car."

"Do you know how far that is?"

"I mean, there's no traffic, right?"

JayB laughed. "It's not an overnight trip, Alana." He regarded her thoughtfully. "Tell you what. I'll drive you."

"Sorry?"

"It'll be fun," JayB elaborated. "I haven't been on a road trip in a long time. If you're going to drive through Kansas, mid-June is probably the best time."

"That would be really nice of you."

Odin glanced at me to see if I knew what was going on, but I did not.

"Well," Maddy interrupted brusquely, "if you think you are going to pile into your Honda with my boyfriend and drive off into the sunset like the end of *Thelma & Louise*, you have another thing coming."

Alana frowned. "Oh, no. Maddy, don't misunderstand. I'm going to meet my boyfriend."

"Oh, right," Maddy mocked. "In Vegas. A guy named Guy."

"Well, hey. You know, we'll all have a lot more fun if I go, too," Rodney ventured.

"That's so kind of you, Maddy and Rodney," Alana praised cautiously, "but the car's pretty small. And obviously, we'll be taking two dogs with us now. There's just no room."

Walter clapped his hands together. "How's this? Let me provide the transportation."

"Uh, what are you saying, Dad?"

"I'm saying, I'll figure out transportation," Walter clarified. "It'll be fun. I haven't been to Las Vegas since the time I was evading that subpoena."

"When was that?" JayB wanted to know.

"Bah. It got dismissed."

JayB looked to Alana. "It's your decision. Do you really want everyone to go?"

Alana took a long pause, then spoke meekly. "Sounds great."

"All right," JayB agreed. "I'll get someone to take care of Kelsey and tell Dominique I can't walk Phoebe for a few days. She'll understand."

Maddy scowled. "Who the heck is Dominique? What, you've got a pole dancer in your basement now?"

"Then it's settled," Walter declared. "We're going on a road trip!"

When we left later without anybody giving a good dog treats, JayB drove Alana and Odin home with us. The moment the car started moving, Alana turned to JayB, looking angry. "What was *that*?"

"Sorry? What was what?"

"The way you put me on the spot, JayB. *It's my decision. Do I really want everyone to go?* Do you understand how that felt?"

JayB was quiet for a moment. "You're right. I'm so sorry. I honestly didn't consider how you'd feel."

Alana turned and stared at the side window.

JayB cleared his throat. "Do you want me to tell them they're not welcome?"

"Of course not. They'd know who was behind it." She sighed. "When he called, Rodney made it sound like I was being invited to the restaurant to discuss the restaurant's finances. I was so nervous on the way down that I almost threw up in the Uber."

"I'm so sorry. I didn't think about that either. I just needed you to paint the picture in broad strokes. I'll deliver the bad news to the three executives."

"Can you believe the deal on the house fell through? I feel like screaming."

"Well, maybe there's a silver lining," my person ventured after a long moment.

"Oh?"

"I was thinking. At the restaurant. We've got all this unused space right off the foyer. What if we opened a little shop? Sold, I don't know, dog toys, leashes."

Alana stared at him. "Dog collars, even," she stated finally.

JayB nodded enthusiastically. "Exactly."

"Dog collars with, oh, I know, Swarovski crystals glued to them," Alana continued flatly.

JayB was silent.

"Does *everyone* know you're trying to . . . what, seduce me into staying by getting me involved in the restaurant business, or is it just you acting alone?"

JayB glanced at her. "I've mostly kept them out of the loop."

"Well, it's not going to work, JayB. I'm really pissed that you'd even try it."

"Okay."

"I didn't come to Kansas City to find a new job. Or a new life, either."

"I get it. I apologize."

"It's not like you're even being subtle."

"I'm pretty bad at subtle."

"I noticed."

"If I were better at being subtle, you wouldn't have noticed."

"Oh my God." Alana turned her face away, hiding a smile. There was a long silence. "Hey," she finally said softly.

JayB raised his eyebrows.

"People do love spending on their pets. The dog toy store? It's a really good idea," she told him, smiling.

JayB smiled back.

*Dear Diary:*

*I can't seem to help myself—this has gotten bigger than just cutting off the cat's food supply. I've managed to maneuver the wonderful moving chair over to the counter more than once, and now all I can think about is that delicious fish meal waiting for me.*

*I wag with extra enthusiasm when JayB comes into the room to see me. I want him to know how much I love him even if I am being a bad dog. He goes to Kelsey's food bowl, which somehow skidded off onto the floor when I licked out its contents.*

*He stands with his hands on his hips looking down at it. "What happened here?" he asks in stern tones. I'm not sure what he's doing and hope that he's mad at the cat. "Clancy, did you do this?"*

*Well, I do hear my name, but how does he know it was me? Surely the more likely candidate is Kelsey, or even Spartan, who was here the other day.*

*"How did you get up there?" JayB goes to the magical moving chair, considering it. "Oh. Oh, Clancy. Bad dog," he lectures. He reaches down and twists something and then pushes the chair and it doesn't move.*

*I hang my head. I have been given the worst news any dog could ever have, which is that I am a bad dog.*

*And obviously Kelsey is a bad cat.*

*Love,*
*Clancy*

# *Nineteen*

Alana fell quiet for quite a while. "It was actually Guy who brought up Las Vegas. Completely out of the blue." She turned and searched JayB's face with her eyes. "He made it sound like it's about the cat, but I can tell it's something else."

"What do you think that might be?"

"Honestly? Where my mind went? He's going to propose."

JayB glanced at her and she nodded.

"I know," she agreed. "I did say he'd never do it. But he's been dropping hints lately. About taking stock of his life, that kind of thing. Like, he wants to say something profound to me, but then he chickens out. And honestly, even Guy wouldn't propose over the phone. So now, all of a sudden, he says we should meet halfway, in Vegas, and he'll bring Rhiannon?"

"Vegas is hardly halfway to LA from here."

"I understand, but Guy hates driving, so probably to him it feels like it is. Anyway, he's not really a fan of my cat, so why pretend to be concerned for her? I can tell something's going on."

JayB mulled this over. "How do you feel about it? Getting married to Guy, I mean," he asked carefully.

Alana sighed. "It's what I wanted from the moment we met. It was a real whirlwind romance at first, you know? I even brought it up a few times—I knew it was a bad move, but I couldn't help myself—and he completely quashed the subject. Not because of me, but because he doesn't believe in marriage, not after his divorce. So, you know, I gave up on the idea."

"Maybe he wanted to wait until you no longer thought it would happen," JayB speculated. "A proposal's a lot more romantic if it's a surprise."

Alana's eyes widened. "Wow. You might be right!"

"You still haven't said how you feel, though," JayB reminded her.

"How do I feel? Guy is the love of my life. I want to be with him forever. Of course I'm happy."

"Of course," JayB murmured.

"So, we'll get on the road, to Vegas, I'll see Guy, grab Rhiannon, come back and sell the house, and then . . ."

"Live happily ever after. And what about Odin?"

I glanced at Odin because my person had said his name. He glanced at me for the same reason.

"It's a good thing you're coming and bringing him instead of staying behind to dog sit," Alana answered. "Give Guy a chance to fall in love with Odin while we're there." She paused. "At least I hope that's what happens," she finished in a small voice.

"You seem pretty sure he's going to pop the question."

"Oh, no, I'm not sure about anything, except he's obviously been working up to something big. And, okay, I'm not a spy or anything, but a few days before my mom died, I accidentally bumped his mouse and when his screen came on it was a jewelry-store website."

"Does seem like an important clue."

I was happy that Spartan was no longer living at our house, and that he wasn't with us when, a few days later, we mounted Phoebe's front steps.

Bedford came to answer the door.

JayB cocked his head. "What's wrong?"

Bedford pursed his lips. "Just some personal stuff."

A moment of awkward silence followed. JayB cleared his throat. "Oh, hey, I'm just coming by to tell you that I won't be able to take care of Phoebe for the next few days. I'm taking a quick road trip with some people."

Bedford's eyes grew wide. "What? No! Listen—" He looked over his shoulder and then stepped out onto the stoop with us. "Okay. Dominique's sister was in a car accident a couple of hours ago."

"Oh, I'm sorry to hear that. Is she all right?"

"No, she's really banged up. She's in the hospital." Bedford put his knuckles to his teeth and appeared to bite them. "I don't know what to do. I mean, Dominique's . . . she's a wreck. She's crying, and I can't help her. I . . ."

"Well, maybe just be there for her," JayB suggested sympathetically. "Where did this happen?"

"Seattle."

I could sense JayB's distress. I could also smell that Phoebe was in the house, but she hadn't come to the door.

"I . . . I'm not good at things like this," Bedford stammered. "I just . . . I don't know what to do."

JayB stood still for a moment. "Well, you have to go there, Bedford."

Bedford peered at JayB in confusion. "What do you mean?"

"I mean, you have to go to Seattle. Like, right now. Dominique needs to be there."

Bedford stared numbly.

"Okay, look. Go get suitcases. You don't know how long you're going to stay, so don't pack only summer clothes. And get your toiletries and all that, okay? For both you and Dominique. Let her know you're going to Seattle with her."

Bedford hadn't moved. "I . . . I just don't know what you're saying to me."

JayB pulled out his phone. Then he opened the door behind Bedford and shooed him into the house. I plunged ahead, sniffing for Phoebe.

"I've got a friend who manages travel for my old company," JayB continued. "He'll know how to get tickets on short notice. Go get me Dominique's driver's license. Do you have yours? I'll call him right now. I need your credit card. Then let's call Uber."

"No, we use . . . We use Lyft."

"Fine. Whatever. Just go get those driver's licenses for me now."

There was so much tension coming off of JayB that I abandoned my search for Phoebe's scent and sat at his feet, watching him with concern. He spoke into his phone for several minutes, and while he was doing so, Bedford came up and handed him a pair of small items. JayB glanced at the items while he talked into the phone. Then he hung up.

"Okay," JayB announced. "He'll text me with the details as soon as he's got your flights nailed down. Where's Dominique?"

"In the bedroom."

"Show me. Come on, Clancy." We walked together down a hallway and turned into a room.

Phoebe was lying on the bed and registered my arrival with the slap of her tail against the covers, but otherwise didn't move. Her head was in Dominique's lap. Dominique was sitting cross-legged on the bed, stroking Phoebe's fur.

"Hey, hey," JayB greeted softly. He knelt and put his hand on Dominique's. "I'm sorry to hear about your sister. You need to be with your family now. Bedford's arranged for flights, so you're leaving for Seattle soon." JayB pulled up his phone and looked at it for a moment. "In fact, your flight is in three and a half hours. So you need to get moving. He's packing for you right now, okay, Dominique? I'll take Phoebe home with me. Everything's going to be fine. You just need to be with your sister now."

Dominique nodded gratefully. She held out her arms and JayB allowed her to pull him into a tight embrace. She was crying when they finally stood back from each other.

"Be sure to lock the doors behind you, okay?" JayB turned. "Bedford?" he called.

Bedford appeared in the doorway.

"You getting packed? Almost done?" JayB asked.

Bedford nodded.

JayB waved his phone. "I'll forward you the text with all the details. You should call Lyft right away. Better to get there early under these circumstances. Got it?"

Bedford nodded again. "Hey, man," he murmured as JayB started walking past him, then reached out and clutched JayB into a tight hug. Phoebe and I watched. People often hug each other even with dogs there.

I was thrilled that Phoebe left with us, though she seemed both confused and upset. As we walked away from her house, she stopped several times to look back over her shoulder. I knew she was unhappy because her person was unhappy. But dogs have to go with people whenever they're on a leash, and JayB walked us steadily down the sidewalk.

My delight only increased when it became apparent Phoebe was now living with us! As the day progressed, JayB let us out into the yard several times (we both lifted our heads alertly when we heard Odin barking at the wind). We had fun but JayB was distracted, putting things in a box and muttering to himself, so we didn't go to any dog parks.

Kelsey tentatively ventured out from wherever she'd been skulking, and I prepared myself for another dog-meets-cat, cat-runs-away encounter—Phoebe was the largest dog that had ever come to visit! So, I was shocked when Kelsey stood her ground while Phoebe pranced up and, wagging, lowered her nose and gave Kelsey a playful sniff. What was Phoebe *doing*? Didn't she know Kelsey was a cat?

When a woman rang the doorbell, Phoebe and I both barked joyously. I was even more elated, however, when JayB handed Kelsey to the woman, who gave Kelsey kisses on the face (who would *do* that?) and carried the cat out to her car.

"I'll phone you when I know when I'll be back," JayB called to the woman.

I could scarcely contain myself. We had traded a cat for a dog—and not just any dog, but Phoebe, the love of my life! Oh, and Spartan had left our home! I adored my person more than ever before.

The next morning JayB had an air of expectation about him as he clicked leashes into our collars and led us outside. He was carrying a box with a handle on it.

"Okay," he said to us. "Are you ready?"

Phoebe and I were manic with excitement, though we weren't sure why. Something was about to happen, or perhaps was already happening.

Soon Alana walked down the street, dragging a box on wheels, leading Odin on a leash.

"Hey, let me help," JayB called, and we all dashed up to her and JayB took her box. Phoebe and I sniffed Odin—was this the reason for the odd air of tension about JayB? That Odin and Alana were coming to visit? Maybe!

"Is it weird that I'm looking forward to this?" Alana asked, smiling.

"No. Me, too. It's . . . a change. Variety, spice of life."

We all stood in the front yard, waiting for something, apparently. Phoebe glanced at me but I had no ideas. Odin was politely examining a tree I'd just marked, and I watched indulgently as he raised his leg on it.

"Did I tell you your dad offered me ten thousand dollars a month to be his financial advisor?"

"You've got to be kidding."

"No lie. I told him that I would look at his bank statements and, in his words, 'get a handle on how rich he is,' but that I'm not an advisor and it would be illegal for me to pretend otherwise."

"So? How rich is he?"

Alana's expression turned grim. "He's broke."

I snapped my head up to look at JayB as his jaw dropped in shock. "What? How can that be?"

Phoebe sniffed my muzzle in concern.

"You ready for some math?" she asked.

JayB nodded numbly. "Sure."

"Okay. Yes, he won the Powerball. One hundred thirty-two million. But that was the value of the annuity. The cash payout was eighty-eight million, which was split between two tickets. So his group as a whole, his syndicate if you will, got forty-four point four million and change. With me so far?"

"Sure. Forty-four point four mil."

"Yes. And then there were twelve people who contributed to their subscription."

"Divided by twelve." JayB nodded.

"So that's roughly three point seven million per person."

"My dad got three point seven million."

"Yes, but then there were taxes. No state, but federal taxes took them down to two point seven-eight million."

"Huh, I didn't know," JayB confessed. "I thought it would be a lot more than that, honestly. I don't play the lotto myself, but I thought we were talking maybe a hundred million."

"No one *plays* the lotto. You hand over your money and fantasize about winning until you lose."

"Still, nearly three million," JayB reasoned. "I don't see how you get from there to broke."

"So he had to put half down on a house in Mission Hills in order to get financed. I mean, it's a great house, and if you could move it to where I live, it would cost ten times what he paid. Then he bought the Cadillac and the Ferrari. Want to guess on the Ferrari?"

JayB wordlessly shook his head.

"With tax, just over three hundred thousand."

"You've got to be kidding me."

"No. But his cars were all cash purchases, so he has some equity. Understand? But that's it for assets. He's spent a lot of money on his investments with Rodney."

"Those are doing well, I hear."

"Oh sure. And, of course, the biggest drain is the restaurant. It's weird that Walter doesn't seem to understand that the salary he's paying himself comes from the money out of his personal checking account. Have you talked to him about Rodney and Maddy?"

"Not yet."

"Why not?"

"Dad won't listen to me about anything to do with the restaurant, or his 'investments,' or money. He sees me as this dud of a son who can't understand the concept of enjoying life, or some such idiocy."

"You sound angry."

"Of course I'm angry! Wouldn't you be angry?"

I wagged a little, concerned. Odin slept through it. Phoebe was staring down the street, watching a squirrel.

"I've just never seen you angry before."

"I've spent my whole life being picked on for making plans," JayB elaborated bitterly. "For thinking ahead. For looking for downsides, for hidden consequences. My brother the ski bum, my father the 'entrepreneur' . . . even my mother would say I needed to enjoy life more. I *do* enjoy life! Only Howard ever understood me." JayB's eyes bulged as a thought occurred to him. "Wait, if Dad sells his house, where would he live? With me?"

JayB turned to look at his house, so I did, too.

"Um, I don't know," Alana replied uncomfortably.

"I do. It happened once before, when I was at KU. He lost his job and got evicted, so next thing I know he's sleeping on my couch. Can you picture what that was like? Walter, walking around in a Jayhawk T-shirt and flirting with all the Chi Omegas."

"Would you do that again, though? Let him move in?"

"It would be the absolute worst thing that could happen to me. But what choice would I have? That's just what you do for your parents."

All the dogs turned their heads to Alana as a deep, strong emotion wafted off her. She raised her hand to her mouth, and I saw and smelled the tears at exactly the same moment.

Dear Diary:

As much as I loathe Kelsey, I love beautiful, wonderful Phoebe. Her odor lingers in my nostrils, as sweet and unforgettable as a dead squirrel flattened to hot pavement under the summer sun. I could chew on her for hours. I could romp with her anywhere. I could lie with her in the back seat of a car or in a shady spot in a yard, though I would prefer the couch. Watching her run excites me more than a car ride with JayB.

Kelsey has never shown me the respect due a predator who is larger, faster, and more attractive. I can charge her, my throat thundering with a menacing growl, and she remains completely unperturbed. If I bark in her face, she insouciantly licks her paw.

With Spartan and Odin, however, Kelsey behaves as a cat should, turning and fleeing in terror.

Phoebe approaches Kelsey with playing and licking. Kelsey leaves the room whenever Phoebe enters, not out of fear, but because of the overly friendly interest.

It's only me, Clancy, that the cat treats with such contempt. No matter what I do, Kelsey won't run away.

How is it possible that Kelsey knows how to behave around other dogs, but not me?

I have been so happy that Phoebe now lives with us, and Kelsey doesn't, that it's becoming easy to lose sight of my most important role, which is to help JayB navigate life.

JayB cares about Alana, and when she's upset, he's upset.

So, for now, I have to concentrate on being his dog.

Love,
Clancy

# Twenty

JayB's face filled with regret. "Oh. I'm sorry, Alana. That was so thoughtless of me."

"I didn't even *visit* my mom."

"I know. I didn't mean to say it that way. I just meant, my parents had a way of making me feel obligated to clean up their messes—especially Walter."

Alana swallowed, nodding.

"I'm really sorry."

"No, it's okay," she murmured. "I have to learn to live with it." She took in a deep breath.

Something told me these people should hug, but they didn't. Odin stood and went to Alana, wagging a little, trying to help.

Phoebe remained on the lookout for squirrels.

"So, your dad . . ." Alana finally continued. "The way things are going, especially with the executive salaries, he'll be out of money by the end of the year."

"Wow. I had no idea."

"Look, the good news is that the restaurant's almost current with all the vendors. That's key."

"I'm in over my head, though," JayB fretted. "I can talk to suppliers and schedule deliveries, but I need help—someone quick on her feet, to put out the daily fires."

"Okay, I knew you'd say that, with all the usual subtlety," Alana responded. "I know exactly what you're doing. But yes. You need to find somebody. Somebody who's not Alana Knox."

"You're saying your mind's made up."

"Yes. Sorry."

"Okay," JayB said with finality. "I won't ask you again."

I felt gusts of sadness from them both, and could tell Odin and even Phoebe sensed it as well.

"So, when are you going to tell your father he's broke?"

"I don't know. Not while we're all in the Suburban or whatever he's renting for this trip. I'll need to catch him alone."

"The longer you wait, the more money gets wasted," Alana warned.

Moments later a car pulled up, one that I could smell contained Rodney and the ridiculous Spartan.

"The Rodster has arrived," Rodney announced.

Phoebe reacted joyfully to their arrival, much to my dismay. Odin didn't bother to sniff Spartan, but I demonstrated proper dog behavior with a dignified lift of my leg, not that Spartan appreciated it. Soon Phoebe had her leash tangled with Spartan's.

I was unsurprised when Maddy pulled up in her own car. She slid out, carrying several bags. "Where's your dad?" she asked JayB.

"My dad, who is not supposed to be driving but left a message saying he's coming over in our, quote, *new mode of transportation,* unquote? *That* dad? He's late. But that's hardly unusual. He's never really been an on-time kind of guy."

Maddy nodded shrewdly. "You could maybe learn from that. I hate it when men have to be taught everything."

Rodney smiled at Alana. "You know, this trip's gonna be good for you. We'll get to know each other and you'll have a chance to think things through."

"What do you mean?"

"I mean, you're going off to Vegas to get your cat and see the guy, Guy," Rodney explained.

"You are so hilarious, Rodney," Maddy proclaimed.

"Thanks! Anyway, so you'll have time between now and then to think about who your real friends are and, you know, how important relationships are. I mean, without human relationships, people would be just, I don't know. Human."

"Thank you, Rodney," Alana replied faintly.

Rodney clapped JayB on the shoulder. "Hey, talk to you for a second?"

"No, I don't want to buy a boat full of Korean pig iron."

"Ha. Funny. Come here."

"Seriously? Another bro conference?"

"Last one."

I was still on leash, so I followed JayB and Spartan behind Rodney, who took us to the side of the house. I sniffed where I had marked earlier and decided it needed another squirt.

Rodney took a deep breath. "I wanted you to know before everyone starts congratulating us. I'm going to ask Alana to move in with me."

JayB stared for a moment. "Move in . . . where?" he finally ventured. "You don't have your own place."

Rodney looked impatient. "Okay, I move in with her, then. It doesn't matter. Point is, I'm making a commitment. Get it? So, it's not open season any longer. You have to back off. She's no longer just my girlfriend, she's my fiancée."

"Your fiancée," JayB repeated. "So you're going to propose?"

I sensed a flash of alarm rising from Rodney's skin. "What? No."

"That's what fiancée means. It means you're engaged to be married."

Rodney wiped his face, his expression blank. "Oh God. Okay, wow, I didn't even think of that."

"Congratulations?"

"Whoa." He focused on JayB. "I guess this makes you my best man, huh? Things are moving so fast, I feel like I need to sit down."

"When are you going to tell Alana? Oh wait, I know! You can get a marriage license in a few hours in Nevada. You'll be in Vegas. This isn't just a road trip, it's a wedding trip!"

Rodney stared. "Whoa," he breathed again.

A little while later, Walter pulled up in the driveway in a large, tall, blocky vehicle. JayB shook his head when Walter jumped out, beaming.

"You bought a bus?" JayB demanded. "Are we a rock band now?"

Walter laughed. "It's no bus, just an extended van."

Alana shook her head. "It's huge."

"Yep. It's a conversion van," Rodney told her.

"I don't know what that is," she confessed.

Rodney threw back his head and laughed. "That's California for you. A conversion van is a *van* that has been *converted* to have swivel seats that are more luxurious, and probably there's a great stereo system, stuff like that. Cabinets, some even have sinks. It's been *converted* from a regular van, so it's a *conversion* van. Get it? Converted, conversion. It's converted by conversion."

"That is so helpful, Rodney."

JayB grinned.

"I thought we'd need the room," Walter explained. "We've got the dogs, luggage . . . and it's a long drive to Vegas. The seats fold down, so we can nap if we want."

"And are you the driver?" JayB wanted to know.

Walter laughed. "Still have a suspended license. I got a lawyer working on it."

"But in the meantime, you're driving all over town."

"Just here," Walter corrected. "No big deal. No cop's going to pull me over in two miles."

For a moment, everyone stood looking at one another, and the dogs picked up on it. Something even more exciting was about to happen.

And then it did!

"Okay. Let's get everything in there and hit the road," JayB announced, slapping his hands together.

Before long, Spartan and Phoebe and I were with Odin in the spacious far back of the vehicle for a car ride. Everyone loaded in. "Hey, Alana." Rodney beckoned from the middle seat. "Why don't you sit back here with me?"

"Oh, no thank you," Alana demurred. "I get carsick if I'm not sitting in one of the front seats."

"I'll sit with you, lonely boy," Maddy declared, moving up to a seat next to Rodney.

Rodney spun his seat in a full circle. "Pretty neat!" he grinned.

Walter's seat was one row back, in front of where our dog pack had gathered. He pulled a lever and his chair collapsed underneath him.

"Cool!" Rodney enthused.

At first, we dogs quivered with excitement, but after a while we could tell it was going to be the sort of car ride that takes a long time. We all settled into position. I tried to lie with my head on Phoebe's back, but she squirmed away from me. She seemed unsure of herself, and I wanted to offer her comfort, but that turned out to be impossible with Spartan sticking his pushed-in face at her.

"I bought sandwiches and put them in the fridge," Walter told the group.

"Refrigerator!" Maddy squealed. "Oh my God, I can't wait to eat a sandwich from a van!"

Eventually the vehicle stopped swaying and settled into a steady droning sound. Gradually, everyone quit talking.

"Denver, five hundred and ninety-eight miles," JayB announced. This didn't seem to make any of the people happy.

"God," Maddy muttered. "Why did they put Denver so far away?"

"Oh, I know," Rodney suggested after a long silence. "Why don't we each tell each other our biographies. You know, the facts of our lives?"

"How do you come up with these amazing ideas?" Maddy wondered.

Rodney shrugged. "Everybody asks that. Okay, I'll go first. So, I think it's fair to say that everyone was shocked when I dropped out of KU, but honestly, I got there and looked around and said to myself, 'Hey, I already know more than anyone here.'"

"That's amazing," Maddy encouraged. "I'll bet you they were impressed with *that.*"

"I didn't graduate from college either," Walter interjected proudly. "And see? Look at the two of us, Rodney."

Rodney smiled affably. "I'd like to tell it, Walter, if you don't mind."

"Oh," Walter apologized. "Sorry."

"After all," Maddy reasoned, "it is mostly Rodney's life. At least so far."

JayB and Alana exchanged a grin.

"Anyway, you can tell where this is going, I'm sure," Rodney continued. "I decided that, you know, instead of going to med school or something, rack up student debt, that I'd be better off if I went to work at the car dealership. I've always been good with my hands, Alana."

"You know," Maddy interrupted, "it's a little irritating that you act like you're telling this story just to Alana. You're supposed to be sharing with all of us so that no one person has the advantage."

"Oh, you're right," Rodney agreed, looking chagrined. "I'm sorry. I know this is interesting to everybody."

"I know *I'm* completely enthralled," JayB agreed.

"So: the car dealership," Rodney resumed. "Instead of going into management right away, I said to the owner, no sir, that wouldn't be right. I'd like to start in the wash rack, and move up from there."

"Wow," Maddy marveled. "You totally pulled your bottom up by the boots."

"Had me a job like that myself, once," Walter observed. He held up a hand when Rodney shot him a look. "Sorry."

"So, I've always been amazing at either building things, or fixing things, or imagining things." Rodney winked at Alana. "Anyway, so mostly that's what I've been doing. I've been a mechanic and a builder and a developer."

"What's the difference between a builder and a developer?" Alana wanted to know.

"I knew you'd ask that," Rodney declared. "See, a developer is like what would have been what we did at the restaurant if it hadn't been for the weird zoning laws. A builder's like what I'm doing right now, which is remodeling that kitchen."

"And how is *that* going?" JayB asked innocently.

Rodney shrugged. "You know, with the Canada trip and everything, I've just been really busy."

"Exactly," Walter assented.

"Bigger fish to fry," JayB suggested breezily.

"Well, my backstory is really about one person," Walter began.

"Well, hey, Walter," Rodney interrupted, looking troubled. "I
wasn't really done yet."

"I think it would be better if you let us absorb all the information
you've given us before you say more," Alana recommended. "We
don't want to be overloaded with complexity."

"Great idea," Rodney agreed. "Beauty and brains, both."

"Which one am I?" Maddy demanded. "And don't say brains. No
one can even *see* your brains."

"Her name is Celeste," Walter pressed on smoothly. "She's the
only woman I have ever truly loved. And my biggest regret is that I
let her go." Everyone was quiet for a moment, and I sensed a change
of mood in the car.

"Man, I get it," Rodney told Walter. "I had this girlfriend for a
few years." He looked at Alana. "This is before I met you, of course.
And we were really serious there for a while. I didn't know what to
think when she told me she was engaged to somebody else, because
there was this pure love between us. I mean, yes, she had moved to
Philadelphia, but that's only a plane ride away, I told her. And I kept
asking when she was coming back to Kansas City . . . and then she
didn't." Rodney held up his hands. "I mean, I gave it my best shot,
but come on. Somebody's got to meet me halfway. You know what
I mean?"

"Maybe," JayB predicted, "you'll get engaged again. *Soon.*"

Rodney blanched.

"It's so romantic that you fell in love with Celeste and you love
her still," Maddy observed with a sigh. "JayB's not like that. He's
flighty. He doesn't recognize a good thing when it's right in front
of him."

JayB glanced at Alana. "I'm not sure I agree with that."

Alana blushed and looked away.

Dear Diary:

Made drowsy by the steady hum in our new car, the fragrance of the other dogs filling my nose, I reflect on one of my favorite memories, made especially notable because it begins with a bath.

I do not understand why humans believe a dog loves a bath. I have had several baths in my life and have been miserable through every single one of them.

I recognize the word, though, especially since it's pronounced with such a phony joy. "Clancy? Want a bath? Time for a bath? Want to take a bath?" This fooled me at first, because it sounded so fun, but now I know that "bath" means a wretched time spent standing inside a big bowl with water running all over me, and a hideous-smelling liquid being run though my fur until all the wonderful odors I've developed since the last bath are rinsed away.

After a bath, I try to rub the essence of my smell back into my fur by rolling on the rugs where I nap, but it's never of much use.

After one such incident, I was trotting around, trying to become accustomed to the horrific smell that was now mine, and wound up wandering into the bathroom, where I was outraged to see Kelsey standing on the edge of the tub where I'd just been, her tiny nose sniffing at the remains of my torment. She was no doubt delighting in my misery.

I didn't even pause to think. I lunged forward and butted her with my head. With a yowl, she plunged into the water!

Instantly she was back out, bedraggled and soaked, and I watched with joy as she fled from the bathroom.

*There was a reckoning, of course—JayB discovered Kelsey, her fur in odd, hilarious tufts, and I knew I was in for some bad dog conversation. But instead, JayB directed all his questions toward the cat. "Kelsey, what happened? Did you fall in? You silly cat, let me get a towel. What were you thinking?"*

*Not a cross word directed at me.*

*Kelsey, of course, knew exactly what I had done. She regarded me with eyes so malevolent, I wanted to squirm with joy.*

*In the war between cat and dog, I was clearly winning.*

Love,
Clancy

# Twenty-one

I think Clancy's dreaming," Walter observed. "He's been twitching and moaning."

I opened my eyes but didn't raise my head.

"Are you dreaming, Clancy?" Alana asked.

"Anyway, leaving Celeste out of it for the moment," Walter continued, "I have a real breadth of professional experience on my resumé. I maintained laundromat machines for a while. When I got bored with that, you know, all those quarters, I worked in a liquor store. That was fun. Met a lot of really nice people after midnight, coming in and wanting to talk or lie on the floor. Then, of course, I got that job at the DMV."

JayB frowned in the rearview mirror. "The DMV? I didn't know you worked for the DMV."

"Oh, yeah. That's why I lived in Omaha."

"I didn't know you lived in Omaha."

"Well, where did you think I was all that time?" Walter challenged.

"Honestly, Dad," JayB snapped, some anger creeping into his voice, "I just thought you were gone. I didn't know *where* you were."

"It's called *parenting*," Maddy retorted.

Alana silently regarded JayB, moving her hand slightly, as if to touch him.

Walter looked down for a moment. "Yeah. So, anyway, I got fired from that job."

Alana pulled on a lever and rotated her seat around so that she was facing us. "You got fired from the DMV? I never heard of anybody getting fired from the DMV."

"I just hate working for other people," Walter explained.

"Oh, man. Me, too," Rodney interjected. "Taking orders, not my thing."

"I hear you," Maddy agreed. "It's even worse in food service because you not only have the managers always being dictator on you for being late or getting the orders wrong, you have customers complaining, too. I'm like, 'If you don't want to eat it, why don't you stay home and cook for yourself for once?' I swear, they should give every waitress in this country the Pulitzer Prize."

"You gotta let every day take care of itself," Walter persisted seamlessly. "Like one time, we went to Mexico. I just told Celeste, 'Grab your bag, honey,' and we didn't even do the dishes. We drove straight to the airport and got on the next flight. Man, we had a blast until they cut off my credit card. And here's the irony—to raise the money to fly back home, we took jobs *washing dishes*."

"Wow—proof that God exists," Rodney observed reverently.

"Well, I wish you'd given some of your DNA to your son, because he wouldn't take a surprise trip if he were kidnapped by pirates," Maddy fumed. "His idea of a fun time is to plan everything out. Like this trip—he's probably got it all figured, no surprises."

"We're driving I-70 across the flattest state in the union, Maddy," JayB responded. "Surprise!"

Alana laughed.

"Seriously learning at the knee of the master here," mused Rodney. "The Mexico trip sounds brilliant."

Walter nodded in satisfaction. "And now here's where I'll let you all in on a little secret. A few days ago, I bought Celeste a diamond necklace. From Tiffany's."

Maddy gasped.

Rodney frowned, "Tiffany's? The breakfast place?"

Maddy leaned toward JayB. "Are you listening to your father?"

"It shows her I'm a man of means," Walter explained. "I'll never have another car repossessed again as long as I live."

"Right," JayB agreed, "because no one will give you financing. Speaking of which, this vehicle is rented, I hope?"

"It's a conversion van," Maddy corrected.

Walter laughed. "Renting is for chumps. This is an investment."

"An investment," JayB repeated. He and Alana exchanged dark glances.

"So, I should probably tell you, Jago," Walter continued, "that with that necklace, I included a message from both of us."

"Huh."

"I said she should come to Kansas City for a family reunion. I'll buy the ticket, first-class. And once she gets here, she's going to see my Ferrari and this van and my house in Mission Hills, and all her objections will melt away."

"That's so romantic," Maddy sighed. "Women love to have their objections melted by expensive stuff."

"Great strategy, Dad."

"Did she say she's coming?" Alana asked.

"Well, not yet," Walter admitted. "I'm sure she's got to straighten it out with Wolfman Twain or whatever his name is."

"Maddy," Rodney put in, "you want to do your bio now, or should I keep going with mine?"

Maddy shook her head. "I need to hear what everyone else says before I decide my story."

Alana frowned. "So your life history changes, depending upon what other people say?"

"It changed when I met JayB, didn't it?"

"Hey," Rodney suddenly asked. "Don't you think it's interesting that no one has asked me why I named my dog Spartan?"

All the dogs looked at Spartan and Spartan looked back at all the dogs.

"Michigan State?" JayB guessed.

"What? How would that make sense? No, it was because of that movie, the one with ripped abs." He glanced at Alana. "I texted you that pool picture."

"Can I see it?" Maddy requested.

Nodding, Rodney pulled out his phone.

"Would you be willing to tell us about yourself before we get another dose of Rodney?" JayB asked Alana.

She gazed at him, then nodded. "Okay, sure. So, not everybody knows this, but I was the youngest child growing up."

"I was the middle child," Rodney interjected.

"My brother and sister were so much older than I was, it was like they weren't even in the same family."

Rodney nodded. "Oh, I can relate to that. There were lots of times when I felt like my family was trying to get rid of me."

"My parents longed to be empty-nesters. They had their whole life planned around my dad's retirement. They just wanted to travel, but then I came along." Alana shrugged. "So I had a lot of babysitters."

Rodney huffed, "Me, too."

"Don't get me started on babysitters," Maddy warned.

I turned my gaze to Alana, feeling a strong gust of sadness coming off her. "And I guess as a result," she continued, "without really feeling like I belonged to my own family, I've always had trouble unlocking the secret to relationships with other people. It's as if there's a bunch of rules that no one told me."

Rodney opened his mouth.

"Rodney," JayB warned sharply.

Rodney blinked.

"Do not say a word."

"Well," Rodney began.

"Rodney," JayB admonished even more loudly, "stop talking."

"I was just . . ."

"Rodney!"

Rodney sighed and shook his head. "Somebody's gone a little crazy here," he muttered.

Alana focused on JayB. "My mom wasn't a saint, you know."

JayB regarded her with curiosity, and I sensed anger in Alana.

She bit her lip. "Did she ever talk about me?"

"Well . . ." JayB replied uncomfortably.

Alana shook her head. "No, I didn't think so. My mom always

bragged about my sister the doctor and my brother the teacher, but she told me I shouldn't 'settle for being a shopkeeper.'"

"I'm sorry to hear that," JayB murmured.

"When we came out to Kansas City, Guy and I, she hated him, but not because he wasn't good enough for her daughter. Because he looked down on *her*. And I have to confess, part of me liked that he did that. I couldn't defend myself to my mother, but Guy had no problem."

There was a long silence. "Can I talk now?" Rodney asked impatiently.

"No," JayB said curtly. He was glancing occasionally at Alana while watching the road. "So, I hear you about the family," he told her. "It was a little disorienting for me when my parents got divorced."

Walter nodded. "I'll say."

"And Howard, that's my stepfather—"

"He's not your real father," Walter interrupted sternly.

"I said *step*father. Dad, are you going to let me tell this?"

Walter and Rodney exchanged "what're you gonna do?" glances.

"Howard was the opposite of Walter. He did tax preparation. He'd go to the office every day at the same time and return home at the same time, five days a week."

"Like that's a life," Walter snorted.

"Amen," Rodney agreed.

"Howard was steady. It's what Mom wanted," JayB pointed out.

"Yeah, and look what it did to you," Walter challenged. "You've gone from being his happy-go-lucky kid to being a dog walker."

I heard the word "dog" and glanced around. People seemed a little uneasy.

"Oh, don't worry," Maddy boasted. "I'm totally making him into a waiter."

"I think I understand what you're saying," Alana encouraged quietly.

"So I kind of think we skipped some of my story, if you want to know the truth," Rodney complained.

"We got sidetracked by the jewelry," Maddy agreed. "Diamonds do that. I hope the men were paying attention."

"Okay, so I'm not sure where I left off," Rodney apologized.

I closed my eyes, listening to the pleasant drone of Rodney's voice.

A long time later (Rodney was still talking), we pulled into a big flat parking lot. The air was much warmer when I jumped out than it had been when we left our house. JayB took all the dogs off-leash to smell some bushes and to make sure we marked them.

"Good dogs," he told us. Odin and Phoebe seemed to appreciate the words, but Spartan didn't react. Rodney took Spartan's leash.

"I'm going to go into the mini-mart," Walter announced, "get some snacks, maybe iced tea. Anybody want anything in particular?"

Everyone shook their head.

I concentrated on hanging near Phoebe as Walter walked up to a small, squat building and passed between glass doors.

Rodney announced, "Well, I need to use the facilities," and, dropping Spartan's leash, walked around the side of the building.

Spartan followed his person and sniffed along the bottom edge of the door that had closed behind him, then glanced at me. Maddy trailed after Spartan.

Another car pulled into the parking lot, near the front doors of the building. Alana and JayB were standing together, watching us.

A man jumped out of the new car, leaving his front door wide open.

JayB recoiled. "Oh my God."

"What is it?" Alana asked.

JayB gave her a grim look. "He's got a gun."

"*What?* Did you say a gun?"

The man who had left his car door open moved briskly from it to the glass front of the building, stepping inside. JayB was afraid of this man, and I felt the fur rising along my back. Odin was alert as well, coming quickly to join me. Phoebe was unsure but she responded by following my lead, her eyes wide.

Whatever was making people afraid, a pack of loyal dogs was there to protect them.

JayB turned to Alana. "Stay here. Call 911. Tell them a guy with a pistol just went into the gas station."

"Wait! Where are you going?"

"Just make the call," JayB said tersely as he walked toward the building. "My dad's in there."

*Dear Diary:*

*Of all the emotions that leap from human skin, fear is the strongest and most primitive. It has a taint to it, designed to grab a dog's attention. When our people are afraid, dogs know we might be required to do something, though we rarely know what. We perceive that there's a threat and we stand ready to do whatever our people need in order to protect them.*

*No matter the sacrifice.*

Love,
Clancy

# Twenty-two

JayB moved briskly across the parking lot, so Phoebe, Odin, and I followed. Spartan, sensing something, trotted quickly to intercept. Maddy was standing outside the door through which Rodney had entered, her arms crossed.

"JayB!" Alana cried. She held her phone to her ear but was running after us. "Stop!"

My person halted, and we did too—except Spartan, who was closer to the building and was sniffing frantically for something.

"What do you think you're doing? He's got a *gun*," Alana pleaded. "Let's wait for the police."

I think we all smelled it at once, though only we dogs reacted, turning our heads toward that open car door, through which floated a delicious scent that I recognized from many late nights at our house. I pictured the object before I saw it in the car: a big, flat box with bread and cheese and meat inside, sitting on the front seat.

"Alana . . ."

"JayB. Please don't go in there," she urged. "Please."

Spartan didn't hesitate; he leaped inside that car.

"Spartan!" JayB called. "Get out of there!"

He and Alana began striding rapidly toward the car.

I could see what Spartan was doing. He had used his collapsed nose to nudge open the lid on the flat box and was eagerly chewing the contents, bolting down cheese and bread as fast as he could. As I advanced, Spartan raised his head, glared at me, and growled. I stopped in my tracks, and so did the other two dogs. There was nothing friendly about Spartan at that moment. This was his meal and he had no intention of sharing.

"Spartan!" JayB commanded. "Come."

"We're at the food and gas station, I-70, Hedville Road exit," Alana told her phone shrilly. "We think there's a holdup—a man went into the building with a gun in his hand. Yes!"

Alana's tone sounded like nothing I'd ever heard from her before. Was she upset about Spartan? I knew I was.

"Spartan!" JayB called again, his voice so stern it caused Spartan to wolf the food down even more quickly.

The glass doors of the building slid open and the same man came running out. He was holding something under one arm and something in his other hand. He ran to the open door of the car. Spartan reacted predictably. As the man approached, the dog growled and snapped, showing teeth.

Spartan wasn't done eating yet.

The guy pulled up short. "What the . . ." He turned and glanced at us wildly. "Whose dog is that?"

"Not mine," JayB informed him.

The man waved the thing in his hand. "Well, get him out of my car. Now!"

"I don't think he wants to get out," JayB replied.

The man turned and looked frantically at the building from which he had just emerged. Spartan kept choking down the food but kept his eyes on this new threat. The man tried a second time to get in the car and Spartan growled again.

"Jesus!" the man cried. He looked at us. None of us wagged.

"You should maybe get going," JayB observed casually. "Cops are on their way."

The man stared for a moment and then spun on his heel and ran, his footsteps loud on the cement as he sprinted toward the road.

"Maybe next time don't leave your door open!" JayB called after him. He turned to Alana. "I think this was his first robbery."

Alana stared at him, shaking her head. "You're unbelievable."

"Hey!" Maddy called, running up to us. "What happened?"

I could tell all the food was gone because Spartan leaped out of the car. To my dismay, Phoebe trotted to greet him, wagging.

"There was a guy with a gun. He just robbed the place," Alana informed Maddy.

"What?" Maddy's eyes were huge.

"I'm shaking," Alana admitted.

"I'm going to throw up," Maddy replied. "You'd think after living with my cousin Gregg I'd be used to this kind of thing, but I'm not." She sat abruptly on the pavement.

JayB bent over her. "Okay, just breathe easy. I'll get some water from the van."

Far in the distance, we heard a loud, thin wail coming toward us. "Police," JayB observed.

Rodney came out of the side door.

"Hey, Rodney," JayB called, "your dog just ate a whole pizza."

Rodney walked up to us and threw up his hands. "Why'd you let him do that? That can't be good for him."

"He seemed disinclined to take instruction," JayB said with a shrug.

"Rodney, you missed the whole crime!" Maddy blurted. "Why did you take so long in the bathroom? You knew I was waiting. I could have been killed!"

Rodney frowned.

The loud wail, a familiar sound made neither by dog nor any other animal, increased in volume until two cars screeched into the parking lot. People jumped out, looking agitated.

This was exactly what I had feared. Spartan was a bad dog, and now angry humans had come to shout at us. One bad dog can spoil the day for the entire pack.

The people yelled, "Get down! Get down!" which is what I'm accustomed to hearing when I'm on the couch, but wasn't sure what to do in this instance. I followed Odin's lead. He dropped to his belly, so I did, too. Oddly, Alana, Rodney, and JayB fell to their knees with their hands in the air, while Maddy sat with her hands on her hips.

"The man you're after just ran down the road," Alana called, pointing.

The people who had arrived, one of whom was a woman, had

spread out and were surrounding us, though Spartan had lost interest and was sniffing some weeds with Phoebe, my precious Phoebe, by his side. She was learning precisely the wrong lessons from Spartan. When people were upset, they needed their dogs.

"Hey!" Maddy snapped. "Do I look like a bank robber to you?"

The new arrivals glanced at one another. One of them dropped his hands and put something on his belt, and then the others did as well. "Ma'am, this isn't a bank. This is a gas station."

"The guy who held up the place took off down the road. That shar-pei over there was in his car and wouldn't let him drive off in it," JayB informed them.

"What?" cried Rodney, delighted. "Spartan? Spartan did that?"

The new people exchanged looks.

"All right," the woman decided, and she and a man jumped into one of the loud cars and sped down the road.

I looked up and wagged because Walter was coming out of the building.

"Dad, are you okay?"

Walter frowned. "What do you mean?"

"Sir, would you put the bag down and step away from it, please?" one of the remaining men requested in a firm voice.

Walter put a bag on the ground, puzzled.

I thought bitterly that it was probably more food for Spartan.

We spent a good part of the day in that hot parking lot. Everybody wanted to talk to everybody else. We dogs were taken for an occasional walk around the property, but that was the extent of any enjoyable activities.

Phoebe found a stick and shook it and then sat down and started chewing it, eventually gnawing it to bits. I eyed it several times, but I knew a stick is more fun with a person on the other end of it. Plus, if I approached her, Phoebe would run away with the stick, but that was not the kind of game I wanted to play right now. I was still feeling ill about the obvious way she'd chosen Spartan over me.

Walter seemed the most agitated. "We need to get moving," he kept saying. He looked repeatedly at his wrist.

Eventually, we all slid back into the big new vehicle. We settled into the same spots where we'd been lying before—Odin and I in the middle with Maddy and Rodney; Spartan and my sweet Phoebe in back, sprawled next to Walter.

"Well, that was exciting," JayB drawled as the car began moving. He glanced at Alana. "Our first holdup together."

She shook her head but was grinning.

"Man, I'm so proud," Rodney boasted. "I mean, my dog saved our lives."

"Did you train him to do that?" Maddy asked.

"Well," Rodney waffled, "sort of. I've trained him for a lot of things."

Alana and JayB exchanged glances.

"We aren't going to make it all the way to Denver, are we?" Walter fretted. "We'll have to cancel our hotel reservations."

There was a silence.

"So now what?" Maddy challenged. "Not only did we not get a reward for the crime spree, but we're too late to inspect our rooms. Now I'll never know what Denver looks like with me in a hotel."

"There's got to be places between here and Denver, though. Doesn't Kansas have some towns?" Rodney asked.

"Might be difficult to find a hotel that'll take this many dogs," JayB observed.

"Just great," Walter muttered.

I could tell that everyone, especially Walter, was unhappy. I looked at Phoebe to see if she understood we were all in trouble because of Spartan, but she was sniffing his face.

Right in front of me.

"I'll start looking for a hotel up ahead that's dog-friendly," Alana volunteered, waving her phone.

"Looks like rain on the horizon. See the cloudbank?" JayB asked.

"It's completely black!" Alana exclaimed. "And we're driving right toward it. Is that wise?"

"We don't really have much of a choice."

"That kind of cloud, out here in Dorothy-land, drops a tornado every time," Maddy declared grimly. "It's why there are trailer parks."

"Man, I remember as a kid, this tornado wiped out a whole block," Rodney bragged. "Blew the roofs off, knocked over trees. *Bam.*"

"Well, Rodney," JayB chided, exasperation creeping into his voice, "do we all think it's a good idea, when you're driving across *western Kansas,* to talk about tornadoes to someone who's never been through one before? Someone like, oh . . . I don't know. Alana?"

Rodney thought about it. "Yeah, he's got a point, Alana. Don't worry, though. I'll walk you through what to do if we get hit by one."

"Are you honestly saying we're driving toward tornadoes?" Alana demanded.

"If we see one, we should pull over and lie down in a ditch," Rodney advised. "Facedown. Cover yourself with plywood, if you've got some."

"Why don't you do that *now,* Rodney?" suggested JayB.

Alana laughed, but she seemed nervous.

"Whatever you do, don't hold a metal pole over your head, even if it seems to make sense at the time," Rodney continued.

"Would you let her look for a place for us to stay, please?" Walter begged. "You're distracting her. I'm sick of the inside of this van."

"I don't think we have anything to worry about," JayB reassured Alana.

"Except that Spartan caused us to fall hours behind schedule," Walter groused. "*That's* what to worry about."

"Patience is a virtue, Dad."

There was a lot of silence in the car this time. No one seemed in the mood to talk. This meant I was able, not only to smell, but to actually *hear* the sudden explosion of odors from Spartan. All the dogs raised their heads in shocked amazement. It was fragrant and tantalizing and thick upon the air, probably the most attractive aroma I have encountered in my life.

Now I was completely disheartened. Spartan was introducing another, even more powerful element into the competition for Phoebe's affections.

"Oh my *God*," Rodney blurted. He contorted and rolled down a window. The roar of outside air swirled in.

"What is it?" Maddy shouted over the noise.

"I think," JayB guessed, "it's what happens when a pepperoni pizza is filtered through a shar-pei."

"Do something, Rodney!" Walter yelled.

"Yeah," JayB agreed, "you've given Spartan all that training."

"Well . . ." Rodney looked a little confused. "I mean, yeah, but I don't think I've ever . . . All right." He twisted back to look at Spartan. "Spartan. *No.*"

Odin, Phoebe, and I all flinched at that word, but Spartan simply stared back at Rodney stonily, filling the interior of the big car with another glorious blast from under his stubby tail.

Alana reached forward and fiddled with buttons. Soon there was air blowing strongly from vents along the front and top of the vehicle. Phoebe nuzzled Spartan, while I watched miserably. Why couldn't I manufacture that sweet smell so Phoebe would want to be with *me*?

Every time Spartan unleashed another volley, the people in the car would make noises, like, "Arghhh!" and "Uhhhhh," and the windows would go down. I could smell a storm, wet and cold. Each blast of outside air told me the rain was rapidly approaching.

"Temperature really dropped outside," Rodney observed. "Feel that?"

"You're just trying to distance us from your dog's farts," Maddy accused. "Maybe instead of acting like a typical guy, you could show a little focus."

"Oh . . ." breathed JayB.

I turned and stared at him, feeling a strong change in his mood as he tensed in his seat.

"What is it?" Alana asked.

"Guys," Rodney protested, sounding wounded, "I don't think you should judge me by my dog's gas."

"If I don't judge it, who will?" Maddy challenged. "He's your dog, so it's your problem, that's the law."

"Everybody shut up," JayB said tensely.

The car fell into a shocked silence. I felt a heavy sensation as we surged ahead. "Okay, listen up," JayB continued urgently. "See that, right at the edge of the squall line? That's a funnel cloud. And it's descending."

"A funnel cloud? And you're going faster? *Straight at it?*" Alana asked shrilly.

"No. I mean yes, but I'm aiming for that overpass up ahead," JayB responded evenly. "The second we get there, I'll stop, and everyone bail out." He raised his voice. "Got it? Climb up the side as high as you can, close up under the steel beams. Okay? I'll be right behind you with the dogs."

## Dear Diary:

When a dog is a bad dog, it makes all the other dogs uneasy.

When we see a dog misbehaving, we can anticipate that the people will be unhappy. Nothing makes us more anxious than unhappy people. Cats, of course, are different. A person can say a harsh word to a cat, or use the most dreaded word of all—"no"—with a cat, and the cat won't care at all.

Spartan is a bad dog. Odin knows it, and I know it. Phoebe doesn't seem to care. Her jovial lack of concern, which I adore so much, makes her accepting of even a bad dog in the pack. That the dog in question is my rival is all the more vexing. I wish her sweetness were reserved for me alone, but that's not who she is.

 Love,
Clancy

# Twenty-three

Now all our people were afraid, and every dog, except bad dog Spartan, was panting in response. Even perpetually joyful Phoebe, when she glanced at me, had her ears back and tongue lolling out. We could feel odd forces pulling at us as our car lurched, its engine loud.

"I don't want to die!" Rodney wailed.

"Nobody wants to die," JayB agreed.

"No, I mean of everybody here, I *especially* don't want to die," Rodney corrected urgently. "I can't die. I have so much I want to *do*."

"I didn't get to say my biography!" Maddy wailed.

"Just do as I say," said JayB, talking loudly over the rising wind and rain. His wipers began slapping at the glass.

"It's touching down! It's on the ground!" Alana gasped.

*"We're headed right for it!"* Rodney screeched. "Stop! You have to stop!"

"Almost there!"

I heard a sound build, oppressive and loud, outside the car.

"Hang on!" JayB called.

We all fell forward as the car slammed to a halt.

*"Now!"*

Everyone scrambled, doors popping open, and JayB's hand snagged our leashes. "Let's go!"

I blinked at the dust and rain swirling in the howling wind as we sprang out onto the wet pavement. The growling roar became unimaginably loud.

We were scrambling up a wet hill that felt like a slick road under our nails. I knew none of the dogs understood—I sure didn't—we only knew we had to keep up with JayB. At the top of the slope, Alana reached for Odin and Rodney grabbed Spartan. The noise got louder and louder. JayB put his arms around Phoebe and me and squeezed into a tight, shallow space like a doghouse with a low roof.

The roar was upon us, so powerful I felt it more than heard it. My entire body vibrated. I sensed everyone's fear, tasted it, but with JayB's arm around me, I knew I would be all right. People are why dogs can survive in a dangerous world. I pressed up against him, taking comfort from his body against mine. I closed my eyes against the assault.

The intensity lasted only moments, but they were long moments. I heard Maddy scream something, and Rodney bellowed back, and I was buffeted by a terrible wind. And then a lessening came: a change in pressure, fading noise and wind. The howling rage of the storm had gone off in pursuit of other people, other dogs.

Now we heard only the rain, a drenching downpour, though we remained mostly dry in our shelter. Nobody spoke, but they were all breathing loudly.

It got quiet enough that I heard a squeal from Spartan's butt, and another cloud of wonderful aroma drifted over us.

"Oh my God, Spartan," Maddy complained.

JayB released his tight grasp and everyone sat up, moving awkwardly under the ceiling pressing down on us.

"I thought for a second there that we weren't going to make it," Walter breathed. He laughed shakily.

"Man, that was intense," Rodney agreed. "I've been through a lot of amazing stuff in my life, but this was, like, a thousand times that."

"Hey," Alana said, peering around. "Where's the van?"

Everyone went quiet.

"Did you leave the keys in it, JayB?" Maddy demanded.

"I don't think anyone stole it," JayB responded.

We gingerly picked our way down the wet slope until we were standing on the wet road. Odin, Spartan, and I all marked the same spot at the side of the road while Phoebe watched us admiringly.

"There, see?" JayB announced, pointing. "Looks like the van took your advice, Rodney. It's lying facedown in a ditch."

We stood in place, safe from the falling rain, and eventually I wagged a little because I saw our car. It was up ahead, just off the road. It was on its side, like Odin when he sprawled out for a tummy rub.

"So, no; we're not going to make it to Denver tonight," JayB advised Walter.

"The next town of any size is Colby, Kansas," Alana observed, peering at her phone. "About an hour west of here."

"You do have insurance, right, Dad?" JayB asked.

"Of course," Walter replied, looking surly.

"It have roadside assistance?"

Walter nodded.

"Time to make the call."

"But what if it's no longer roadside?" asked Maddy. "Does it cover cornfields?"

"Maybe if you hadn't panicked," Rodney accused JayB, "the van would be okay."

JayB shrugged. "Sure."

"He look like he was panicking to you?" Alana demanded. "Because he looked like the opposite to me."

Everyone was staring at Alana, shocked by her savage tone. She turned to JayB, her hands trembling as she pulled him to her in a tight hug. "You saved our lives," she murmured into his shoulder.

Rodney slapped JayB on the arm. "We're a good team, JayB."

Moist, fragrant air brought us smells of vegetation and stone, of unknown animals and richly complex soils. We dogs all lifted our noses, wanting to explore, but we were still on leash.

"Okay," Alana announced, "I found a hotel up ahead in Colby that takes dogs. Should I reserve rooms?"

"Please," JayB requested. "If the van's not drivable once the tow truck gets here, we'll figure out how to get to Colby."

"Colby," Rodney snorted. "You know what that reminds me of?"

"Cheese?" Maddy guessed.

Rodney laughed. "Exactly. Good one."

We waited for a long time, standing on wet ground, leashes limp in human hands. Phoebe nosed me playfully, but whipped her head around at another emission from Spartan. She was, I recognized dismally, a dog who fell in love based on odors, which was common but disappointing. Except for his magnificent smells, what else did Spartan have to offer?

"Can't believe how long this is taking," Walter grumbled. "I'm going to complain to Triple A."

"They should have a squad of trucks standing by, waiting for a call from somewhere in the middle of a cornfield in Kansas," JayB agreed cheerfully.

I think we dogs all expected that when the rain stopped, we'd leave wherever we were and go someplace else, but we only traveled a little way, to sniff around our car before returning to the same patch of pavement.

Spartan barked gruffly when a huge, beeping, growling truck arrived, several men jumping out of it. I was excited to see them—to see anything, really—and Phoebe wanted to play as well, but we were held back while the truck made small movements and the men shouted at each other.

When our car was back upright, I anxiously watched JayB climb inside it without me. Our car backed up, then drove forward, then steered one way and then another, and then JayB jumped back out. "We're good!"

Walter mournfully ran his hand along the one side of the car that had been lying in the mud. "All busted up," he noted. "Looks like utter crap."

"She'll get us there, though," JayB countered cheerfully.

"What if your mother shows up? This doesn't look like the sort of thing a man of means would drive."

JayB stared at him. "My mother?"

"She called and left a message, gave me her cell number. Thanked me for the flowers. I texted her and told her to meet us in Vegas."

Maddy had joined us. "She gave you her cell phone? Oh, she's leaving the wolfman for sure."

Walter brightened. "You think so?"

"Let's go, everybody!" JayB called.

The car made a new rattling sound as we headed out onto the road. Tired from all the unusual activities, we dogs collapsed in our customary places.

"Okay," Maddy announced after a while, "so everyone got to tell their story except me, which is good because I didn't know about the robbery and the tornado yet."

JayB shrugged. "Since we all know about those, I'm not sure you need to include them in the story."

Maddy scowled. "Fine. I'll say nothing then, all the way across Kansas. Talk about naming the chickens!"

Alana glanced back at us. "So, Maddy. Why don't you tell us your biography?"

Maddy shook her head. "I don't think it's fair to call this my biography because I'm not dead yet. But anyway, my first boyfriend had a normal name. Elliott Turner. So you can see how JayB is a real challenge for me."

Rodney nodded. "When I was in high school people called me The Rod. Or, the Rodster. Still do, obviously."

"This wasn't high school yet! Are you even paying attention? It was sixth grade."

"God, sixth grade," Rodney lamented. "That's when I got my braces. Remember that, JayB?"

"Now that you mention it, no."

"Now my *high school* boyfriend, since everyone wants the plot spoiled, was Cliff Zodd," Maddy continued. "He acted a lot like you, Rodney, only better looking. I'm pretty sure my so-called friend Samantha had a crush on him, because when I got suspended for that thing in science class, all of a sudden they were having lunch together. I was heavier then. I wasn't permitted to exercise because of my mom's fistfight with the gym teacher. Then Cliff moves to Kentucky with his parents, so you know what senior year was like. I had this pet turtle I had renamed Cliff . . . and now what? That was before salmonella."

"I keep thinking of going back to college to get my degree," Rodney reflected.

Walter snorted. "What would be the point?"

"The *point*," Maddy seethed, "which I am making, is that my college boyfriend had the same name!"

Alana frowned. "Sorry, same name as . . . ?"

"Terry!"

Alana glanced at JayB, then back at Maddy. "I'm a little lost."

"Terry was the name of my turtle before I changed it to Cliff. Anyway, so when I started dating Joey, naturally I became a vegetarian."

JayB nodded. "Naturally."

"You may not believe this," Rodney warned, "but there are some vegetables I can't stand."

Alana regarded Maddy curiously. "Are you still a vegetarian?"

"What? Of course not. Joey and I broke up a long time ago."

"So you only stopped eating meat because of your boyfriend?"

"That's the biography."

Rodney held up a hand and ticked off his fingers. "Brussels sprouts. Spinach. Kale. Hummus."

Alana sighed. "I did that."

JayB glanced at her. "What do you mean?"

"I became a vegetarian for a while because of the man I was dating."

Maddy smirked. "That's nothing. You probably think I always lived in Kansas City, but the best plot spoiler is that I moved with Nolly to Houston. And I don't even like football!"

Rodney still had his fingers up. "Let me think, I know there are others. Oh, lima beans . . . wait, are beans considered vegetarian?"

I opened my eyes because Alana pulled on a lever and spun her seat around so that she was facing Maddy. "Why do we do that? Why is it always the woman who has to sacrifice for the man, and not the other way around?"

Rodney grinned. "Whoa, where did that come from?"

Maddy shrugged. "It's just how it's always been, I guess. Ever since women got the vote."

"I do what you do, Maddy. I mark my life's milestones by my

boyfriends," Alana marveled. "I never even realized I did that until just now."

Rodney nodded. "I'll bet when my ex-girlfriends get together to talk about me, they see it as a big phase."

Maddy and Alana were gazing at each other. "There are lots of nice neighborhoods in Los Angeles," Alana said evenly. "But Guy will only consider Marina del Rey, because that's where he grew up. Period. So that's where I live."

Maddy processed this, then nodded and turned to the window. "I'll do the rest of my biography later," she murmured.

Alana swiveled her seat back around to face the front.

Night was falling, and, periodically, Spartan filled the inside of the car with his astounding new scent and everyone allowed the roar of air in through lowered windows.

A little while later, I noticed that Rodney and Walter were both sleeping with their heads tipped back. Maddy had sagged sideways. The rain had diminished as quickly as it had come, and we were driving through the darkness.

"So, back there at the gas station, were you scared?" Alana asked JayB softly.

He thought about it. "No, not really. I mean, the guy was pretty far away, and he had a handgun. I hadn't heard any shots, so I figured Dad was okay. I just prayed the guy would leave us alone. It was a shock when Spartan wouldn't let him into his own car."

Alana nodded, but she was gazing at him thoughtfully. "Were you thinking anything else?"

JayB shook his head. "Well, not really. Why?"

"Do you know you stepped in front of me?"

JayB regarded her silently.

She nodded. "Yeah, here's this guy with a gun and you stepped right in front of me. You even swept your hand back to keep me behind you. You don't remember doing that?"

"I guess I do."

"You were protecting me, JayB. You could have gotten shot."

"Well, I mean, I couldn't let the guy just *shoot* you, right?"

Alana didn't say anything for a long time after that.

We all wagged when the car stopped. A new place! The people jumped out of the car and stretched. Alana and Walter walked into a big building that had glass doors. Soon, Alana shaking her head, she and Walter came back out.

"Well, bad news," Alana announced gravely. "They do take dogs, but the weight limit's twenty-five pounds."

Even though I heard the word "dogs," something told me this wasn't an occasion for wagging.

*Dear Diary:*

*There are many times in a dog's life when we must wait for some indication from our people as to what we are doing, and what we will do next.*

*We don't actually need people to provide direction. A dog can sit patiently, smelling the world going by on the wind, or sniffing up interesting scents from the ground, or curling up into a nap. But when the sense of expectation is high in people, when there's a tension to their movements, we become alert and remain so, watching for a signal.*

*In fact, one of the most perplexing things about humans is the impatient restlessness they display so often when there are wonderful smells to behold all around them.*

*And then, when something happens that justifies all that nervous human anticipation, it can be completely incomprehensible to dogs.*

Love,
Clancy

# Twenty-four

"Twenty-five pounds? Well, that's certainly interesting," JayB observed. "Guess we'd better put them on a diet."

"That can't possibly be legal," Maddy objected. "It's not *their* fault they're fat!"

"The hotel will let us out of the reservation because of the misunderstanding if we want to keep going," Alana advised.

"I have to say, I'm exhausted," Walter interjected. "I really need to sleep."

JayB thought about it. "Okay. Well, I guess as the official dog walker of this expedition, I'll spend the night in the van with the dogs."

"Oh, no," Alana protested. "That's not fair. Odin isn't your dog. I'll do it, too."

Maddy's eyes narrowed. "Oh, no. Do you think I can't see what's going on here?"

"Maddy—" Alana started to say.

Maddy held up her hand. "Just stop. You are not spending the night in the love van with my boyfriend. End of story."

"Yeah," Rodney agreed. "I mean, I'm not comfortable with the idea, either." He shrugged at Alana.

"Okay," JayB said with false enthusiasm, clapping his hands together. I wagged at the gesture. "This should be fun. Me, Alana, Rodney, and Maddy in the van with the dogs."

Everybody turned to look at Walter, so I did too. He shook his head. "I'm going to get a good night's sleep." And with that, he left us.

What a great night! The people put the seats down and we all stretched out *in the car*. There was light filtering in through the windows and I could see all of them and smell all of them, especially Spartan.

"These seats are surprisingly comfortable like this," Alana observed.

"Oh, come on," Maddy responded scornfully. "Are you trying to say this is the first time you've ever slept in the back of a van? You're describing my whole early twenties."

"We used to do this a lot when I was a kid," Rodney noted.

"Spend the night in a Hampton Inn parking lot?" JayB asked innocently.

Alana laughed.

Rodney shook his head. "We'd go camping, my whole family." He turned to Alana. "Do you camp much?"

"Rodney, I live in Marina del Rey."

Now JayB laughed.

"You're in for a whole new human experience," Rodney promised. "I'll take you to the Ozarks. You've never seen a natural wonder like the lake down there—they made it by damming up this huge river."

"But stay away from the boys in that area," Maddy warned. "That's where my sister had her first baby, or at least one of the places, anyway."

"You don't need to worry about boys when you're with me." Rodney chuckled.

"Everything you're hearing is true," JayB assured Alana with a smile.

There was a long silence. I yawned, content to be with my dogs and people in such a small space.

"Okay, well," Rodney announced, "the part of my bio I held back is the story of the car that JayB and I bought in high school."

JayB groaned and put his palm against his forehead with such force that we all heard the slap. "You've got to be kidding me."

"If JayB doesn't want you to tell the story, it's got to be good," Maddy speculated. "My brother's like that about his plastic surgery."

Rodney sat up. "Okay, here's the deal. Sixteen years old. I was helping my dad in the garage, stuff like that. And JayB had a job at the Dairy Queen, which he'd been doing since he was like nine."

"Sure," JayB agreed affably. "Nine years old."

"And JayB . . . well, you know the kind of guy he is," Rodney continued. "He never has any fun. So he kept every dime he ever made, stuck it all in a bank account. Can you picture someone in high school with a bank account?"

"I had a bank account in high school," said Alana.

Maddy snorted. "I don't have a bank account *now*."

"So JayB and I decided to pool our money together and go and buy a Toyota MR2 that we saw for sale."

"Right," JayB concurred. "By pool our money, I think you mean, I supplied the money."

Rodney shrugged. "Whatever. The point was, this guy—that wasn't his name, by the way—was asking $5,150. But I figured, because I'm good at this kind of thing, that I could probably talk him down because of cash on the barrelhead. All we had was $4,842. No more."

"That's the part I want to speak to," JayB interjected. "Rodney's method of negotiation was to start the bargaining by saying, 'Hey, all we've got is $4,842.'"

Alana looked over at JayB and grinned. "Sounds like a tough negotiator."

"Exactly. The guy never knew what hit him," Rodney agreed. "Here he is. He wants $5,150. The next thing you know, we're driving out in this beautiful machine and we got it for what . . . like, almost a grand less?"

There was a long silence.

"I can't do the math," Maddy finally admitted.

"To be clear," JayB corrected, "we didn't *drive* out of there because it wasn't running. We had to tow it."

Rodney nodded. "But that's not the most exciting part. We took it to my dad's garage to work on it, and let me tell you, there was a *lot* wrong with that car."

"Right. Another part of the plan had been to inspect it thoroughly, but Rodney elected to go straight into tough negotiating."

"Absolutely. I worked on that car for months and months."

"Meanwhile," JayB prodded, "did I do any work?"

"Oh, yeah. I mean, sure, you'd hand me tools and stuff."

"Right. That's what I did. What else did I hand you, Rodney?"

Rodney looked completely dumbfounded by the question.

"Well, I still had a job," JayB hinted, "and we had to buy parts. So what else did I hand you?" He held up a hand and rubbed his forefinger against his thumb.

I looked at it curiously.

"Money?" Alana guessed.

"I was going to say motor oil," Maddy added. "Or electricity."

"Okay, yeah," Rodney agreed tiredly. "The Dairy Queen job. I get it. I was working on the vehicle 24/7, doing what we call 'sweat equity,' so we could sell it and split the profit."

"But what did we do instead?"

"Can you let me tell it? So, what JayB's talking about is that I took it up to Ward Parkway." He turned to Alana. "That's this beautiful stretch of road on the Missouri side. The houses are awesome and it's mostly a flat straightaway."

"Okay," Alana replied cautiously.

Rodney nodded. "So obviously I raced that puppy."

"Obviously," JayB agreed dryly.

"Puppy?" Maddy repeated with a frown. "I feel like you just trapped us in a different story."

"No. I raced the car. Like, I put my foot to it. That little MR2, man, she could take off. I mean, I couldn't beat a Corvette or something, but up against like a minivan, I blew those people away. Kids looking out the windows, crying."

"So far it's a great story," JayB admired. "And then what, Rodney?"

Rodney thought about it. "Okay, the thing I have to tell you, Alana, and you're going to think this is really strange, but they have these traffic circles on Ward Parkway. They're big circles where the cars are supposed to go around."

"I know what a traffic circle is, Rodney."

"And I went into this crazy circle and I drifted a little bit, and I sort of hit this wall. I mean, I smashed into it sideways. Look, I know what you're thinking and you're right. It's a miracle I survived."

"So, this is, in the end, a story about a miracle," JayB said in summary.

"Then get *this*," Rodney added dramatically, "I lost my driver's license until I was eighteen. It was absolutely ridiculous. I wasn't the one who caused the accident. The car couldn't handle the speed."

JayB was silent. Alana was silent. Maddy reached out and touched Rodney's shoulder. "I can so identify with this," she murmured sympathetically.

"And what about car insurance?" JayB asked.

Rodney shook his head. "You know the answer to that one."

JayB turned to Alana. "You see why I don't like this story? Rodney goes drag racing and he winds up flying across a couple of people's yards and smashes into a brick wall. He's fine. The car is not. But there was no car insurance. We were supposed to leave it in the garage until it was running."

"It *was* running," Rodney pointed out.

"Why didn't you tell me? I could have gotten it insured."

"I wanted it to be a surprise for you, and *this* is how I get repaid," Rodney complained bitterly.

"That was so nice of you," Maddy praised Rodney. "You risked your life for JayB."

We spent a restless night in the car. The people were not sleeping well, I could tell. And occasionally, Alana or JayB would slide open the side door and let the dogs out to squat and sniff around. Gradually, the pungent smells were leaving Spartan's system, but I feared the damage to my relationship with Phoebe might well be permanent—she still stuck close to Spartan whenever he lifted his leg.

The next morning, the sun came in through the windows and JayB sat up, yawning.

Alana stretched and looked around. "I'm going to need some coffee," she announced.

Maddy and Rodney stirred.

Walter approached the car and slid open the side door. I lifted my nose to him. He'd never given me a treat, but a dog can always hope.

"All right," Walter greeted cheerfully, "that was great. How about I let you use my room for showers?"

"I'm first," Rodney responded instantly.

JayB shrugged. "Why don't we let Alana go first?"

Rodney blinked, looking perplexed.

"Oh, in fact," JayB continued, "this'd be a good time for you to take all the dogs for a walk. Don't you think?"

"Me?" Rodney replied incredulously. "What am I paying *you* for?"

"Rodney, you're *not* paying me."

Grumbling, Rodney grabbed up dog leashes, though I stayed with JayB. I knew who my person was. Odin moved slowly while Phoebe, lovely Phoebe full of life, danced with excitement.

"I'll take Clancy out in a minute," JayB added.

I wagged slightly at the mention of my name.

"Come on, Alana. I'll show you the room," Walter offered.

The two of them left, so now I was sitting in the vehicle with Maddy and JayB.

"Why did you have Alana go first, and not me? Aren't I built to be a woman?" Maddy challenged.

JayB nodded reflectively. "You know, you're right, Maddy. I'm sorry. I was trying to introduce Rodney to the notion that maybe we should be thinking about people other than him, but I completely missed the opportunity to suggest that you go instead."

"That's okay, because I have to talk to you about something really important."

"Oh," JayB protested, "please don't."

Maddy scowled. "No, this is it, JayB."

"This is what?"

"I need to know point-blank, and you need to be honest with me for once in your life and not just make up facts. Are we getting back together, or not?"

I sensed an acute tension between Maddy and JayB, so I sat quietly looking between the two of them. I was not sure what they were doing, but JayB, in particular, seemed unhappy.

"Well?" Maddy demanded. "Are you just going to stand there like a mouse in a trap, or are you going to answer my question? I deserve to know. Are we going to stay together, or are you going to break up with me? *Again?*"

"Maddy," JayB began, "I really appreciate that you took all the trouble to come up with however many rules we're at now, and that you've always been honest with me in your desire to see me be a completely different person."

Maddy waved her hand. "Well, any woman would want that. I shouldn't get all the credit."

"Okay, I'll give you just partial credit for that. But I am being as straight with you as I can. I just honestly don't think the two of us are meant to be together."

Maddy searched his face with her eyes. "Okay," she decided abruptly, "so can you fix me up with Rodney?"

JayB looked startled. "What?"

"Rodney. You're his best friend. Use your man-code words and tell him he should ask me out."

"Actually, I'm not his best friend, but even if I were, I don't know how to fix people up. If I could fix someone up, I'd fix myself up."

"Yes, okay, it's all about you . . . but seriously, I need you to throw me a life raft here. I really think Rodney might be the one. I get that you're hurting over our relationship; it's like a phantom limb for you, but I'm hoping you'll look past that."

JayB nodded. "Okay, I'm past it."

"I know I said you were the one, but this is really different. He's handsome, for one thing. And he's got such interesting stories."

"He does have a lot of stories," JayB observed.

"And your dad is right about Rodney. He's got this passion for life. You, no offense, are like an ugly microwaved potato with nothing on it . . . just blah."

"Why would I be offended?"

Alana came out of the big building smiling. Her hair was wet and she ran her fingers through it. She walked up to us and I wagged. I'm always happy to see Alana.

"Hot coffee and a cool shower," she announced. "I feel like a new woman." She held up a small piece of plastic. "Here's the key. Who's next?"

JayB turned to Maddy. "You should go, Maddy. You're a woman."

She shook her head. "I'm not playing that game. We're all equal here. I'm offended you'd even bring that up."

"Oh, sorry."

"I think you should go, JayB. Alana and I want to have some women talk, and no, not about gynecology."

JayB looked back and forth between them. "Okay." He handed my leash to Alana. "Would you hang on to Clancy?"

"Of course," Alana agreed.

I watched in confusion as JayB walked away from us. What was happening? I looked up at Alana in concern, not knowing how long I could stifle a whimper.

Where was JayB going without me?

## Dear Diary:

As it turns out, people don't like to sleep in a pile, not even when they spend the night in the same car together.

Dogs are different. A dog knows that nothing is softer than another dog.

I try to entice Phoebe to sleep up against me, but she inexplicably curls up against Odin. Spartan, as always, is aloof, but Odin gives me a look before setting his head down with a sigh. I think he knows how much I love Phoebe, and he's feeling guilty she decided to lie with him.

Odin is a good dog.

 Love,
Clancy

# Twenty-five

Maddy turned to Alana. "I'm glad we're going to have this time to talk."

"Sure," Alana agreed cautiously.

"So, get ready for this: JayB and I just broke up."

"Oh."

"This isn't like all the other times. This time it's for good."

"Um, how do you feel?"

"Liberated, of course. Slightly nauseated. I've got some cramps. I might be getting a zit on my chin."

"I see."

"So that's good news for you, right?" Maddy gave Alana a shrewd look. "Right?"

"I'm not sure what you mean."

"He's out of jail free, okay? You can have him. JayB's all yours, including any warts."

"Oh. No. I'm sorry," Alana protested. "I think you misunderstood something. I already have a boyfriend."

"I've used that one before. Sometimes it works. The boys get jealous and then, you know, they flip out and make a big move. Maybe buy you something. Other times, it flops like a dropped pancake. JayB's the kind of person who backs off when you say you have a boyfriend, so you should maybe switch tactics, here."

"It's not a tactic, Maddy. Guy really does exist. We're on our way to see him right now."

"Oh, sure," Maddy sneered, "in Las Vegas. Right."

"Why do you say it like that? Why would I have us get in that van and drive all the way to Las Vegas if not to see my boyfriend and pick up my cat?"

"Okay, first," Maddy responded, "cats are easy to fake. And, second, there's a chapel on, like, every block in Las Vegas. You can marry somebody without them even knowing it. I think we both know JayB's going to step into a McDonald's or something and then, boom, man and wife."

Alana stared at Maddy. "That never occurred to me. About Vegas."

"Sure. Whatever. I see through your plan and I have to say I'm in favor of it. If I can get Rodney to go along, we can make it a double wedding."

"Oh, Rodney . . . okay. I didn't know you were interested in Rodney."

"Oh my God," Maddy marveled, "who *wouldn't* be interested in Rodney? He's like what would happen if a man and a woman got together and made a living person."

A short time later, JayB came back. I whimpered with joy, pawing at his legs.

"He's been crying off and on since you left," Alana advised.

"Clancy, you are such a silly dog," he murmured to me.

I loved hearing my name come from my person's lips.

Soon we were all back in the big car. For some reason, we only jumped in and out of the doors on one side, now. Our people were mostly silent as we drove, staring out the windows.

"This is not at all what I pictured," Alana remarked. "It's so green. I thought Kansas would be all dust. Like in the Westerns."

"I think the Westerns are mostly filmed in Arizona. It's drier there," JayB suggested.

"Kansas is like Ireland," Rodney declared.

"Seriously? Ireland?" JayB replied. "Have you ever *been* to Ireland?"

"He was just in *Canada*," Maddy hissed angrily.

JayB didn't have anything to say to that.

"And it goes on and on forever," Alana observed after a while. "Miles and miles."

"Yeah, it's driving me crazy," Walter sighed. "Look, Alana"—he leaned forward—"would you do me a favor and see if you can book me a flight from Denver to Vegas?"

Everyone was quiet for a moment.

Walter looked around. "I'm too old for this crap," he explained defensively. "I'll meet you guys there. Be your man on the ground. Find the best dog-friendly hotel."

"Sounds like a good idea," JayB opined neutrally.

Maddy turned to Rodney. "We're going to have *fun* in Las Vegas," she proclaimed pointedly.

Rodney considered this. "Well, yeah, of course. Have you ever been there?"

Maddy shook her head. "No, I was waiting for the right person."

Rodney frowned at her. "Okay, sure."

We burst out of that side door with manic energy when JayB pulled the car off the road. We were in the most amazing place; a wide, open space with no fence for as far as the eye could see.

I knew what she was going to do before she did it. Phoebe simply couldn't resist the sight of all that terrain. With her ears back, she took off at a dead run, headed just nowhere.

And I, of course, pursued.

I loved watching her gallop. I loved the way her feet rose from the ground. As she pulled away from me, her scent trailed behind her and I drank it in. Behind us, Spartan kept pace for a few steps, then halted his stiff, bulky body. Odin, of course, wasn't going to run at all. He remained by JayB's side.

I could have kept running forever, but I pulled up short when I heard JayB calling me. Phoebe slowed as well. I didn't know what I would have done if she had kept going, but when she wheeled around, I knew we were headed back and I tried to stay ahead of her. Of course, this was futile. She was so swift. When we returned to JayB, Spartan ran into her with his chest, in his usual wooden fashion. She play-bowed and wagged as if this was a game and not an obnoxious way for one dog to greet another. I looked at Odin, who glanced away.

JayB gave us water. Back inside the car, the people had unwrapped sandwiches, so I went on alert and noticed even Spartan doing the same. JayB served us, in our own bowls—crunchy morsels that I bolted down so quickly I almost couldn't taste them. Finished, we dogs inspected each other's bowls, disappointed to find nothing left in any of them.

Soon after the car started moving again, Walter fell asleep, and Alana swiveled her seat to face us.

Maddy sighed in displeasure. "What happened to squish everything so flat here? It's like a parking lot with corn."

"Probably from dinosaurs walking all over it," Rodney speculated.

JayB frowned. "I think this was once the bottom of a sea."

"In *Kansas*?" Maddy hooted. "This look like a yacht club to you?"

Alana nodded. "JayB's right, I'm reading about it; this was once the floor of an ocean."

Rodney shook his head. "Nah. I'm gonna stick with the dinosaurs. You know how heavy they were? Like, two million tons."

I heard a noise as JayB tightened his grip on the steering wheel.

Maddy reached out a hand and touched Rodney's shoulder. "It's like you know everything, Rodney. How do you keep it all in your head?"

JayB glanced back. "I wish you *would* keep it all in your head."

Alana laughed.

Rodney shrugged. "I've just always had this talent for facts." He paused, reflecting. "Tell you what I'm thinking. I'm going to take my half of the money from the Korean pig iron and buy a radio station. Then I'm going to have my own talk show. People are naturally interested in what I have to say, you know? They want to hear my opinions on things before they make up their own minds."

Maddy smiled. "I'm going to use my half to open a beauty shop. But not for just anybody—customers can't make appointments. I'll decide who gets to come in, and when."

Alana cocked her head. "That's interesting. So you'd call me to say, 'Hey, Alana, come in for a color and cut on Tuesday at four?'"

"Well, not you. No offense."

"So, Rodney gets half and Maddy gets half," JayB noted. "Doesn't the person who puts up the money usually get most of it?"

Rodney spread his hands. "Walter can have as much as he wants as long as I get half."

"Well, it's not coming out of my share, that's for sure," Maddy warned.

"Got it," JayB said. "So the topic of your radio show would be math."

Alana laughed.

Rodney scowled. "What? No, of course not. It would be like, what I think about current events, that sort of thing."

"I'd listen to it," Maddy assured Rodney.

He nodded. "Of course you would."

"So, what *do* you think about current events?" JayB wanted to know.

Rodney waved a hand dismissively. "I don't meant current like *now.*"

"Don't even listen to JayB," Maddy advised. "If there were political parties, he'd be nominated wet blanket."

Rodney laughed. "Right? But I guarantee he'll call in, like, every day. He's the type we'd have to block eventually."

Maddy leaned forward. "I know a game we could play to keep time from stopping. It's one I made up. I call it 'Book or Band.'"

Alana looked intrigued. "How do you play?"

"I think of a name and then you guess if it's the name of a book or the name of a band."

Rodney brightened. "Cool! Do all bands, though, because I don't really read books."

"You get a point for every right guess and lose a point for every wrong one," Maddy continued.

"I'm going to kick butt!" Rodney boasted.

Walter made a slight snoring sound.

"Ready? Okay. Here's the first one. Light Song with a Rock."

"Band!" Rodney shouted.

Maddy nodded. "Correct."

Alana seemed puzzled. "I don't think I've heard of that one."

"Well of course not," Maddy explained patiently. "These are names I'm *thinking of,* like I said."

"Ah."

"The Rodster's out in front," Rodney crowed.

"You're quick," Maddy praised him. "Everyone else was like a deer with their headlights off. Okay, another: The Long Standing Marker of Goodbye."

Rodney looked thoughtful. "That's a tough one, even for me."

"I'm guessing . . . book?" Alana speculated tentatively.

Maddy tapped the back of JayB's seat. "JayB, what's your guess?"

"No, thank you."

"Since Alana said book, I'll go with band," Rodney guessed.

"Rodney's right."

Rodney pumped a fist. "Yes!"

"So, Alana and JayB are both at negative one," Maddy informed everyone primly, "and Rodney has two points."

"Why do I get a negative?" JayB objected. "I didn't say anything."

"You lose points for not guessing," Maddy explained.

"This game is brilliant," Rodney enthused.

Maddy beamed. "Thank you! The attraction is mutual."

JayB glanced over his shoulder. "Hey, Alana, I know you're enjoying Maddy's sophisticated car game, but could you help me look out for, um, prairie dogs running across the highway? I wouldn't want to hit one."

"Of course, but it'll take all of my attention." Alana reached down and grabbed a lever. "Maddy, I'm so sorry I can't play anymore." She pulled the lever and spun her seat around to face the front. "Really sorry," she murmured.

"Prairie Dog . . . that would be a good band name," Rodney suggested.

Maddy shook her head. "No, it wouldn't."

"Book?"

"Nope."

Rodney threw up his hands. "This game is hard!"

Maddy leaned forward to speak to JayB. "If you can't see the prairie dogs, maybe you should use cruise control."

JayB nodded. "Good idea—except, if you run over a prairie dog with a van, everyone gets seven years of bad luck."

Maddy reflected on this. "I've heard the same is true for hamsters."

Soon, we changed direction—I could sense it by the position of the sun. We stopped and Walter wrestled around with some of the bags and grabbed one that I recognized as smelling like him.

"All right, thanks for the lift. I'll see you in Vegas," he called with a cheery wave. He slid the side door shut. I watched him go.

Whatever was happening was nothing a dog could possibly understand.

We drove off without Walter.

"I've never seen the mountains of Colorado before," Alana marveled. "They're beautiful."

"Soon we'll be *in* the mountains," JayB replied.

"What's it like in Marina del Rey?" Maddy asked. "Is it close to the mountains of Los Angeles?"

"Oh, yes, it's actually considered part of Los Angeles." Alana looked over at Maddy. "You've never been?"

Maddy shook her head. "I never get to go anywhere. Usually, I'm in court trying to get my money back."

"Ah."

"There's no way we're going to make it all the way to Vegas tonight," JayB observed. "Maybe we should book a hotel and stop and foil another robbery."

Everyone smiled at this.

"I'll remind you, though," Rodney interjected, "it was actually me and Spartan who caught the robber. You guys were just standing around with your hands in the air when I came out of the bathroom."

"That's exactly how it happened," JayB agreed.

Maddy reached out and touched Rodney's shoulder. "It's a word that gets used too much, especially in the restaurant business, but you're a hero, Rodney."

Rodney shrugged. "Actually, I'm just a man, but like all men, I won't just stand by when something wrong's going down."

A little while later, I woke up because the car had pulled over to the side of the road.

"Buffalo viewing area," Rodney pronounced.

"You dogs ready to see some buffalo?" JayB asked.

We heard the excitement in his voice, so we all leapt to our feet, wagging when the door slid open. JayB reached in and seized all our leashes in one deft grab.

Everyone was stretching and yawning. Alana followed JayB as he led us to a fence we could mark. My nose twitched at the smell of foreign creatures.

"I think I know what's going on with Guy," Alana murmured to JayB. "Something Maddy said made me realize it."

JayB waited.

"There's a reason he was so particular about wanting to meet in Las Vegas. Vegas, of all places." She stopped and searched JayB's eyes with hers. "It's not just to propose. It's because of the chapels. We're getting *married*."

*Dear Diary:*

I don't think any of the dogs knew, when we first climbed into this big car, that this would be our life—riding and even sleeping overnight in the vehicle, lulled into a continual drowsiness by the low, steady drone of the tires on the road. Given our new circumstances, I decided to take the opportunity to reflect on the members of the current pack and their relationship to our people.

Spartan pretends he doesn't care about humans, but I know from the way he greeted Rodney's return after a long absence that he is a devoted dog—he just doesn't display emotion. Does that mean he also adores JayB, the most wonderful human a dog could ever love? I would have no way of knowing.

My love, Phoebe, is a happy dog, always wagging and ready to play. She doesn't seem at all perturbed that Dominique and Bedford aren't with us. Some dogs are like that, willing to follow anyone with a kind voice or a treat in their pocket. I'm not that dog—JayB is the center of my world, and I am so glad he's along for this car ride.

Odin, of course, is the opposite of Phoebe. Though it has been many days since some people took Helen away, he still mourns for her. Odin misses Helen in a way that can never be fixed.

How does he feel about Alana? I think he's reached the same conclusion that I have—our humans have resolved that she is Odin's new person. He will accept this, of course, because dogs must accept what people decide, but I am pretty sure he still can't imagine life without Helen.

*A larger concern is the hesitancy from Alana, a lack of commitment. When a human loves a dog unconditionally, the dog knows it, and knows that human is his person. But the same reluctance I sensed in JayB, the obvious withholding of complete devotion to Odin, is present in Alana. She hasn't yet given herself to Odin, either.*

*My friend knows I see this pain in him. His wise, sad eyes often meet mine in an exchange of information, telling me what it's like to be Odin in this world—a dog who has lost his person.*

Love,
Clancy

# Twenty-six

L ook at the buffalo!" Maddy yelled from over by a sturdy fence. "They're huge!"

I could smell and see massive creatures moving slowly away from us in the distance. They carried a pungent odor, very attractive, but as much as I wanted to pursue their scent trail, I was not going to go anywhere near those ridiculously enormous animals. Instead, I focused on JayB, because I felt him tensing up as he regarded Alana.

"Married?" he repeated in a whisper. "Are you sure?"

Alana bit her lip. "It's just that Guy hates to drive. Whenever we're on the freeway, he swears constantly and is always hitting the horn. If this is only about the cat, why not ask me to come all the way to LA? That'd be more like him. Plus, he's always told me that Vegas is for fools. He's also been so evasive, lately. I'm not sure, but what else could be going on?"

"Wow."

Alana looked over JayB's shoulder. "Let's talk more later."

Maddy grinned as she and Rodney joined us. "Those buffalo really make you appreciate cows, don't they?" she said.

"More than ever," Rodney affirmed.

JayB pointed to a row of small, plastic-smelling buildings. "I need to jump in there for a minute."

"I'll take Clancy and Phoebe," Maddy offered.

Alana held out her hand for a leash. "I've got Odin."

"Yo, Spartan," Rodney called. "You're with me, dog."

I was ecstatic to be paired up with Phoebe. I lifted my leg to let her know I was not intimidated by the giant beasts foraging in the grass. Alana and Rodney walked off together and were soon near our big car. Maddy waited a moment, then followed silently, pulling Phoebe and me. While I checked anxiously for any sign of JayB emerging from the plastic buildings, Maddy stopped on the other side of the car and held still, listening to Rodney and Alana.

"Okay," Rodney told Alana, "this is as good a time as any."

"As good a time as any for what?"

"To tell you my truth, what you've been suspecting. I mean, it's obvious to everyone else, I'm sure." Rodney gave her a nervous laugh.

"What're you talking about?"

"I'm in love with you, Alana. You're the best thing that's ever happened to me."

I saw and felt Maddy react. Phoebe sensed it too, a sharp and immediate change in her mood.

"Oh, Rodney," Alana responded awkwardly, "I don't know what to say to this. You do know that I have a boyfriend."

"Right, some guy." Rodney laughed. "Get it? Some guy?

"I get it."

Maddy pushed away from the side of the car and strode toward the plastic buildings, from which JayB was emerging. I wagged happily.

"Well, I've been in worse places," he advised Maddy, reaching for my leash.

"You'll never guess what I just overheard," Maddy huffed.

"You're probably right."

"Alana and Rodney are making out on the other side of the van, saying they're in love with each other."

JayB's eyes went wide.

"I guess," Maddy speculated, "that means I'm back with you. I know it's not what either one of us would've wanted, but we can't let them get away with this without some sort of payback."

"You sure you heard right?"

"Oh my God," Maddy exploded, exasperated. "Yes. I mean they're talking love, L-O-V-E. I appreciate that Rodney's not afraid to use that kind of language. Maybe if you ripped a lesson from his text-book, we could spark some passion ourselves."

JayB didn't reply.

"Well, you don't have to act like I'm second prize, or something.

I'll remind you we've got a lot more world history together than you and Alana could ever have."

"I guess I can't believe it."

"Yeah?" Maddy put her hands on her hips. "Men don't see something even if it bites your nose despite your face. Well, you just wait. They can't hide. We get back on the road, I'll prove it to you."

"How're you going to do that?"

"You'll see."

Later, the sun was gone from the sky and we were driving through darkness. Maddy was in the back seat with her arms folded in a stiff posture. Rodney kept leaning forward to speak to Alana, who had swiveled her chair to face the front.

"You like hiking, Alana?" he asked. "I love it. it's like running, only you have hiking boots."

"Sure," Alana agreed faintly.

"Oh, so the two of you are *going hiking*?" Maddy challenged significantly. "Together? *Alone?*"

"Sure!" Rodney confirmed brightly.

Maddy snorted. "And then what? Out to dinner?"

"Sounds like a plan." Rodney grinned.

Alana looked troubled. "Well, I mean . . ."

Maddy leaned forward intently. "What about a cruise? Those can be pretty romantic, if you don't get food poisoning."

Rodney beamed. "Now *that* would be fun! When's a good time to go? Once we move that Korean pig iron, I'm going to need a well-deserved break from it all."

"So, you and Rodney on a cruise off to the sunrise, while JayB and I stay behind and do your dirty laundry," Maddy sneered. "Sounds like quite a *hike*."

Alana twisted to peer at Maddy. "I'm not sure what you're saying, Maddy."

"That's okay. I know. JayB knows. Rodney knows. And you know, too," Maddy accused. "Don't pretend you've got your hands behind your back, here."

Alana gave JayB a helpless look.

"Alana," JayB probed delicately, "have you fallen in love with Rodney?"

"Whoa!" Rodney exclaimed.

Alana shook her head. "Of course not."

"Well—" Rodney started to say.

"So, Maddy," JayB interrupted, "you can see you were wrong about that. Alana and Rodney did not spend all of Kansas getting romantically involved."

"I know what I saw when the lights went out in Georgia," Maddy retorted.

Rodney turned to Maddy. "What did Alana do to make you think that? It must have been obvious. Just curious."

Maddy scowled at him. "What did *you* do, should be the question here. If you weren't so cute, I'd be sick to my stomach."

Rodney raised his eyebrows. "You think I'm cute?"

"Just about twenty more miles 'til Grand Junction," JayB interjected. "Be good to get out of the car." He grinned at Alana. "You did tell the hotel how much our dogs weigh, right?"

"Oh yeah, they know. They promised they're dog-friendly."

That night, we slept in a whole new room. Phoebe and I wrestled and wrestled, full of energy from all the car naps. JayB kept saying, "Cut it out," which was not a familiar phrase to me. I could see Phoebe didn't know it either.

The next day, we were back in the car before the sun had time to fully light up the sky. Everyone was quiet, sipping coffee.

"Your dad's text says that he got us all upgraded rooms in a hotel that welcomes dogs," Alana said after a long while. "I'll put the address in the GPS."

"My favorite thing to do in Vegas is the slots," Rodney declared.

"Me, too," Maddy beamed.

"Right? Because there's a skill involved," Rodney elaborated. "I mean, you go and you play blackjack or whatever . . . well, those are just cards coming up at random. The slot machines are completely different. You pick the right one, you win big."

"Sounds like a good system," JayB praised.

Alana put a hand over her mouth and looked out the window. A long, long silence followed. I slept. We stopped a few times, but JayB couldn't find a dog park, so we got back in the car. I slept some more, but opened my eyes when my person spoke.

"How are you doing?" he asked Alana quietly.

"Honestly, I'm a little nervous."

"Is Guy at the hotel yet?"

She held up her phone. "Not yet. He'll arrive right after we do, I think. I'm really looking forward to seeing my cat."

I heard that word, "cat," and I wondered why such an awful subject would be introduced at a time like this.

"Oh my God, look! I see the Eiffel Tower!" Maddy exclaimed. "How did it get here? Did we go to war without knowing it?"

"Ah, no," Rodney told her. "Let me explain. We'll see the Statue of Liberty, and the space needle from San Francisco. In Las Vegas, it's like you can get anything you want. If you want Paris, they have Paris. If you want Greece, they have Greece, right? If you want—I don't know, Alaska—they've got Alaska."

"Alaska?" JayB repeated skeptically.

"Las Vegas is the one real place in the world. You wait. With the buffets and all, you're gonna feel like royalty."

"Will they carry me on their shoulders in one of those chairs?" Maddy asked, excited. "I've always wanted to do that. *Let them eat cake.*"

"Well . . . I don't know about that one," Rodney admitted. "They have golf carts, though."

Maddy waved a hand. "That's okay. I'll do it when I go to Egypt."

"Oh, they have Egypt," Rodney assured her. "More than one."

We pulled into a driveway and a nice man came and opened the door for all of us. JayB watched as they put all our bags on a cart, and then I wagged because Walter was there, smiling and handing everybody something wrapped in little pieces of paper.

"Welcome!" Walter greeted. "You're going to love it here. It's like a carnival."

"You lose much money?" JayB wanted to know.

Walter shook his head. "No, I'm up, way up. Blackjack's my game."

Rodney groaned. "See, I disagree there. Blackjack's not nearly as fun as the slot machines."

Maddy reached out and touched his arm. "Let's go hit the slots." She spun and gave Alana a deep, significant glare. "You don't like slots, *do you,* Alana?"

"Oh no, not at all," Alana assured her. "Besides . . . Okay, he's here. Guy. Guy's here!"

Everybody looked around.

"Where?" Rodney asked.

"He's coming. He's got Rhiannon!" Alana was grinning broadly.

I could sense a change in JayB's mood, a quietness. Odin glanced at me—he felt it, too. Then I saw a man with dark hair approaching. He was not smiling. He held a bag in his hand, and from that bag came the unmistakable odor of cat.

It was a cat bag.

With a squeal, Alana ran across the parking lot and threw her arms around the man, who set the bag down and hugged her back. They kissed briefly and she stuck her arm through his. Then she reached down and grabbed the cat bag and put her face to it. Next, the three of them—Alana, the new man, and the cat bag— approached us. Alana was smiling. The new man still wasn't.

"Everybody, this is Guy."

"Yo, Guy," Rodney hailed. "I'm Rodney. I know there's a lot going on, but I just want you to know, whatever Alana has told you about me, I'm basically a good guy. Honest. Person, I mean. A good person, I should've said. No offense about your name."

"Sure," Guy said.

"He's the best knife in the drawer, even if he doesn't mean to be," Maddy put in.

Everyone decided to stick their hands out to the new man, saying their names.

All the dogs turned their attention away from the cat bag to assess the man. We knew something about him, knew it instantly. Odin and I exchanged glances, and even Spartan seemed to react.

This was a man who did not like dogs. There are few such people in the world, and I've never understood them, but it's obvious from their scent and body language.

I didn't know why Alana would be happy to see him any more than I understood why she suddenly had a cat. I just knew that a man who doesn't like dogs cannot be trusted.

"We probably should grab some man time and talk, Guy," Rodney observed. "You know."

Guy frowned.

Maddy was looking the new man up and down. "Hi, Guy. For some reason, I pictured you being taller."

JayB smiled a little at this.

All of the canines went back to being focused on that bag, but only Phoebe was wagging. She probably didn't know what a waste of time it was to wag for a cat, even one in a bag.

"And this," Alana announced grandly, "is Odin, the dog I told you about."

The man looked down at Odin without saying anything. Odin did not wag.

"Um, JayB?" Alana said, grinning shyly. "I guess . . . would you watch Odin tonight? I'll take Rhiannon with us."

"Sure," JayB agreed. I heard some unhappiness in his voice and wondered what it meant.

"Okay—goodnight, everybody." With her arm around the new man, she turned and they walked through the glass doors, taking their stupid cat bag with them.

I didn't understand any of it, except we were still in the parking lot and JayB felt sad.

"And there she goes," he murmured.

*Dear Diary:*

*People make a lot more sounds than dogs, and I've never understood why—especially since, during the bland exchange of tones between people, it seems as if feelings are seldom communicated. Usually, their smells are a better indicator of what's going on.*

*When dogs vocalize, it's easy to know what they're experiencing. A dog will bark with glory at another dog; cry to be allowed up on the bed; and growl at cats. There's no mistaking the meaning of any of it, and every dog within earshot will be affected.*

*Humans, on the other hand, will talk and talk without clarity. Only the strongest of emotions come across in human voices—joy, anger, sorrow. Otherwise, people drone on to each other without any obvious purpose.*

*After a time, some elements of conversation emerge that a dog can recognize, like "Clancy" and "dinner." Normally, therefore, when a person is speaking, all dogs can do is listen and hope to hear something they understand.*

Love,
Clancy

# Twenty-seven

Maddy poked Rodney in the ribs. "Ready for the slots? I'd love to go home with a few thousand bucks putting holes in my pants."

Rodney grinned. "Now you're talking."

Walter turned to JayB as Maddy and Rodney walked off together, Spartan snuffling along at Rodney's feet.

"Will they actually let Spartan on the floor of the casino?" JayB wanted to know.

Walter shrugged. "I don't know. I've seen some dogs and cats there, but for all I know they were . . . what do you call it? Emotional support dogs." Walter eyed JayB. "So what do you want to do? Go get a drink?"

"No, Dad, thanks," JayB demurred. "I'm really tired. I'm just going to take the three dogs and get in bed."

Walter was assessing JayB. "You'll be okay, son. Look, I'm no stranger to this, to heartbreak, and I'm not going to lie to you. It never completely goes away. When someone walks out of your life, it's like they leave a hole, and every time you pass by that hole, a little of you is sucked through it into the void. Anyway, that's what it felt like to me. But I'm here to tell you that as you get older, it gets better, all right?"

"Sure. Thanks."

"You're a good man and I'm proud of you, even if you let some woman beat you up at your own office."

"Thanks."

Walter clapped JayB on the shoulder. "All right, have a good night."

We were all taken outside to lift our legs, and then we stood in a room where it felt like my stomach was dropping out, and then we

were escorted down a long, long hallway. I knew Phoebe wanted to
gallop, and I did too—the place was made for running!—but JayB
kept our leashes taut. We eventually found our way into a room that
was very chilly. Without Spartan there, Phoebe and I resumed our
wrestling where we left off, while Odin sighed and curled up in the
corner.

"Cut it out," JayB kept saying.

I still didn't know what that meant.

The next morning, JayB led us outside. Alana met us at the door,
and I was surprised to smell that she persisted in carrying a cat in
a bag.

I could not imagine why anyone would want such a thing. I could
see the cat peering out from within the bag. There were holes along
the side, through which she could see that she was in the presence
of superior beings—people and dogs. She peered out with typical
cat hostility. Alana kept saying the word "Rhiannon," so I concluded
that Rhiannon was the cat's name.

We were taken to a dog park, a very small one with spongy plastic underfoot, from which wafted the enticing scent of the urine of
many, many dogs. We all reacted by making our own marks—even
Phoebe squatted.

JayB held our leashes, which was unusual in a dog park. Apparently having a cat in a bag changed everything.

"Where's Guy?" he asked delicately.

"He likes to sleep in," Alana explained. "I ordered some coffee
and left a note telling him to come to the dog run when he's up."
She eyed him in concern. "Look, I know he came across a little unfriendly yesterday. But he's actually a really nice person."

"It's okay. So how do you want to do this?"

Alana considered his response, then nodded. "Let's start with
Odin; he's the biggest worry."

"You sure?"

"I know my cat," Alana replied simply.

I'd hoped Rhiannon would stay in the bag, but she didn't. Instead, Alana put the bag down and unzipped it and the cat waltzed

arrogantly out, giving the assembled canines the barest of smug glances.

Kelsey's not bright enough to know she's safe when dogs are restrained by leashes, but this cat apparently knew that JayB was preventing us from attacking.

We all stared at Rhiannon, who was strolling languidly along the fence line, seemingly unaware of any danger. Phoebe was wagging madly and actually play-bowed—as if you could play with a cat! Odin's tail went stiff and Spartan's gaze remained unblinking.

Alana took Odin's leash. "Okay. Let's try this."

Keeping him on a tight leash, Alana allowed Odin to approach the cat. His shoulders hunched as his claws dug into the plastic.

Much closer and this would be the last of Rhiannon.

The cat finally deigned to notice that there was a dog grunting and straining to hunt her. I knew she'd run now.

Except she didn't. Her ears went back, her fur puffed out, and she opened her mouth. A moment later she lunged straight at Odin's face, slashing the air in front of his nose.

I watched in amazement as Odin nearly fell over himself backing away from this terrible creature. And the cat kept pursuing! Odin dashed back toward where we were watching, yanking Alana behind him.

The cat sat and calmly licked a paw.

Phoebe was still wagging, but the rest of us were shocked and afraid.

"Wow," JayB admired.

Odin appeared both wounded and baffled. He looked to me for an explanation, but I'm an expert in *frightening* cats, not *attacking* them. Especially one so full of aggression.

"How about Spartan?" Alana suggested.

Spartan looked up at his name. He watched Alana switch his leash for Odin's, but when Alana tried to pull him over to the evil cat, Spartan did a resolute Sit. I didn't blame him.

"Clancy?" JayB asked.

Oh, no. I flopped down onto my tummy. If Alana wanted me

near the cat, she was going to have to drag me. When she tugged my leash, I whimpered.

JayB laughed. I gave him a beseeching look.

"It's okay, Clancy," he told me.

I sagged with relief when he took my leash back, but I remained on the ground just in case.

Phoebe was dancing around at the end of her tether, wagging frantically. The cat stonily watched this display. Alana slowly and cautiously guided Phoebe over. Phoebe positively radiated affection for Rhiannon but was wise enough to stay just out of reach of those claws. Even a loving dog like Phoebe recognized menace.

Later, Alana's new friend with the dark hair came out to join us in the dog park. He smelled of sweat and some sort of stale food. He was the same height as Alana, shorter than JayB. She seemed to really like him and held his arm and smiled at him. Neither the man nor JayB smiled; they simply nodded at each other.

"I guess Spartan and Phoebe don't want to poop on the artificial turf," JayB observed. "I'll take them for a walk, find some grass."

I was unhappy when JayB took Spartan and Phoebe with him somewhere, leaving Odin and me to sit in the shade and avoid looking at Rhiannon, who was sniffing along a line of bushes. Odin kept giving me hurt, accusing glances, but the cat was not my fault.

Alana sat with her friend on a bench. I eyed him distrustfully. Clearly, he still did not like dogs.

"Odin is such a good, sweet dog. No trouble at all," Alana told him. "And Rhiannon already put him in his place."

The man sniffed.

"I've grown really attached to him."

"Already hot here," the man replied.

Alana was silent a moment. "Sure is," she finally agreed comfortably. Alana seemed relaxed and happy, but the man was tense. "I have to tell you," she continued, "it was a real eye-opener to drive here. I've never been in that part of the country, and I just assumed it was all going to be dirt and dry rock, but it's not. Utah's beautiful. Colorado's beautiful. There are rivers and trees. It was just wonderful. And the weather was perfect—except maybe for the tornado." Alana laughed lightly.

"Yeah?"

"Why the look?"

"Why the look? You cruise through beautiful Colorado with waterfalls and I drive from California across the Nevada desert. It's got to be the ugliest stretch of road in the world."

"I'm sorry," Alana apologized in a small voice. "It was your idea, though."

"Yeah, and you didn't really thank me. I mean, I brought your cat and some clothes."

"That's true," Alana agreed. "Thanks. But you did come. . . . Why Las Vegas, of all places? I would have been happy to go to LA." Alana gave him a speculative look, a small smile playing on her lips.

Her friend glanced away. His agitation seemed to be increasing. "Why are you still in Kansas City? You never said you'd be gone this long."

"Well, it took a lot more time to go through my mom's things than I thought it would."

The man glared. "It's just *crap*, Alana. Throw it away."

Alana looked wounded. "Well, no, not all of it is crap. Some of it I'm keeping."

"Oh, I know all about that," he snorted scornfully. "Who do you think's been answering the door to UPS?"

"Right, I know. I'll find a place for it. I'll get a storage unit." Alana sighed. "I got an offer on the house and it fell through at the last second. I didn't take any backup offers because that just seemed wrong. I mean, you make a deal to sell people a house, but only if somebody else drops out? Didn't seem right to me."

"Oh, for God's sake . . ." Guy muttered with a shake of his head.

They were quiet. Odin sprawled on his stomach, his tortured eyes on the cat. I knew what he was feeling: he just wanted the world to go back to being the way it used to be.

"Are you okay, Guy? What's going on? You've been acting strange this whole time."

I glanced at the man because his tension seemed to be peaking. He looked away from Alana. "So, I should tell you—I got a room-mate, to help with the rent."

"What do you mean?" Alana objected. "I've been sending my half this whole time."

"Well, I didn't know if I could count on that. Come on."

"You could count on it, because I've been mailing checks."

The man turned back to Alana, scowling. "It doesn't matter now. She's already moved in."

Alana was silent for a moment. "*She's* already moved in?"

"Don't make a big deal out of this."

Alana looked troubled. "Don't you think you should have talked to me before you let someone move in?"

"Yeah? Well, I had to make a decision quickly. There wasn't time to reach out to you in Prairie Town."

"Okay. So, tell me about this woman roommate."

The man shook his head. "There's nothing to tell."

"Well, sure there is. What's her name?"

The man turned away and peered at the cars driving by. He said something in a soft voice.

"What?" Alana demanded sharply. "What did you say?"

"Nikki," he repeated.

"Nikki. *Nikki*—your ex-girlfriend, Nikki? That's my new room-mate? You moved your ex-girlfriend into our home?"

"Look, you've been acting really weird. I had no idea when you're coming back."

"I told you when I'm coming back: when I sell the house."

"Sure. In the red-hot real-estate market of Kansas City."

"I don't even know what to say to that."

"Where's the gratitude that I was fighting traffic all the way here just so you could be with your *cat*?"

"And to see me," Alana replied pointedly, "right? You came to see me. Or did I dream what happened last night?"

"Sure."

"I'm very unhappy that Nikki has moved into our home without you telling me!"

"Oh really?" the man shot back. "You know you never asked *me* before you started shipping crap to LA. Every day I'm stacking another box on the guest bed."

Alana regarded him with a cold expression. "And where exactly is Nikki sleeping, if the guest bed is covered in boxes?"

The man looked away. There were no cars going by, but he was staring at the same place anyway. "I was going to tell you, but then you left."

"*What?*"

Odin and I both glanced up at the strong emotions cutting the air.

"It started as just a lunch, but then . . ." The man sighed. "You left."

Alana jumped to her feet. "Because my mom died, Guy. She *died.*"

"Sure, but it was really bad timing."

"Oh my God."

"Look, Alana. Things haven't been great between us anyway. So, I brought you your cat, because she said it was the decent thing to do."

"She being *Nikki*?"

He looked at his wrist. "You know what? I have to go."

"No," Alana disagreed firmly. "We have to talk."

"No, we don't." The man stood up. "You know I hate when you act all . . . demanding."

"Demanding? How am I being demanding?"

"You've changed. Remember how easygoing you were at first? Now all I get from you is a bunch of lip."

"No, *you've* changed," Alana said through angry tears. "You said you would never hurt me. You promised. You were gentle and kind, but now you're a . . . where are you going? Guy? Don't just leave!" She stared after the man as he strode away. He did not look back. She wiped her face and I licked her wet, salty hand.

*Dear Diary:*

*It is the job of every dog to keep people cheerful, so we are always alert for the first signs of human sadness. After living with JayB for so long, I've learned that there are many sorts of sadness swirling within him, though outwardly he always seems as happy as Phoebe.*

*I have felt the creeping loneliness in him when we've spent days in our house with only a cat for company. I have noticed a bleakness when he's eating—he'll gaze off at nothing and forget to finish his meal. I nudge him to let him know that he could cheer himself up if he only shared a little of what's left on his plate.*

*When Alana came into our lives, JayB's moods began to swing from one extreme to another. I can't tell if, in the end, Alana is good for him, or not—if she makes him happy, or not.*

Love,
Clancy

# Twenty-eight

We spent a long time in that small dog park. Alana was so, so sad—I could taste it on her skin. She kept wiping her eyes until Odin put his heavy head in her lap.

Rhiannon, of course, made no effort to comfort her, so it was up to Odin and me. We were better suited for the task, anyway.

Eventually Alana pulled out her phone. "No, Guy's left. I'll meet you in the parking garage—the bellman has my luggage," she told it.

A short time later, a nice man loaded all the boxes into the car. Alana put the bag with the cat in the front. We all took a last leg-lift (except Phoebe, who squatted) while our people made obvious preparations to go for a car ride.

Maddy was excited. "The trip back's gonna be a *blast*," she gushed enthusiastically. "Like time travel, only in reverse."

When Rodney climbed through the big sliding door, Maddy reached out and put her arms around him.

He backed away. "Whoa," he cautioned.

"Come here, you," she leered.

"Okay, let's just, you know . . ."

"What I know is that last night was wonderful, times a thousand."

"No, no. Stop, Maddy," Rodney objected. "I need to explain something to you. I don't know if you've ever heard this, but it's state law. What happens in Vegas stays in Vegas."

Maddy was smiling. "Yeah, I know, but not *that*. *That* doesn't stay in Vegas. That goes with us. Forever and ever."

"No. That, exactly *that*. They're talking about *that* when they say what stays in Vegas."

"My life has changed forever," Maddy told Alana, who didn't respond.

Finally, we were all settled into our places in the car. Even Walter.

Cool air began to flow. The car was vibrating, but not moving.

"Well, I'm not at all looking forward to the drive back," Walter said with a sigh.

JayB didn't answer. He was regarding Alana carefully. "You okay?"

Alana sighed and wiped her eyes. "I just had a pretty big fight with Guy."

"Oh?"

She nodded, pressing her lips together. "I think we broke up. We did break up."

"What?" JayB replied. "Oh, I'm sorry."

Alana gave him a weary look.

Maddy leaned forward. "Well, that's just what they do. Men always leave, like a rat from a sinking ship. It's in male DNA to walk away from what's good for them. If it weren't for women, there would never be any babies." Maddy reached over and patted Rodney's arm. He moved it out of her reach. "You know what you have to do now, Alana? You have to go after him. Prove you think he's worth the effort. See, Guy only left because he wants you to chase him down. Otherwise, it means you don't really love him."

JayB frowned. "That doesn't sound like particularly good advice to me."

Rodney was nodding. "Yeah, no, I agree with Maddy. If a woman's really into me and I dump her and she keeps coming around and she wants me, I'll take her back for a while, even if she's not that hot."

"You have such a big heart, Rodney," Maddy praised.

Rodney shrugged. "Well, yeah."

"I wonder if anyone would ever think I was worth chasing after," Alana pondered. She turned to JayB. "What do *you* think I should do? Do you think I should go after him? Would that be *your* advice, JayB?" Her voice had an odd edge to it.

There was a long silence. Walter leaned forward. "Alana, the worst mistake I ever made was letting Celeste walk out on me. I have forever regretted that I didn't go after her. I was hurt, and I let my hurt make my decision for me. I think this is one of those moments that is a pivot point in life, and I think you should go after the person you love. Don't be like me. Stand up for yourself."

Alana remained focused on JayB. "JayB? Do you have anything you want to add?"

JayB pursed his lips. "I think you should do what your heart tells you to do," he advised at last.

There was a silence, then, "Okay," Alana blurted suddenly. "Oh my God, okay. JayB, will you watch Rhiannon and Odin for me? Just for a few days, I promise."

"Sure. I'm expanding into all kinds of new species."

"Way to go," exulted Maddy. "Take him down, like a cheetah taking down a kangaroo. That's what I did." She patted Rodney's arm again. He looked unhappy.

Alana gave a quiet little scream. I wagged, confused, as she jumped out of the vehicle and grabbed a bag from the back. "Okay, I'm taking a cab. I'm going to the airport. Thank you so much, JayB. Thank you, everybody."

The door made a loud *clang* as it slid shut. We all sat there silently for a moment. I watched as Alana ran to a bright-colored car and jumped in the back seat. The car drove away.

Odin and I exchanged glances. Alana had left and the cat had not. Neither of us understood.

"Well," JayB drawled, "that was certainly dramatic."

"It's like the time my sister shot her boyfriend," Maddy agreed. "So romantic."

"She *shot* him?" Rodney repeated, looking worried.

Maddy nodded. "Just with a pellet gun. Of course, my sister didn't know that. I mean, it *looked* like a real gun. Everybody was disappointed."

"I'm sure they were heartbroken," JayB observed blandly. "All right, everyone ready to go?"

All the dogs settled down and let the familiar vibrations wash over us. There was a long, long moment of silence. The other dogs slept, but I remained sitting, my attention rooted on my person. His voice was normal—cheerful, even—but I could feel his distress. I looked around for a squeaky toy or a ball or anything to comfort him, but couldn't find anything.

"Lots of traffic," JayB remarked. "Should have gotten an earlier start."

Walter leaned forward. "I think you kids would be happier if I went back on my own. JayB, turn around and take me to the airport, would you?"

"You should have gone with Alana." JayB sighed. I felt the car changing direction.

"Drop me, too," Rodney requested. "I need to get home."

JayB raised his eyebrows. "How come?"

Rodney sighed wearily. "This Korean deal's going sideways. I'll probably be on the phone all night."

Walter slapped him on the shoulder. "And if it doesn't happen, don't worry about it. Things always have a way of working out, and if they don't, other countries have pig iron, you know?"

"That could be our family motto," JayB suggested.

"Well, I'm going with you, Rodney," Maddy insisted firmly. "We're like two peas in a pot from now on."

"And what about Spartan?" JayB inquired mildly.

We all looked at Spartan, even Phoebe, but he didn't look back.

"Oh, well," Rodney said awkwardly. "I mean, you *are* the dog walker."

"Of course."

"Wonderful," Walter beamed. "I'm glad things are working out."

JayB laughed but didn't sound happy. "It's so wonderful."

We took a car ride to a hot, dry place with lots of noise. Everyone jumped out except JayB, the dogs, and a cat in a bag.

"Okay, then," Walter told JayB, "we'll see you back in the city. Drive safely."

"Sure," JayB said. "What *really* happens in Vegas is that everyone leaves me to drive the animals."

The people walked into a big building. I was unsure what this meant, but I felt fine because I remained with JayB.

We were going for a car ride! Whatever the others were doing, it could not possibly be as fun as that.

The smells were familiar: dry air, heat, and dust. We stopped occasionally for water and to run around, and nice people handed sacks of food to JayB through his open window. He gave us dog food, but he also shared a small amount of what was in the sack.

I loved JayB.

The cat in the bag sat where Alana had been seated. It made almost no noise at all, and occasionally JayB would say, "Are you doing okay, Rhiannon?"

Phoebe allowed me to sleep near her, but if I pressed too close, she would get up and shake. Then she would make her way up to between the front seats and put her face on the seat with the cat and sniff the bag.

"Go sit down now, Phoebe," JayB always instructed. "Go sit."

We all knew Sit, though those of us who were already lying down felt that no additional action was necessary.

We stopped at one of those big buildings with a lot of rooms, but we all stayed in the same one this time. JayB held us by our leashes for a while so that Rhiannon could jump around on the furniture and sniff it and eat some Kelsey-smelling food from a small can. Odin refused to acknowledge the cat was there. Phoebe stretched at the end of her leash toward Rhiannon and seemed delighted. Spartan sprawled on his stomach, unmoved. The cat ignored us all. Eventually, she crept back into her bag.

"I'm zipping it up for the dogs' protection," JayB told her. "You have a good night, Rhiannon."

Fed and watered and content after such a wonderful day, we all found places to sleep. Spartan, Phoebe, and I climbed up on the bed. Rhiannon slept in her bag on top of a piece of furniture with drawers. Odin slept on the floor, as far from Rhiannon as possible. I admired his principled stance.

My person kept letting out exhalations, each sigh laden with sadness. I watched him roll himself over and back under the sheets. I was concerned that, even with dogs lying next to him, JayB was full of loss and despair.

The next day, JayB got up early. The air was cold and still as we climbed into the car after squatting and lifting our legs. We found our usual places and sprawled out for what was our new life: a constant drone of tires, warmth rising from the floor, cool air blowing from vents, and JayB sitting silently.

He pushed at something and a voice filled the car. *"Hi JayB, it's Dominique. Sorry to have missed you. I'm just calling to tell you I'm going to be home late Tuesday, and I'm wondering if you'd be okay bringing Phoebe over on Wednesday?"* Phoebe raised her head, looking confused. *"Call or text me back if that won't work. Otherwise, I guess I'll see you then. And JayB? I'm really looking forward to seeing you again."*

JayB made a long, low noise, a little like a whistle. "Did she just say she was looking forward to seeing her dog-sitter?"

I didn't hear my name, so I put my head back down.

Quite some time later, I heard a different voice.

"Hey, JayB."

"Hi, Alana. How's it going there?"

"Oh, things have been pretty . . . Well, let's just say they're different than what I expected."

"Okay . . ." JayB replied cautiously.

"Anyway, I have a question for you."

"Shoot."

"How far away are you from Grand Junction?"

JayB sat up straighter. "Let me think. It's been about an hour, I guess."

"It's been? You mean you've already passed Grand Junction?"

"Yeah. I got an early start this morning." There was a long silence. "Alana, you there?"

"I'm here. So, would you consider coming back?"

"What do you mean?"

"I'm at the airport in Grand Junction. I just landed. It's complicated. I'd like to explain everything in person."

JayB became very alert. "Sure." He looked out his side window. "I'm practically at an exit now. I'll be there in an hour."

"Thanks. See you then."

I sensed a change in direction. The sun shifted. Odin glanced at me to see if I knew what we were doing, and I acted as if I did. Spartan and Phoebe continued to snooze. The cat stayed in the bag. When we stopped, I wagged because I recognized the scent of the person opening the side door. It was Alana!

All the dogs stood at attention, even Spartan.

"Oh, good dogs. Good dogs," she told us.

She did not have any treats, but we knew she loved us. What I didn't know was how Alana had gotten here. Humans can do all sorts of astounding things.

She slid into the seat next to JayB. They sat there, regarding each other.

"Hi," Alana finally said.

## Dear Diary:

Odin is not happy that there is a bag with a cat in it, especially this cat, Rhiannon, who radiates such malevolence that I can't bring myself to meet her glare. I have the very real sense that if JayB opened the bag and let her out, she would kill us and eat us.

Unlike Odin, Phoebe seems delighted about the cat. She wriggles up into the space between the two front seats and pushes her nose forward as if to try to climb in the bag. She is wagging and happy. Why any dog would be happy to see a bag full of cat is beyond me. Spartan, of course, is neither happy nor unhappy. He has decided to ignore the cat, the same way he ignores everything else in the world.

I have to admit that, in the case of Rhiannon, this seems exactly the right thing to do.

Love,
Clancy

# Twenty-nine

Alana reached out and touched JayB's shoulder. "Good to see you," she murmured softly.

"Good to see you, too," JayB replied.

Alana reached into the bag and pulled out Rhiannon, who made a cat sound at her.

"Oh, sweetie. Oh, sweetie. How did she do last night?"

"She's negotiated a grand truce," JayB advised. "Odin and Spartan find her invisible. Clancy glances at her sort of furtively, but seems terrorized. Phoebe wants to be best friends."

"I think Rhiannon could be friends with a dog, but it would have to be on her terms."

I felt the car gaining speed and knew we were back to going wherever it was we were going.

"So," JayB prodded, "you want to talk about your, uh, side trip?"

Alana sighed, "Well, not really, but I think I should. I sort of owe you an explanation, don't I?" She laughed softly. "Okay, first off, you need to understand that Guy's really smart. As in, brilliant. He works on AI algorithms. You know, computers that can learn?"

JayB nodded. "Heard of it."

"Right. Of course. So anyway, I kind of think he wrote an algorithm on me. Meaning, he learned exactly what I needed. What I wanted to hear. He seemed so kind, so perfect. 'Let me handle that for you,' he'd say. So I think I got to the point where I sort of let him take over my life. I stopped *thinking*. And when I started having doubts, I sort of shrugged them off."

"And did you finally get a chance to talk to him about that?" JayB asked.

Alana laughed again. "Let's just say, things did not go well. When I let myself into my apartment—a place I'm paying rent on, by the way—it was clear that Guy was shocked to see me. He had just arrived himself and was sitting there having a glass of wine with this woman. Her name is Nikki. He and Nikki used to go out."

"Okay," JayB responded neutrally.

"No, I should have figured this out. I don't know why I thought showing up would fix anything. Nikki's been back in the picture for a while and I didn't know it, but clearly the moment I left for Kansas City, she made her move."

"So you're saying that she started seeing Guy on the side, even though you were living with him?"

"That's exactly what I'm saying."

"Wow."

Alana shook her head. "I don't know why I just explained it the way I did. It's like I work so hard to sugarcoat everything. I *had* figured it out. By the time my plane pulled back from the gate, I *knew* what I was going to find in Marina del Rey. I *knew* Nikki would be there. I let everyone's encouragement convince me to, in Maddy's words, take him down like a kangaroo. Then I was so busy trying to make the flight—barely got to the jetway before they closed the door—that I didn't have time to think until we were wheels-up, and then I second-guessed my whole decision. I felt sick inside, but I went home anyway. My *former* home."

"Maybe if you hadn't, you always would have wondered if you should have."

"Maybe. No, probably not. Guy was pretty clear with me; I just didn't want to hear it. Seeing Nikki's smug face pounded it into me in a way I really didn't need."

"I'm so sorry."

"The second I saw his expression, I knew how foolish I was being. In the end, it wasn't because of Nikki that Guy didn't want me there. He didn't want me there because he didn't want *me*."

"That must have been awful."

Alana nodded. "I couldn't breathe. I turned around and left, and while I was waiting for Uber, I kept listening for him to come running after me. But of course, he didn't. I'm the only person dumb enough to do something like that."

"You're not dumb. Everyone in the van told you to go."

Alana stared at him. "Everyone but you."

"I had ulterior motives."

"Yeah? Tell me."

There was a shift in the mood between the people then. I sensed it, and Phoebe raised her head as well. Odin was asleep.

JayB shrugged. "It's just that I've wondered for a long time what would happen if there were no guy named Guy."

"What do you want to happen?"

"You're going to make me spell everything out, aren't you?"

"Please."

JayB nodded and cleared his throat. "The night we were in a Disney movie?"

"The fireflies."

"Right. The reason why that felt a little overpowering is because it was. Overpowering. For me, I mean. You said what . . . that you were swept up in the moment?"

"Something like that."

"Well, that's exactly how I felt. I didn't even think about it, we were just kissing."

Alana regarded him intently. "You make me feel different than anyone has. Empowered. Like I can do things. Like I'm . . . capable."

"Because you *are* capable."

"You said I should do what my heart tells me. But what if there's no clear signal? What if my heart is confused?"

"Then, maybe take your time? Think things through?"

"Or maybe *don't* think things through. Isn't that what we both do, so much that everyone complains about it?"

"It's one of the eight simple rules," he admitted.

"So maybe I should stop doing that. Maybe I should just be in the moment. Like I was the night of the fireflies. Make a bad decision and own it, instead of stewing in regret."

JayB looked troubled. "So kissing me was a bad decision?"

"It felt like it the next morning. So, what did I do? I ran from it, ran from you. The way I run from any situation I think I might come to regret later. I'm a coward, JayB. I don't have any spine at all."

"So you regretted our kiss?"

"No, I regretted that I was afraid to kiss you again."

JayB gazed at her a moment before looking back at the road. "So you're saying the next time your heart tells you something . . ."

". . . I'm going to listen," she finished for him.

JayB smiled. "Sounds like a plan."

"It's a lack of a plan," Alana corrected.

"Got it. So now . . . What happens next?"

"I don't know. I arranged for my stuff at the apartment to go into storage and I bought a ticket, hoping you'd pick me up as you drove past Grand Junction. I didn't expect you to have passed it already."

"It was worth turning around."

They didn't say anything for some time, then JayB frowned. "I'm not sure what I'm seeing up there." I could sense that he was alarmed, so I sat up and focused.

The vehicle came to a halt. As it did, the other dogs jumped up, yawning in anticipation of fun.

"Why're all the cars stopped, I wonder?" Alana asked.

JayB nodded to the window. "I've been watching that cloud. See that black cloud? I thought it was a storm, but now I think it might be a fire."

Alana lowered her window and all the dogs raised our noses.

"I don't smell any smoke," JayB noted. I could tell that Odin and Phoebe were reacting to the same thing I was—the clear, acrid scent of smoke on the air. Spartan, of course, didn't change his expression.

"We're not moving," Alana fretted.

"Why don't we get off here in Glenwood Springs?"

Alana was looking at her phone. "It *is* a fire. The interstate's closed up ahead. We can't get any farther east on this road today."

JayB thought about it. "Is there a way to go around?"

Alana continued to stare at her phone. "Yeah, but it's some distance. You got to get south, through Aspen, and then go north on 24. Looks like we'll add several hours to the trip." She glanced up at him. "We should just stay here, see if they put the fire out."

JayB nodded. "Good idea."

I felt the car yaw as JayB swerved and drove very slowly. Soon, we pulled up in front of a building like many we had seen the past couple of days—lots of windows in the front.

"My treat," Alana announced, opening her door. "You wait here with the dogs, okay?"

Alana was inside for a while, long enough for us dogs to settle down. Then she came out and walked around to JayB's window.

"So"—she waved something at him—"with the fire, they're completely booked. I got the last available room."

"I see."

"I told them about the dogs, and it's okay with a deposit, which I paid, but it's all of us bunking together."

"That's fine," JayB observed carefully. "I can take the couch."

Alana gazed at him levelly. "What if my heart is telling me I want to sleep in your arms tonight?"

That night, the dogs were not allowed to lie on the bed for some reason. I wondered if it had something to do with Rhiannon. The next morning, JayB took us for leg lifts and squats, and then we piled into the vehicle. He stood watching Alana load bags in the back.

When she slammed the back door shut, he said, "Fire's out and the road's back open. Want to drive for a while, then stop for a meal?"

We did a car ride, and then the people sat outside at a table and ate things while all the dogs scrunched uncomfortably at their legs. We all smelled the bacon up there, and tried to press as close to the humans as we could. Phoebe even put her head in Alana's lap, which I thought was a pretty good maneuver. We sat there for quite some time. Even after a woman came and cleared away the plates, taking the fragrance of bacon with her, we still sat.

"So, this newspaper is pretty interesting," JayB observed. "It's full of want ads."

"For what?" Alana wanted to know. "Selling skis and snowmobiles?"

"Well, sure; that, but also, they're looking for people. Like, everybody's hiring here, and they're offering pretty good money. Actually, very good money."

"Really? To work here in the mountains?" Alana glanced around. "It's beautiful, although I don't know what the winters are like. I mean, there's still snow up there."

"I know, because I just read about it. They get more than three hundred days of sunshine a year. It snows, but then the sun comes out. There's skiing and snowshoeing."

"It sounds like you should work for the tourism department," Alana said with a smile.

"They're one of the places that is hiring, in fact," JayB responded, grinning back.

"What's going on here that there's such a hiring boom?" she asked.

"I think I've got it figured out. They're offering high salaries, but there's no place to live. The rent in this county is so expensive. To move here, you really need a chunk of money, down payment on a home."

Alana gave him a shrewd look. "You're saying that very deliberately, so there's a point you're making, right?"

"Well, I've got a free and clear house in Prairie Village. Originally, I moved there without any sort of plan. Maybe I thought I'd get closer to Walter, but I think he's going to adopt Rodney instead."

Alana laughed.

"And, I don't know, I've never wanted to be a ski bum like my stepbrother, but it's a fun sport. That's in the winter. In the summer, there's biking and hiking, and the weather here is glorious."

"So, you're thinking of selling your house and moving to, what, Summit County? Here? Frisco?"

JayB gave her a frank look. "It might be an interesting thing to do. Pull up roots, make a fresh start. New challenges and experiences. I could afford a nice place, and then get a job. I do have skills. I mean, I'm considered one of the top dog walkers in my field."

Alana laughed delightedly.

Soon we were back in the big car. I was content. I slept.

After a long time, JayB said, "How about you?"

"How about me, what?"

"Back when we were at breakfast, what we were talking about. How would you feel about pulling up stakes and moving someplace acutely different? Being, I don't know"—he arched his eyebrows—"spontaneous."

Alana smiled at him, but the smile faltered. "I don't know. I'm not sure what I want right now."

"Okay."

"JayB. I don't . . . I wouldn't read too much into last night."

He shot her a glance. "Is this like the morning after the fireflies? You're feeling regrets?"

"No, no regrets. But I don't know . . . that was one thing, but talking about moving to Colorado? Together? That's a whole different deal."

"I get it. What happens in Glenwood Springs stays in Glenwood Springs."

Alana laughed. Then her mood turned serious. "Part of listening to my heart is making sure it's *my* heart. If I went from living with Guy to living with you, I'd be repeating a pattern I've been stuck in my whole adult life."

"I understand."

Alana nodded. "You really do, don't you?"

They were quiet long enough for me to settle into a nap, but I opened my eyes when Alana spoke again. "Oh, hey, I sold the house."

"Again?"

"This time it's people who claim to have all cash. Unloaded their place in California and have a ton of money. Picked Prairie Village because it's such a good place to raise a family."

"I thought you wanted to meet the people first, though, make sure they weren't Hannibal Lecter."

Alana shook her head. "Guy said that was ridiculous, that I shouldn't care. That I should just take the highest bidder."

"Okay."

"God," Alana groaned.

"What is it?"

"I'm just . . . stupid. I always let Guy tell me what to do about *everything*. I didn't visit my mom or even talk to her for more than two years." She pounded a fist against the side of the car. "I *hate* that I did that. Why did I let him tell me what to think?"

"Hey, why don't we pull over at this rest area, take a break? Breathe in some Kansas air."

We dogs were delighted when the car stopped and the door slid open. A new place!

## Dear Diary:

Alana is angry, I can tell. But she is not angry at us dogs—I can tell that, too. When people are angry at dogs, they speak sternly to us. Usually, we don't understand the reason for the harsh tones, but we believe we've been bad dogs and feel ashamed.

Alana doesn't seem upset with JayB, either. Often when people are angry at other people, they shout, but other times they say nothing. When one person is unhappy with another, dogs can tell. That makes us feel like bad dogs, too.

People are supposed to be happy around dogs. That's why there are dogs.

The only thing that would not make me feel like a bad dog would be if Alana were angry at the cat in the bag. Rhiannon is mean to dogs—a bad cat, in other words, deserving of stern words from Alana. But Alana only speaks soothingly to the cat.

So who is she mad at?

Love,
Clancy

# Thirty

JayB gathered our leashes and walked with Alana.

She turned to JayB. "You know what? I never stand up for myself. That's my problem."

"You did say that, but I'm not sure I agree."

"Well, who are you to disagree with that?"

JayB dropped his eyes. "I'm sorry; I just see a person who's being hard on herself for no reason. I think you're stronger than you're making out."

Alana looked around. "How far away are we now?"

"It will be after sunset when we get there, even though in June it feels like the sun doesn't go down until midnight."

"Then we should get back in the car," she suggested curtly. "Why did we stop?"

"I just thought you could use a moment."

"So you decided for me that I needed to stop, and I went along with it because I have no free will," she observed bitterly. "I just let everyone walk all over me. Rodney and Walter invited themselves to Vegas and I couldn't say no. They told me to chase after Guy, so I did. I don't make a decision for myself, ever." She glared at my person. "I allow men to run my life."

JayB said nothing and remained quiet for the rest of what turned out to be a very short walk. Then we jumped back in the car for more car ride, which had all us dogs wagging with excitement. I couldn't tell how the cat felt.

For a long time, we drove with no people talking.

"At least one problem is solved," Alana finally observed.

"Which one?"

"What to do about Odin. I told the leasing company to look for a place that takes dogs. Odin? You're going to live with me in LA, okay?"

Odin flapped his tail but otherwise didn't move.

I recognized the scents as we approached home. I knew where we were and so did Phoebe. We stopped in a driveway, and when JayB opened the sliding door, Spartan jumped out. He was wagging that little stub of a tail of his as he trotted up to the front door. I smelled Rodney when he opened it and I wagged a little in greeting, but I stayed in the car with Alana and the rest of the dogs. Rodney waved, grabbed Spartan's leash, and trotted across his yard and up to Alana's window. She sat, looking at him, and he laughed and rapped his knuckles on the glass, so she lowered it.

"Hey, Alana," he greeted. "Oh man, are you a sight for sore eyes. How was the ride? I didn't realize you were going to be here this soon. So, did you dump the guy, is that why you're back after just one night? Did you fly back to KCI or what?"

"I don't want to talk to you right now, Rodney," she replied.

Rodney looked nonplussed. "What do you mean?"

"I mean," Alana repeated evenly, "I'm tired and I don't want to talk to you right now."

Rodney laughed. "You're not serious." He put a hand on his heart. "You got to me." He was still grinning when Alana put the window back up.

JayB slid into the front seat. "Ready to go?"

She nodded.

JayB started the car and glanced at her. "Look, why don't you come to my house. The sitter dropped off Kelsey; we'll introduce the cats to each other. I'll make you a late-night snack, maybe have a glass of wine?"

He seemed very awkward.

"It's getting pretty late."

JayB nodded. "Just a bit? Unwind after the trip?" He gave her a shy smile.

She was expressionless and then she shook her head and laughed softly. "Why not."

I was happy to lead the charge of the dogs into my house, to show Phoebe it was still my territory. Odin followed willingly, and

Phoebe, as always, was delighted to trot along with us, though she kept turning to stare at the cat bag. I sensed Kelsey fleeing our arrival the moment we opened the front door. She had probably been in the window the whole time we'd been gone, glaring out at the world, hating everything.

"Hang on," JayB requested. "I'll put Odin and Phoebe in the back room and keep Clancy here on his leash. I'm not worried about Rhiannon around the dogs, but Kelsey's terrified of Odin."

We were in the kitchen. I registered JayB strolling with Phoebe and Odin down the hallway. He put them into a bedroom and shut the door.

"Kelsey . . . Kelsey," he called. "Kelsey, Kelsey, Kelsey. Where are you, kitty kitty?"

Cats sometimes come when they're called, but only if they feel like it.

Alana reached into the case and set her cat silently on the floor. Rhiannon immediately started to lick her paw, looking around contemptuously. I knew that she was probably missing all the signs that she was here as my guest—not that I had any expectation of anything but rank hostility from her.

JayB rustled Kelsey's food bag. There was still an open can of food up on the counter, but he was going to give her even more to eat. This never happens to a dog.

Soon, I sensed Kelsey padding her way silently down the hall toward us. She walked into the kitchen and caught sight of Rhiannon. Kelsey *screamed*.

It was a sound I had never heard her make before, and it was absolutely chilling: a high, deep-throated, full-bodied cry. She immediately squatted and made a puddle of cat urine on the floor. Then she turned and fled down the hallway.

JayB shrugged. "Well, that went pretty well."

Alana laughed. "I take it Kelsey's never had a roommate before."

JayB shook his head. "No, but I think people and cats should get used to different circumstances, don't you?"

Alana folded her arms and leaned up against the counter, regarding him as he unspooled some paper towels. "So that's how it's going to be?"

"Meaning . . ."

"You're going to continue making all these supposedly subtle points? People and cats should get used to different circumstances, huh? Like, move to Kansas City, start a doggie gift shop in a restaurant?"

"This will all go easier if you just pretend I'm as smart as you are," he replied with a smile.

"I feel like Kelsey."

He cocked his head. "You feel like you're going to pee on the floor? Because I'm almost out of paper towels."

Alana shook her head, not smiling. "No, I mean I feel like my world was perfectly normal and predictable and I was happy, and then my mother died and everything changed. Suddenly I've got to find a new place and my boyfriend and I broke up and I've got a dog. How's that for different circumstances? Is that good enough?"

"It's pretty good," he admitted, wiping up the cat urine. I could still smell it even after several scrubbings. I knew Phoebe would be most intrigued.

"I'm already under a lot of pressure, JayB," she continued quietly. "Could I ask you to just not add to it? Maybe give me a break?"

"Of course."

"I've had a lot of decisions thrust at me all at once."

"I completely understand."

She gave him a small smile. He smiled back. I wagged because I could feel the anger leaving the room.

"So, hey, what do you want to eat?"

"Do you have any fruit?"

JayB pulled out some raspberries. "Of course! I am a full-service—" He stopped.

"A full-service what?" Alana inquired, regarding him sternly. "You weren't going to say full-service *boyfriend,* were you?"

JayB grinned sheepishly.

Alana gave him a long look. I wagged tentatively. Finally, she shook her head. "You're really giving yourself a promotion there, big boy."

JayB stepped up to her. "Sorry. I didn't mean to violate protocol. I know in the manual it says you have to post for the position and interview all the candidates before making the final determination."

"And then I have to have a security guard present, in case some woman shows up to punch you in the nose."

"That's also in the manual."

She looked intently into JayB's eyes. "I can't move this fast, JayB," she whispered. "I'm not at all sorry about last night, but I'm also not ready to make life-changing decisions."

"How long is your leave of absence?"

"They told me to take as much time as I need."

"Okay. I'm telling you the same thing. Take as much time as you need, Alana."

He reached out his arms and Alana stepped into them. I watched with interest as their mouths came together. I felt myself wagging because of the emotions pouring off of them, and I wondered if I should try to jump up and wriggle in between their hug as they clutched each other. I was preparing to do that when I heard a loud rap on the door, followed by the doorbell. I, of course, barked. It's my responsibility to do so whenever someone comes to the door. I heard Odin and Phoebe responding from down the hall.

Rhiannon acted unfazed by the barking. Kelsey was still cowering under a bed somewhere. JayB and Alana were staring at each other.

The doorbell rang again.

JayB stepped back and blinked. "In order of who I don't want that to be, I'm going to go with Rodney, then Maddy, then my father, then the FBI."

JayB opened the front door.

"Hey!" a man boomed. I wagged because it was Walter. "Why'd

you lock your door?" He pushed inside. He held a big bottle in one hand.

"To keep people from walking in without knocking, I'm guessing?"

"I'm not interrupting anything, am I?" Walter asked with a chortle. He presented his bottle and smiled. "We have cause for celebration."

"And this is such good *timing* for that celebration," JayB responded.

Alana laughed.

"Hello, Alana, you're looking lovely as always," Walter greeted. He grinned at JayB. "You'll never guess."

"You and Rodney are investing in a drug cartel," JayB speculated.

Walter guffawed. "Nope. You ready? *Celeste is coming to visit.* Time for some champagne."

I looked up at JayB because he seemed stunned. A long silence followed.

"You know," Alana stated carefully, "I think I'm going to go back to my house and unpack and everything. You two can talk."

"Sure," JayB agreed faintly.

"Walter, I'm sorry," she said regretfully. "We haven't had a moment to talk about your bank statements yet. I've been . . . preoccupied . . . with other things. And obviously this is not a good time. But we need to do it soon." She and JayB exchanged meaningful glances.

Walter grinned. "Money can always wait."

Alana put Rhiannon back in the bag, retrieved Odin, and left. Phoebe tracked them to the door, then stopped, puzzled, when it shut behind them. She looked to me for an explanation. I didn't know how to tell her that this is just what people do. Humans come and go, with or without dogs.

"So did I hear you correctly?" JayB asked finally. "Mom is coming to visit?"

"*Exactemente,*" Walter responded. "Where are your champagne glasses?"

JayB wordlessly pulled two tinkling glasses from a cabinet. With a flourish, Walter played with the bottle in his hand and there was a sudden loud *pop* and a dog toy flew up, hit the ceiling, and bounced on the floor. I jumped on it, but then let Phoebe have it. She lay down and began chewing on it vigorously until only bits remained.

"When is she coming?" JayB asked his father.

"She gets here Thursday."

"Thursday, as in, day after tomorrow? Wow." He held up his glass and touched it briefly to Walter's before they sipped.

"So, what do you think?" Walter asked slyly. "Maybe her marriage isn't as solid as you said it was."

JayB shook his head. "I didn't say anything about her marriage," he corrected. "I don't talk to Mom about Twain."

"Twain," Walter snorted derisively. "What kind of name is that?"

"We've been through this," JayB responded patiently. "So, all right, she's coming. Do you know for how long?"

Walter shook his head, but then gave a wink. "I'm hoping I can talk her into staying for a while. But if she wants to go somewhere else"—he shrugged—"Maui, Paris, whatever she wants. We'll go."

"Okay . . . but, those sound like expensive trips," JayB agreed cautiously. "Maybe wait until we've had a chance to sit down with Alana about the numbers. Okay, Dad?"

Walter waved a hand. "Nah. This is one of the happiest days of my life, son."

JayB nodded carefully. "Well, be sure not to tell her that."

Walter stared in surprise.

"Look, all I'm saying is, you need to go slow. You know how Mom's going to react if you take the position that her coming here means she's leaving her husband for you? That might not be what's going on. People don't like to be rushed into things, especially when it comes to relationships."

Walter thought about this.

"You need to give her space," JayB concluded.

"Is that what you're doing with Alana? Giving her space?" Walter challenged shrewdly.

"Actually, before you showed up, there was very little space. I'm just saying, remember why Mom left in the first place."

"She left because I was broke," Walter contended. "That's not the case now."

"Is that really why she left?" JayB asked.

*Dear Diary:*

*I'm noticing that, over time, a change has come over Odin. It's subtle, but something is tiring him out from within and slowing him in obvious ways. This is beyond his suffering over the loss of his person. This is physical.*

*He smells a little different as well. Again, subtle, but something is going on; it's on his breath. Our eyes meet—he knows that I know.*

Love,
Clancy

# Thirty-one

The next day, Odin did not come to greet us when Phoebe, JayB, and I stopped at his house.

"How goes the packing? Need any help?" JayB asked.

Phoebe went into the kitchen to sniff along the floor, but I padded over to where Odin lay in his bed and lowered my nose to him. He tiredly raised his head. I knew he would not want to walk with us, but he'd go if JayB asked, because that's what dogs do.

"There's not much, actually. Thanks anyway," Alana said. "You still want me for dinner?"

"That's why I came by, to make sure you didn't try to get out of it." Alana laughed.

We took a long walk, just Phoebe and JayB and me. I was so happy. I pictured chasing Phoebe around in the old dog park. If that mean, brown dog showed up to challenge her, I would show her that her dog Clancy could be there for her, too. Unless he threatened to bite me or something.

But we didn't go to the dog park. Instead, we turned up a sidewalk that was familiar to me. This was Phoebe's house. Phoebe strained at the end of her leash.

JayB pushed a button. The door opened and Dominique fell to her knees. "Phoebe!" she cried.

Phoebe wagged and whimpered, climbing around and around Dominique, kissing her face out of absolute joy. I couldn't help but wag.

Dominique smiled up at JayB. "She looks great. Thank you so much for taking care of her."

"No problem. How's your sister?"

"Come on in, please." We followed Dominique into her house.

She waved her hand. "Don't pay attention to the living room. The furniture in there was all Bedford's, and he took it when he left."

"I see," JayB observed neutrally.

"My sister's fine. Thanks for asking. It was really bad at first. I was so scared. But she's going to make a full recovery."

"Glad to hear it. That's great news. So Bedford . . . took his furniture?"

Dominique rolled her eyes. "He just couldn't handle any of it. Completely folded in a crisis. Couldn't make a decision. We're there and my sister's in surgery and he leaves to go find a gym. I mean, who does that?" She shook her head. "We were already having problems, but this sort of cemented it for me." She focused on JayB. "He told me, though, how you helped. He explained about the plane tickets and everything. I knew he couldn't have put that together on his own. Thank you, JayB." Dominique stepped forward and gave JayB a tight hug. Both Phoebe and I did a reflexive Sit, reading something in the room that hadn't been there before. "So, how's the dog-walking business going?"

"Well, actually," JayB answered after a moment's pause, "I'm running a restaurant now."

Dominique's face reflected her surprise. "Oh, nice. I didn't realize you were in that line of work."

"I wasn't. It's a long story."

"Okay." Dominique smiled. "Maybe sometime you'll tell me that long story?"

"Of course. I'm still walking dogs, but now I only do it for the glamour."

Dominique laughed, then frowned. "So, is this a sneaky way of telling me I'm going to have to find someone else to walk Phoebe?"

JayB nodded. "Pretty soon. I don't want to leave you in the lurch, but I really only sort of stumbled into dog-walking by accident. It's—"

"Another long story?" Dominique guessed.

"Exactly."

She pouted. "Well, I'm sorry to hear it, if I can be honest. I realized as I was flying home just how much I've come to look forward to seeing you when you come over."

"Oh," he fumbled. "It's . . . always nice to see you, too, Dominique."

She smiled, reaching out to smooth the fur on Phoebe's head.

We left a little while later. "What the heck was that, Clancy?" JayB asked. "Am I completely wrong, or was she dropping hints? And why *now*? It's like some sort of cosmic joke." He looked down at me. "You know what 'cosmic' means, right? Of course you do."

I picked up on my name and wagged, not sure what he was saying. I hoped it was something like, "Let's go back and get Phoebe," but he didn't say her name at all.

Later, I wagged instead of barking when I heard a light tap at the front door, because I smelled Odin on the other side.

Alana was standing on the front steps, carrying a box. "I brought you gifts," she told JayB brightly.

JayB peered into the box. "So, I take it you think I need to change my shampoo."

Alana laughed. "These are just some things from the house that I'll wind up not using. Shame to throw them away. A half a bottle of shampoo is better than none."

"That's what I always say." JayB took the box. "So, how many days?"

"I'm leaving Saturday," Alana replied, following him into the house. "Right after the closing. I met the couple buying the place. They're really nice. She's pregnant and they've got a dog."

"Oh, good," JayB replied. "I've been wanting to grow my business. Babies are like dogs, right? You just need to let them out in the yard to pee every so often." He smiled at her. "Any chance the deal might fall through like the first one?"

Alana shook her head. "All cash."

"So that's it, then. Saturday. Three days, and then you and Odin are back on the road."

"Today, tomorrow, Friday. Three days," she affirmed. "I don't have a new apartment yet, so I'll probably do Vrbo."

"You want company again for this road trip?" JayB asked tentatively.

Alana gazed at JayB for a long, long moment. Odin and I both understood something significant was happening in the room. My reaction was to do Sit. Odin's was to move slowly into the living room and settle into his corner with a mild sigh.

Finally, she shook her head. "You know what the expression 'on the bounce' means?"

"Sure."

"What?"

"Well," JayB pondered, "on the bounce is when someone jumps out a window and you try to grab him and you miss—you can catch him on the bounce."

Alana laughed delightedly. "You totally got me with that one." Gradually, her smile faded. "Losing Mom has affected me far more, and in far more ways, than I would have thought. It's as if I was living on auto-pilot, and when she passed, the auto-pilot disengaged. Now that I've taken over, I need to figure out how to fly the airplane."

"So it's the *airplane* that bounces."

"Every bad decision I've ever made in relationships came when I was on the bounce. Like I am right now, from Guy. If I . . . moved here. Stayed here . . ." Her eyes searched his. "Wouldn't that be going back on auto-pilot? Letting the airplane fly itself?"

"Wouldn't moving back to LA and going back to the job you dislike be the same? Auto-pilot?"

"That is . . . a very good question," she conceded. She focused on him. "Do you think . . . I don't know. Would you ever consider moving back to California?"

JayB thought about it. "That would feel like a step backward to me. I'd be willing to go almost anywhere else, but I've *done* California."

Alana nodded. "Fair enough. But you grew up here. You've done that, too."

"Kansas City's not so bad."

"I know. Everyone who lives here seems to love it, almost like you're all in a cult or something. But I need to figure out my next move. I've done what I came here to do—the house is sold, and my mom's stuff is gone. Time to turn the page."

"You're standing up for yourself."

Alana gave him a wry smile.

"But it isn't really Kansas City keeping me here," JayB explained. "If you'd like to know the truth, I'm looking forward to turning the restaurant around. Get it money-making. And then on to the next spontaneous adventure."

"I do get that part. Wanting to save the restaurant. It's gotten to me a little, too. You know what we should think about putting on the menu? Dog treats. Gourmet, homemade, I mean."

"Fantastic idea. You're amazing."

Alana blushed. "Thank you."

"So how do we get something like that started?"

Alana held up a hand. "*We* don't, because I'm not going to be here. Look, JayB, I *really* don't want to be talked into anything right now. Can we just enjoy the next few days together?"

"Sure. Except I told Walter we'd go to his place Friday. Day after tomorrow. To go over all his numbers. Not exactly fun. I'll do the heavy lifting, but when it comes to the facts—like I said, he'll listen to you."

Alana sighed. "I won't enjoy it, but sure."

"What you *will* enjoy is my Cajun spaghetti."

Alana laughed. "*What?*"

JayB looked sheepish. "Okay, I called DesMoines and she had me tell her what I had in the pantry and she gave me the recipe. It's pretty good."

When Alana and Odin left that night, he was moving very slowly.

We did not go to get Spartan or Phoebe the next morning, but we did take a walk. Odin and Alana were waiting on our front steps when we returned.

"Why didn't you just barge into the house like everybody else?" JayB asked her.

Alana laughed. "You ready for me to buy you lunch? An ad came up in my feed this morning for a place where the dogs can run in a fenced-in area."

"Let's go."

We walked to JayB's car and I hopped in and wagged, but Odin sat on the ground and looked at the leap to the seat as if it were too much. JayB lifted Odin into the back seat and leaned over him. "Are you okay, Odin? You're not in any pain, are you?"

"What's wrong?" Alana asked, concerned.

Odin flapped his tail once. It reminded me of when he crawled on his belly to his person and then rolled on his side. He was in the same position and his tail wagged the same way. It was Odin's way of responding to a person's love.

"He just seems to have run out of gas all of a sudden," JayB replied apprehensively.

"Should I take him to a vet?"

JayB gave her a long, searching look. "Yeah. I think it's a good idea. I've got probably the best vet in Kansas, Dr. Deb. I'll call her for you." He straightened. "Rain check on that lunch?"

"You're worried about him."

"I am."

"Then, sure, I think I'll take him in right away."

Odin took a short nap in the car while Alana walked up the street to get her vehicle, then JayB moved him to the back seat of her car. I wagged, completely confused but accepting the situation, because when it comes to car rides, people know what they're doing.

The day was odd, because JayB was busy washing things and moving around but not doing anything a dog could identify as fun. I watched him, alert for any ball-throwing he might undertake, but he did nothing of the sort.

We were out the door the moment Alana's car wheeled into the driveway. I could smell Odin in the back, but he remained there while Alana slid out and went to JayB. They embraced in a long hug, and then Alana stepped back, wiping her eyes. She held up a piece of paper, her hand trembling a little. "It's called hemangiosarcoma."

"So, cancer?"

She nodded.

"Oh, no. Poor Odin."

My person was now as sad as Alana. I nosed his leg.

"Inoperable and incurable," Alana elaborated. "The vet—you were right, she's amazing—says that it's a fragile tumor by his liver. Fragile meaning it bleeds internally sometimes, which makes Odin feel really weak, like he is now. Then he'll improve, because a lot of blood and nutrients flow to the liver, so the bleeding heals. With some dogs there's pain, and when that happens you have to . . . well, you know . . . Other times, most dogs, they just live with it awhile, and then one day . . ." Alana gave JayB a dismal smile. "Gone."

JayB opened the back door and knelt next to Odin. I sniffed curiously.

"Odin," my person whispered softly. "I'm so sorry, buddy. You're a good dog." He looked up at Alana. "There's nothing we can do?"

"Not really. Might have to carry him to the car and certainly up stairs. But he could go on like this for a long time, just really tired all the time. Keep him comfortable, she said."

JayB stared down at Odin. I stared at JayB. "He is an old dog, I guess."

"That's what Dr. Deb said. That we all have to go sometime, and that of all the things that can happen to big dogs, this is one of the least painful. Like I said, she was wonderful."

That evening I was a little shocked to see JayB put a pillow on the couch and lift Odin onto the pillow. Odin sighed contentedly, but didn't eat when my person put a little food out for him in a bowl. To help as best I could, I ate the food myself.

JayB and Alana had people food and laughed a lot. I wagged. I realized then that, though I had not managed to coax Dominique and Phoebe into living with us, Alana was around all the time now, with Odin. So I guess my charm worked.

Alana kissed JayB after dinner, but stepped back from him. "I can't sleep over tonight," she whispered.

"No, of course. I knew that."

"I'll see you tomorrow morning, though. To go with you to Walter's."

Odin, sensing departure, shook and jumped off the couch.

JayB smiled. "I guess he's good to walk home."

That night, I sensed a deep sadness in JayB and slept pressed close up against him. He was restless and up out of bed shortly after the sun rose.

We drove to Alana's, which was unusual—it was such a short walk. Odin joined me in the back seat and Alana sat up front.

"How'd he do?" JayB asked.

"Fine," Alana replied. "Normal, even. Ate breakfast."

"And how about you?"

"Hardly slept. Just . . . so much to think about. You?"

"Same," JayB told her. "Exactly the same."

The car ride did not last very long. When we all got out, I knew I had been to this house before. In back, it had a great yard for running in, but we didn't do that. We followed JayB as he knocked on the front door.

Walter opened it, because it was his house. "Hey, there," he greeted us with a grin. "This is an unexpected surprise."

"Unexpected, in that I told you we were coming?"

Walter chuckled. "Come on in."

We all stepped through the door. Odin immediately curled up on a rug.

"I got your text. Is the dog okay?" Walter asked.

"He's moving fine this morning," said JayB. "Doesn't seem to be in any pain or anything at the moment."

Walter gestured to the other room. "I was just going to make some breakfast for myself. Are you two hungry?"

"I'm good," Alana replied as the two of them followed Walter into the kitchen. I did a Sit beneath the table, because a dog always has hope, even with Walter.

JayB cleared his throat. "So, Dad, Alana reviewed your personal financials like you asked, and we're here to tell you the conclusions."

"Excellent." Walter beamed.

JayB nodded. "Well, okay, I don't know if I would use the word 'excellent.' There are other words, but that's probably not the one."

I looked up with a wag because I heard someone approaching. A woman I had not met before descended the stairs and stepped into the room.

JayB stared at her.

"Hello, everyone," she greeted graciously.

I wagged harder.

JayB took an audible breath. When he spoke, his voice sounded strained. "Hi, Mom."

*Dear Diary:*

*When people meet dogs for the first time, they often extend a hand, knuckles up, as if hiding a treat. And sometimes there is a treat, but usually it's just a hand.*

*Sniffing the offered fingers tells a dog a lot about a person. A lick does an even better job, but some humans jerk away when I do that.*

*This new woman smells strongly like flowers, and strongly like Walter. She seems nice.*

Love,
Clancy

# Thirty-two

I wagged as JayB stood and the woman came across the kitchen to hug him. He kissed her on the cheek. I could tell by her scent that I had never met her before.

"Mom, this is Alana."

"So nice to meet you, Alana. I'm Celeste." The woman held out both hands and Alana, a little awkwardly, stepped into an embrace. "Walter has told me so much about you."

"Whereas Walter hasn't told *us* much about anything," JayB noted.

"There's my Jago, always loading his words with extra meaning," the woman observed with a smile. "We do need to catch up. I came on short notice. Can we do lunch today?"

"Sure."

"Terrific."

Walter gestured to the kitchen. "Celeste, would you like me to make you some eggs?"

She shook her head. "No. I'd like to get back to the hotel and freshen up." She turned to JayB. "I'm staying at the Raphael on the Plaza. Would you swing by? Around, say, twelve-thirty?"

"Fine. I'll get us reservations somewhere."

"Okay. Bye-bye." She waved her fingers and turned and walked out of the room. I glanced up at JayB, who gave no indication that we were going anywhere. I got no clear sense of what he was feeling.

"Bye, honey," Walter called after her.

The nice lady left the house, and there was a short silence in the room.

"Well, Dad, your face is the very definition of smug right now," JayB commented.

"Who wants coffee?" Walter offered expansively. "I've got this new gizmo. It makes espresso and cappuccino and foofoo and Wi-Fi."

"Sure, yes, that would be nice," Alana replied.

Walter pointed. "Jago, would you make us some coffee?"

My person stood and went to some cupboards, opening them and pulling things out. I glanced at Odin to see if he understood that the sounds we were hearing might lead to treats, but he wasn't interested.

"So you're still planning to leave for California?" Walter asked Alana.

"Tomorrow night. We close the house sale at three, then I'll get on the road."

"Well, then. I want to throw you a surprise goodbye party," Walter declared.

JayB turned from where he was running water at the sink. "Surprise!"

Alana laughed. "Really, that's not necessary, Walter. It's sweet, though."

"I insist," Walter told her. "At the restaurant. We'll give you a proper send-off. It'll be us, Celeste, Maddy and Rodney, and the dogs."

"Okay." She nodded.

"Coffee's ready in a few minutes. So, Dad, you know why we're here. Alana wants to show you what she came up with when she analyzed your financial situation."

Walter rubbed his hands together. "What's the good news?"

"I hate this," Alana moaned. "I hate disappointing people."

"Why would I be disappointed?"

JayB took a deep breath. "Because at your current burn rate, you'll be out of money by Christmas."

Walter's face froze. Then he opened his mouth and very sharply said, "Ha!"

"You've got some money left in the bank, but the restaurant is blowing through that pretty quickly," Alana explained.

Walter gave a weary sigh. "Alana. You yourself said you're not a financial advisor. I'm sure if we went to a professional . . ."

"It's just math, Dad," JayB interrupted. "You don't need to be a genius, you just need to be able to subtract."

Walter glared at JayB. "Don't talk to me like I'm stupid."

JayB sat at the table and leaned forward. "Dad. There's some good news here, but you're going to have to proceed carefully. We looked up the book value on your cars. Combining the van with the Ferrari, you'll have more than three hundred thousand dollars. That's a lot of money, and you'll still have the Cadillac to drive when your license is reinstated."

"I am not selling the Ferrari," Walter snapped. "You should have seen Celeste's face when I showed it to her. I know your mother, and that car sealed the deal."

"Did you tell her you're not allowed to drive it?" JayB challenged.

"Funny." Walter scowled.

"Walter," Alana interjected softly, "you asked me to look at the restaurant cash flow, and I did. And you asked me to look at your personal situation, and I have."

"My God, I wish I'd never even heard of that restaurant." Walter put his head in his hands.

"The thing is," Alana continued optimistically, "people are bringing their dogs and letting them run in the pens while they eat and watch them play. Like, a lot of people. There's been real growth in the past few days."

"Then let's sell it!" Walter cried desperately.

Alana and JayB glanced at each other.

"It's still losing money, Dad. And even if you could sell it, you're not going to recoup anywhere near your investment."

"Celeste flew in last night. To see *me*!" Walter gestured around the kitchen. "To see *this*! To see the Ferrari!"

"When does she fly back?" JayB asked softly.

Walter glared at JayB with narrowed eyes.

"I know Mom, and she's not going to stay here, Dad. She's just not."

"Stand back and watch me work," Walter proclaimed.

"Did she really spend the night here?"

"That's between your mother and me."

"Fair enough. But what about Twain?"

"Ask her, not me. All I have to say is, you've been wrong before, and now that I'm rich, Celeste and I are getting back together."

JayB tilted his head at that, then looked to Alana. "Well, since this is the point in the conversation where we're ignoring reality, you might as well tell Dad your conclusion about why the restaurant's losing money."

Walter held up a hand. "If you're going to try to sell me a bunch of doom and gloom, I don't want to hear it."

JayB sighed.

"It's not all doom. I mean, there's some hope," Alana allowed carefully.

Walter shot JayB a triumphant look. "Thought so."

"So . . . this is really awkward for me," Alana lamented. "But okay. Walter, you and Rodney and Maddy take more money out in salaries than the place generates in profit each week. Like, by a huge amount."

"There are always start-up expenses," Walter grumbled.

"The thing is, though, those three paychecks are *killing* you financially," JayB added. "So, here's my offer: I've been working every day, and I will continue to work every day, but only if Rodney and Maddy make what you do, which has to be *zero*."

"Zero? I'm not telling your mom I'm making *nothing*. Oh, wait, what are *you* making?" Walter asked pointedly.

"*Nada*. Same as you. Same as I've made from the beginning. Nothing. Zero. I don't need the money." After a long silence, JayB stood. "Coffee's ready; who wants some?"

Walter wordlessly shook his head. JayB poured hot, fragrant liquid into a cup for Alana and one for himself.

"I'll go down and give Maddy and Rodney the bad news," JayB continued. "I've had a little experience with things like this."

Walter roused himself. "You'd better make sure there's a security guard this time."

JayB grinned. "*Touché*. I also need you down there, Dad, to back me up. I don't think either of them will believe me."

Walter turned a morose gaze on Alana. "You said there was good news."

"I said there was hope," Alana corrected. "And it's this: you're no longer having to buy your food at the grocery stores, and your liquor is no longer cash-and-carry. Revenues are up. Eliminating the three 'executive' salaries puts you in the black. Soon you can even start taking a small salary again. Meaning just you, *not* Maddy and Rodney."

"Imagine that, Dad. Walter Danville, successful business owner," JayB marveled.

Walter gave him a sour look.

"I'll come down with you if you'd like," Alana offered. "Be there to go over the numbers with Rodney and Maddy."

"Really?" JayB seemed surprised.

Alana nodded grimly. "I need to force myself to sit through stuff like this, or everyone's going to continue to see me as a doormat."

"I would *never* see you as a doormat, Alana. But I understand what you're saying. So, yes. I doubt they'll be much interested, but it would be great if you came with us." JayB looked to his father. "Why don't you call 'em, Dad. Tell them there's an ultra-important, top-executive meeting, stat."

Walter stood. "This is not how I thought the day would go. I'll call them, shower, get a ride, and meet you down there."

A little while later, we were in the car for a car ride. I was in the back seat with Odin, who was deep into his sleep.

"How was that for you, seeing your mom?" Alana wanted to know.

"Uh, I think the word I'm looking for is 'unreal.' I've never really been able to figure out my mother. She's an enigma."

"I wish I had that quality. I feel like everyone can read me like an open book."

"I can't. I still don't really understand why you're going back to LA. Why not hang here and see what happens once the three executives are gone from the payroll? Just for a while?"

"I told you, I'm not going to stay here for the restaurant."

JayB took a deep breath. "Alana. The night in Grand Junction . . ."

She flashed him a warning look, and I shrank from the emotions filling the car.

"No, please, just listen," JayB urged. "I know you think it was a mistake, but I don't. I've never felt so certain. I mean, it wasn't just about you being on the bounce, was it?"

Alana gave him a contemplative look. "Remember Maddy's autobiography? It was all about who she's dated. That's her definition of herself. And as she gave us her bio, I realized you could say the same for me: I've always lived for other people. I lived to please my mother, and then had a couple of relationships that were the same as what I had with Guy—I did whatever they told me."

"I'm not telling you. I'm asking you."

She shook her head. "I need to figure out a way to seize control of my life. I mean, what about me? What do *I* want?"

"That *is* the question," JayB agreed. "What *do* you want, Alana?"

She looked out the window and didn't respond.

I figured out from the smells that we were headed to our personal dog park. I was surprised and excited to see so many dogs there. I started to wag, but then Walter arrived and I went to sit under a picnic table with him, Alana, and JayB. Odin touched me with his muzzle, communicating something, a request, and when I flopped down, he lay against me with a groan. Whatever internal disturbance made him want to press up against another dog, I was happy to oblige.

"You're having lunch with Celeste?" Walter asked JayB.

My person glanced at his wrist. "That's right."

"Well, don't bring her here, okay? I want to get it spruced up for tomorrow's party before she sees it."

"Okay."

"Good thing I know the owner," Alana observed. "Other people are actually having to wait for a table." She smiled at JayB.

"We're busy all day, now," JayB agreed. "People bring their dogs, work on laptops . . . the woman who came up with this dog-park concept saved a lot of jobs."

"She sounds like a smart person," Alana teased.

"Oh, she is. She certainly is." They gazed at each other, smiling.

Maddy and Rodney soon joined us. I wagged, but remained loyally pressed against Odin. To my satisfaction, Rodney led Spartan away from us and penned him with a squat, stuffy-seeming dog. The two of them ignored each other.

"Getting warm today," Rodney observed by way of greeting. "I'm thinking we need a new HVAC system in this place."

"What would something like that cost?" Walter asked.

Rodney shrugged. "Pays for itself."

JayB nodded. "That's interesting."

"Well, listen," Walter announced, "I've got good news. Celeste flew into town, and she's going to hang here for a while. I thought we should have a big party tomorrow night. Not just to celebrate her arrival, but since Alana's going to be hitting the road, we should give her a proper send-off."

"Excellent idea, boss," Rodney praised. "You can count on me to be the guy to put the 'animal' in 'party animal.'"

Walter turned to Alana. "You're getting on the road by when?"

Alana looked uncomfortable. "Well, the closing's at three, so I don't know. Six, maybe?"

"Perfect." Walter beamed. "You come by as soon as the closing's over. We'll kick things off here at four, put on a big spread. Not just the best items from the menu, but *everything* from the menu. You can load up. Take some food with you for the road. It'll be a grand time. Plus, there may be some big news from Celeste and me."

I heard JayB make a slight groaning sound.

"Count me in," Maddy agreed eagerly. "Although I don't want DesMoines serving us. I got some permanent issues with her that I'm gonna put in her performance review."

"Be sure to run that past the HR department," JayB instructed her tactfully.

"Oh, no," Maddy responded scornfully, "if you think for a moment I'm going to slow down our progress, you are wrong, wrong, wrong."

"Anyway," Walter continued, turning suddenly to Alana, "go ahead and tell them what we all decided."

*Dear Diary:*

*I am often conflicted when we arrive at our personal dog park. Because it has grown so popular, there is often a bounty of new urine scents to drink in—and, if the situation calls for it, mark over.*

*The situation always calls for it.*

*Running with Phoebe gives me great joy, and if there are other playful canines, I need to make sure they understand that Phoebe's willingness to engage in wrestling does not mean she doesn't already have a dog named Clancy.*

*But these and other considerations are in direct conflict with my duty and desire to be with JayB. He is my person, and a dog belongs with his person.*

*When I'm in the fenced-off area, I pine to be with JayB. When I am lying at his feet, I am content, save for the longing to be in one of the pens with Phoebe.*

*It isn't easy being a dog.*

Love,
Clancy

# Thirty-three

Everyone looked expectantly at Alana, who gave Walter a pained stare.

"Thank you for that introduction, Walter," she began. "Okay, well—to start, Walter's salary, starting immediately, will be zero."

"Whoa!" Rodney exclaimed, his eyebrows raised. "Well, I guess you can afford it, big man. I remember one time I had a job and they cut my wages and of course I didn't stand for it. I let them know, you don't bring on somebody with the quality of Rodney Spitz and expect to get him on the cheap."

"Right . . . about that . . ." Alana continued.

JayB leaned forward and touched her arm. "No, let me do this. Rodney, Maddy, you can continue to work here, but you're going to get paid the same as my father."

Rodney and Maddy stared at JayB silently.

"I don't understand," Maddy finally admitted.

"It's pretty simple. This restaurant is going broke. We're making progress, but we'll never be profitable with the overhead of your salaries. So, effective immediately, those salaries are zero." JayB focused on Maddy. "If you'd like some hours as a server, I'll speak to DesMoines, and of course you can keep your tips." JayB sat back. "Any questions?"

"Hold on, JayB," Rodney objected. "Just hold on. I know you probably forgot, but I'm the one who found this place. There wouldn't even *be* a restaurant if it weren't for me. So, it's only fair that I am compensated for my contribution."

JayB nodded. "I actually think paying you zero *is* compensation for your contribution."

"You must have learned HR from the devil," Maddy spat. "You're supposed to be thinking of ways to pay us *more*."

Rodney slapped his hand on the table. I cringed from his temper, and Odin stirred uneasily. "Do you think I work for free?"

"No," JayB countered. "I think you cost whoever you're working for quite a bit of money. But that ends, as of today."

"Well, sorry, but you forget that I outrank you here, pal."

"When it comes to matters like compensation, HR sets the policy," JayB replied primly. "It's in the manual."

"Do I need to remind you that Rodney's been traveling *internationally*? You can't do this to a man without a country," Maddy seethed. "This is treason."

"Do you understand that I don't even have a place to live now?" Rodney shot back. "The place I've been remodeling violated my contract and kicked me out. So, feel good about that, JayB. You're making me a homeless person, living in the gutter with—with rats, and leaves, and . . ." He turned to Maddy.

"Firecrackers?" Maddy suggested.

"Gutter stuff!" Rodney finished angrily.

"Well, of course you're not homeless," Maddy soothed. "You can live with me, honey."

Rodney didn't reply to this.

"Thank you for your opening bid," Maddy told JayB, "but I'm not coming back as a waitress. I've done that my whole life. Now that I've tasted being an executive, I know that's what I was born to do, so I'll only serve duty in that capacity."

"That's reasonable," JayB replied. "We don't have an open position for an executive on sabbatical right now, but when we do, I'll let you know."

Rodney turned to Walter. "I think you need to step up here, Walt. You can't let JayB ruin a good thing for all of us. Do you think you're worth *nothing*? That Maddy's worth *nothing*? Me? Rodney, your right-hand man, who's been leading the charge? This is a prince turning on the king."

Maddy was nodding. "You're like a father to me now, Walter. So I need you to support me like any father would."

Walter bit his lip. I could feel his distress.

JayB turned and looked at him. "Dad," he prodded, "what do you say?"

"I say." Walter looked helpless. "I mean, can't we come up with some sort of compromise here?"

Alana opened her mouth, but JayB held up a hand. "No, Dad. We can't. There's no compromise possible. This is about survival. Alana showed you the numbers."

"Oh, sure," Rodney jeered. *"Numbers."*

"Like Alana hasn't been looking to get her fishhooks into your flesh from the moment she saw you," Maddy snarled. "Of course she'd use numbers. What else has she got?"

"Okay, well, then, like JayB said . . ." Walter began.

"I can't believe this!" Rodney stood up. "You need to think real hard about what you're doing here. Come on, Maddy."

"Don't even think of trying to stop me from following Rodney," Maddy stormed at JayB.

I wagged as Rodney and Maddy walked away. They took several steps, conferred briefly, then came back. I wagged uneasily at their return, hoping there wouldn't be any more anger.

"Okay, see how bad it could be? What if we *left for real*?" Maddy demanded. "Then where would you be?"

"Walter. No more bluffing," Rodney declared, his voice low. "I get that blood drains thicker than water. But this was never about building up your empire so that your son could inherit the earth. We're here with our final offer, and"—he glanced at JayB—"no *human resources* need to get involved."

"As if human is even part of this!" Maddy scoffed.

"Here it is. Maddy and I just had a conferral about it, so we're a unified bloc," Rodney informed Walter icily. "Either JayB goes, or we go." He looked at JayB. "No offense. Like they say in the mafia, this is business—nothing personal."

"I'm with the mafia on this one," Maddy agreed.

Sounding extremely unhappy, Walter appealed to Alana: "You're my financial advisor. . . ."

"No, I'm not. I just did you the favor of some adding and sub-tracting."

"It would be wrong for her to give an opinion in this relevance anyway," Maddy interjected. "This is family."

"I've always said heart was more important than money," Walter murmured helplessly.

"Yes!" Rodney exulted.

"You know what, Dad? I agree with you. And when your money runs out—by Christmas—you'll still be rich in heart. No one, not even me—*especially* me—would disagree with that."

"Okay, I can't be the only one who thinks we've gotten off the train tracks here," Maddy fumed. "You're saying JayB needs to buck up and butt out, right?"

Walter gave Alana another pleading look.

"You want me to tell you what to do," Alana translated flatly.

Walter gave a slight nod.

"Wow. Just . . . I suppose you get what you ask for," she marveled. "I said I needed to learn to be the bringer of bad news. And here it is."

"Exactly," Maddy agreed supportively.

"Okay, then. Walter." Alana leaned forward and put a hand over one of his. "This isn't really a choice at all. Keep on this course and you'll be wiped out. You can show Celeste your house and the fancy cars, but it won't matter, because by next year they'll all be gone. Or you can let JayB help you build on what you've got here. You could make a lot of money. But not if you run out of cash."

There was a long silence. "So, wait, are you saying he should keep paying us or not?" Rodney asked suspiciously.

"I think," Maddy declared, rising to her feet, "she's doing what all women do, which is to stand right in front of you and stab you in the back."

"Or threaten to shoot you in the back if you turn around," JayB added.

"I knew you'd say that," Maddy retorted.

Walter finally spoke again. "I'm sorry, but no more executive salaries for now."

"Let's go, Rodney," Maddy stormed. "These straws have broken our backs for the last time."

I wagged uncertainly as Maddy and Rodney stomped off again. I saw them stop and open a gate and hook Spartan up to a leash and then they vanished around the corner.

"Hey!" Walter cried after them. "Don't forget the party tomorrow. Four o'clock!"

There was no reply.

"Oh my God," Walter lamented. "I've become one of those people who fire other people. This is the worst day of my life."

I sensed his anguish and nosed his hand. What I knew, but had no way to explain, was that if he only carried around a few treats in his pocket for moments like these, it wouldn't take much to cheer him up.

"Yeah, but think of what it means," said JayB. "What if this really were successful, this business? Picture greeting parties of people at the door, saying, 'Welcome to the Dog Park Restaurant.'"

Walter gave my person a sour look. "Picture being the hostess, in other words."

Alana laughed. "Come on, Walter, where's the eternal optimist? Where did that man go? There's so much potential here. Can't you picture how rewarding it will be to build on what you've started here?" She turned and gave JayB a sharp look. "Rewarding for Walter and you, I mean," she told him sternly.

"I didn't say anything," he replied innocently. He dug his phone out of his pocket. "Okay, I need to get you home so I can meet Mom for lunch."

Walter's mood instantly improved. "Tell her I'll pick her up at six."

JayB gave him a steady look.

"I'm taking her to dinner, and then dancing," Walter explained.

JayB looked to Alana, then back to Walter. "I'd like to not be in the middle of any of that," he said delicately.

For some reason, that afternoon I stayed alone with Kelsey. I paced, nervous, worried JayB had forgotten where I was and was out there looking for me. I reacted joyously when I heard a noise at the door, smelling my person on the other side.

I wanted to greet him with kisses and cries, but he quickly snapped a leash into my collar and we strode briskly up the street to Odin's. When we were at the door, Alana yelled, "Come in!" and we entered. Immediately, I smelled Rhiannon. Odin was lying on the floor and flapped his tail in greeting.

Alana came out of the kitchen. "So . . . how'd it go? With Celeste?"

"Well," JayB responded, "my mom and I have figured out a way to talk to each other without really getting into anything that's bothering us."

"What happened between them last night?"

JayB sighed heavily. "Turns out Twain left her for another woman."

"*What?*"

"Walter knows, I know, and now you know, but otherwise she's keeping it quiet."

"So she came back? To be with your father? Like he's always dreamed?"

JayB shook his head. "I did *not* ask about that. I have no idea why she's here, or what she's thinking. I try to stay out of it."

"Is it . . . painful for you?"

"No, not really. I was upset when she and Howard split, even more than when the marriage to Walter fell apart, if you want to know the truth. But I've never had a relationship with Twain. Anyway. How are you? Can I help you with anything?"

Alana looked around the marvelously empty room. "Nope. They picked up all my other belongings from our—" She paused. "From Guy's apartment today." Her mouth settled into a bitter line. "Guy *and Nikki's* apartment, I guess I should say."

"Buy you dinner tonight?"

Alana shook her head. "No, I think what I want to do tonight is just be alone, if that's okay. I'll take a bath and then, you know, walk around and remember seeing my mom in this place the last time I was here."

"What about the bedroom stuff, the remaining furniture?"

"Donated. They'll be here tomorrow. Then the cleaners, and the new owners will be here the morning after that." She gave him a weak smile. "All done."

"All done," JayB agreed sadly. "Well, if you change your mind about being alone, I'll just be hanging out with Kelsey and Clancy. But I'll see you tomorrow at your going-away party."

"Yeah," Alana responded cautiously, "about that. Do we really think Maddy and Rodney will be there?"

"I don't know. Usually in a situation like this, you don't hear from people again. But what do I know—the last person I fired came back and punched me in the nose."

Alana laughed. "I don't see Rodney doing that, but I wouldn't put it past Maddy."

"Honestly? I think they'll show. They're off somewhere, planning some last-minute appeal to Walter. They had such a good thing going, they won't give up after just one try."

"And your mom will be there?"

"I guess. You'll get to know her better. All the dogs, you, me. It'll be like old times in the van."

On the way out, I gave Odin a final sniff before leaving. He didn't open his eyes.

*Dear Diary:*

*Humans probably don't even realize how many wonderful things they have discovered for dogs. Canines never could have figured out that cars can be used for car rides, or that refrigerators contain so many wonderful scents that they're worth swooning over.*

*Beds are amazing—soft things layered in softer things with large, rounded, even softer things on top of the layers, designed to entice a dog into the deepest nap ever.*

*Dog dinner is much better than anything I've scarfed down furtively on my own, because there's more of it and the aroma is heavenly. Some of the things I've eaten off the floor I didn't even like.*

*A table can be a glorious place. Built to accommodate a dog or two underneath them, tables are where humans set out foods to be handed down in small pieces to the receptive and appreciative dogs at their feet.*

*Sometimes, though, people will sit at a table and talk instead of eating. This is perplexing behavior, but there's nothing a dog can do about it except lie there loyally and wait for the situation to change.*

*It's all different, though, when a dog's person is upset, or sad. JayB is that way now, cycling through dark moods that are so unlike him.*

*I am lying under the table now, not because I'm waiting for him to toss down cheese, but to let him know that whatever is making him sad can probably be fixed if he only remembers he has a dog.*

*Though, I wouldn't turn down the cheese.*

Love,
Clancy

# Thirty-four

Back at our house, JayB didn't say much to me, and he fed the cat without a word. I watched as Kelsey haughtily leaped up on the counter, and then I realized something: I was happy, of course, because even with Kelsey making her tiny, disgusting chewing noises, I was with my person. But I felt even happier when Alana and Odin were with us. JayB carried a lightness with him when Alana was in the house. Also, Odin terrified Kelsey, which lifted everyone's mood.

These were delightful elements of life that, in my opinion, should be experienced daily. I didn't understand why things that were so obvious to a dog were so difficult for a human to understand.

The next day, I knew something fun was happening because of how long JayB stood in the shower with water pouring on his head. He pulled several things out of his closet before getting dressed, and I wagged as we got ready for a car ride. It was exciting to go back to our personal dog park. I couldn't pick up Phoebe's scent, however, except as a lingering presence in the pen where she and I had last frolicked. I took this to mean that Phoebe would not be coming today.

For a while, JayB and Walter waited in a big room in the back of the building. Walter was pacing.

DesMoines brought in a tray of food and set it down. "I'll hold off on the rest until everybody else gets here."

Walter nodded.

"Are you going to be okay?" she asked him.

He gave DesMoines a startled look. "Why do you ask?"

"Because you seem really agitated at the moment."

"Right. But it's a good agitation," Walter explained. "Like the best kind."

"Okay." DesMoines looked between the two men. "I guess you and I have different definitions of good agitation."

"We're having a going-away party for Alana," JayB explained. "Would you like to join us?"

She shook her head. "We're too busy up front, but thanks." She cocked her head at him. "Are *you* going to be okay?"

"Me?" JayB smiled. "I'm fine. Thanks, DesMoines."

She turned to Walter and handed him a small piece of paper. He stared at it numbly.

"It's my phone number," she told him. "I think you could use a friend right about now, Walter. A good friend. Call me. Maybe I'm that person."

After she left, Walter leaned forward. "I drove the Ferrari here," he whispered.

"What? You're not supposed to drive *anything*," JayB objected. "There's probably not a cop in town who doesn't recognize that car."

"It's important that your mom see it parked out front when she arrives," Walter explained.

I sniffed hard and wagged: Maddy and Rodney were here! So was Spartan, but I was learning to tolerate his presence. I watched expectantly, then stopped wagging because Maddy and Rodney wore grim expressions as they stepped into the room. They ignored JayB, both staring intently at Walter. Maddy, as usual, smelled angry, but Rodney smelled like Maddy—and also angry, I realized. I wondered if Maddy's anger had worn off on him, the way her other odors had.

Spartan, of course, was oblivious to everything. He didn't even glance my way or raise his nose toward the food on the table.

"I'm going to be very fair here," Maddy warned Walter. "We've come up with eight simple reasons why cutting our pay would be a huge mistake and destroy everything."

"You sort of ambushed us, Walter," Rodney added. "I mean, yes, I'm quick on my feet, and I can handle adversity better than just about anyone you've ever met. But still . . ."

"In fact, adversity is one of the eight simple reasons," said Maddy.

Rodney frowned. "We said that one was mine."

Maddy nodded. "Oh, of course it is, honey. I was just giving him a preview of the coming attraction."

"Celeste!" Walter called, rising to his feet.

The nice lady I had met at Walter's house, the one with the strong fragrances, strolled into the room with a smile. Walter hugged her affectionately. He called her Celeste enough for me to understand that this was her name. JayB, by calling her Mom, was only confusing matters for the rest of us.

Rodney and Maddy seemed cowed by the new arrival. They said their names to make sure I knew who they were, then stopped talking and filled small plates from the platter in the center of the table.

"Is this all?" Maddy challenged. "Because if I were putting on the party here, which"—she turned to Walter—"in my position I'm in charge of, I would make sure there was a lot more food."

"But not an *unpaid* position," Rodney reminded her.

"Right. No salary, no food. The customers can starve, for all I care."

"We're going to wait until Alana arrives before we serve the rest of it," JayB advised.

"But *I* can't wait." Walter grabbed a big bottle out of a bucket of ice, making a swirling sound. He started twisting at the top. "You guys are not going to believe how cool this is going to be."

"It seems like that must be true," JayB said agreeably.

With a loud *bang*, Walter suddenly had a dog toy in his hand. He threw it on the floor, where it bounced between Spartan and me. I seized it, of course, but it felt like less of a victory because Spartan didn't care.

Meanwhile, Walter had shoved a finger into the neck of the bottle, squelching the strong odors that wanted to escape into the room. "You ready?" he asked in a tone that suggested he was about to give us some treats. I watched with eagerness as he vigorously shook that bottle.

"Dad . . ." JayB cautioned.

When Walter took his finger out of the top of the bottle, it sprayed foam everywhere. He directed the spray at the wall in front of him. I found this to be a very interesting development. A sweet-smelling liquid painted the white surface and dribbled to the floor. I eased over to it and sniffed. Though it didn't smell like anything I had ever eaten, I gave it an experimental lick, deciding instantly that I didn't like it.

I lapped at it anyway.

"Well, I don't get it," Walter muttered after a moment.

"What's not to get?" JayB responded. "You just took a perfectly good bottle of champagne and sprayed it all over the wall. Now the wall will have to be scrubbed and probably repainted. Well, you were right: we can't believe it. Clancy, stop that."

I heard my name and the tone of voice and shrank away guiltily.

"No," Walter corrected testily, "I mean, there are supposed to be words. I looked it up online. You're supposed to be able to read the words I wrote ahead of time, revealed like magic."

"I think it's cool anyway," Maddy assured him.

JayB nodded. "Okay, then. What would the words have said if we could read them?"

Walter blinked. Then he turned and his face changed. He smiled broadly at Celeste. "Celeste."

Celeste looked alarmed. "Oh, Walter."

He held up a hand. "Here's what I painted on the wall that was supposed to appear by magic. *Will you marry me, Celeste?* And what I mean by that is, marry me again, and for good this time?"

Everyone except the dogs seemed to suck in a breath. The room went utterly quiet, save for the steady dripping of the sweet liquid making its way onto the floor.

"Oh, Walter," Celeste said again. "Can we talk? Alone? This isn't something I want to play out in front of strangers."

Maddy arched her eyebrows at Rodney. "So now we're demolished to strangers?"

"Life can turn on you in a second," Rodney agreed bitterly.

Celeste gave them both a blank look before walking away. I

followed her and Walter out the door, thinking that's what we were all doing. When it shut behind me and I discovered I was alone with them, I was disconcerted. Looking back at the door separating me from JayB, I settled uneasily onto the floor while they sat on a bench.

Walter was still smiling. He seemed very happy. "I guess this comes as a shock."

She shook her head sadly. "Oh no, Walter. You've been telegraphing this for months."

"Well, your arrival changed everything."

Celeste put a hand on his. "Look at me, Walter."

Walter looked at her, his grin faltering.

"I'm going to tell you something now, something you may find hard to hear."

I sensed an uneasiness in Walter as Celeste pinned him with her stare. "I told Jago what I told you, that Twain and I are getting divorced." Walter made a slight noise, but Celeste held up a hand. "It isn't easy for me. It feels a little like, three strikes and you're out. But that doesn't mean you and I are getting back together. That's never going to happen."

"I don't understand," Walter murmured hoarsely. "Haven't the past forty-eight hours proven what I've always said, that we belong together?"

Celeste sighed, then regarded Walter with a long, sad look. "Many years ago, I had a date with a man who captured my attention. I think at the time you were selling automobiles, and you picked me up in a brand-new Lincoln."

Walter nodded. "It was a dealership demo."

"And you were dressed so nicely. And you took me down to Crown Center and we watched the ice skaters. And then we drove back and the lights were on, the Christmas lights in the Plaza. And it was so beautiful. And we went inside. I think it was called the Ritz-Carlton back then."

"It's changed hands a lot. Now it's the Intercontinental."

Celeste shook her head. "Let me tell it, Walter. We went in and there was a wedding. The party was in full swing, and no one stopped us when you escorted me out onto the dance floor. And we danced and danced. And the new couple was so beautiful, and everyone was so elegantly dressed, and I felt enveloped in your strong arms. The way you looked at me . . . no one had ever looked at me like that before. Part of me felt we were all alone under the lights. And when you whispered that you thought you could get us a room upstairs, I never hesitated."

Celeste's eyes were moist as she gave him a sad smile. "And that was the start of our romance, Walter. You're a romantic to the core. Remember how you picked me up and carried me across the threshold into that hotel room? That's how every day felt to me at first. Like you'd swept me off my feet and were carrying me in your strong arms, carrying me into a wonderful future. Do you remember?"

Walter's voice was a whisper, immeasurably sad. "Of course."

"I accepted your invitation to come visit you here because I do care about you, and to try to see if I could recapture a little bit of that magic. I wanted to close my eyes and feel as if we had just left the dance floor, hand in hand, ascending in that glass elevator, seeing all the beautiful lights as we sped to the penthouse. I wanted to know if that young woman, that girl, still lives." She touched her chest. "Lives inside my heart."

"She does. You haven't changed, Celeste. You look exactly the same."

Her smile was wry. "Thank you. I would say you haven't changed either, but I'm not sure I would mean it as a compliment."

Walter frowned. "I don't think you understand." He gestured. "This is my restaurant. I'm a businessman now. I have a Ferrari, and a beautiful home. When you and I split, I had not a penny to my name. But I can support you now, Celeste. And we don't have to live here. We can move to Florida or wherever you want. Paris, even."

Celeste was silent.

I glanced uneasily back toward where I could smell JayB. What if he left without me?

"What do you say, Celeste? There's never been anyone else but you, not since the day we danced at someone else's wedding. Whatever we do, wherever we live, let's go *together*."

*Dear Diary:*

There are many human emotions a dog must be attuned to. Anger, fear, joy—these are all vital to a dog's survival. But the most important feeling is love. When people love dogs, dogs know it like a strong scent, coming to us in warm waves.

Love is as simple from a human to a dog as it is from a dog to a human. There are no complications or conditions. Behaviors can upset the peace—a bad dog can hear "Get down!" for forgetting that a couch is off limits, or "No!" for digging into the bin of delicious food left open for us to sniff and drool over. But no matter how sharp the word or strong the temper, we love our people, and nothing can change that. Usually, even behind the sting of an angry voice, dogs feel our people loving us back just as strongly.

The way humans love each other, however, is far more complex. Messy clouds of doubt and ambiguity disturb any sense of clarity. I sense that Walter and Celeste love each other, but it doesn't come without confusion for both of them. I feel sadness and regret and frustration radiating off them, interfering with the otherwise lucid connection.

This has been true of all my people: Maddy and Rodney and Alana and JayB have completely disrupted the currents of love flowing from each of them. This new, odd way of loving was already growing among my humans before Celeste's arrival, but by joining our pack, she clearly provoked disturbed emotions in Walter.

Maddy, Rodney, Alana, JayB, Celeste, Walter—they are

*all good people, but in my opinion, they'd be much better off if they stopped worrying about so many things and just lived their lives like dogs.*

Love,
Clancy

# Thirty-five

Celeste's expression was one of kindly amusement. She regarded Walter fondly. "Paris . . . There's my romantic. I've never been to Paris. But it was never really about the money, Walter. I'm glad you're rich. And yes, when we were struggling, it would have been nice to be able to buy things. But that's not why our marriage failed. It was the chaos. It was about how you just kept changing what you wanted to do and where you wanted to live. And I eventually realized I wasn't meant to exist like that. Especially when Jago came along. He was my responsibility."

"Mine, too."

"Yes, but I used that word very deliberately. 'Responsibility.' If you had stayed with one thing for more than a few months, if you had managed to hold down a steady job . . ."

Walter groaned. "Come on, Celeste. Is that what you want? A nine-to-fiver? Somebody who punches a clock? Does the same boring thing over and over again? Isn't it better to have vision? Isn't it better to have joy?"

Celeste nodded. "Those are certainly good things, Walter. Fine things. But when you have a baby, your focus is on a reliable situation, a place to live that doesn't keep changing."

"Okay, well, Jago's grown up now," Walter pointed out.

"He is. But I'm content where I am, Walter. I'm going to keep the home that Twain's giving to me as part of the divorce."

Walter snorted. "Twain."

"Please listen to what I'm saying. I like my garden and my tennis club and my friends. You're exciting and surprising—I would be the first to admit that. But I don't *want* surprises. My life has washed up on very comfortable shores now. Everything you've got going on here is wonderful, I'm sure. But it's not for me." Celeste glanced away. "Oh, Walter, you still look at me with those same eyes. I would be lying if I didn't say I'm tempted. That's why I've decided to leave here as soon as possible."

Walter jerked. "What? No!"

Celeste stood. "You've given me many wonderful moments to remember. I've always been grateful for that, and I'm thankful for the new memories we made these past few days."

Walter also stood, then reached out and took her hand. "Celeste. Please sit back down. Jago was right; he said not to press you. I'm sorry. Let's take things slow . . . but please don't leave me now."

Celeste raised her eyebrows. "Jago said that? He's grown to be such a smart man. We can be proud."

"I'll do anything, Celeste."

She put a hand to his face. "I know you would. But what I learned by coming here is how different I am from that giddy girl on the dance floor at a stranger's wedding. Okay? You *deserve* romance, Walter. But with someone else. The real reason I came was to tell you not to send flowers or leave me any more messages. But then you did what you do, and the next thing I knew . . ." She shook her head, her eyes wet. "Being with you is like trying to live on a diet of desserts." She pulled out her phone. "Let's go say goodbye to the others. My Lyft will be here soon."

I was beyond relieved when Walter opened the door and I was able to dart back inside. Thankfully, JayB was still there. Spartan too, but I didn't mind as long as I could keep my eyes on my person.

JayB did not seem any happier than when I'd left, and now Walter was sad. These people had one very good dog and one pretty deficient dog in the room, but it didn't seem to be making much of a difference. I wished Phoebe and Odin were there.

"Everyone," Celeste proclaimed, "it has been so nice to see you, and I'm so glad to have met all of you. I'm sorry that Alana isn't here for me to tell her goodbye."

"You're leaving, Mom?"

Celeste nodded. "I've already called for the car. We'll swing by the Raphael. The doorman has my bags ready to go."

"I love you, Celeste," Walter grated hoarsely.

Celeste's eyes started getting wet again. "I love you too, Walter," she replied softly.

They embraced, but I didn't wag. What I felt from them now was grief.

Celeste broke away from the hug and turned to JayB.

"All right," he stated with finality and hugged her as well. He didn't seem sad, only wistful.

She glared at him, pointing a finger. "You need to call me more often, and you need to come visit again soon." She smiled.

"Maybe this winter," JayB agreed.

"All right. Good, good. Bye, everybody." Celeste waved.

Walter didn't say anything. Everyone else said goodbye, and I watched as she glided out of the room. I had no idea what was going on. I only knew it was stirring up powerful emotions.

"Is there any of that champagne to drink?" Rodney finally asked.

We sat around, the people not talking much while DesMoines came in with more food.

"Aren't we a cheerful group," DesMoines noted. She looked to Walter. "I saw Celeste leave."

Walter nodded. "Yeah."

"Stop by the bar later, why don't you," DesMoines suggested. "I'll buy you a drink." She smiled at JayB and left the room.

The food perked me up, but my people weren't in a dog-feeding mood. Spartan either knew this or he didn't. When it comes to treats, he waits for them to be handed to him. He's not willing to work for it like I am.

Rodney wiped his mouth, glanced at Maddy, and nodded. "Right, okay. This is now. Walter, since the business case didn't work, I'm going to have to appeal straight to your sense of decency."

"This is going to make me cry," Maddy declared fiercely. She pulled out a tissue and crushed it in her hand, glaring.

"I know you have a heart, Walter, a good one," Rodney lectured. "So here's the deal: I don't have a place to live."

"Well, except you're moving in with me," Maddy objected.

"Maddy, let me tell it," Rodney complained.

"Well, sorry, but you make it sound like you're living on the streets or something."

"With rats and firecrackers," JayB agreed.

"The point is, the people I was working for kicked me out." Rodney shook his head in disgust. "They expected their kitchen to be done like magic or something. What I do is way more complex than anybody understands."

"Of course it is, honey," Maddy soothed. "And don't worry. I've supported a lot of men before in my life. After all, I am a waitress. Speaking of which, I think we all feel disappointed about this party so far. Clearly this restaurant isn't going to run *itself* into the ground."

"Uh, Maddy, we're not doing business talk anymore," Rodney corrected her impatiently. "Now we're trying to make him feel sympathy."

"Well, women can multitask," Maddy informed him archly. "Sorry if I interrupted your monorail."

"I don't know why Alana's so late. She hasn't responded to my texts," JayB interjected.

"Hey!" Rodney snapped. "We need to focus on what Walter's doing to me, here, and you guys keep changing the subject."

Walter was gazing at the table as if there were something in front of him. He finally lifted his red eyes and narrowed them. "You know what, Rodney? You—and you, Maddy—can drink my booze and eat my food, but I'd appreciate it if you both kept your yaps shut about the restaurant. And everything else, for that matter."

Rodney sat back. "Well, I don't know what's gotten into you, but if that's the way you want to play it, okay. I'll just leave here tonight and go sleep in a ditch somewhere."

"Nicer at my place, I'll bet," Maddy wagered.

"What's *gotten into* my father is, he just proposed marriage to a woman who said no and left to go to the airport," JayB told the pair. "Perhaps we should give Walter a bit of a break here."

"Your dad," Rodney sneered. "Like I can't see nepotism when I see it."

Maddy nodded. "Exactly. I'm not sure what that is, but I can smell it, too."

We all turned when Odin came in the room, followed by Alana. She carried that bag in her hand, and yes, there was still a cat inside. She put the bag down on the table and held out her hands to me.

I wagged my tail and licked her fingers.

"I'm so sorry I'm late," she apologized. "The closing took longer than it was supposed to."

"That's okay. You missed all the excitement," JayB informed her. "Dad applied a fresh coat of champagne to the wall. Maddy and Rodney filed an emergency appeal. Celeste left."

"Oh." Alana looked at Walter. "Are you okay?"

"I don't know," he responded in a small voice.

Alana sat next to him and put her hand on his shoulder. "I'm so sorry. I know that must've been very tough for you."

Walter looked down in his lap.

"About Celeste," Maddy interjected, "I don't think she gets what she's missing. There are plenty of women my age willing to date a rich, older man." She was talking to Walter, but he did not react.

"So, what time are you leaving?" JayB asked Alana.

"I really appreciate this party and everything," she said. "But I want to get on the road, put some Kansas miles under the tires."

"Well," Rodney said dismissively, "good luck."

"I won't text you back until you apologize," Maddy threatened.

"Pass those chicken nuggets," Rodney added.

"You mean . . . you're leaving *now*?" JayB asked.

Alana nodded solemnly. "I think so."

Alana was still looking at JayB, but now she turned to Walter, touching his shoulder again. "Goodbye, Walter. You're a good man. Please believe that."

Walter still looked miserable, but he nodded.

Alana stood. So did JayB. "Clancy and I will walk you to the car," he offered stiffly.

"Bye, all," Alana said, a bit haltingly.

JayB and I walked with Odin and Alana out the door.

Alana forgot to leave the cat.

We walked across the parking lot to the car that I recognized as belonging to Helen. The air of the night had turned a little cool, and Odin and I both lifted our noses to it. Mostly, I smelled cat.

Alana opened the passenger door and put Rhiannon inside. Then she opened the rear door and JayB reached down and picked Odin up and placed him gently on the back seat. Then he turned to Alana.

"I guess this is it," he observed solemnly. "I really hate that you're doing this drive alone, you know."

Alana nodded. "I'll stay safe. And honestly, it's alone time that I think I need right now. I want to make sure I'm making smart decisions."

JayB took a deep breath and let it out. "That's what I want for you, too."

"Okay, then."

They embraced. I did not wag. Though I sensed the love between my humans, an inner frustration was blocking it from coming out into the open.

Alana walked around and slipped in behind the wheel, and JayB leaned into the back seat. He put his face to Odin's. "Odin, you are a good dog. A good, *good* dog. I'm going to miss you so much. Take care of Alana."

Alana, watching, wiped her eyes.

JayB looked back at me. "Clancy? Say goodbye to Odin."

I could tell by JayB's tone and motions that I was supposed to go and sniff Odin, and that it would be the last time I ever did so. I put my front paws in the car and Odin and I touched noses. We both knew what was happening. We gazed into one another's eyes, each smelling the sadness in the other.

I dropped back down on all fours and JayB stepped forward again, leaning over my dog friend. "And, Odin, I know you'll be leaving us soon. That's okay. That's what dogs do. But you've brought us so much joy by being in our lives. We will never forget you. Okay, Odin? Good dog." JayB pressed his lips tenderly to Odin's head.

Odin gave a single tail thump, but otherwise didn't react.

"I'm never going to see you again, buddy," JayB murmured. "Goodbye."

## Dear Diary:

Goodbye is what people say when some of them are leaving and some of them are staying. Whenever JayB and I leave the house together and I see Kelsey in the window, I think, Goodbye, Kelsey. I don't want you here when we get back.

When dogs do Goodbye, we never know if we will see the other dog again. Humans always seem to know, though, and it can be heard in their voices. There is a big difference between when they say "Goodbye" while knowing there'll be another "Hello" tomorrow, versus the "Goodbye" that means we won't be saying "Hello" again soon.

Or ever.

Love,
Clancy

# Thirty-six

When my person stood and closed the door, Odin's smell diminished and I felt a lonely sadness settle over me. We were doing Goodbye.

JayB approached Alana's open window. "Please let me know how it's going. I want to know you're safe."

Alana nodded, swallowing, her eyes shining.

"Like, text me every thirty seconds."

Alana laughed, but there was so much sadness in the sound, my ears drooped and I lowered my head, as if being scolded.

"Goodbye, Alana."

"Goodbye, JayB."

We watched as the car pulled away. It honked once, a forlorn little wail as it left the parking lot. JayB didn't react.

We turned and trudged back into the big building and found our way to where Walter was sitting alone. The smell of Spartan lingered, but Maddy and Rodney and Spartan had left.

"Hey, Dad. How are you holding up?"

Walter gave him a surly look. "How are *you* holding up?"

JayB sat down. "Not so good, to tell the truth." They sat in heavy silence for a long time. "Sort of parallel circumstances for the two of us, don't you think?"

Walter stared at him for a moment, then vehemently shook his head. "Not the same at all. Celeste is leaving me for her 'comfortable life.' For her flower club. Alana's leaving you for *nothing*."

"Gee, thanks, Dad."

"I mean it. Celeste just told me what she wants." Walter's face twisted and he made his voice mocking. *"Her house. Her garden. Her friends.* And she also told me what she doesn't want: *me.* Did Alana say that to you? Did she say *anything* to you?"

"Something about not liking my shampoo."

Walter scowled. "You make a snide comment about everything, like nothing matters to you, you know that? Do you never feel any anger?"

"It's one of the eight simple rules, I've heard."

Walter sighed, shaking his head. Then he leaned forward. "Jago. *Stop evading your feelings.* Stop pretending like nothing matters to you!"

I cringed because Walter was shouting.

"It *does* matter," JayB protested mildly. "The truth is, I don't *know* why she's leaving. She says she always makes the same mistake every time, getting together with someone immediately after some guy dumps her. 'On the bounce.' She said she has to change her pattern."

"Can you see how stupid that is? You didn't try to argue?" Walter made his tone urgent. "The worst mistake I ever made was letting Celeste walk out on me. Not this time, the first time. I have forever regretted that I didn't go after her. I was hurt, and I let my hurt make my decision for me. I think this is one of those moments that is a pivot point in life, and I think you should go after the person you love. Don't be like me. Stand up for yourself."

"What are you suggesting?"

"I'm saying you should get in your car and go after her. You can't let her just *leave*. What's wrong with you? Have you got no spine at all?"

JayB sat silently for a moment, then exploded to his feet. "You're right." He snapped his fingers at me and we hurried for the door.

"JayB!" Walter called.

My person stopped and turned.

"Take the Ferrari. It's faster." Walter flipped his wrist and JayB caught something. Then we were out in the parking lot and hopping into Walter's car. I was panting with agitation because I didn't know what we were doing, but it sure seemed like it was going to be exciting. We drove in a way that was unusual for JayB: every time we stopped, I was thrown a little forward, and every time we sped up again, I was thrown a little back.

My person seemed extremely tense. "Come on," he muttered. "Come on!"

All of a sudden, he sat up straight. "There she is, Clancy!"

I heard my name but didn't know what might be required of me other than to do a good Sit and wait to see what happened next. I felt the car surge forward and then heard honking.

JayB was looking next to us and motioning with his hands. "Alana! Look at me! Come on!" he called. "Would you look? Hey! Alana! Hey! Okay, finally. Wow."

Slowly we steered off the road and stopped on the shoulder. JayB and I jumped out. So did the driver of a parked car in front of us: Alana.

"What's wrong?" Alana asked, wiping her face.

"What? What's wrong?" JayB responded. "What *isn't* wrong? Why are you crying?"

Alana shook her head. JayB approached her. I could smell Odin in the back seat and Rhiannon in the front.

"Why the tears?" he asked more gently.

"You just let me go," she finally choked out. Her wet eyes searched his. "Why didn't you try to stop me?"

JayB looked helpless. "I thought you said you wanted everyone to let you make your own decisions."

"Not about something like this. I wanted to hear you say, 'Don't go.' Even Maddy knows you're not supposed to just let someone *leave.*"

"I didn't. I came right after you."

She shook her head. "It's too late now."

"How can it be too late? It's only been eight minutes, and for six of those you wouldn't pull over."

"I was worried it was a carjacking."

"In a *Ferrari*?"

Alana laughed, then pulled out a tissue and blew her nose.

"Look, we both know going back to LA won't be good for you. I get that there's plenty of reasons to want to live there, but there's plenty of reasons to want to live *anywhere*. And I think the most important reason is when there's a man standing right in front of you who loves you."

Alana didn't say anything.

"And what I said before, I'm taking back. If California is absolutely the only place you'll consider, then I'll move back to California. I'd rather pick someplace else, but I can't lose you, so if it's got to be California, that's where I'll go."

"What about the restaurant?"

JayB shook his head. "My dad's a grown-up. Let him hire Rodney back, I don't care."

"No. You care. You want to see it through to the end. You can taste victory."

"And you do, too, don't you? Come on, you know you do."

Alana opened her mouth, then shut it.

"So fine. Let's get the joint up and running—together—and after that, go someplace else. Take it minute by minute. And the moment you say we're done with the place, we're done."

"I don't know."

"I can't believe I just told you I love you, and we're talking about the restaurant!"

Alana smiled. "Maybe I just want to hear you say it again."

JayB put his hands out and gently took hold of Alana's arms. "I love you. Watching you walk out of my life eight simple minutes ago, I realized that from that moment on, I'd be exactly the same man as my father. I'd always talk about you, always tell people about this one regret, this one amazing woman I let go. And I'd never forget you. You're the one for me, the *only* one for me. And, damn it, if you look into your own heart, don't you feel the same? Aren't we gumming up the works with all these other considerations? I'm in love with you, and have been in love with you since you almost killed me with a toy gun."

Alana gave a small laugh.

JayB's return smile was tremulous. "I love your sense of humor. I love how you examine yourself and you grow. You're good for me because you'll teach me how to change, and I'm good for you because I'll never tell you what to do. I'll never run your life. I'll never control you."

She gave him an odd look. "Aren't you running my life now, or trying to, anyway?"

He shook his head. "I'm giving you a *choice*. Don't go back to Los Angeles. *Please*."

She cocked her head playfully. "Except you're forgetting, I sold the house. I don't have a place to stay."

JayB's grin broadened. "Well, turns out I've got a spare room."

They stood looking at each other for a moment. And this time, when they came together in a tight hug, their mouths pressing together, I wagged. This time, the love between them was uncomplicated and easy, the way dogs do love.

*Dear Diary:*

*My living arrangements seem unsettled. Odin and I are a pack, one that frequently expands to include Phoebe—and, unfortunately, Spartan—but Odin and I are the only dogs who sleep in the house with JayB and Alana. Is this a permanent arrangement? I don't believe it's possible, because as Odin and I sleep, Kelsey and Rhiannon prowl. We tolerate it because we know that if we attacked, JayB would be angry. And also, Rhiannon would hurt us.*

*Surely I am not living with two cats.*

*Odin is my ally in this. He and I often exchange mournful looks when a cat prances past our noses.*

*Otherwise, though, Odin is happy. There is no longer any hesitation from JayB and Alana in accepting him: he lives with us and they love him. He will always mourn for Helen, but I can tell he's adjusted to his new people.*

*He is a good friend. I can sense, though, that whatever is wearing him down from inside is getting worse. JayB and Alana seem to know it too, and spend a lot of time stroking Odin and telling him he is a good dog.*

*One night, I am conscious of Odin easing out of his dog bed and padding silently out of the room. Curious, I leap to the floor and follow him as he moves slowly down the hallway and through an open doorway to curl up on the floor of a seldom-used bedroom. His breath is coming raggedly. I don't sense any pain in him, but some sort of change is overtaking him. I go alongside him and lower my nose to his. He opens his eyes and focuses on me, giving his tail a single thump. I ease down on the floor and place my head on his chest. It rises and falls with his labored breathing.*

*I am with him, he is aware of me, and he knows that whatever he is facing now, he is not alone.*

*Part of the night passes. His breathing slows. Odin is*

leaving us and I will miss him terribly. He has been a wonderful friend to me, but it is his time. A dog can sense these things. I press against him so he can feel my warmth and my love.

Suddenly, he jerks. He lifts his head and is alert the way dogs are when a person enters the room. I turn and look in the direction he's staring and see only an empty doorway. There's nobody there, but Odin is wagging his tail. Then he does something I saw him do a long time ago. He crawls forward on his belly, carefully moving across the floor. I get the real sense that he knows he is being a very good dog. When he reaches the doorway, he flops onto his side, stretched out for a tummy rub. His tail flaps vigorously and I feel the love pouring off him. It is the love of a good dog for their person. I still see no one beside him, but I think I understand what he's doing.

And then, with a final wag, Odin's tail stops moving. He sighs contentedly, and that is his last breath.

I regard him in the stillness of the gloom. He is bathed in stark moonlight filtering in through a single window. His form is still stretched out, as if expecting hands to stroke his tummy.

I'm sitting, being a good dog, watching over him. I am remembering all the walks we took together, all the times we lifted our legs in the same spot. I will never forget him.

Odin was a good dog.

I know what to do now. Out the window, I see the moon high in the sky, and it is toward the moon that I lift my head and give voice to a long, mournful howl.

When I hear the people stirring down the hall, I howl again.

Love,
Clancy

# Thirty-seven

Odin's scent gradually evaporated from the surfaces of our home. His customary spot on the rug was the last to surrender his presence—one day, I noticed it was gone and couldn't recall the last time I'd encountered it. Outside, I found places where he had lifted his leg, and I saluted these. Eventually, though, a blanket of snow descended on the world, and my nose lost this final connection.

I missed him most powerfully at our personal dog park, always half expecting to see him lying beneath his favorite tree. Phoebe came with me many days, and Spartan was often brought by Rodney or Maddy, or both, but even when Millie and Tillie joined us, our pack felt incomplete without Odin.

A new room had been forged out of one of the big decks off the side of the restaurant. It had glass walls that slid open on warm days. It made for a comfortable, dry place, with dog beds provided for naps. One wintry day, JayB and Alana led Phoebe and me through the side door into this new room, and I wagged because DesMoines was waiting for us in there. She carried bacon in her pocket, which she fed us.

I loved DesMoines.

"Is Walter back yet?" JayB asked her.

"No, still at the farmer's market." She gave JayB a close look. "So today's the big day, isn't it?"

"The big day?" Alana repeated.

DesMoines nodded. "The day you tell him your decision. I've never seen him so nervous. He's so sure you've picked Colorado, he's already talking about opening a second restaurant out there. Which"—she held up a hand—"don't worry, I won't let him do." She offered Alana and JayB a wan smile. "You know, if I had a vote, I'd ask you to stay."

Alana and JayB glanced at each other. "Well," Alana started to say.

I wagged because the door slid open and Rodney came stomping into the room, shedding snow from his boots. I did not wag for Spartan, who ignored Phoebe and me and trotted with his typical arrogance to lie in the bed he always claimed as his.

Rodney looked disturbed. "I really need to talk to you guys," he announced, "stat. That means—"

"I know what stat means, Rodney," JayB interrupted mildly. "What's up?"

I was disappointed to see DesMoines turning away. I had thought the day might steer itself back to more bacon. "I'll leave you alone for some stat talk," she said dryly.

"Let's have a seat, Rodney," JayB offered. The three of them sat at a table, but without food. I glanced at Phoebe, and we both settled into beds.

"Hey, I have to say you did a really good job turning this deck into a glassed-in porch," JayB told Rodney, gesturing around the room.

"We really needed the extra space," Alana added.

Rodney nodded. "Yeah. Well, it was pretty hard to get it done, because you kept coming over to check things, so I felt like I had to keep working."

"Huh," JayB replied. "Interesting. So what's going on?"

Rodney leaned forward. "It's about the snowblower."

"Something wrong with it?"

Rodney shook his head. "No, the issue I'm talking about is me on the snowblower."

Alana looked unhappy. "Well, it's really important to keep the dog runs plowed out, so that the dogs don't get all wet."

"Right. I just wanted you to know," Rodney replied.

JayB looked puzzled. "Know what? Are you saying you don't want to do the snow-thrower any longer?"

Rodney looked annoyed. "Oh, no, of course not. Are you kidding? It's the most fun job I've ever had. But that's the point."

"I'm sorry—what's the point, exactly?" JayB asked.

"That it's a *job*. This isn't my *career*, okay? This is just something I'm doing until my ship comes in."

"So you've got more pig iron somewhere?"

Rodney shook his head. "No, it's an expression. You've never heard this, 'my ship comes in'? It's like the one about the Rolling Stones not getting any moss."

Alana nodded thoughtfully. "I've heard that one."

JayB smiled. "Well, Rodney, I don't see it as your career either. I mean, I wasn't thinking you'd still be throwing snow in *July*."

Rodney frowned. "I know that. I'm saying, I'm helping out around here as something temporary to make money, but it's not how I'm going to get rich."

"Ah. Okay."

"Though," Alana interjected, "if you're done with clearing snow for today, that dishwasher still isn't draining properly. Could you take a look?"

"Sure." Rodney stood up, snapped his fingers, and he and Spartan left the room. Phoebe flapped her tail because she wagged at everything.

"I guess our handyman's leaving us to become an investment banker," JayB observed with a sigh.

"I'm not worried about that, but I feel bad that Walter's anxious."

"Probably good for him."

Phoebe and I both wagged when Maddy, carrying a box, climbed the outside steps and kicked at the bottom of the sliding door. JayB opened it and Phoebe and I sniffed at the snow she tracked in. "Snowing guns and roses out there," she declared and set her box down on the table with a thump. I could smell nothing interesting in it. "These are just *some* of the dog shampoos I have to memorize," she advised. "It's like I have to reconstitute knowledge of everything known."

"But you're getting along better with your instructor?" JayB asked cautiously.

"Oh, yeah." Maddy waved a hand. "She says I'm the most unique person in dog-grooming school. She means in history. We stopped fighting once I realized she wasn't after Rodney. Is he here?"

"In the kitchen," Alana replied.

"Since the dog tub hasn't arrived yet, I've been practicing on him at home, which is why he probably smells like flea juice."

"You've been dog-grooming Rodney?" JayB asked with a delighted laugh.

Maddy shrugged. "Spartan won't go near the tub anymore, so yeah. It wouldn't make sense for me to do it on myself." She squinted. "Why, do you think I should cut my hair?"

"No, not at all," Alana assured her.

"I'm going to go talk to him. He asked me to a movie tonight, so it's open season." Maddy stood up and waved at the box. "Help yourself."

She left. Alana reached into the box and pulled something out. "Clancy? Do you want to smell like mango?" she asked me. "Or"— she pulled out something else—"lavender?"

I loved Alana. I wagged, hearing in her voice that we were soon going to have extra fun.

Moments later I heard, saw, and smelled Walter as he charged into the big main room of the restaurant, pulling a cart stacked with boxes. "I'm here," he called loudly.

Walter's boxes smelled deliciously fishy, and as we all approached, DesMoines was peering into one of them, probably thinking of feeding the dogs. "Nice tomatoes," she observed.

"Okay. Don't be mad," Walter warned, "but I got something that wasn't on your list."

"Again? Color me surprised," DesMoines said with gentle sarcasm.

"So here's what happened," he continued, unabashed. "The fish guy got in a shipment of bluefish, but then the people who ordered it didn't show up, and he said you can't freeze it, so he offered me a great deal. So, you know . . ."

"Well, he's right," DesMoines agreed. "You can't freeze bluefish. It turns to mush."

"Maybe Alana could make it into dog food?" Walter suggested.

DesMoines gave Walter a pitying look. "Bluefish might be ugly, but you forget I'm from New Orleans. You taste my blackened bluefish, you're never going to want to eat trout again."

Walter grinned. "I knew you could do something with it."

"I'll get to work." DesMoines took Walter's cart and headed to the most delicious-smelling room in the place. I was crushed, because Spartan was back there—was she going to give the fish to him?

JayB gestured with his head. "Come on back to the glassed-in porch. We can talk there."

Walter gave a reluctant nod and we all followed JayB. The room still smelled like Phoebe and me, and we both returned to our beds.

"Man, the market was crazy today," Walter proclaimed, sitting down across from Alana and JayB. "This storm fouled up deliveries. Good thing I have a standing arrangement with the hothouse— some of the other buyers went empty-handed. The bluefish thing was just pure luck, but I thought I'd take a chance."

"It seems like every day is a wild experience for you," JayB observed.

Walter nodded. "Yeah, keeps me on my toes."

Alana had a small smile on her face. "But you like it, right? You like doing that?"

"Oh." Walter thought about this, then nodded. "Yeah, I kind of do. It's exciting. I've made friends, and no matter what I bring back, DesMoines can turn it into something. She's the most amazing cook in the universe. Hey, I should tell you, I got a text from your mom."

JayB cocked his head. "Celeste texted you?"

Walter nodded. "Yeah. I sent that photo of DesMoines and me in Florida."

"What did her text say?" Alana prodded.

"She said we make an attractive couple."

JayB raised his eyebrows. "What did you say to that?"

Walter frowned. "Well, nothing. I don't see us as a 'couple.'"

"Is that right?" JayB challenged. "But isn't it true that when her lease expires, DesMoines is moving into your house?"

"Well, sure," Walter agreed uncomfortably, "but she's there every night anyway. It's ridiculous that she's paying rent just to have a place to put her shoes. I've got lots of closets."

"You know what you should do?" JayB replied. "You should show Celeste's text to DesMoines."

Walter looked puzzled.

"Because," Alana continued for JayB, "you *do* make an attractive couple. If you show her what Celeste said, DesMoines will understand that you and your ex-wife have moved on from each other."

Walter's face was blank for a moment and then he nodded. He stood up. "Okay." He made to leave the room.

Phoebe and I both raised our heads because we picked up on something between Alana and JayB.

"Wait, hang on. We need to talk, Dad."

Walter's shoulders slumped. He settled reluctantly back in his chair. "Okay, before you say anything, I need to tell you something. All right? Just listen."

JayB shrugged. "Sure."

"I may not be as involved in the day-to-day, but even I can see that you and Alana are the only reason this whole operation works. Not just because of the dog park. It's the way you manage the people, JayB. And the improvements you're always making, Alana. And your dog shop, I mean, that's going well, right, making a profit?"

"True," Alana agreed.

"Business is good. No, it's more than just good. Because of you two, DesMoines is free to run the kitchen, and now people come for the *food*. So I know the plan is for you to move on. You're like me in that, JayB."

"Well . . ." JayB started to protest mildly.

"Hang on, because I put a lot of thought into this. You ready?"

There was a pause, and JayB nodded, "I guess we're ready."

"Okay. I'm having the papers drawn up to give you fifty percent ownership of this place." Walter gestured expansively, while Alana and JayB glanced at each other in surprise.

"Wow," JayB said softly.

"And when I pass—which, you know, should be ten, forty, many years from now, you can have the other half. But only under two conditions."

"Dad . . ." JayB started.

Alana put a hand on his arm. "What conditions?"

Walter held up a finger, and I contemplated how much more attractive it would be if he had a gob of peanut butter on the end of it. "Number one is, you have to stay. You have to commit. I don't know for how long, but for a long time. I'm talking years. Otherwise, no deal."

"And the second condition?" JayB prompted.

"Whether I'm still alive or not."

"You're only sixty-one years old, Dad. Come on."

JayB was grinning, but Walter looked serious. "The other condition is, no matter what happens to me, you keep DesMoines. She gets to work here for as long as she wants. I mean it." Walter sat back in his seat.

I inhaled, taking in the wonderful odor of fish clinging to his clothing.

"You've surprised us, Walter," Alana commented carefully. "We never even considered this."

JayB nodded. "Didn't see it coming."

Walter shrugged. "Owning things is only important if you can share them with the people you care about. Come here, you two."

Walter stood and held out his arms, and first Alana and then JayB stepped into them. The three of them hugged while Phoebe gave me a look of complete non-comprehension.

"Now, Jago," Walter grated hoarsely, "I know I haven't been the greatest father in the world, but I feel like I've really changed, and I promise you I'll do better."

"You haven't been a bad father," JayB protested. His voice was too.

"So." Walter stepped back and looked at Alana and JayB. "What's your answer?"

JayB and Alana glanced at each other again. "You don't have to give us anything, Walter," she replied. "We were already going to stay."

Walter blinked.

"Yeah, we talked about it," JayB affirmed. "We've been talking about almost nothing else for the past six months. We like it here. You're right. Alana innovates, I implement. You come back from the market with squid milk and flaming cactus and lava worms and DesMoines turns them into something amazing. So, there's no need for your kind offer. You were operating under false assumptions."

Walter shook his head, smiling. "No, I wasn't. I meant it; without you two, this ship would sink. I'm insisting on making you partners. It's good business." He looked at his wrist. "Speaking of, I'm meeting that guy I told you about—got a repossessed inventory from a liquor store to sell off."

"Okay, just . . ." JayB looked pained. "Make good decisions."

Walter waved his phone. "Don't worry, Rodney programmed my phone so I can look up the prices for anything." He turned and left the room.

"That's Google," JayB softly told Walter's back.

Alana and JayB sat back down. I glanced at Phoebe. As usual, I couldn't tell what, if anything, she was thinking, but I knew my mind was on the fact that we often were served food in this room, and therefore we should probably continue to do a good Sit just in case.

"Well, this really changes things," Alana observed, "I know he said we would *both* have ownership, but you're the heir. It rightfully belongs to you."

JayB shook his head. "No—if not for you, this place would have collapsed. Not just because of the marketing and the dog shop, but everything else. You and DesMoines are really in charge of the restaurant. I keep the parts oiled, but you two *invented* the parts." JayB patted his stomach. "Well . . . I also do taste-testing of new menu items."

Alana smiled. "We've got to get you back to walking dogs."

"Yes, we do," JayB agreed. Then he gave her a meaningful look. "So we're partners. This deal sort of forges us into a forever kind of relationship, don't you think?"

"Oh?" Alana responded warily.

JayB nodded. "You live with me, we work together, and now we co-own half a restaurant. So . . ."

"So?" Alana repeated, mock-stern. "I'm picking up another one of your subtle hints here. But if you're talking about something other than the restaurant, spell it out."

"Okay, then," JayB said agreeably. He stood up, walked over to where Alana was sitting, and then dropped to his knees. Alana's mouth opened in a silent gasp. "I have a question for you, Alana."

He reached into his pocket. I didn't smell any dog treats in there, but suddenly the room crackled with nervous energy—and, underlying it all, real happiness—so I did what any dog would do under the situation: I jumped on top of JayB, knocking him over. Instantly, Phoebe crashed into me, so the two of us were straddling JayB, who covered his face as Phoebe inadvertently stepped on it.

"Dogs!" JayB sputtered. I licked his face.

Giggling, Alana joined us in the pile, and now there were two dogs and two people, rolling on the floor together.

They were happy. And I was happy, too.

## Dear Diary:

It turns out I do live with two cats now.

It's twice as bad.

Kelsey and Rhiannon do not live with cats, or at least they pretend they don't, because they each refuse to acknowledge the existence of the other. There is a big couch in the living room and Kelsey has one end of it and Rhiannon has the other. That's pretty much the only room they ever occupy at the same time. At night, when I'm sleeping on the bed, first Kelsey and then Rhiannon will take turns running in and leaping silently onto the mattress. They always come to me purring, as if I'm supposed to be happy to see them.

I am never happy to see them.

When I'm lying in my dog bed and just trying to be a dog, one of the cats will come up and curl up with me. This is not appreciated, but they don't care what I think.

It took only a few days after Rhiannon moved in before I reeked of cat stink. They breathe their fish breath on me and make me smell like that, too.

We drive to our personal dog park almost every day. The cats never come, but they're always in the house when we return.

Alana and JayB spend nearly all of their time together. They make each other happy.

We often stop and pick up Phoebe on our way down to our personal dog park. I was chagrined the first time I saw her, conscious of how much cat smell clung to me. I didn't know if she would reject me. I was somewhat surprised when she didn't—instead, she seemed thrilled to see me, sniffing me up and down and wagging furiously.

Now, when we're at the dog park, Phoebe plays with me almost exclusively. I don't know what I did to change her mind, but I'm happy that she loves me and that she is not repelled by my cat smell.

Sometimes we go and pick up Spartan from Maddy and Rodney's place. I've never been inside, but I often see one or both of the people come to the door with Spartan. Phoebe, I observe to my delight, also ignores Spartan now. And when we play, Phoebe and I, Spartan stonily looks away from us. I often think that if he lived in our house, he would occupy one end of the couch or the other.

And that is my life. My name is Clancy and I am a good dog. I live with my person, JayB, and Alana, who I love just as much. Phoebe now knows we belong together. Everything is wonderful.

Except the cats.

Love,
Clancy

# Acknowledgments,
# Meandering Thoughts, Song Lyrics

Ironically, when I say I write fiction, it's a nonfictional statement. That doesn't mean, though, that everything I type is true, not even in the acknowledgments, which are generally supposed to be accurate. So when I say, "Thank you, Jeff Bezos and Elon Musk, for both giving me your entire fortunes," I'm obviously forgetting about Bill Gates. Or when I thank Beyoncé for all the love letters, or *People* magazine for making me "Sexiest Man of this Century," I am clearly exaggerating—it was *last* century. They haven't even voted for this century yet, though I understand Beyoncé is lobbying hard for them to pick me.

*Love, Clancy* is a work of fiction, though for me the characters feel so real, I have this ironic feeling that I should thank them first. Without Clancy, JayB, Alana, Maddy, and the rest, I couldn't have written this novel—so thanks, guys, for showing up and insisting I quote you accurately.

I should also thank anyone (you!) who reads the acknowledgments in any book, because they can be really granular ("Thank you, Uncle Bob, for pointing out my shoe was untied"), obscure ("Thanks, Rosemary Gluck, for your information on the impervious hermetical seals of the nineteenth century"), dubious ("Thank you, Beyoncé, for the wonderful weekend where we spent all my Bezos money, you can stop writing me love letters now"), or overly broad ("Thank you, everyone in France and the rest of Europe and the planet Earth, living, dead, or not yet conceived, I love you all and invite you to breakfast on Tuesday").

I'll point out that if you read the dedication, you'll see that *Love, Clancy* is dedicated to a man I admire and appreciate, Scott Miller, without whom there really wouldn't be any reason to thank anyone else, because no one would read any of my books except Beyoncé. Scott's my agent at Trident, which sounds like a toothpaste.

Sheri Kelton is the CEO of my career, I tell people, and works impossibly hard to get my stock price up. Her official title is manager. She loves me even more than Beyoncé does. Gavin Polone is my *unpaid* manager—he works tirelessly to find ways to produce my work as movies, television shows, operas, and fourth-grade dance recitals. He also models tracksuits. Thanks to both of you for all you've done to help my work become more widely seen and appreciated.

Thanks, Ed Stackler, for your deft, professional editing, it makes me look smarter than I am.

Scott Miller tells me how lucky I am to (a) be so delusional and (b) have all of my books, whether they are for younger readers or adults, published by Tom Doherty/Tor/Forge/Starscape. And I do feel lucky, especially with Linda, Lucille, Eileen, Sarah, Kristin, Susan, Kristin, Tom, and all the other hard workers who get behind my writing and *push*.

The people who reach out to others and say, "Can we have Bruce come speak to our library? Would Bruce come to our school district? Would Bruce please stop eating all the cookies?" are wonderful humans unless they are members of another species. Thank you, everyone who reacted to the end of Covid restrictions by trying to set up appearances at schools, book events, and dental appointments. I do enjoy meeting people, especially children, who are at the crossroads of love for dogs and books. I so appreciate the invitations and hope to see you all soon! Maybe breakfast Tuesday in France?

Few people know this, but I did not invent the internet. Early on, though, I was quick to recognize it was worthless for flipping pancakes. I also concluded that it might be useful in providing ways for people to connect with my work and to hack into my bank account. Mindy Wells Hoffbauer, Jill Enders, Julia Hart, Chase Cameron, Elliott Crowe, Breeze Vincinz, and Susan Andrews have all worked to keep people reminded that I do exist and I did eat the cookies. Because of them, there is a secret group of *A Dog's Purpose* fans on Facebook (friend Susan Andrews if you'd like to join) and a less secret "fan" page where people can talk about my books, their dogs, my hygiene . . . whatever is on their minds. I so appreciate their work.

Thank you, Olivia Pratt, for keeping the boat afloat in 2020–21, and thank you, Lisa Michie, for swimming to it. Andrew Solmssen keeps the computers talking to each other but I don't like what they're saying.

Thank you, Sammi Rose, for not being squirrely. Thank you, Theo, Sonata, and Matisse for drinking morning tea, feeding Tucker hot dogs, and leaving me cookies.

The people at Apogee, especially Marlene Passaro and Betty Bennett, invented really cool electronic gizmos for me to use to dictate early drafts of my novels. That's right, "gizmos," sorry to be so technical with my jargon. But they've saved me a lot of typing, so my fingers thank them.

Thank you, Dr. Deb Mangelsdorf, for being my go-to for all questions about veterinary medicine, and for physically dragging me to a passing grade in geometry.

You know how your true friends are those you can call at three o'clock in the morning to come bail you out of jail? Well, I don't have any of those. But what I do have are friends who have always encouraged me when my path became steep, rocky, narrow, or led too often to Dunkin' Donuts. I can't possibly remember everyone, but if I were to load a lifeboat I'd have to at least include Robert Schaumburg, Henry Cox, Andy and Jody Sherwood, Diane and Tom Runstrom, Tim Whims, Gary Goldstein, Diane Driscoll, Margaret Howell, David Leinberger, Robin and Barb Foster, Amy Ephron, Alan Rader, Leslie Rockitter, Carolyn Pittel . . . okay, the boat's overloaded. Turns out that when I asked myself who has been really, really supportive, a gusher of names came back. I can't name or even think of everyone, but if I haven't told you lately how much I appreciate how you've had my back all this time, then shame on me. I'll thank you personally in France on Tuesday.

Thank you, Samantha Dunn, for being an astounding talent, and for featuring me in all the publications you edit, and for allowing Jimmy and Ben to help me win the Super Bowl.

I wouldn't get very far in life without my family. My older sisters, Amy and Julie Cameron, have consistently forced people to read my books. My parents, now deceased, did everything they knew to do back when I wasn't selling anything I wrote, and they continued to help me when that changed. My children show up for events, buy books, and reproduce. Thank you, Georgia and Chelsea, James, Gage, Gordon, Sadie, Arlo, Eloise, Garret, and Ewan, for giving me the reason why life is so good. Thank you for your service, Chase, and I look forward to expanding the family soon. Speaking of family, thank you, Evie, for loaning me your daughter, and to Ted, Maria, Maya, Ethan, and Jakob for inviting me in. Thank you, cousin Jen, for getting that I got it. All my other cousins, nieces, nephews—I'm not going to name you but I love you all.

Teachers, librarians, and space aliens who read my books to students or assign my books to be read: thank you very much. I'd send cookies but I involuntarily ate them.

Finally: the main reason I have a Hollywood career isn't because I look like a young George Clooney. It's because there's this woman, Cathryn Michon, my partner in life, who has worked so tirelessly by my side. Actually most of the time she's across the room; I'm speaking metaphorically, here. We have one of those relationships where we support each other in every way. She directs, acts, produces, writes, and stars in movies. I stand by craft services and eat. See? Support. We've been business partners since around the time I was named *People*'s Sexiest Man in Bruce's Apartment. I'm so grateful for all you do, Cathryn. "Thank you" seems an inadequate sentiment here, but you know how I feel.